There can be only one!

He sat in the middle of the alley and waited. The morning light grew stronger. Finally, he filled his chest with air and yowled "I am king! I am king!" The echo had hardly faded when One-Eye came out from behind a box and glared at him.

"I am king!" One-Eye yowled back.

Instead of leaping at head height, he leaped low, butted One-Eye in the gut. His long teeth found One-Eye in the upper thigh. He bit and savagely tore left, right, left, ripping the muscle. One-Eye fell upon his back, screaming and clawing and biting, but his back made it hard for One-Eye to gain purchase.

He thrust up and to the right with his rear legs. One-Eye fell over onto his side before scrambling up, rear leg lifted off the ground. He could taste One-Eye in his mouth and grinned at him, long teeth showing red. "There can be only one!" he yowled, and charged again. One-Eye tried to stand and meet the rush but could not, lurched to his injured side. This time he leaped high, came down upon One-Eye like a thunderbolt from the sky. His teeth met through One-Eye's ear. He closed his eyes and shook his head, nearly deafened by One-Eye's howls of pain and shame.

After a few moments of bliss, he let go, stepped back. One-Eye struggled to his feet but kept his head low.

"Who is king?" he urred.

"You are," panted One-Eye.

—from "I am King!" by Edward Carmien

Mystery Date, **edited by Denise Little**

First dates—the worst possible times in your life or the opening steps on the path to a wonderful new future? What happens when someone you have never met before turns out not to be who or what he or she claims to be? It's just a date, what could go wrong? Here are seventeen encounters, from authors such as Kristine Katherine Rusch, Nancy Springer, Laura Resnick, and Jody Lynn Nye that answer these questions. From a childhood board game called "Blind Date" that seems to come shockingly true . . . to a mythological answer to Internet predators . . . to a woman cursed to see the truth about her dates when she imbibes a little wine . . . to an enchanting translator bent on avenging victims of war crimes . . . to a young man hearing a very special voice from an un-plugged stereo system . . . these are just some of the tales that may lead to happily ever after—or no ever after at all . . . .

Fellowship Fantastic, **edited by Martin H. Greenberg and Kerrie Hughes**

The true strength of a story lies in its characters and in both the ties that bind them together and the events that drive them apart. Perhaps the most famous example of this in fantasy is *The Fellowship of The Ring*. But such fellowships are key to many fantasy and science fiction stories. Now thirteen top tale-spinners—Nina Kiriki Hoffmann, Alan Dean Foster, Russell Davis, Alexander Potter, among others—offer their own unique looks at fellowships from: a girl who finds her best friend through a portal to another world . . . to four special families linked by blood and magical talent . . . to two youths ripped away from all they know and faced with a terrifying fate that they can only survive together . . . to a man who must pay the price for leaving his childhood comrade to face death alone . . . .

The Future We Wish We Had, **edited by Martin H. Greenberg and Rebecca Lickiss**

In the opening decade of the twenty-first century, many things that were predicted in the science fiction stories of the twentieth century have become an accepted part of everyday life, and many other possibilities have not yet been realized but hopefully will be one day. For everyone who thought that by now they'd be motoring along the skyways in a personal jet car, or who assumed we'd have established bases on the Moon and Mars, or that we would have conquered disease, slowed the aging process to a crawl, or eliminated war, social injustice, and economic inequity, here are sixteen stories of futures that might someday be ours or our children's, from Esther Friesner, Sarah Hoyt, Kevin J. Anderson, Irene Radford, Dave Freer, and Dean Wesley Smith

CATOPOLIS

EDITED BY
MARTIN H. GREENBERG
AND JANET DEAVER-PACK

DAW BOOKS, INC.

DONALD A. WOLLHEIM, FOUNDER

375 Hudson Street, New York, NY 10014

ELIZABETH R. WOLLHEIM
SHEILA E. GILBERT
PUBLISHERS

http://www.dawbooks.com

First Printing, December 2008
1 2 3 4 5 6 7 8 9

DAW TRADEMARK REGISTERED
U.S. PAT. OFF. AND FOREIGN COUNTRIES
—MARCA REGISTRADA.
HECHO EN U.S.A.

PRINTED IN THE U.S.A.

ACKNOWLEDGMENTS

Introduction copyright © 2008 by Janet Deaver-Pack
"Gut Feeling," copyright © 2008 by Esther M. Friesner
"Black," copyright © 2008 by Richard Lee Byers
"I Am King!" copyright © 2008 by Edward Carmien
"Old Age and Sorcery," copyright © 2008 by Lee Martindale
"Kitty and the City," copyright © 2008 by Paul Genesse
"For the Birds," copyright © 2008 by Jana Paniccia
"Eye Witness," copyright © 2008 by Donald J. Bingle
"Mentor of the Potala," copyright © 2008 by Bruce A. Heard
"The Guardian of Grimoire Hall," copyright © 2008 by Christopher Welch
"After Tony's Fall," copyright © 2008 by Jean Rabe
"Ink and Newsprint," copyright © 2008 by Marc Tassin
"Burning Bright," copyright © 2008 by Elaine Cunningham
"To Cat, a Thief," copyright © 2008 by Robert E. Vardeman
"The Scent of Death," copyright © 2008 by Elizabeth A. Vaughan
"The Persian, The Coon, and Bullets," by Matthew Woodring Stover
"Father Maims Best," copyright © 2008 by Ed Greenwood
"Cat Call 911," copyright © 2008 by Janny Wurts

TABLE OF CONTENTS

INTRODUCTION, OR "PROPAW"

As most of you know, I've lived with cats for much of my life. A gorgeous, elegant long-haired gray and white lady I christened Star because of the markings across her face adopted me when I was four. Apparently, life in the house three doors south of my home wasn't to her taste. With very little encouragement, and ignoring the strenuous protests of my mother as only a cat can, Star became "my" pet. (My oldest sister fed her, encouraged her to stay, and blamed it on me.) Star and her numerous offspring became close friends, homework helpers, and playmates as I grew up.

I began to suspect that there was more to "domestic" feline society many years ago. I couldn't get any of my furry associates to tell me more than snippets of things going on in that hidden level of existence. They didn't want me to get in trouble with either the humans I had to live with, or with other cats. And especially not with the Goddess Bast, who might have taken offense and squashed my earliest investigations. She seemed amused instead. I persisted, trying to discover more of the unique society I knew must be brimming just beneath the human stratum. The longer I lived with cats, the more sure I was that they had communication and rich lives beyond what I saw.

Prince, son of Star, was not the most talkative of cats. An almost-feral, I persuaded him from the garage to the back porch with treats. He liked his comforts too much to imperil them by whispering to me the secrets of his kind. But he loved curling up in my lap, sighing, and making vague references to things I, a grade-schooler, couldn't quite put together.

After Prince died of old age, Ari Mithral Shannonn and I had a very close relationship. That 16-pound Blue Point not-quite Siamese and I talked a lot during his too-short life. He was my first Guardian, and he took his duties quite seriously. It was through him that I learned how large a cat's vocabulary can be, both in catese and in human words. He adored music and listened to me practice singing for hours from the top of the piano, a smile on his face as I worked on Mozart, Johann Strauss, Jr., and art songs. Shann was also my first analytical cat: He'd play with strings until he realized where their motion stemmed from, then all he wanted was my hands and fingers. After him, Bastjun Amaranth was a tabby that gave nothing away but the barest hints, but Canth Starshadow (my first black cat) started me on the road to understanding more of what cats do while they appear to be napping. He also offered suggestions as to why cats sit on anything printed and why they sometimes stare at walls for extended periods.

After all this time, I began to understand.

I've gleaned much more through close living with my current trio. Tabirika Onyx has extensive conversations with crows when the windows are screened during the summer months. She also tells the deer when they're too close to the house and monitors the crazed hollering of the chipmunks. Her information network is extensive, and she keeps a paw on everything going on in the neighborhood from our windowsills. Syrannis Moonstone, who is half Abysinnian, gets odd expressions on her face, then studies walls and corners as if expecting them to speak. It's as if she sees ghosts of the past or future against the paint and wallpaper. Baron Figaro de Shannivere, my rare mist cat, is an analytical creature who turns doorknobs and has a huge vocabulary reminiscent of Shann's. He won't play with a laser pointer because he's figured out that its motion comes from my hand. Trouble is, he told Syri, and now she won't play with it either.

All of this information slammed together in a headache not too long ago. That's when the idea for *Catopolis* was born. Cat society, as thick and varied as that of humans, exists in a stratum below ours. We see only a fraction of it. It is there, our feline companions allowing us to know bits and pieces of its tapestry, while they watch us with knowing eyes.

I started keeping notes about a Catopolis society. My cats, after they became accustomed to my knowledge about their secrets, contributed a goodly proportion of the details. We believe this has Bast's approbation, because our notes haven't disappeared in flames, been shredded by ghostly claws, fluttered away without the agent of wind, or destroyed by soggy organic means. The authors telling the tales within these pages offered to flesh out the rest, building on our initial descriptions.

And we all had a lot of fun.

So welcome to Catopolis, the city of felines that exists on the same plane with humans, yet is hidden. Here you'll find Guardians, mentors, detectives, Robin Hood-second story types, demon-fighters, guides, kings, strays, oracles, true love, incredible friendships, and those hoping to win elected positions via mouse ballots. (Those may have to be rethought before next time: there were too many missing for an accurate count).

Enjoy!

Janet Deaver-Pack
Tabirika Onyx
Syrannis Moonstone
Baron Figaro de Shannivere
Williams Bay, Wisconsin
Autumn 2007

CATOPOLIS

GUT FEELING

Esther M. Friesner

The small, plump tabby female sat before the massive black and white tom and did her best not to let him see her shiver. *Courage, Lulu!* she told herself. *He can't kill you. He wouldn't dare.* But even as she did her best to hold onto her last few shreds of valor, an insidious afterthought whispered: *He can't kill you . . . yet.*

Unaware of the female's fear, the big tom gave her a long, cool stare from beneath half-lowered eyelids. "Well, kit? Have you reconsidered my . . . request?" he drawled.

"I have," Lulu replied, keeping her voice steady. "My answer's unchanged. I won't betray my gift by making a false prediction."

"Ah, but would it be false?" The black and white tom licked one paw lazily, then opened his mouth so that one of his minions could pop in a KrunchiYum cat treat. "I *will* be the sole, undisputed ruler of Catopolis. It is fated. Your prediction will simply hasten the happy day."

Despite her fear, Lulu scowled. "If you're so certain it's predestined, you don't need my services."

"Oh, but I do," the tom replied. "You see, kit, I am not the most patient cat in this city. Even nine lives end some day. I want the power I deserve while I can still enjoy it for a long, long time. You are this city's respected Seer. Your prediction will make all accept the inevitable *immediately!* You shall perform the Reading I desire at the next full moon, when—"

"No," said Lulu. She pressed her forepaws closer together to steady herself. "If I don't interpret the omens truthfully, I dishonor the goddess Bast, who gave me my powers. I'd—I'd sooner die."

A low, warning ululation welled up from the big tom's throat. It was echoed by his attending minions, a cadre of seven muscular felines, scarred victors of many battles. The most vicious looking of them all, a street cat born and bred, took a step toward Lulu, fangs bared, eyes flashing. She cringed, awaiting the slash of pitiless claws.

"Stop!" the big black and white tom commanded. "Don't lay one paw on her, Hss'shah! She is still of use to me."

Lulu opened her eyes in time to see the black and white tom looming over her. He was smiling, and it was not a comforting smile. "Did Hss'shah frighten you, my dear? It was his idea of a joke. A crude one. What do you expect from a feral?" (Lulu's stomach churned at the subtle insult. Her mother was a feral cat, too.) "But if you were so afraid, why didn't you call upon Bast to protect you?"

"I—" Lulu bowed her head. "Lady Bast is a great goddess. She has more important things to do than look after me."

"If she looks after any of us," the big tom purred. "If, in fact, she even exists as more than just a story to make kittens behave." Lulu stared at him, horrified at such blasphemy. This only made him laugh. "Why don't you stop worrying about our so-called goddess and look after yourself? Reconsider my request. I'll make it worth your while." She answered him with silence. He lifted one wispy eyebrow. "No? Then go. We shall meet again soon enough. Oh, and don't bother running to tell the Elders about our little meeting tonight. My comrades here will swear I was nowhere near you. You'll have no proof to back up any accusations against me. What do our human servants say? That the proof of the pudding is in the eating?"

For an instant, his urbane smile turned into a grimace of such deadly menace that even the street cats in his service were taken aback. Then, as swiftly as that demonic expression had flashed over his face, it was gone. He brought his muzzle close to Lulu's ear and murmured, "In the *eating*, kit. The proof of many things is in the eating."

As soon as he stepped back, she bolted, but as she raced away, she heard him calling after her, "Whether or not you *wish* to serve me, you *will*. So speaks Señor Pantalones!"

In the days and nights that followed, Lulu's mind was haunted by apprehensive thoughts of Señor Pantalones' sinister intentions. *If he can't have my cooperation, he'll twist things so I have to help him, whether I want to or not. But how will he do it? O great Bast, help me!* Such anxieties wreaked havoc with her disposition and her digestion. Thus it was nothing extraordinary when the two-days-from-full moon looked down on a city alley and saw Catopolis' Seer in an all-too-familiar position.

"Argh!" said Lulu as she crouched, bug-eyed, in the lee of a garbage can. The sentiment was soon followed by deeper, more throaty sounds. Had the humans with whom she deigned to reside been within earshot, they easily would have read the omens in those guttural eruptions.

This did *not* mean that Lulu's humans shared her wondrous powers. It merely meant that after two years of living with her in an apartment of pure white wall-to-wall carpeting, they could instantly foretell an incipient regurgitation and shot-put her into the tile-floored bathroom or kitchen before you could say "Jack Robinson" or, more likely, "Not on the rug, goddammit! *Not on the rug!*"

There were no rugs in the alley, nor any fussy humans. Lulu let nature takes its course uninterrupted, unmolested, and—so she believed—unobserved. When she was done, she set to tidying herself. She had a fair distance to cover between this night's lonesome rendezvous point and the high-rent East Side apartment building her humans maintained solely for her pleasure and comfort. She would not—*could* not—be seen on the streets in an uncleansed condition. She had her pride.

She was almost done with her ablutions when a small, sarcastic voice from the darkness caught her with her right forepaw up and her tongue in midlick extension. "Well, that was disgusting," it said. "And by 'disgusting,' I mean 'disgusting even for a barfing cat.' *That*, my friend, sets the bar damn high!"

Lulu tensed. "Who's there? Show yourself!"

The small voice chortled. "Who died and made you the boss of me? No, let me rephrase that: I *know* who died. I saw her die, and then I followed the cats who killed her. I watched them bring her to you and I saw you rip her open, guts and gizzard. Say, do mice even *have* gizzards? Ah, what the hell, you get the picture. And then you *ate* the picture. I mean the mouse. I mean Shirley. Poor critter never knew what hit her, thank Seeds."

"Shirl—the Reading I just gave was a friend of yours? I'm sorry." Lulu felt odd, apologizing to the unseen critic, but the words escaped her mouth unbidden.

"The *Reading*? Is *that* how you think of her? As a *thing*? Look, furbag, there's more to our lives than being your toys or your four-legged pu-pu platters!" Abruptly, the voice changed its tone from harsh to conciliatory. "Y'know, I want to set the record straight: I'm not cheesed with you for *eating* Shirley."

Lulu was puzzled. "You're not?"

"Nuh-uh." The hidden speaker was firm. "Cat eats mouse, that's the way it goes, the big, bad food chain, the balance of nature, the circle of Disney copyrighted songs, the end of an old life, the beginning of a new heartburn."

"If you're not mad that I ate her, then why—?"

"You couldn't have done her the courtesy of keeping her *down?*" the small voice shrilled. "It's no shame to die if you're going to become nutrition, but what's Shirley now? Wasted. And not in the good party-hearty way! It's one thing to kill my friends when you're hungry, but it was pretty obvious that you were already stuffed when you gobbled her down in two big gulps, mostly because you horked her *up* again just as soon as the other cats got their ugly mugs outta here. She was nothing more than a snack to you, but she was my friend, and she deserved better treatment than you gave her. She deserved to be *appreciated*. She deserved to be *savored*. She deserved to be *digested*. She deserved to be—"

"I get the idea." Lulu was under enough strain without the added *agita* of dealing with this strident phantom. She switched her bushy tail angrily as her pale green eyes plumbed the shadows. As excellent as her night vision was, she could not locate the source of the snide diatribe, and it made her bristle. "How about *you* get the idea of shutting up?"

"If you can't take the truth, move your overfed butt out of my alley."

"*Your* alley? You don't sound big enough to lay claim to a sock drawer. I don't take orders from mice."

"Shows what you know." There was a soft, rustling sound followed by the faint tap-tap-tap of miniscule paws trotting across pavement. Only a few ragtag splotches of light touched the alley—the glow of moon and stars, the faint radiance of not-so-distant streetlamps, the borrowed wattage from apartments with less than desirable views. Now, as Lulu watched, a ball of golden fluff sauntered right into the middle of one such splotch with as much devil-may-care attitude as a rock star claiming his place on stage.

"I am *not* a mouse."

Lulu narrowed her eyes. "So what are you, then?" she growled. "A tailless dwarf rat? A stunted groundhog?" (She had seen the beast in question when her human servants watched a February 2nd newscast, and she hoped she'd never have to behold such a monstrous rodent again.)

"I've never been so insulted in all my life!" The downy-furred golden animal sat up on its haunches. "I'm a *hamster*, you preshrunk puma!"

This latest insult was one too many for the badly stressed young cat. "Oh, so *what?*" she snapped. "Go away before I pounce on you where you stand and flatten you like a pizza!"

"I'm shaking," the hamster replied dryly. "And I'm *not* going to go away. I'm the one who lives here, not you."

"I don't have time for this." Lulu stood up and started back for the city streets. "Good luck not becoming someone's lunch, with that attitude," she declared as she stalked off. "Good luck and goodbye."

"And good luck to *you* with Señor Pantalones!" the hamster hollered after her.

Lulu froze, every hair on her body standing upright. She could scarcely draw a breath. Her paw pads felt dank and cold. "How—?" The word was a hoarse whisper. She turned and regarded the hamster nervously. "How to you know about Señor Pantalones?"

"Same way I know about lots of things." The hamster met Lulu's curious gaze with a complacent smile. "I know that the thugs that killed Shirley are Señor Pantalones' minions and that he sent them here to test your limits. *Again*. They'd rather see if you can read the future in your *own* entrails, but they're willing to wait for that. No matter what you see in the omens on the night of Catopolis' full moon conclave, the final score's going to be Señor Pantalones, 1; you, dead."

"Why—?" Lulu's voice was barely a whisper. "Why are you telling me all this?"

The hamster ran its dainty pink paws through its whiskers. "Because you're my best hope for payback on Pantalones for Shirley, even if you are a cat. The enemy of my enemy, right? I was just a pup when I escaped from my cage and found my way here. I didn't know the first thing about surviving in the wild. Shirley taught me how to keep my freedom without ending up as kitty chow. Funny how I wound up learning that lesson better than she did." He wore a wistful smile. "I told her to stick close to her nest tonight, but she said, 'And miss toss-out-the-stale-cheese day at the corner deli? I'll be fine.' Sure, *now* she wishes she hadn't been such a know-it-all. *Now* she's all, 'Oh, if only I'd listened to you!' *Now* she's—"

"—dead," Lulu cut in. "Why do you make it sound as if she's still speaking to you?"

"Uh, because she *is*." The hamster gave Lulu a let's-not-allow-you-near-any-sharp-things-just-yet look. "And she'll keep on speaking to me until I manage to give her remains a decent cover-up." He cast a mildly sickened look at the spot where Lulu had relieved her belly. "I can't say I'm looking forward to it, but if I don't send her off properly on the Last Cheese Hunt, she'll be on my case about it until she decomposes all the way."

"This is nonsense." Lulu shook herself vigorously, as if she'd been caught in a rainstorm. "I refuse to believe that your dead friend talked—*still* talks to you!"

The hamster uttered a contemptuous sniff. "And how many cats believed *you* the first time you claimed you could read the future in the entrails of dead rodents, O Oracular One?"

Lulu's eyes went wide. "Oracular One? That title is *secret!* It was Lady Bast's gift to me when she consecrated my powers! How do you, a mere rodent, know it?"

"Well, duh," the hamster said, quite calm. "There's nothing mere about reading minds."

"You can do that?"

"How do you think I knew about Señor Pantalones and his moggy mob? I can't see *everything* going on inside someone else's head, but accessing their life story's always a piece of seed cake. You're Lulu, child of the feral female Yurrrrr and a miscellaneous tomcat. You and your littermates were discovered behind a bookstore, in a discarded shipping box for one of the Harry Potter novels and taken to a no-kill shelter from which you were all happily adopted. You discovered your special gift at six months old when you had some kind of vision."

"The dream," Lulu whispered, awestruck. "The dream Lady Bast sent to me."

"You and a couple of other cats. They were your witnesses, right?"

Lulu nodded. "When I told the Elders about the dream, the other two cats confirmed it, as Lady Bast commanded."

"All of which mystic hoo-hah officially made you the Seer of Catopolis. Nice work if you can get it. You have the admirable power to gaze into the future, though I can't say I care for your methods. Ever consider using something *besides* my kinfolk's entrails? You know, there's more than one way to skin a—"

"Who are you?" Lulu demanded. "*What* are you?"

"My name is Huey. As for what I am—"

"Besides a hamster," Lulu put in quickly.

"Shush, you're ruining the moment." Huey struck a dramatic pose. "What am I? I am, like you, one of the few, the gifted, the chosen, the Oracular!" He paused for a reaction from his audience of one, but Lulu only stared, gape-jawed and gobsmacked. At last he said, "Kitty, close your mouth before someone sticks a cheeseburger in it. This is real simple: I am an Oracular hamster, you're an Oracular cat, together we fight crime!"

That fetched her. "We do what now?"

"It's not a crime to eat rodents you're only going to barf up two seconds later? I saw how miserable you were when you ate Shirley. The cats who brought her were watching every bite closely, as if they *wanted* you to quit. Hey, *you* looked like you wanted to quit, too! Why didn't you?"

Lulu sighed. "Once a Seer has examined and interpreted the pattern of the entrails, she must ingest all traces of the Reading."

"And if you don't, won't, or can't eat the whole thing?"

"Then it's a sign that the omens in the Reading are reversed inescapably. Seekers who don't like what I see in their future always hope I'll overlook the last bite."

"Like the cats who brought you Shirley's body," Huey concluded. "I could tell they were really dissatisfied customers even before I read their minds."

"Reading minds . . . speaking with the dead . . ." The impact of being in the presence of such power was too much for Lulu. She pressed her belly to the ground and hid her face against outstretched paws. "Huey, your gifts outshine my own. I am but a dust-bunny in your presence."

The hamster affected a modest look. "Reading minds and talking to the dead just lets me know about what's going on in the here-and-now. *You* can see the future. Closest I come to that is a little recreational seed-reading. The results are unreliable. That's why Shirley laughed off my warning tonight."

"Seed-reading?"

"That's the way my kind foresee the future. It's a lot like your method, finding the answers to a Seeker's question in a pattern, only the Reading material's not so messy-bloody-sticky-hork-hork-hork-*bluargh!*" He winked at her. "The Seeker brings me some sunflower seeds, I throw 'em into the air and interpret the design they make when they fall. Then I have to make the Reading vanish, just like you do, or it won't come true." He puffed out his cheeks happily. "Being Oracular *rules*; we always get to eat!"

Lulu murmured something under her breath.

"Say again?" Huey pricked up his ears.

"Don't like . . ." The rest was lost.

"Don't like what?" the hamster persisted.

"I don't like—I don't like eating *rodents*, okay?" Lulu yelled so loudly that Huey was bowled backwards, tail over toes. "I *loathe* having to eat the Reading afterwards." She shuddered with revulsion. "The smell, the taste, the fur in my throat, the crunchy bones, the way the liver always pops in my—"

"*Enough!*" Huey groomed himself frantically, a sure sign of anxiety in hamsters. "These are *my* kin you're talking about! Our lives are short enough without you making them shorter *and* dissing our livers! Do you know *why* so many of us have died for your stupid Readings lately? So this Señor Pantalones creep can find out just how big a Reading has to be before it's *impossible* for you to eat it all!"

"So that's it." Lulu looked grim. "I thought that they were getting larger, night after night."

"Yeah, you'll probably have a wharf rat on your plate before this is over," Huey said bitterly.

"They can't do that," Lulu said. "The holy rules that govern Seekers and Seers alike come from Lady Bast herself, great goddess of cats since the days of ancient Egypt. Her words must be obeyed, for she commands the kitty-flap in the doorways of space and time, and is mistress of the Broom of Admonition and the Water Pistol of Chastisement! She decreed that because we assured our future as treasured masters of the human race by keeping the granaries of Egypt free of mice, only mice can bring us the secrets of that future."

"A big, *fat* future, in your case, if Señor Pantalones gets his way," Huey put in. Abruptly, he frowned. "Uh-oh."

"Uh-oh?" Lulu repeated. "I don't like the sound of that."

"You shouldn't." Huey chewed one claw, agitated. "There's this mouse I know, Big Rudy. His mama was pet store stock. Lucky girl escaped on snake-feeding day, but rumor has it she got a little too . . . *friendly* with one of the Guinea pigs in the shop before that."

"Is that even possible?"

"Seeing is believing, and if you ever saw Big Rudy— which no one has, lately. He vanished a week ago." He gazed at Lulu with bleak eyes. "*They've* got him. I'll bet my last seed on it! If Señor Stinky Pants wants a mouse fat enough to turn your prophecy on its ear, he'll never find one to equal Big Rudy. That'll make *two* good friends of mine he's killed." He began to cry.

Very carefully, so as not to alarm him, Lulu patted Huey gently with the tip of one paw. "Maybe not. Even if they've *got* him, that doesn't mean they've killed him. If he were dead, wouldn't you be able to 'talk' to him?"

"Not if they ate him."

"But they *can't* eat him! They need to keep him alive and gaining even *more* weight until the full moon conclave. That's when Señor Pantalones is going to turn your friend into a weapon of mouse destruction for me. I don't need a glob of entrails to see what's coming: as a Seer, I answer all Seekers' questions, but at the conclave I only perform Readings concerning the future of Catopolis itself. As soon as the Elders ask if anyone wants such a Reading, Señor Pantalones will claim he dreamed that Bast appeared to him and named him our sole ruler. His minions will swear they had confirming dreams, but because of the magnitude of his claim, my gift will be called upon to verify it."

"Except there *was* no 'I'm king of the cats' dream for Señor Stinky Pants. Game over, right?"

"Not until I eat the Reading," Lulu said. "All of it. Him. Big Rudy."

"Oh," Huey said. "Oh, crabapples."

"And thus the Reading will be deemed reversed and binding. Every Reading is a word spoken in the goddess' own voice and must be obeyed. It won't matter that we've never had a lone ruler before. If it's the 'will' of Bast, it must be made so." Lulu laughed without joy. "After he's in charge, it'll be simple for Señor Pantalones to have me killed. He'll replace me with a false Seer, one whose predictions will always ratify his desires. I'm doomed."

"But you look like a house cat," Huey said. "You could stay safe at home. He'd never be able to get at you there."

"I am a *Seer*," Lulu said staunchly. "It's my duty to make my powers available to my kin. If I die, I die, but I will always honor Lady Bast's gift as I honor my goddess."

As she finished speaking, she glanced to where Shirley's body lay. Her chin rose. An air of purpose possessed her. She strode toward the mouse's remains and began gathering bits and pieces of alley debris around the corpse.

"What are you doing?" Huey asked, scuttling beside her as she worked.

"Giving Shirley the best burial I can manage," Lulu replied. "I feel responsible for her death."

"You didn't kill her!"

"But she still died because of me. Let me do this, Huey, for your friend and for you." She found a half page of old newspaper and dropped it onto the pile of blown leaves, discarded candy bar wrappers, and crushed soda cans covering Shirley.

"That's—kind of you, kitty." Huey cocked his head as if listening for something. "And it worked. Her spirit's moved on. I hope someone does the same for Big Rudy, when the time comes."

"You're my colleague, a fellow Oracular One. It was the least I could—" Suddenly, inspiration flashed in Lulu's agate eyes. "Yes," she said, half to herself. "It *was* the least I could do. But the least is *not* enough! I am a Seer, an Oracular One, a servant of the goddess! If I stand back and let Señor Pantalones fight me on his terms, I might as well show him my underbelly. No. Never. By Lady Bast's sacred name, I'm going to take the battle to *him*."

"Oh, my Seeds, you're gonna try to save Big Rudy!" Huey exclaimed. He raised his forepaws to his temples. "Your thoughts are blaring about how you know where Señor Pantalones' hangs out with his minions, how that's where they're probably holding Big Rudy, how if he's set him free, there's no way they'll be able to catch another mouse his size in time for the full moon conclave." He lowered his paws and grinned at her. "Good plan. Let's roll."

"I don't remember inviting you," Lulu said.

"You need me and you know it!" Huey declared. "Any lookout can keep his ears open, but I can keep my *mind* open and let you know if Señor Stupid and his goons are heading your way even before *they* do! Whaddaya say?"

Lulu thought about it for a moment. "I say . . . let's fight crime."

*   *   *

"Well, *that* could've gone better." Under the icy moonlight, Lulu raced down the center of one of many paths snaking through the city's foremost public park. "Did we lose them?"

This question was tossed back to the hamster clinging desperately to the red collar around her neck. Huey cast a fearful look behind them. "I can't tell. All they're thinking about is what they're gonna do to us when they catch us."

"Son of a—" Lulu grumbled and put on a little extra speed. *If only I didn't have to stick to the open road!* she thought. *I'd have a better chance of shaking them if I could dive into the shrubbery. None of those toms is small enough to follow me there.*

"Why don't you?" Huey asked.

"Why—? Hey! You're supposed to be reading their thoughts, not mine!"

"You *should* go into the bushes," the hamster persisted. "That's what saved Big Rudy, once we upended his prison box. Man, I never saw so much mouseflesh move so fast! If only he could've made his getaway a little more quietly—"

"The important thing is, he's *safe*, and Señor Pantalones is left empty-pawed for the conclave," Lulu said. "We did it, Huey! We thwarted his plan to corrupt my Reading!"

Huey was not sharing her optimism. "Ever think he might have a Plan B? I'm telling you, get the heck off the road and into the bushes, unless you *want* Señor Pantalones' minions to rip you open like a Christmas present! Are you even *listening* to—? Oh!" Huey's paws tightened convulsively on the fur under Lulu's collar. "Oh, no, you don't mean it. That's just too stupid to—"

"What are you babbling about?" Lulu snarled. Her paws were hurting, her ribs were on fire, and she felt ready to hit the wall.

"You're doing this for *me*!" Huey cried. "Don't deny it;

it's *screaming* at me from your thoughts. You're afraid that if you hit the underbrush, I'll be knocked off your back by a branch and the Pantalones mob will get me."

"You're welcome," Lulu said, her voice hoarse with weariness.

"*Have you lost your mind?*" the hamster squealed.

"You . . . are not the boss . . . of me." Lulu slowed, then stopped. She sat down in the middle of the path, breathing hard. She looked unable to move, but Huey learned differently when he tried to make a break for it. Her paw fell on him like Divine Judgment. "Where do you think you're going?"

"Away from *you*, crazy cat-lady! I won't let you put yourself in danger."

"Tough seeds, rodent," Lulu countered. "We're in this together."

"Oh, *please*. Teaming up to put a kink in Señor Pantalones' tail is one thing, but a cat protecting a hamster? That's like a cop protecting a donut!"

"Huey, you're no donut," Lulu said solemnly. Then she frowned. "Did that sound as dumb as I think it did? Never mind. What I'm saying is, we're not just cat and hamster any more, predator and prey; we're partners. We share a gift. We can see and hear things that others can't. The power's the same, whether it touches a hamster or a cat."

"Cue violins," Huey said wryly. "As long as you're not related to them."

"Look, if you want to be snarky, fine, but all the snotty one-liners in the world won't change what I *know*: Lady Bast gave me my powers for a reason, and I worship her best by using them rightly."

"By throwing away your own life to save mine?" The hamster was not convinced. "Why would a cat goddess want you to take care of a *rodent*?"

"I believe that Lady Bast is a goddess first, a goddess of cats second. What kind of god or goddess places a limit on love?"

Huey looked up at Lulu in awe. "Is your faith *that* strong? I can hardly—"

Before the hamster could finish, the shrubbery to either side of the path erupted as seven lean, muscular tom cats shot out of the darkness. The foremost one knocked Lulu to the ground. She lost her hold on Huey in the tumble, but before the hamster could gather his wits and run, a second feral sprang forward and pinned him down. As Lulu squirmed impotently in her captor's grasp, she heard the bushes rustle again. Though her head was pressed to the path, she was able to turn it just enough to see the large black and white fulfillment of her fears amble up to seat himself a whisker-length away from her nose.

"Poor kit," he said sweetly. "I'd hoped it wouldn't come to this. You should have given me what I wanted, but at least you've ended by presenting me a revelation worthy of one of your own gut-dabblings. When you and this . . . snack—" he gave Huey a blood-chilling smile. "—sneaked into my lair and freed that stupid mouse, my first reaction was to ask why I'd tolerated your existence for so long. Then it came to me: I only need you because you are Catopolis' Seer. But *why* are you Catopolis' Seer? Because you said you were! You claimed Bast appeared to you in a dream, and two other cats swore they'd shared it. Only two." His gaze drifted over the faces of his seven waiting minions. "I think I can swing that."

"You can't just proclaim yourself a Seer!" Lulu shouted. "You haven't got the gift!"

"Sometimes, kit, the gift of prophecy lies in the Seekers, not the Seer. What a difference a title makes! Call yourself a Seer, and they all stand ready to believe you *can* see! Fill your prophecies with vague, 'mystic' words, and your Seekers blame themselves when their foretold futures don't come to pass as predicted. Such a clever trick."

"That's not how I serve Catopolis, and you know it!" Lulu protested.

"But it *is* how I will do things when I take your place." Señor Pantalones looked as though he'd fallen heir to a catnip factory.

"Our kin will find out you never had Lady Bast's blessing," Lulu said. "You won't be able to fool them for long."

"Long enough to remake Catopolis in my own image. As for Bast's blessing, don't make me laugh! How can a scrap of some ancient cat's imagination bless anything? You put all your faith into a pretty fable, staked your life on a myth, and where did it get you? Where's your so-called goddess now?" He smirked, then told the cat restraining her: "Let her up. I want her to have a clear view of this."

As Lulu shakily got to her feet, Señor Pantalones made a terse gesture with one paw. The minion holding Huey grabbed the hamster by the back of the neck and dropped him in front of his master. "My first Reading," Señor Pantalones said, his whole body rumbling with wicked delight. He lifted one paw for the killing blow.

"No!" Lulu exclaimed. She tried to reach Huey, but her feral guard shouldered her back. "*Please.* Spare him and I— I'll read the omens any way you want! And if you want to replace me as Seer, I won't stand in your way. I'll confine myself to exile among humans. I'll never show my face in Catopolis again!"

"All that, for *this*?" Señor Pantalones sneered at the hamster in his clutches. "Have you a reason, or have you simply lost your mind?"

"This creature is a greater Seer than I could ever hope to be," Lulu declared. "He can speak to the dead."

"Any minute now," said Señor Pantalones.

"He also has the power to read minds."

The big black and white cat threw back his head and guffawed. "Is that so?" He looked down at Huey. "All right, little snack, prove it. Look into my mind and tell me how I'm going to kill you."

The hamster regarded Señor Pantalones calmly. "You think you'll do it by slitting me open throat-to-tail. Of course now that I've said that, you're thinking you'll make it tail-to-throat, just to be a wiseass. You're also thinking that as soon as you're boss of Catopolis, you'll never have to associate with smelly trash like your feral buddies over there." Huey waved a paw at the seven street cats.

"Bah! Nonsense!" Señor Pantalones huffed. But a nervous look twitched over his face and he refused to meet his minions' eyes. "That will be enough out of—"

Undaunted, Huey forged on: "*Plus*, you think you'll be able to fool the other cats with your stupid 'I had a dream from Lady Bast making me a Seer' plan, except you're all ego and no brains. Otherwise you'd to realize Lady Bast can send *real* dream-visions to every cat in Catopolis, telling them what a big, fat phony you are. Which is something your feral buddies will already know when you kick them to the curb like a bag of empty Tuna NomNom cans. And what's more—"

"I said *enough!*" Señor Pantalones' bared claws slashed down. The force of the big black and white cat's blow tore Huey open from throat to tail, as the hamster himself had predicted. Lulu yowled.

And then, a miracle: Instead of the expected gush of blood and innards, Huey's ravaged body erupted with a surge of blinding light. The humble park pathway became a carpet of fragrant lotus blossoms. Silver stars danced in swirling midair streams. As the awestruck cats stood witness, a lithe, graceful feline as tall as a royal palm tree ascended from the fuzzy shell at Señor Pantalones' feet. Her ears and paws were adorned with rings of pure gold. Her flanks were the color of the immortal desert, and her eyes were green mirrors of the moon.

She showed the big black and white tom teeth like a row of scimitars. "*Surprise*, moth-brain."

Señor Pantalones stared openmouthed, faintly uttering the feline version of homina-homina-homina-homina until he regained control of his tongue. He then flung himself flat and called out, "O great Lady Bast, have pity!"

"Way ahead of you," the goddess replied. "For your name alone, if nothing else. *Señor Pantalones*? What *were* your humans thinking? Remind me to smite them with a plague of locusts, or at least make them lose their car keys. But aside from that, it's impossible *not* to pity someone whose main goal in life was to become the sole ruler of Catopolis. You actually thought you had a future *herding cats*?"

"My lady, I—"

"*Ffffftttt!*" She silenced him with one admonitory hiss. "Señor Pantalones, your crimes are many. You doubted my divinity. You attempted to corrupt my chosen Seer. When she refused to serve your purposes, you sought her death. You have brought about the self-serving slaughter of so many of this city's mice, endangering the food supply for my feral children, that I was compelled to assume rodent's guise in order to intervene. Do you have any idea of how humiliating that was for a cat goddess? Do you think I *enjoy* this whole *felis ex machina* gig?"

Señor Pantalones raised his head. "Sweet Lady Bast, I swear I'll—"

"Save your breath. I call your own minions to witness that you are banished to the sole company of your human servants from now on. If you ever dare to show so much as a whisker in the streets of Catopolis—" The goddess raised one paw. A gigantic water pistol appeared in midair. An unseen hand pulled the trigger.

Lulu was still laughing long after Señor Pantalones' drenched and caterwauling flight from the park was a faint memory. His minions too had fled, sharing their erstwhile master's soggy fate. When she caught her breath again, she asked the goddess, "Once he dries off, do you think he'll stay in exile?"

"He'd better. His former minions will see to that. Remember what I said about how he was going to dump their butts once he came to rule Catopolis? They'll remember that, too. He may be a power-mad fool, but he's not stupid enough to venture onto the streets as long as seven strong ferals are holding a grudge with his name on it." The divine feline smiled. "But enough of him. My kitten, this night you have shown steadfast reverence, faith, honor and compassion. Tell me, how may I reward you for all this?"

"Welllll . . ." Lulu took a deep breath. "Could you please rewrite the rule that says I have to eat the Reading, after? Because like I told you when you were still a hamster, I really, *really* don't like to eat—"

"—rodents? Then let me see what you do like to eat, sweet Seer." Bast placed one forepaw on Lulu's head and closed her eyes in concentration. "Aha!" she exclaimed at last, looking well pleased. "Hear me, O Lulu, my Oracular One! From this night forth, you are empowered to read the omens of the future in a splash of milk, a scattering of kibble, yea, in anything my beloved children lay before you. And whatever form the Reading may take, through my sacred power it shall become your favorite food once it touches your lips."

"You mean—?" Lulu scarcely dared believe the blessed fate awaiting her.

"Yes," said the cat goddess gravely. "Turkey. And the good kind, from the deli; not the cheap supermarket store brand. So let it be written! So let it be done!"

Lulu bowed low. "Hail, Lady Bast! A fowl future never looked so fair!"

That was when Bast got out the Broom.

BLACK

Richard Lee Byers

Black cats were disappearing.

Silent was black as midnight from nose to tail, so it might have been prudent to lie low. But he was also one of the Queen's knights and an initiate in the Mysteries of Bast, so duty and pride alike demanded he investigate.

First he went to ask the dogs. Rude, barbaric creatures, dogs didn't have one supreme ruler, but Ragged Ear was as important a chieftain as any.

Silent found the pack in a park the humans forsook after sunset. Twenty dogs were foraging, sniffing about the ground and overturning garbage cans to rummage inside.

Silent padded across the street and onto the grass. He made no effort to go unseen, and a long-legged mongrel with spotted fur came stalking out of the gloom.

"Hello, Howler," Silent said. "I just want to talk to your boss. Can we do it the easy way?"

Howler bared his fangs.

Silent called on the Aspect of Brother Lion and roared like thunder. Howler recoiled, his pungent urine spattering the ground.

"You see?" Silent said. "The easy way is better."

"I'm not so sure," rumbled Ragged Ear. Silent turned to

see the big Doberman standing in front of a confusion of curved, colored pipes built for human children to climb on and crawl through. Brother Lion's voice had scared every other dog into keeping its distance, but not the alpha. "I might be willing to go to some trouble to pay you back for your tricks."

"Do you really want to start up that old fight again?" Silent replied. "What's the point, when Her Majesty has already taken the prize?"

Ragged Ear snorted. "What do you want, shaman?"

"Black cats are going missing."

"And you think I deserve the credit?"

"No. Even if you had some reason to hunt blacks and blacks only, you're not cunning enough to catch so many. But your pack ranges all over the city. Perhaps you've noticed something odd."

"Maybe I have, but why would I tell you?"

"I'll owe you a favor."

"I don't need anything from the likes of you."

"No? You have white hairs on your muzzle that weren't there the last time we talked. You're favoring your right foreleg, and that has tooth marks on it. You're getting old, and others are starting to challenge you for mastery of the pack. A day may come when you need a charm to help you win one of those duels."

Ragged Ear cocked his head. "You'd do that?"

"Why not? What do I care which hound is the boss?"

"Well . . . you know downtown? The part with the narrow brick streets and old, sooty buildings?"

"Of course."

"It stinks of power. Your kind of power."

Silent waited a moment. "Is that all you have?"

"Yes. We're not stupid. We cleared out as soon as we caught the scent."

"So really, you barely know anything at all."

The Doberman grinned. "But I did know a little, and you agreed to trade for it."

"Don't worry, I'll keep my end of the deal." Not with any great enthusiasm, but honor demanded it.

It took two days' travel to reach the center of the city, and Silent's paws were sore by the time he arrived. He couldn't smell anything except the vile, hot spew of the countless cars, trucks, and buses, but then, he wasn't a dog.

Stained by the shadow of a high-rise, the cathedral looked like a clump of dirty icicles growing upside down. A sort of antimagic, feeble but cold and forbidding, seethed in the pale stone walls.

Silent glowered at the church. Even before Ragged Ear steered him to the district, he'd suspected he was going to end up here, but he'd hoped otherwise.

He bounded up the steps and waited. When a human opened a door, he slipped inside.

The interior of the cathedral was quiet, cool, and dim, the stained glass dull for want of sunlight. The votive candles smelled like rotting flowers. Silent prowled onward, searching for priests. The third one he found wore a silver ring. It had a sort of raised cross on it, but, scrutinized closely, the emblem was also a hammer.

Silent stalked the human, waiting for him to move from the cavernous nave to some secluded area. Then something hissed from overhead.

Silent looked up. Yellow eyes in a black feline face glared down from the choir loft. The priest reached inside his jacket, then staggered and collapsed before he could pull anything out.

Astonished, Silent faltered for an instant, then screeched at his fellow cat. Calling on Sister Cheetah's Aspect, he raced for the stairs leading upward.

The assassin was gone by the time he reached the loft. But at least the priest was shaking off the effects of the curse. Assisted by people who'd come running when he fell, he clambered to his feet.

Silent jumped on top of the railing enclosing the loft and crouched there waiting for the priest to look up and see him. He was poised to spring for cover if the man reached for his weapon again, but he didn't. He just gave a tiny nod.

Eventually the priest convinced the other humans that it was safe to let him alone. Then he led Silent down a hallway and stepped inside a room.

Despite everything, this could still be a trap, and Silent followed warily. But the priest, a round, bald man with muddy brown eyes, was alone. He sank down behind a desk in a cluttered little office.

Silent jumped onto a chair. "Do you have the Gift of Siegfried?" he asked. If not, he'd have to expend some of his own power to establish communication.

"We call it the Blessing of Saint Francis," the man replied, "but yes, I understand you. Strange as it seems, I saw you scare the other cat away. So I suppose I ought to thank you."

"Thank me by explaining what's going on. My Queen sent me to look into it."

The priest blinked. "You're a black cat yourself. Don't you know?"

"All I know is that others like me are disappearing. Until I saw the black attack you, I suspected the Inquisition was persecuting our kind as you have in times past."

The human frowned. "Those who came before me didn't mean to 'persecute' anyone unjustly. They believed they were fighting Satan's servants. Because, as you probably understand better than I, the Devil gave gifts to all cats, but to blacks most of all, with the promise of even stronger magic if they would bow down before him."

"Yes," Silent said, "but what you and those like you have always refused to understand is that very few of us have ever taken the bait."

"You say that," the inquisitor replied, "but suddenly there's a whole little army of black cats with their power to hex and jinx awakened. They're using it to attack the clergy and others who perform good works. Making people sick and causing accidents. I think that if you hadn't chased it off, the one that came for me would have given me a heart attack."

Silent didn't want to believe what the priest was saying, but he'd just seen proof that at least one black had bartered himself to the Old Serpent. "What's the Inquisition doing about it?"

The human sighed. "Not much. Maybe you don't realize, but there really isn't any such Office anymore. The world has changed, and even the Church doesn't want to believe in magic, demons, or animals that talk. We in the Society of the Hammer try to continue the work of the witch hunters, but there are only a handful of us. I'm the only one for several states around, and evidently I'm no good at my job, because I haven't been able to accomplish anything."

Silent would never have expected to feel sympathy for one of his kindred's traditional foes, but now he did. A fleeting twinge of it, anyway. "At least you figured out that blacks are going wrong. That puts me farther ahead than I was before."

"Then you mean to stop what's going on?"

"Yes. Cats are free to do almost anything they like, but not to give themselves to the Fallen Star. It's against Her Majesty's laws."

"Then maybe," said the priest, a plea in his tone, "we can work together."

"I'd like that," Silent lied, "but unfortunately, no human

could keep up with me through the narrow spaces and over the rooftops while I hunt for answers. I'll come back if it turns out you can help."

"Well, all right."

"Meanwhile, can you let me out of the building?"

Once outside, Silent pondered what he'd learned and wished there were more to it. It was good, if also daunting, that he now knew who the enemy was, at least in general terms. But he still didn't understand how the Old Serpent's agent was making contact with black cats, how the corruptor could persuade so many to surrender to the wicked side of their natures, or where they were all hiding.

It was three days later that, pacing along a sidewalk, dodging the feet of striding, oblivious humans, he peered down an alley and saw several cats foraging amid the refuse in a row of dumpsters. Two were black. They were reckless to show themselves in broad daylight, but perhaps they hadn't heard about their fellows disappearing. Felines were the most cultured, sophisticated species in the world, but even so, they had no means of rapid universal communication such as mankind enjoyed.

Silent supposed it was up to him to warn the pair. He started down the alley. Then a yellow tom staggered a step and let out a puzzled meow. He flopped over onto his side in the open pizza box in which he'd been standing.

Over the course of the next several moments, somnolence overtook all the cats. Some jumped out of the dumpsters and tried to bolt, but they couldn't outrun a danger that was now inside their bellies. Something was wrong with the garbage.

The last of them, a Siamese, collapsed beside the tire of a parked car. Then a door in a brick wall opened, and two men in gray coveralls came out. The garments had ANIMAL CONTROL stenciled on the backs. Silent couldn't read human language any more than he could speak it without a spell in place, but he'd learned to recognize certain symbols and labels, and this was one of them.

He hadn't hesitated to invade the cathedral, but he faltered now. Perhaps it was because the Inquisition was mostly a terror in the tales of generations past, while Animal Control still hunted cats every day.

But Silent was Her Majesty's knight, sworn to protect her subjects, and with luck, Brother Lion's roar would frighten humans as effectively as it startled dogs. He invoked the Aspect, drew a deep breath, then saw what the men were doing.

Each human moved to pick up one of the blacks, stepping over other slumbering cats to do it. After they collected the pair and carried them around a corner, they came back for the others, but even so, it was obvious which prizes they'd truly wanted to capture.

Silent had hoped to scare them off. Now he would have been happy to hurt them. But he'd seen the "animal shelter," a gray concrete fortress of a place not far from the cathedral. It wouldn't be as easy to infiltrate as the church had been. So perhaps there was a cleverer way to handle this situation.

He trotted toward the nearer of the men. He meowed as if hopeful for a petting or a morsel.

The human exchanged glances with his partner. Then he squatted down and crooned, "Here, kitty, kitty, kitty." There was a smile on his long, narrow face, but he had the malicious eyes of someone who'd rather yank a cat's tail than stroke its head.

Silent stayed where he was. He didn't want to appear *too* unwary, lest it arouse suspicion.

Moving slowly, the human extracted a plastic bag from a pocket. He took a white pellet out of it, and the mouthwatering smell of fish suffused the air. "Here, kitty, kitty, kitty."

Silent trotted forward and took the oily meat. Even knowing it might be tainted, it was hard not to gobble it down. For cats had many virtues, but self-denial wasn't chief among them, not even for champions of the realm.

He suffered the human to pick him up and carry him around the corner, then put up a token struggle when his captor sought to stuff him into a cramped steel box. The man did it anyway, clanged the barred door shut, and went back for other prisoners. Silent spat out the fish, then batted it out onto the floor of the cargo bay where it couldn't tempt him anymore.

After the men gathered and caged all the cats, they shut the back of the truck, and then the vehicle shuddered into motion. Silent lay down in the stuffy, rumbling, rattling darkness and hoped he hadn't just made a fatally reckless move.

The first several rooms in the animal shelter weren't as horrible as rumor claimed. They lent credence to the accounts of those animals claiming to have survived imprisonment here, who to some degree refuted the tales of neglect and mutilation. But the man carrying Silent's box didn't stop in any of those spaces. He took him through two more doors and into nightmare.

The back room reeked of filth and festering wounds. Some animals bristled, snarled, barked, or hissed when one of their captors appeared. Others cringed to the backs of their tiny cages, and a few didn't even seem to notice, as if they'd fled deep inside themselves.

The human shook Silent out into a wire cage, one of many stacked in rows. The food and water bowls were empty, and they stayed that way. Silent's mouth grew dry, and he ignored the discomfort as best he could. At least he was sure his captors wouldn't let a black cat die of thirst. That wasn't what this was about.

He asked some of his fellow prisoners what they'd experienced here. Their answers sickened him.

The sun set. Sealed in a room with no windows, he couldn't see it, but like any black cat, he could feel it, and he was glad. Maybe he shouldn't have been. Demons and their servants were more powerful at night. But so was he.

The door opened, and the men who'd captured him came back through. The one with the narrow face opened a cage and dragged a dachshund out. The little black dog tried to bite, but its teeth couldn't penetrate the human's brown leather work gloves.

The other man, thickset with blond hair sheared very short, jabbed a hypodermic into the dachshund's flank. In a few moments, its frantic struggles subsided to an almost imperceptible squirming. The man holding it laid it atop a steel table, and his partner set down the needle and picked up a cordless power drill. He pressed the button, and the bit spun and whined.

Silent had no obligation to act, for it was only a dog quivering helpless on the table. If he were as cunning as a magus was supposed to be, he'd wait to learn more before making a move. But he was simply too disgusted.

He called on Brother Tiger and swiped at the door of his cage. It flew open and dangled askew, hanging by one hinge. He leaped out onto the linoleum floor.

The humans pivoted in his direction. He charged them and ripped at the leg of the one with the drill.

His claws cut to the bone, the gashes spaced more widely than seemed possible, because at present he wasn't just a cat but rather a fusion of cat and tiger. The man screamed and dropped, his blood spurting. The captive animals clamored.

Silent pivoted toward the man with the narrow face. His eyes wide, the human backed away and lifted a pocket pistol.

The gun was a problem. It likely wouldn't kill Brother

Tiger, but it could put a hole in Silent that would kill him when the Aspect departed.

He darted under the table. The human would be waiting to shoot when he reappeared, but at least this way he didn't have to cover the entire distance running straight at the muzzle of the gun. Instead of charging directly at his foe, he swung left.

He bounded into the open. The pistol banged, and the bullet cracked into the floor beside him.

Silent closed the distance and tore the human's leg out from underneath him. His foe fell down, and, his arm now shaking, tried again to point the gun. Silent leaped and clawed at his hand, half severing it and knocking the pistol away. The man convulsed.

Silent spun around to check on his other adversary. Still supine, the man was only shivering and twitching. By the looks of it, there was no fight left in either one of them.

Silent stood and panted. It wasn't difficult to roar like a lion or run like a cheetah. But even for an adept, generating the strength and shadowy semblance of a tiger's size and weight was a more taxing feat.

The other prisoners begged him to free them. He wanted to, but perhaps it would be better to scout now and come back for them later. He was still considering when the door opened once again.

A slender, raven-haired woman dressed in an Animal Control coverall entered the room, with several black cats padding at her back. The maimed men whined, evidently begging for her help.

When she answered, even a cat could recognize the note of scorn in her voice. She raised her hand, and each man jerked and then lay still. Points of light flew up out of their mouths and into her grasp. She squeezed them together, mashing them into a jelly, which she then licked off her palm and fingers. Now perceiving her true nature, the caged animals cowered.

Her repast complete, the demoness shrank and became a black cat. In heat. The scent of her evoked an instant pang of desire, even though Silent recognized her for what she truly was. It was surely a ploy to addle him, and he struggled to clear his head.

Perhaps she could tell that he was straining, for she laughed at him. "Silent," she purred. "When I heard what happened in the cathedral, I suspected we'd meet by and by."

He didn't like it that she knew his name, but then, he didn't like anything about this situation. "Who are you, and what are doing here?"

"When I wear this shape, some people call me Barb." She lifted a paw and unsheathed gleaming claws to display their secondary points. "As for what I'm doing, haven't you guessed?"

"You've taken control of the animal shelter, or at least a part of it, and turned it into a place of torment. You offer the black-cat prisoners a way out, but only if they agree to become what you want them to be."

"Actually, it's a little more subtle than that. The prisoners never associate me with captivity and abuse. That's all done by humans under my control. I'm the shadow that comes in the night offering comfort, hope, and liberation if only the blacks will join me in a war against mankind. And why wouldn't they? By that time, most of them are only too eager to strike back."

"But what's the point?"

"Why, to corrupt souls. To create living weapons, wield them to assail servants of the good and spread misery and despair, and, in time, to pass them along to human warlocks to serve as their familiars. With any luck, to stir up the old mistrust between men and cats all over again."

"Her Majesty won't allow that."

"Your Queen isn't here, only you, and you can't stop me. But you *can* join me."

"Why would I do that?"

"To save your life."

"It's no use keeping your body alive if you kill your spirit to do it."

"I'm not asking you to lose yourself. I'm asking you to *become* yourself more fully than ever before. Lucifer's gift has always been a part of you. Haven't you ever wondered how it would feel to use it? Imagine the wonderful things you could do if you married that power to the magic you've already mastered."

For a moment, the prospect tempted him, or maybe it was simply the smell of her nether parts, still wafting on the air. He gave his head a shake. "I'm not interested."

"Why? Because you love the humans? Have you looked around at this horrible place they built? It was a house of misery and death long before I arrived."

"Maybe so, but for every one that hates us, there are ten who are our friends, and for every cruel deed, a hundred acts of kindness. I suppose I do love them. And even if I didn't, I love the Queen, and I've already pledged *her* my allegiance."

Barb sighed. "What a shame. We could have sinned such magnificent sins together." She glanced around at the cats arrayed behind her, no doubt to order them to attack.

With the enemy blocking the only way out of the room, Silent poised himself to fight as hard and die as well as possible, for die he almost certainly would. The conversation had given him a chance to catch his breath, and he had faith in his own powers, but they couldn't protect him from a dozen tainted blacks all giving him the Evil Eye at once.

Then inspiration struck. "Wait!" he cried.

Barb turned back around. "Changed your mind?"

"Partly. I won't just surrender myself. But I will *bet* myself." According to feline lore, demons loved to gamble.

Barb's green eyes narrowed. "What do you have in mind?"

"You and I will fight. *Just* you and I. Your stooges will stay out of it. If you render me helpless, then I'll let you change me as you've changed these others. If I win, they revert to what they were."

"Ridiculous. They gave themselves of their own free will."

"That's not the way I see it. You boasted yourself that you tortured and tricked them into it, and that means they deserve another chance."

"Whether they do or not, you're proposing to wager one soul while I risk more than twenty. You value yourself too highly."

"Do I? Does the chance to turn an Adept of Bast come along every day? You want me, demon. Quite a bit. Maybe you shouldn't have let me know, but it's too late now."

Barb glared.

"What's the matter?" Silent asked. "You're a champion of Hell. Are you afraid of one lone cat? Don't you think you can beat me without a bunch of slaves backing you up? I hope the other demons don't find out. They'll laugh their tails off."

"All right," Barb spat, "it's a wager."

"Good. After I kill you, how do I change the other blacks back to normal?"

Barb turned her head. Following the motion, Silent saw a stack of parchments sitting on the floor. It hadn't been there a moment before.

"Covenants," the demonic cat said, "sealed with paw

print and fang mark, blood and spit. If I die or yield, they'll catch fire instantly."

"All right," Silent said. "Shall we fight outside? There's more room."

"As you prefer, magus. Wherever we do it, the outcome will be the same."

She and her servants led him to an exit, doors opening of their own accord when she neared. Once he was clear of the building, he had to stifle a craven urge to bolt. He wasn't used to feeling so afraid, but he was certain Barb was the most formidable foe he'd ever fought, and he had no real idea of the extent of her abilities.

For his part, he could do a great many things with spells, but he couldn't cast them quickly enough to be of use in a duel. He'd have to depend on the Aspects, and accordingly decided to cloak himself in the power of Sister Leopard. She wasn't as big and strong as Brother Tiger, but she was quicker and more agile.

The procession wound up in a dark self-service parking lot. A couple of cars still sat in their spaces, but most had departed at the end of the workday. Barb's minions positioned themselves around the perimeter of the space. The gleam of the sickle moon caught in their eyes.

"Is the dueling ground acceptable?" asked Barb.

"It'll do," Silent said, widening the distance between them.

"You know, you can yield right now and avoid a lot of pain."

"Or you can give up right now and not get killed."

She charged, and as she did, she changed. She swelled big as a lynx, and her fangs and claws glowed like red-hot iron. The flesh around them charred, but it didn't appear to cause her any distress.

Silent waited until she'd nearly closed, then sprang to the

side. He clawed and tore open her shoulder. Her blood burst into flame on contact with the air.

She wheeled and swiped at him. He jerked back, and barbed, smoldering claws missed him by a hair. He leaped, bore her down beneath him, and reached to bite her throat. He supposed her blood would burn his mouth but it couldn't be helped.

She writhed and blurred beneath him, and suddenly he didn't have a secure hold on her anymore. Clad in the form of a python, she whipped scaly lengths of herself around him and pulled the loops tight, and now he was the one being gripped. The pressure was painful and relentless.

Barb raised her wedge-shaped head to leer down at him. "Surrender," she hissed.

He couldn't reach her with his fangs or fore claws. He groped with his hind paws, found a part of her, and raked hard.

She jerked, and her hold loosened an iota. He heaved with all of Sister Leopard's might and broke free. Barb swirled around him, seeking to wrap him up again. He struck at her, bashing her head to the side, and sprang away from her sliding, twisting coils.

The jump obliged him to turn his back on her. Just for an instant, but when he spun back around, she was gone.

Had he killed her, and her body then disappeared? No, surely not, that last blow hadn't hit solidly enough to break her spine. He turned around and around, seeking her in vain. Did she have the power to become invisible? Or had she shrunk into something so tiny it was impossible to spot?

Whatever she'd done, he couldn't locate her, and his nerves crawled with the certainty that she was stealing closer. Then he noticed the attitude of one of the other cats. It wasn't looking at him or anything else on the expanse of asphalt with its oil spots and painted lines. It was peering up at the sky. Silent followed its gaze to the winged shape plunging down at him.

He sprang out from underneath, just in time to keep the huge owl's talons from driving deep into the center of his body. But one claw still tore his hindquarters.

Hissing away the shock of the injury, he whirled, struck, and ripped the owl's wing. Barb snapped at him with her beak. He recoiled, and his right hind leg almost buckled beneath him.

For what it was worth, he'd hurt Barb, too. She flapped her wings but couldn't take flight. So she melted into the form of a gigantic, bone-white spider with a ring of lambent scarlet eyes. Silent noticed that the new form didn't appear wounded. Evidently, whenever she changed shape, the new creature joined the battle fresh and strong.

Silent wished he had some comparable advantage. As he and Barb circled one another, he hobbled, his gashed and bloody leg more painful by the moment.

Still, he managed one more spring, onto the spider's back. His claws and fangs scratched the thing's chitin armor, but couldn't penetrate to the soft parts beneath. Barb whirled, flung him off, and leaped after him. He only barely managed to roll and scramble clear.

Silent let his link to Sister Leopard dissolve. She couldn't help him prevail against a foe impervious to her natural weapons.

Barb let out a low hiss that somehow conveyed gloating satisfaction. She probably thought he'd let go of Sister Leopard because he was too weak to hold her any longer, and she wasn't far wrong at that. He was quickly reaching the limits of his strength and could only hope enough remained for one last trick.

He crouched. A mere lamed, gasping cat facing a horror. Barb scuttled at him, and he pretended to try to dodge. She raised a foreleg, whipped it down on top of him, and pinned him to the asphalt. The several horny points on the bottom of the limb dug into his flesh.

"You fought well," said Barb. "Now give up."

"No," he said.

"So stubborn. But I can't say I mind." She spread her pincer-like serrated jaws wide and lowered her head. She still wanted to inflict agony and terror, not kill him outright, and so she poised herself to take the first nip with daintiness and deliberation.

It gave Silent time to invoke one final Aspect. If he could.

Calling up Grandfather Saber-tooth was a difficult feat at the best of times, because the great progenitor had departed the world so long ago, and because it was a strain for any vessel to contain his transcendent power. For a terrible moment, nothing happened, but then Silent felt a god-like strength and ferocity exalt him.

He twisted and struck with the enormous teeth that were invisible to most eyes, yet as real as anything in the world. They punched through Barb's chitin and deep into the juncture of her head and body. He ripped them down through her thorax.

It was all he could manage before Grandfather Saber-tooth's majesty slipped from his grasp. He fell unconscious without knowing whether he'd succeeded in slaying Barb or not.

But when he woke, the heavy, bitter-smelling mass of her spider body sprawled leaking and motionless on top of him, so that was promising. His hind leg throbbing, he dragged himself out from under her and looked her over. She appeared about as dead as any carcass he'd ever seen.

But even so, he couldn't quite bring himself to turn his back on her until the other black cats rushed over to him. Their show of gratitude and concern made it plain that their cold malevolence had withered away, or at least dwindled back into nothing more than a seed.

"I'm all right," Silent panted. "I know a charm that will help my leg. The tricky part is going to be figuring out how to open all those cages back in the shelter before any other humans show up."

I AM KING!

Edward Carmien

He looked over his kingdom with a practiced eye. Black tar that stung his feet in the hot months stretched between the four edges of his world. Humming silver boxes squatted, all sides barred by empty air. Blocky shapes were distant and beyond his concern—he could not walk there. His kingdom, his, and he yowled that to the sky as he did each day: "I am king! I am king!"

Some days there were answers from below, beyond the edge. There were other kings there, false kings in some other kingdom he could not see. Other echoes he could not name, echoes that perked his ears and stirred his loins, occasionally a lament he didn't understand.

His belly was flat and empty, and so he prowled the four corners of his kingdom, one quiet step and a pause, another quiet step and a pause. Water puddled near one of the humming silver boxes. That one was good for shade in the hot months. One of the ledges with glass sides was often better shelter, though it was a climb and a leap with no ground below, down and back again. One quiet step and a pause. The next box was warm in all weather, and the evening-sun side was out of the wind, best for the cold months. One quiet step and a pause.

Tail, first languid and waving, went rigid. He heard the coo of a stinking bird. It was out of sight, so he trotted to the near corner of the silver box that sometimes clanked as well as hummed, then froze. In his mind's eye he saw the thing: dim, slow, fat, stinking of feathers that oiled his tongue and face when he fought through them to the meat and the blood.

In his mind he saw the coiled leap, foreclaws out, head low, chin thrust out, rear legs rising in anticipation of the first strike, the clawed forepaw strike that captured, the clenched bite, the stinking bird's death an eyeblink away, hind paws raking out and down, grinding crunch of bone between his jaws, soft resistance to his belly-ripping hind paws, solid thump to the ground, flight arrested forever, guts soiling his lower legs and belly, salty warm blood washing away the taint of feathers.

Yes. He charged forward. But a shadow whisked the ground to his side.

He arrested his forward lunge, crouched belly-flat to the tar, launched himself sideways. Not enough. Fast as he was, the thing struck. Fire laced his flank, and he screamed with rage and pain, turned and lashed out—hit nothing. Solid whumps of air furrowed his eyes to slits. There before him was a stinking bird, but no prey. This bird had claws the size of his head, wings nearly the span of a silver box, and a very different stink. The smell of old meat made his lip curl.

"You hunt," whump, whump, the giant wings were straining, "my prey!" It had a voice like the wailing that came from below from time to time, a sing-song shriek that started faint, grew loud, then grew faint again.

"I am king!" he screamed back, settled onto his haunches to leap, but the thing was gone, risen in the air like any stinking bird escaping from his claws, his teeth, from death and scattered feathers. He gazed into the sky, limped into the shade of a silver box and licked his wound clean. By night he'd killed and fed despite his wound. There was no sign of the stinking bird with huge claws and a voice.

When the moon rose, he heard the strange lament from far below, a faint echo in the quiet, windless night. The shouts of apes echoed also, and soon the lament fell silent. He slept and dreamed of apes he'd known, soft-handed, living in a room with a glass wall, a wall that opened onto a ledge just a leap and a scrambled climb away from his kingdom. He dreamed of the day he'd found the apes gone, the room empty and silent, glass wall shutting him away from their soft hands. He dreamed of the stinking bird's voice, heard the whump of its wings on the air, dreamed of his jaws finding the joint between neck and shoulder, biting, biting, biting.

He awoke in the midmorning, mouth sore, flank hot. Water. His legs were weak, and he lurched to the drip-fed puddle and drank his fill. Turning, he looked across his kingdom and with fierce pride yowled, "I am king! I am king!" To his shame, that exhausted him. He could not hunt that day, but he felt well enough the next dawn to prowl the circumference of his kingdom, alert for prey.

This time the shrieking bird struck without warning, slamming him to the side. Claws struck deep, but he rolled like a flash and lashed out, feeling satisfaction with a hind rake. He flipped to his feet only to discover there was nothing but air beneath him, falling, he was falling to the sound of stinking bird laughter, laughter that shrieked "My prey! Mine!"

His eyes couldn't focus on the bricks that blurred past him. He struck them, a stinging abrasion that raised a howl of pain. He scrambled to arrest his fall, but his claws tore uselessly. A shadow rose from below with inescapable speed. It slapped him into darkness.

*   *   *

"Wake up," he heard, and he felt an unfamiliar yet thrilling sensation: something was licking his fur. "Wake up." Pain crept upon him from many directions. The old wound in his flank throbbed, a lesser pain. Three sharp points of hurt poked his shoulder. And around all was a stiff soreness. He opened his eyes.

It was dim like twilight around him, though twilight it was not, only some hours from midday. Another like him was speaking. "Wake up," the other said.

"I wake," he replied, and was immediately astonished by the croak of his voice. "Water?"

"You are not dead!" said the other, who was a hunter like himself, smaller in size with dark striped fur, light eyes. As he gazed at the other, it twitched away for a moment before looking back at him.

"I am king," he said, feeling a bit stronger, and rose to his feet. The ground was black and slick beneath his paws, the color of tar but soft and cool. It was like a small hill made of rounded black shapes. He ignored his hurts and looked about.

"Better not let One-Eye hear you say that," said the other. "Good, your blood stopped flowing. What's your name?"

"Name?" he burred back, finding speech like this strange. It felt raw and rough in his throat. "I am king!"

"But One-Eye is king here," said the other hunter, and he smelled the other, and thought: her. She. Her scent made him think of the echoed lament he'd heard in his kingdom. Without knowing why, he looked up. The midday sky was nearly blocked by towering walls. Above was his kingdom. He would return there, somehow, he would find the shrieking bird, kill it, regain his place on the black tar amid the humming silver boxes. But for now, he was thirsty. "Water?"

"This way," she said, and led him down a stack of bulging

slick black shapes. "It is good you awoke. Soon these will be gone and you with them."

"Where do they go?"

"I don't know. The apes take them, then bring them back, one at a time, until there is a mountain again. Finally, they take the mountain." She led him to a puddle not unlike the one he knew beside the silver box. The water had a bad taste, but he lapped it up until he was sated.

A great confusion of scents came upon him, and he sniffed up, down, left, right. There were several others. And a strange, dank smell undercut everything. "There are others here," he said, only half a question as he took stock of his grooming.

"Oh, yes!" she said. "I'm Flinch. One-Eye is king. Beckett, Rumble, Hurry also live here."

"Here?"

"The alley," and she sniffed each way up the narrow path between the walls.

"What's Flinch?" His coat was not so bad as it could be; she had cleaned the worst of his wounds by the time he'd awoken.

"Flinch is me," she said. "Who are you?"

"I am king," he said with a puzzled urrrr. He didn't like being puzzled, wasn't sure what a name was.

"Better watch that around One-Eye," she said again. "Don't you have a name?"

"There can be only one king," he said, sure in his seasons of experience that this was so.

"That's right," said a new voice, low and husky. He whirled about, came face to face with a pug-faced orange and white animal. One eye was a ruined mass of scar, and his ears were notched and cut. "That's right," said One-Eye, "and that king is me."

He didn't hesitate, but hissed and leaped. Flinch's voice

came from somewhere far away, "No, no!" One-Eye didn't leap, merely stood up on his rear legs and met his charge with a solid chest. He felt as if he'd hit a wall and fell back, rear legs scrabbling to claw, but One-Eye bore him down to the ground, the strongest thing he'd ever gripped. Shameful panic overwhelmed him, and he mewled for escape. This was worse than the shrieking bird: He was beaten by his own kind, with tooth and claw.

"Only one," One-Eye said, and bit his ear. His mewl changed to a yowl of outrage, but there was nothing he could do as One-Eye tore his flesh. The pain was lightning. He had no more strength in him to fight. The shrieking bird's attack, the great fall had left him with nothing but limp panting breaths.

"Only one, right?" One-Eye said again, and he measured his words carefully in reply.

"So you say," he said, sick inside with defeat. One-Eye got up and walked away, tail erect and swaying.

"I told you," Flinch said just as a growling, clanking sound entered the alley. "Quick, to the side, the apes have come for their things."

And so it went for him as he healed. The black slick bags were slung on the pile one by one. The bags contained things that were good to eat, but the hunters had to contend with the rats, rats that carried a dank, lip-curling stench. What the rats left they hurried to eat, and he ate with distaste the food from the bags, some bland, some sharp on his tongue, but enough to quiet his flat belly, and more.

One good thing was the shrieking stinking bird never appeared here; one bad thing was the prey birds, the stinking birds he'd eaten most of his life, never came near enough to catch, but perched instead on metal stairs above the alley. He was sure there was a way to catch them, but One-Eye forbade hunting them, saying "Enough to eat in the bags. Don't leave the alley, the apes will get you."

They called him Bit-Ear, but each morning he reminded himself: "I am king."

The light-furred other named Hurry grew fatter and fatter until one day he asked Flinch why; she laughed and said, "She will have kittens soon." As quickly as she'd laughed, she grew somber, tail low. "And then she will lament."

"Lament? Why?" As he asked he remembered the echoes, but she would say no more.

It happened one day when the air grew crisp in the early morning. Hurry had disappeared beneath a metal box that grew from one alley wall, and just as he reminded himself that he was king, he heard tiny mews that quickly grew silent. He crept forward and peered at Hurry, who hissed at him in a friendly way.

"Away with you, Bit-Ear. Let me enjoy them while I can."

"While you can?" he asked, backing away. The kittens were tiny and squirmed. It seemed impossible he had once been so small. A dim memory of huddling in the palm of an ape's hand came to him, along with the sweet taste of milk. Hurry did not answer, but a rustle behind him did. His lip curled with disgust as the smell of rats wafted over him. In the dim morning light he watched them come, quiet and purposeful.

They scurried forward, edged their noses beneath the metal box. Hurry hissed and spat, and he shouted "No!" in unison with her, but they were already snarling and biting. He leaped for the nearest without knowing why; they stank and did not seem like good prey. The rat shuddered as he struck its back, then squealed as his teeth bit home in the nape of its neck. He turned his head a fraction to the side and bit again; the rat squealed anew, and the others pulled their heads out from under the box, dead and dying kittens in their mouths.

His long teeth slid on bone at the base of the rat's skull, he felt a final crunch, and the thing went limp.

The biggest of the rats dropped the kitten so it could speak. "What do you do?"

He was keenly aware that there were five rats facing him. More of them dropped what they held and bared teeth that disturbed him—they were sharp and narrow and looked formidable. Though he was larger than each of the rats arrayed before him, they were five and he was one. He thought about the question. What was he doing?

"Kittens . . . not prey," he finally said.

"New here?" asked the big rat, his brown fur becoming clearer as the dawn progressed. The big one didn't let him answer. "You are. If you weren't new, you'd know. These are ours. Live in the alley? Our alley. Our babies, very tasty. Best warm. Going now." He picked up the kitten he'd dropped, as did the others.

He hissed and urrred with displeasure, but there was nothing to do. The rats returned down their hole. It led into shadow. One after another, the five rats began to disappear into the black until only one remained. Then a kitten mewed from under the metal box, and the last rat froze, turned to face him. "One more for us," it said.

"No," he hissed, and arched his back.

The rat paused. "What do you do?"

"This one stays," he said, and charged.

This rat turned and fled. He chased it down the hole. The path plunged down at first, turned right, left. It was nearly pitch black, but his eyes adjusted and he found he could see. "I am king!" he yowled into the tunnel, scrambled on. He heard the scratching of rat claws ahead of him.

The path opened, and he was assailed with the smell of

rat. Around him he could see rats standing up and sniffing the air in a rough burrow with a low ceiling. Other exits led from the horror he'd stumbled into, a lair of rats, more than he could easily count.

"Fat one, I have a gift for you," squealed a rat triumphantly, surely the rat he'd chased. At one end of the burrow a knot of rats raised their snouts and sniffed. "We have the babies," a huge mass of a rat said. "What else?"

"Smell him," the one he'd chased said, and he realized the rats could not see well in the dark burrow, but relied more on their noses.

The huge rat sniffed. "What do you do?" it said.

"Kittens . . . are not prey," he said, unsure what to say.

"You are prey," the huge one said, and as one the rats in the burrow surged toward him, a dark shadowy wave. He turned and raced through the first open tunnel behind him.

He ran around a tight corner and flailed the open air before him, sensing something just above his head. This was not the path to the alley. Once again he fell, feet first. In the dim light there was not much to see. By the time he hit the water, it was dark, dense darkness he had never seen above ground. It took all his strength to struggle to the air. Even in rain he'd never been so wet. Ground, he needed ground, but in the racing water and the darkness there was no ground. As his strength ebbed, his head slipped beneath the water once, twice. He thrashed, dreading the end, wishing for sky, for air. In the distance, he heard a splash through the sound of the water. Then it was over.

He coughed and spat water, felt his fur heavy and flat over his entire body. He was filled with the urge to twitch violently, scatter this water off his limbs and body, but caution made him freeze. Something large was nearby. He heard it breathe, slowly hissing in, out, in again. A sharp smell came to his nose, and it itched him in a way he didn't recognize.

"You are awake," said a voice, a rumbling giant voice, bigger than the shrieking voice of the clawed bird, bigger than the yawps of apes.

He could not help it any longer. He stood and twitched, spraying water everywhere. Though he was cold, he was a bit dryer and would soon be warmed through by the moist, hot air around him.

"I pulled you from the water, tiny panther," said the voice. "Speak to me, tell me of yourself, of your journey here."

"Rats. I ran from rats and fell," he said, afraid to remain so near to the giant beast but unsure where to go. The darkness was absolute, not even a pinpoint of light to be seen. He sat down.

"Rats do not hunt panthers. I eat rats, I know their tastes, their suppers and lunches and snacks. Panthers hunt rats, or they can if they wish."

"What is a panther?"

"A panther is you, little panther. Four legs, sharp ears, good eyes in night and day, climber of trees, hunter with tooth and claw."

"What is a tree?"

With this the giant voice huffed and hurred. He fell to the side and scrambled away, hit a wall with his head and sat back down. After a moment he decided the creature was laughing, and he gave the fur on his right foreleg an experimental lick. He would be forever grooming this mess.

"I understand, you are as much out of your proper home as I am, little panther. But I am not like you, furred one. My bones know the sun, sun that warms through and through, sun that warms the water. My bones know the log that shades, the bank that prey step upon, the crunch of bone, the salt of blood!" Instead of speech came a *clomp!* noise that made him flinch. "I remember, though I have never seen. I know the names of all that swim and fly and walk, and you are panther, though very small. When I caught you, I tasted you, knew your name, brought you to shore."

"Thank you," he said, shivering. From the cold, he told himself, though the air was warm. "But you said rats do not hunt panthers. They hunted me. I entered their den to stop them from eating kittens. The rats are many."

There was a pause when all he could hear was the long, slow breathing of the giant.

"Furry things must learn, they don't know in the bone like my kind know. If you are not panther, what? Did not your kind teach you?"

"I . . ." he could not answer. Instead he found himself telling the giant about his kingdom, about the stinking birds he'd learned to eat, about the clawed bird that had knocked him into the air, about the alley and the others that lived there, about the lament, about the stronger king. The giant was patient and waited for silence before answering.

"The clawed bird was a hawk, perhaps even an eagle. And if you are king, you must be king."

He quailed inside and said in a small voice, "But One-Eye is king. He is big and strong and . . . tore my ear."

Again the giant whuffed with laughter. "You told me each day you claimed to be king. If One-Eye is large, you must not fight him as large. You tell me of catching birds with a leap and a bite. You tell me of rats who smell their way through their burrow. You tell me the ways you can be king. If you are panther, or tiny-cousin-of-panther, you know how to be king! Now go, go back to the light and find your way to your kingdom!"

Something moved to his side, and he scrambled away from it. It scraped against the ground in a wide swath around him. He ducked left, ran right, but could not escape and was knocked back into the water, water that felt cold after the warm air.

"And if you think of me, little panther, send rats to the water you fell into, send me many rats to eat!"

As he was swept along in the water, the last thing he heard was the giant's whuffing laughter. Around him the air grew close and near; then, as the water began to test his strength, he was scraped along a wall. Soon the air lightened around him, and he paddled fiercely, blinking madly against the splashes that covered his face. There was ground ahead, and he made for it as best he could, claws slipping then finding purchase on smooth round shapes at the edge of the water. He hauled himself up, drenched again, and lay panting with the sound of rushing water in his ears.

He shook himself and groomed himself bit by bit. A narrow path led away, and he twisted and turned along it until the light brightened above him. Now the sound of apes walking came to him, their two-footed pattern distinctive even at a distance. He followed the sound and came to a scraping narrow place, then a climbing place that tested his claws. Soon he was peering out into a sunlit day and filling his chest with cool air.

The giant had said to find his kingdom, but how? He sniffed the air but found nothing familiar other than the smell from the end of the alley, taints and wisps of ape and metal, with an undercurrent now and again of ape-food, the kind of thing he'd found in the bags in the alley. He waited and watched, but no inspiration came to him. The light failed and shadows formed. He slunk from shadow to shadow, careful to avoid the apes. A barking, growling thing chased him for a few steps before it yelped in pain and stopped, caught short by an ape it was tied to. "Fool!" he hissed at it before trotting away to a new hiding place.

On his way he stopped and stared. To one side of the street the tall walls full of apes fell away, and instead of bricks there were—things. He crossed the street at a trot and peered at tall poles that rose from ground that was covered not with pavement or tar but with soft ground and thin stalks. "Trees," he said, "Trees and grass, just as the giant remembered." Scent told him prey lived here: birds and small scurrying things like rats but less dank and not so oily. And water. There was good water here.

Back on the street he thought again of his wish to return to his old kingdom. He did not know how to get there, and wise as he felt he'd become, he could not think of a way to fight the shrieking bird, be it hawk or eagle, as the giant had said. But the place with trees and grass was promising.

There was an alley, but it wasn't his alley. He smelled rats, but he didn't think they were his rats. Their smell was dryer, somehow, less dank and more oily. Tired, he slept in the smallest hiding place he could find, a dreamless sleep that was troubled only by a memory of the bags the apes brought by hand and took away in the snorting, clanking machine.

He woke with a start and heard the machine snort nearby. Stretching quickly, he ignored his flat stomach and raced toward the sound. Apes climbed on and off the machine, which moved in starts and lurches down the street. There was morning light in the sky, and other apes were entering the street again, forcing him to skittle from hiding place to hiding place behind the machine.

He had almost forgotten what victory felt like, but he felt it wash over him when the machine turned into an alley. It was his alley; the scents of the others washed over him, along with the dank smell of his rats. He waited for the apes to finish taking their bags away and strode into the alley, head and tail high. No one noticed him.

He sat in the middle of the alley and waited. The morning light grew stronger. Finally, he filled his chest with air and yowled "I am king! I am king!" The echo had hardly faded when One-Eye came out from behind a box and glared at him.

"I am king!" One-Eye yowled back.

"Bit-Ear!" cried Twitch.

"*I am king!*" he yowled again, and a plan formed in his mind. One-Eye was not a stinking bird to be leaped upon, chest to chest. One-Eye was big, too big to leap well. One-Eye would fight him the way he'd fought before, up on his hind legs before crashing down upon him, crushing him backwards. He charged forward, feinted a leap. One-Eye rose on his hind legs, paws wide, jaws agape. There would be no mercy this time. One-Eye would kill or maim him if he could.

Instead of leaping at head height, he leaped low, butted One-Eye in the gut. His long teeth found One-Eye in the upper thigh. He bit and savagely tore left, right, left, ripping the muscle. One-Eye fell upon his back, screaming and clawing and biting, but his back made it hard for One-Eye to gain purchase.

He thrust up and to the right with his rear legs. One-Eye fell over onto his side before scrambling up, rear leg lifted off the ground. He could taste One-Eye in his mouth and grinned at him, long teeth showing red. "There can be only one!" he yowled, and charged again. One-Eye tried to stand and meet the rush but could not, lurched to his injured side. This time he leaped high, came down upon One-Eye like a thunderbolt from the sky. His teeth met through One-Eye's ear. He closed his eyes and shook his head, nearly deafened by One-Eye's howls of pain and shame.

After a few moments of bliss, he let go, stepped back. One-Eye struggled to his feet but kept his head low.

"Who is king?" he purred.

"You are," panted One-Eye.

"Not for long."

It was a rat. More than he could count had crawled out of their hole and crouched in a half-ring around the cats. In the center of the arc was the bloated, huge rat. Their leader, he decided, and acted without hesitation.

"Get onto the silver box!" he shouted, and cleared the way himself, hissing and spitting as he lunged forward. The surprised rats parted before him. Halfway there he saw Hurry back out from beneath the box, a dark shape dangling from her jaws. He leaped up, was soon joined by Twitch and the others, all but One-Eye.

One-Eye yowled defiance at the rats who ringed him, but his bad leg gave him no chance to flee. "He's crippled," hissed the huge rat, and they were upon him, a squirming wave of tail and squeal. One-Eye's voice went from defiance to anger, then pain.

On the silver box he saw Hurry had a kitten in her mouth, a kitten she placed tenderly up against the wall. "You saved it," she said to him before settling down next to it. The kitten mewed once then was silent. The rats ringed the box, and a few put their forepaws up on the sides. The hunters hissed and spat and darted clawed paws at the rats, who stayed out of range. To the sides a few smaller rats climbed the bricks like flies, but they were too few to dare the top of the box.

"Safe for now," said the huge rat, smeared with blood from snout to throat. "But you'll go hungry up there. And thirsty. Was that a baby I heard? Give it, give it and we let you go. Stay in the alley all you want, just give us babies. We like them warm."

"No, no," said Hurry in a small voice. "Not this one too. Please."

He thought and thought, then bared his teeth. "No deal, rat. How about I eat your babies? The ones in your burrow?"

With a scream he leaped off the silver box, over the heads of the rats, and dove into the hole. He turned and twisted until he reached the burrow. Despite the mob of rats outside, the hole was still busy with rats, but these were younglings and mothers. Behind he heard the rush of his pursuers, each hissing with anger. He stepped to the right and sniffed. Yes, this was the passage he'd taken by mistake before.

Yowling with disdain he charged down it, stopping just before the edge of the fall. He sprayed the wall and leaped upwards, catching his paws on a rounded thing he'd sensed in the near total darkness. He strained and pulled and climbed atop it just as the rats arrived below. He screamed defiance at them, and they charged. Confused by his scent, they fell into space, squealing with terror. Some rats heard, said "Stop! Stop!" to the ones behind, but the mob pressed on, and more fell.

He heard the huge rat, lumbering along last. He dropped down in front of it, hissed "Your rats have fallen to the giant below, the giant with jaws that clomp and a laugh that whuffs, big as the wind."

The huge rat paused and showed his teeth. "Truth of rats: always more. Truth of cats: never enough."

Before it finished speaking, he charged the bloated thing. The tunnel was too low to leap, so he offered his bared teeth to the rat. It stuck forth its neck to bite him. His paws latched onto the rat's head, and as he yanked his head away from the rat's formidable teeth, his rear legs came forward. Three deep, heavy swipes of his rear claws was all it took to open the huge rat's neck. Blood sprayed.

It was hard work to get past the huge rat's body, but after a time he made it, sticky with blood and panting. He stopped in the burrow to scream at the rats there. They scurried away.

The huge rat had been right, he thought: There will always be more rats.

The sunlight was welcome when he struggled out of the hole. He went to the puddle and drank, ignoring the other's questions until he was sated.

"The rats are gone," he said finally. "Though there will always be more." He wondered what the giant thought when uncountable rats swam through his domain. He imagined giant jaws clomping over and over, and smiled. "Now rest. Tonight we have a journey."

They rested. Twitch helped him with his fur, and by night he was presentable again. He spent some time looking carefully at Hurry's kitten. There rose in him a strange urge to kill it, to bite it until it was dead, but he shied away from it; the memory of rats eating kittens was too strong in him. He knew it was not his kitten, but his nose told him there would be a chance to make more kittens soon, and those kittens would be his own.

He waited until the streets quieted and the apes grew few and far between. Then he led them out beyond the alley, from shadow to shadow, taking long rests for Hurry and her kitten. He came to the green place, and they entered, looking in awe at the round posts called trees that rose from the ground, at the leaves and the grass ripe with a dozen different scents.

"Here," he said when they came to a place far from the miniature streets strong with the scent of apes, a protected hollow. "Here is right for us."

As they settled, he asked Twitch, "What are we? I met a giant who called me a panther. But the huge rat said I was a cat."

"We are cats, of course!" said Twitch. "Why don't you know this?"

He explained about the glass box, the soft-handed apes.

"You were the first other-cat I'd ever seen," he said, and sniffed around her ears and neck. "So we are four legs, sharp ears, good eyes in night and day, climbers of trees, hunters with tooth and claw?"

"Cats is cats," Rumble said in his low tones. "And you brought us to trees."

"You need a new name, Bit-Ear," Twitch said.

"Ratkiller," suggested Beckett.

"No, Kitten-Saver," said Hurry, already huddled around her little one.

"How about King?" said Twitch.

"I am King!" he yowled to the skies, just showing a taste of dawn. And that was that.

OLD AGE AND SORCERY

Lee Martindale

The life of a Free Cat was not without its dangers. Even when one's territory was a long-abandoned inner-city freight depot where food skittered abundantly about, the most extreme weather conditions weren't all that extreme, and shelter options were both copious and reasonably comfortable, things could still take a turn for the fatal without much in the way of warning. Sometimes, a Free Cat's venerable age and rumored abilities created dangers in and of themselves.

"Oh, bugger," Myrrrthin Starfur muttered, looking up at what he'd wrought. Commending his soul to Bast, he bent his head, closed his eyes, and waited to be torn limb from ancient limb.

He'd warned Ambrose, the Warlord of Lower Greenville, even while being rather vigorously persuaded into his presence, that frivolous demonstrations were an unworthy use of his talents. He'd gone so far as to swallow his pride and mention that his control had been a trifle . . . well . . . uneven of late. But Ambrose insisted, using the compelling arguments of bared teeth and low growls. And so Myrrrthin closed his eyes, visualized the nonaqueous contents of the lobster tanks at Vincente's Seafood Restaurant, and called them to the loading dock platform that served as The Warlord's throne.

When Myrrrthin opened his eyes again, it was to the sight of the usually pristinely white big tom, his harem, his courtiers, and his lieutenants buried up to their whiskers in the noxious, soggy, reeking, inedible-by-carnivores contents of the dumpster behind Velma's Vegan Paradise. But it was the pink lace doily and florescent orange and chartreuse paisley party hat jauntily perched on Ambrose's head that convinced the old feline that his doom was truly sealed.

Silence lay like drenched dog fur over the scene. No one and nothing moved until a ball of rotting bean sprouts slid off the end of the dock and smacked wetly to the concrete beneath. It was followed shortly thereafter, not by an order for Myrrrthin's disembowelment, but by laughter. Loud, belly-deep, prolonged solo laughter. The Warlord of Lower Greenville was in the throes of a giggle-fit of profound quality and volume.

In due course, the top cat wound down enough to look at the aged feline in front of him. "That was funny, old one," he rumbled. "I do believe I like you. I will like you even more if you make this mess go . . ." he flicked one ear in a dismissive gesture, "somewhere else."

"Of course, my lord," Myrrrthin replied smoothly, adding a bow of his head. He made a show of settling into proper spellcasting posture and began an impressive-sounding chant of chitters, growls, and other vocalizations. His tail undulated, sinuously weaving intricate patterns in time to the chanting. Volume and degree of movement increased in slow crescendo until, finally, his tail lashed forward toward the mess, and his chanting ended on a single, sustained yowl.

For the space of perhaps five heartbeats, nothing happened. Then the mess simply disappeared. All but the doily and the hat. Myrrrthin blinked, scowled, lashed his tail again, and uttered something that sounded almost like a bark. Hat and doily followed the garbage to wherever it had gone.

In the silence that followed, Myrrrthin began to shake like a cat just escaped, by the width of one claw, being reduced to bits of bloody fur by a marauding dog pack. Chitters of amazement, followed by applause, began to sound around him and, after getting control of himself, he acknowledged it as might a warrior victorious but exhausted from single combat. Those around him, especially the alpha tom watching him so closely, need not know that his was the exhaustion of terror, his shaking that of abject relief. No, indeed, they did not need to know that.

"Bravo!" Ambrose bellowed, applauding. "That was wonderful! Come, Starfur, sit here beside me. I have a proposition for you." As Myrrrthin made his way slowly up the stairs on one side of the dock, the tom turned to the female on his immediate left and convinced her, with a hiss and a cuff, to move.

"I've heard tales about you for as long as I can remember," Ambrose confided as Myrrrthin settled himself into the vacated spot. "I was half convinced you were a myth until I started getting reports from sentries who'd claimed to have marked your passage. Just between the two of us, I think you started getting sloppy."

I think I started getting old, Myrrrthin replied in his head. He smiled in deprecating fashion toward his host. "Well, that could be, my lord. Or it could be that your sentries are an observant lot, keen in their senses."

"They're my get," Ambrose laughed. "Of course they're sense-sharp. But what I want to know is the real story. Which of the several myths about you is the true tale?"

Myrrrthin looked thoughtful. "To answer that, my lord, I'd have to know what myths you've heard."

"I suppose you would," the younger cat mused. "Let me see. There's the one that, more generations ago than anyone can count, you were served by the creatures who built this place and that they left you behind when they abandoned it. Another claims this place was already long abandoned when you, yourself, were dumped here." The big tom fell silent as he rifled his memory. The female who'd been displaced from her position next to him crept cautiously close to a place near his back and began grooming him.

"In some myths, you're called The Great Protector and The Paw Of Bast. There are stories in which you single-handedly vanquish entire huge armies of wild dogs, calling lightning from the sky as an ally and weapon to achieve that feat. I've heard you called Magician and Mage and Wizard." For the moment, the alpha tom paused before adding, in a voice touched by sly teasing, "I've even heard your name invoked as the monster that snatches up and devours kittens who wander too far away from the den without proper supervision."

"Oh . . ." the old cat blinked, "my."

"So which is it, ancient one? Which of the stories is the true one?" Ambrose narrowed his eyes a bit and cocked his head to one side, his ears both pointed forward. "And what exactly are you?"

Myrrrthin glanced around, noting that every feline in sight was watching the dock with rapt attention. "Well, now, I'm not at all sure how to answer that. If my being used to keep kittens from going walkabout serves that purpose, then . . . I suppose I'm an imaginary monster, and a bit of a depressing thought that is. It would seem far better to think of me as a useful tool to their survival, don't you think? As for the other tales . . . my days have been long, and there have been encounters with dog packs and other more mindless dangers. I have, somehow, survived them, and it may well be that, in my doing so, others who happened to be in the vicinity have also survived. Have I called down lightning as a weapon? It seems fanciful, and yet . . . . I *almost* recall it. It . . . could be." The last he said almost to himself before growing silent for a long while. Then he smiled engagingly.

"As to what I am, I would think it obvious. I am old unto ancient and venerable unto decrepit. In my prime, I was exceedingly handsome, and exceptionally long legged and lean. But time, as it so often does, has turned me gaunt and a trifle scraggly. My coat, which was at one time a dark wizard gray, is now more gray than dark, and the white markings from whence came my name are no longer quite as white or nearly as much like five-pointed stars as they were in my youth. My hips are stiff, my senses not as keen as they once were, and what prey I catch falls less to skill than to wiles and plain dumb luck these days." He chuckled, and Ambrose joined in. "But the question, my lord, is what I am—or might be—to you. You mentioned having a proposition for me?"

"I want you to join my household. Move from wherever it is you've been living to accommodations nearby and under my immediate protection. Entertain my mates, instruct my offspring, make me laugh, and provide counsel when I ask for it. You said yourself you're slowing down, and your chances of continuing to stay fed and ahead of snapping jaws get slimmer by the day. Join me here, and you need not worry about such matters ever again."

Myrrrthin half-closed his eyes, considering the notion. "I must say, my lord, that's an interesting offer. It seems quite self-serving on your part."

Ambrose blinked, and his lips curled back from his teeth. He blinked again and began to laugh. "Well, of course it's self-serving. I'm a cat, after all. An old, clearly inferior male moving freely through my territory, without regard for my authority, might give some of the young toms ideas that I'd rather they not entertain."

Myrrrthin chuckled. "Indeed. That could present a terrible inconvenience for you. So, if I agree to this bargain, you get the benefit of my service, wisdom, and experience, not to mention getting rid of what might appear to be defiance of your position as alpha. And I get . . . ?

The younger cat's face went entirely still, his eyes holding level on Myrrrthin's. ". . . to live."

The old cat grinned. "Then how can I possibly refuse?"

Myrrrthin had to admit that there was much to be said for being part of a warlord's household. His belly hadn't been empty since taking up residence; food, fresh killed or barely breathing, appeared regularly and with pleasing frequency. Led by a long-forgotten memory into the bowels of the building behind Ambrose's loading dock, he'd claimed a cozy, secluded, and dimly familiar niche for his own, within the area over which sentries and guards kept constant watch. For the first time in more years than he cared to count, there was no need to sleep lightly with senses on guard, and for the first time in more years than he cared to count, he slept soundly.

His duties were just as pleasant. A portion of each day was spent instructing the young in the mundane skills that had served him in eluding pursuit and evading capture or worse. That he included lessons in customs, history, lore and legend seemed to do no harm, nor did they elicit comment. A larger portion of his day, thanks to his age and the perception that calling him a tom was more a courtesy than anything else, involved keeping enjoyable company with the females in the community. Those actively adding to the number of Ambrose's subjects found his distractions and encouragements welcome additions to the birthing process. Those nursing the newest members of the colony—in truth, all the females—found his stories, songs, and small magicks (even those that didn't turn out quite as he planned) highly amusing. Similar entertainments provided for Ambrose and his court completed his daily duties. The whole left him delicious amounts of time for numerous naps, stretched out in well guarded patches of sunlight or cool, cozy shade.

It was, all in all, a comfortable existence, and a far better way to end his days than Myrrrthin had ever expected to see. He wanted for nothing except, perhaps, his pride.

There were times, when a bit of magick went slightly awry, when the result was something unexpected and ridiculous, when laughter saluted his efforts and continued survival dictated his adoption of the demeanor of a clown, that he chafed. Through an accident of birth and bloodline, or some odd mutation in his mother's womb, he'd been born with knowledge and power. It became evident, early on, that he possessed abilities unlike those of his siblings. The ability to wield power, to affect things around him had, indeed, been his, and had probably been the reason he'd been left to fend for himself in a deserted truck depot when barely past kittenhood.

And fend for himself he had, for many years and rather well. In his prime, he'd been a well favored, healthy tom whose speed and cunning served most of his needs. His extraordinary talents were rarely used, except in unusual circumstances affecting his own or others' safety. Although he kept to himself, he always stayed aware of the warlord in whose domain he resided. And, over the many years, he'd had occasion to influence the outcome of potentially harmful encounters between one or more members of the warlord's household and the dangers that periodically wandered, slunk, or coursed into his territory.

The story Ambrose had asked about that first day, of his having called lightning to his paw to deal with a ravening dogpack, had been a true one. Apparently, Ambrose did not recall, being hardly more than a toddler at the time, that one of the cats Myrrrthin had saved during that particular incident had been the future warlord himself. Not that the old cat intended to mention it, of course. He had a hunch that reminding Ambrose of a blood debt owed would result in blood better left flowing in Myrrrthin's veins.

So Myrrrthin occasionally chafed at his waning hold on his magick, and he wondered now and then if it might not be better to wander off into the jaws of a swift death. Mostly he spent his days resigned to playing the role into which circumstance had cast him and his nights reliving his youth and power in dreams.

One afternoon near the end of a particularly hot, particularly dry summer, Myrrrthin lounged on a shelf in the nursery, playing a fuzzy ball of conjured light across the floor and watching kittens bounce after it with great enthusiasm and adorable lack of grace. Females draped in relaxed postures around the room, either dozing or conversing in low tones that added to the drone of insects that would likely turn into the next kitty toy when the young ones tired of chasing the light ball.

The drone suddenly changed into warning hisses. Kittens scrambled in all directions, disappearing into hiding places with remarkable speed. Myrrrthin sat up and scanned the room, stopping at the doorway where Ambrose's second-in-command stood, in violation of all law and custom. Without a word, the young tom locked eyes with Myrrrthin. The summons was clear. The old cat took gallant, if hasty, leave of the females, and followed.

He found Ambrose sitting on the very edge of the loading dock, making not the slightest effort to hide either the tension in his body or the fact that every sense was cast to the edge of feline perception. "We may have a problem," he said without turning. "A pack of adolescent demons have come across the border, and reports have them circling through the outbuildings. It's not that uncommon, but this time the guards say their passage is marked with a scent that raises their fur and makes them uneasy."

No sooner had he finished speaking when a young female approached at full speed and skidded to a halt directly below the loading dock. "The demons are close, my lord," she managed to get out between gasps, "and have gathered around one of their rolling monsters. They seem to be watching the section of the border directly in front of them, as if waiting for something, and they each are holding a long, strange-smelling stick."

The sound that issued from Myrrrthin's thin body was like nothing Ambrose had ever heard. It snapped his head around, and made his whiskers tremble. The old cat stood rigid and quivering, his eyes wide and unfocused. A sudden impression crossed Ambrose's mind: that the light was on, but Myrrrthin was nowhere near home.

At last the old cat spoke, his voice odd and distorted, as by distance and time. "Death rings us 'round. The appearance of safety is only that: appearance. Illusion."

"This is hardly the time for riddles, Starfur," Ambrose snarled impatiently. "What do you mean?"

Myrrrthin trembled harder, going deeper into whatever vision held him. It seemed to take him even farther away. "They hunt," he finally said in the same odd voice, "but not for food. They hunt for sport, for the pleasure of the kill. We are their prey, and they've set a closing trap meant to drive us along a path of their choosing if it doesn't consume us outright." Then, between one heartbeat and the next, every bone in the ancient body seemed to dissolve, and he melted into a fur-covered heap.

Ambrose, too, was trembling as he nudged and licked Myrrrthin's head. "I don't understand, old one. What kind of trap? How do I save my people?"

The old cat's eyes opened, glazed and still far away, but he pushed himself to a sitting position and shook his head as if to clear it. Before he could speak, something on the air, something acrid and irritating, caught his attention. He raised a twitching nose to sample it further. "The trap is sprung."

Ambrose, too, tested the air, and a look of near panic widened his eyes. "Smoke."

"The demons have laid fire all around us," Myrrrthin explained as he pushed himself onto shaky legs, "except for one path they want us to see as the way to safety. That's where they wait to deal us death with the sticks in their hands." As if in illustration, several sharp cracking sounds and a short yowl, abruptly cut off, reached their ears.

"We must move quickly, my lord," the old cat continued. "As dry as it's been, brush and wood will catch quickly and burn hot. We have little time." More sharp pops, all from one direction, were joined by small explosions and crackling from all around them. "We cannot go through, but we can go below. Call all your guards and hunters to you. Send everyone to the nursery."

Ambrose nodded to several young toms, who streaked away in all directions, then followed Myrrrthin inside. "What are you thinking?"

"There are more kittens than mothers to carry them in the short time we have before this place begins to burn. Each cat, male and female alike, will have to take a kitten to the hiding place."

"Males do not ferry kittens," Ambrose huffed.

"They do if you expect to have subjects when this is over," Myrrrthin snapped back.

"But carry them where? What hiding place?"

"That," Myrrrthin replied, "is what I'm going to find out."

"The females won't allow it," the younger cat yelled at Myrrrthin's retreating tail.

"You're the alpha. Convince them."

The memories he followed were dimmer than the dusty light through which he moved as swiftly as age-stiffened joints allowed. They came as if remembered from someone else's life lived in safety and love and years gone. But the farther Myrrrthin went, the stronger his memories became, the tighter his grasp on that other life, and he followed them until he found the door he sought.

He sent a thankful thought to Bast that the door hadn't been shut tight. It was unlatched, and a bare sliver of a crack separated door from jamb. He tore out claws on both front paws convincing long-rusted hinges to give him an opening large enough to get his head through, ripped holes in his fur and bruised his shoulders wrestling the opening wide enough that he could squeeze the rest of his body through.

Beyond lay darkness deeper than any night, and he sent a ball of conjured light bouncing down the stairs. Leaving bloody paw prints in the accumulated dust, he followed it down, calling up another light at the landing and sending it farther down. It came to rest at the foot of the stairs and, when he joined it, showed him what he sought.

The chamber was as featureless and bare as he remembered, unbroken by window or door. So, too, the floor, except for a medallion of heavy iron in the center of the inwardly sloping floor, two cats'-length in diameter and pierced by small holes. He'd remembered the room as being bigger, but that couldn't be helped. It was the best chance they had, and it would either serve or it wouldn't.

Protesting joints and tired muscles carried him back the way he'd come, every step up and out increasing the volume of frightening sound. The flames around the building no longer crackled, they roared. Even with his mind shielded, he could feel the fire as a living thing, a monster bent on devouring everything.

Rounding the corner into the hallway that led to the nursery, a new fear seized him. He had expected a cacophony of yowls, hissing, growls, feline voices raised in fear, anger, and endless combinations of the two, loud enough to drown out the sound of the flames. What he heard was nothing at all.

The fear lasted until he turned into the nursery space and every head turned to face him. He hadn't realized there were so many. More than a hundred, he estimated, and somehow Ambrose had managed to get them organized while Myrrrthin had been gone. At the center of each small group was a female, her litter at her feet. Around her sat females, bred and unbred, and toms of every age from adolescent to mature.

Ambrose sat above the throng, on a shelf against the back wall. Myrrrthin caught his eye and nodded.

"All right!" the warlord shouted. "You each know your duty. Take up your charge and follow Myrrrthin. Single file, stay calm, and we'll get through this. Let's move!"

Ambrose was putting a confident face on things, and Myrrrthin could do nothing less. He waited for the first group to get hold of its kittens, then gestured to the mother cat, Ambrose's alpha female, to take her station immediately behind him. He moved off, tail proudly weaving in the air, leading the way toward sanctuary. Behind him, he could hear an ever-increasing number of soft pawfalls joining the parade, and the squealing protests of kittens being carried by those with no practice in the art.

So far, Myrrrthin thought to himself, *so good*.

Had he been alone as he made the turn into the long hallway, he would have frozen in his tracks. Solid sheets of flame, just outside the windows, lit the hallway in ways it had never been lit before, casting demonic shadows and assaulting the ears with a roar that was almost a scream. Looking up, he saw sparkling among the rafters that could mean nothing other than the roof was beginning to burn. Hoping that the train of felines behind him could manage, he quickened his pace.

Reaching the stairway door, he turned and began a steady, confident mantra. "Single file, all the way down to the bottom. Kittens and their mothers into the corners and as close to the walls as possible. Everyone else, drop your kittens with their mothers and then fill in the center. Cozy in tight, and we'll get through this." Again and again he repeated it, one eye on the line squeezing steadily through the opening, the other on the bits of burning debris that had begun falling from the ceiling. After what seemed like an eternity, the last cat in line, Ambrose, slithered through the door, a kitten in his mouth and another clinging to his back. With a last look up at the now fully engaged rafters, Myrrrthin followed him down.

Pausing on the landing, the old cat surveyed the scene below him. The floor of the room appeared carpeted in gently-undulating, multicolored fur, so tightly woven that nothing of its surface showed through. Cats who wouldn't come within yards of each other without display of tooth and claw pressed tightly together without complaint, and toms who, in any other circumstance would take the opportunity to kill young ones not their own, stood over those same young ones, protecting them from being crushed by the greater press of bodies. Terror lay as thick as the bodies, palpable and close, but none of those below him gave it voice. Only the wide flash of eyes showed their fear.

Never in all his years had Myrrrthin seen the like, and he felt a moment of pride for his species.

That moment was cut short by a loud thudding crash above them that shook the room and sent dust raining down. Almost immediately, the temperature in the room began to rise to a near-painful level. Myrrrthin leaped to a spot two steps above the crowded floor and, without preamble or show, gesture or affectation, closed his eyes and began to chant.

From the firestorm above, he pulled great amounts of hot and mindless energy. He reached below and pulled more, the energy of life that danced cool and delicate. From the emotions that rose in waves, he latched onto some of each: fear, the trust they had in Ambrose to lead them through this, maternal concern and willingness to sacrifice for the little ones. From Ambrose he snagged a sense of duty and pride of position. And from himself, he pulled his own doubt, his fear that his grasp on power had faded with his youth, that he was nothing more than a buffoon, a pretender, that his skill, even with the need so great, would fail him. All of it he pulled together into a great, invisible mass, shaping it with mind and will, charging it with purpose and need. And then he flung it out into the air above.

One beat. Two. A third. And nothing happened.

The old cat screamed his frustration, a sound more at home in a cougar's throat than his own. The wrenching, bloody sound reverberated against the hard walls and collided with the massed energies. They flared with the intensity of an explosion, then began dividing to the purposes he'd set. Some of them soaked into the ceiling, giving strength to heat-weakened concrete and iron. A part of them hardened into a protective dome just below the ceiling. The rest coalesced into a cool mist that coated the walls, soaked into fur, and quenched the heat in the air.

Suddenly weak, Myrrrthin swayed before melting across the step. He was drained and exhausted. He could feel his heart pounding painfully in his chest, breath rattling in his throat, every muscle burning from strain, every nerve electrified and screaming. When the agony began to fade, he was thankful. Then sight dimmed along with his hearing, and he decided that he must be dying, a thought that he discovered didn't particularly surprise him. As the last sensation began to fade, he hoped that his would be the only death this day.

Myrrrthin rose to consciousness with the thought that Bast had a rather nasty sense of humor. Wet and cold was not how one expected to arrive in the Lands of the Dead, and yet he was definitely wet and decidedly chilly. And tired beyond telling. Which made the repeated calling of his name several degrees past annoying. He'd earned his After-life, and he bloody well intended to enjoy it.

Again his name was called, and this time he growled. "Go away, you twit, and stop bothering me. Can't you see I'm dead?"

Laughter was the unexpected reply to his grousing, followed by a voice that sounded familiar. "You are many things, Myrrrthin Starfur," it said, "but dead is not one of them. No one is!"

Obviously, a witty, biting remark was called for. "Huh?"

"I don't know how you managed it," the voice continued, "but you saved the lot of us. A bit of singed fur on a couple of the outermost guards. And one's got part of his tail missing—he's already trying to impress the females with his battle scar. A good many cases of the shakes, and every cat indignant about getting wet, but . . ." the voice—Myrrrthin decided it was the warlord's—dropped in volume as emotion filled it, "you did it, Old One. All alive and accounted for, thanks to you." The voice dropped even lower in volume. "This is the second time you've saved my life, and both times in a spectacular manner."

Myrrrthin's eyes remained closed, but a subtle movement of muscle beneath fur told Ambrose he'd been heard. "Yes," the younger cat continued, "I do remember your calling the lightning. And for that time, and this one, I'm grateful."

Myrrrthin decided to cover his own emotion with gruffness. "Then go away," he grumbled, "and let me rest until things cool down enough to see what's left."

Ambrose laughed. "Already done, so long have you been lazing. We've found plenty of sound, safe places in the building next to this one. A new nursery is already occupied, and I've found a niche that you might find acceptable for your own den. Hunting may be a trifle lean for a little while, but we'll make do. Now open your eyes, and let's get you up and moving."

Sighing the sigh of a severely put-upon cat, Myrrrthin cracked one eye open. The other opened also, and he swiveled his head in the direction from where Ambrose's voice had come.

The Warlord of Lower Greenville looked like a drowned rat. Or rather, a nearly drowned cat. His fur had dried ungroomed, and it stuck out in spikes pointed in all unkempt directions. His whiskers drooped from the weight of ash and soot, and he was covered in black mess from tip of claw to tip of tail, from shoulders to hips.

But what caused Myrrrthin to wonder how he'd been allowed to wake up at all was what was perched, jauntily askew, on Ambrose's head: a soggy pink lace doily and limp florescent orange and chartreuse paisley party hat.

"Oh," the old cat whispered, "bugger."

KITTY AND THE CITY

Paul Genesse

Cassie sat on the dark rooftop, hating to admit that she was one of those cats who always had bad luck in relationships. She thought she had met the perfect tom until he turned his golden eyes away from her and got up to leave. After weeks of dating, she knew their brief romance was over.

Cassie leaned her white face forward. "*Wait.*" She vocalized a soft *meow* for added urgency. Her gray and brown striped ears stood up straight and her sea-green eyes opened wide, giving him an unmistakable sign of her feelings for him.

But he turned away without reacting—cold and distant as usual—and slipped away, padding across the roof. Then he hesitated and faced her, his large body with perfect tuxedo markings almost cloaked in darkness. His white chest, feet, and face glowed faintly in the city's twinkling lights as he whispered, "I just can't settle down right now."

Cassie's tail sagged. His musky scent faded as if he'd already gone. "Why are you so scared to get close to me?"

"I might be leaving the city. Permanently."

"You weren't even going to tell me?" Cassie felt so betrayed. The idea of another failed relationship smacked her in the nose like a slammed door.

He regarded her with a sad expression. "It's just bad timing, Kitty."

She figured this would be the last time he called her by her nickname. He probably wanted to be gentle as he broke up with her, but using it was just too cruel.

"I'll see you around." He disappeared into the shadows, his overly large paws silently carrying him away into the night.

When he was gone, Cassie sank to the stone and turned her head toward the sparkling lights of the vast metropolis below her. *In a city full of felines, why do I always find toms with commitment issues?*

In the end, Mr. Big-Paws had been just like all the rest.

After midnight, when she couldn't take the cloying smells of flowers and pigeon droppings anymore, she made her way down the central stairs—past the penthouse where Big-Paws lived—to the tenth floor of her swank building. She went out through the hall window and navigated along the ledge to her human's large balcony. The glass door was open, but she didn't go in. Cassie lay down, letting the cool breeze blow across her fur. The pain in her heart had become a dull ache, and she hoped she wouldn't wake up for a very long time.

When the afternoon sun warmed her body, Cassie finally dragged herself off the balcony. She moped around the apartment, trying to cheer herself up with a jaunt into the master bedroom closet. Dozens of designer shoes lined the shelves or lay scattered across the floor. Cassie had been planting compulsions into her human's mind to buy all the expensive brands for several years now, and the closet was overflowing. A shoe fetish was not uncommon among her kind, and Cassie was a very discerning feline. Her sense of style had helped propel her human's career as a top writer for a fashion magazine. Cassie prided herself on having impeccable taste and didn't go for the counterfeit knockoffs. They never smelled right. Her human always got the real thing: Prada, Manolo Blahnik, Fendi. They were all there.

The smell of new Italian leather cheered her up for a moment, especially when she got a whiff of the new calfskin t-strap sandals by Jimmy Choo. Cassie had always thought of them as "Chews." She had nibbled lightly on a few of them, and only when they were out of season.

She resisted chewing on the new Choos until she remembered how Mr. Big-Paws had dumped her, then she buried her teeth in the succulent leather. Glorious flavor filled her mouth as she thought of her ex-tom. Out of all the cats she had ever dated, he was by far her favorite. Not because of his access to vast wealth, or his calm demeanor that balanced her excitability. He made her feel like a queen when he was around.

Cassie was also sure he would have been the best lover she ever had and would have made a great lifelong companion. They both loved the same things: long naps on silk pillows, Mediterranean catnip, and gourmet food—especially anything with lobster or pheasant livers.

The worst thing was that they had spent weeks dating, and she still hadn't gotten her itch scratched. If Cassie was ever going to get satisfaction and have kittens, it had to be soon. Her feline clock was ticking. Fast.

Time was getting away from her in more ways than one. She had to meet her friends for lunch, and she was already late. After a quick look in the mirror, Cassie decided that she looked dreadful. Her fur was matted on her haunches, and her face needed a good tongue bath. She had once won top prize at a fashion show featuring American Shorthairs, wearing *haute couture* of course, but the way she looked now—like a common street cat—would get her immediately thrown into a horrid pen with fifteen other tabbies at the local animal rescue association.

Cassie straightened her favorite Versace collar, designed by Luciana herself. The well-known Italian feline was the most famous fashionista in the cat world. Luciana worked through a subservient family of generally competent human designers, but it was well known that she ran the show. Cassie flipped the gold charm that displayed her name in cursive script. The "i" was dotted with a flawless one-and-a-half-carat diamond that set her apart wherever she went.

She then licked her haunches, trying to smooth out her coat. It was hopeless. She was having a bad fur day and that was that. Cassie gave up in disgust. After hopping onto the balcony railing, she made her way along the ledge to the open window into the building. This section of the hallway reeked of the fake-flower perfume that the lawyer lady down the hall slathered herself with. The stench had seeped into the carpet, and Cassie suspected the high-powered—but fashion-challenged—woman had gallons of it fermenting in her apartment.

The fetor faded as Cassie pulled herself up the stairs to the sixth floor, where she was to meet her friends for lunch. She pawed at Abigail's door and *meowed*, sending a mental command for the human to open up. The woman came quickly, as she usually did, and Cassie accepted a generous amount of petting. She then slipped through the woman's apricot-lotion-scented hands and into the kitchen, where Cassie knew the queens were chatting and snacking on what smelled like fresh salmon.

Abigail greeted her first. The fluffy white Persian's face fell when she saw Cassie's bedraggled fur. "What's wrong?" Abigail's large yellow-gold eyes filled with worry.

Cassie hung her head and sagged in front of her three best friends, showing them her snow-colored tummy.

Maureen—an orange tabby with a constantly twitching tail—came over and touched Cassie's nose. The smell of a caramel latte flavored with a little espresso was thick on Maureen's breath. "You okay?"

Cameron—a slinky Siamese with a sapphire-studded collar that matched her eyes—stopped eating the salmon and sat back on her perfectly sculpted haunches.

The delectable fish scent did not even tempt Cassie. She closed her eyes and put a paw over her delicate pink nose. "Big-Paws broke up with me."

"No!" Abigail's fluffy fur seemed to flatten a bit. "Cassie, I'm so sorry." The Persian came over and licked her friend's face. Abigail always resorted to grooming when there was trouble.

Maureen got that scary look, so common among female orange tabbies. Every orange tabby Cassie had ever known seemed to be have a flaw in their genes that predisposed them to bouts of insanity. "I have an associate in the D.A.'s office who knows a human sergeant in Animal Control. If you want him gone, I'll take care of it."

"No thanks, Maureen," Cassie said after considering the offer for one tail flick. "I guess we just weren't right together."

"Honey, how do you know that?" Cameron asked with her annoying up-city accent, which reminded Cassie of the way humans with old money spoke to everyone else. "Did you finally see if he had it where it counts?"

"*Cam!*" Cassie bared her teeth a little. "I'm not that kind of kitty."

"You might regret it someday." Cameron raised her hindquarters suggestively. "I keep telling you to enjoy it while you're young and fabulous."

Cassie batted a paw at Cam, wondering if her friend were really a tom trapped in a queen's body.

"Have some fresh salmon." Abigail licked her own lips, trying to divert the conversation. "It was flown in today, and it'll make you feel better."

"I'm not in the mood for fish." Cassie's tail lay still and her friends stared at each other in horror.

Moments later a delicious-smelling leather shoe with a shiny four inch heel—one of Luciana's approved designs— a cloth sparrow flavored with intoxicating catnip, and the current issue of *Feline Fashion* lay beside Cassie's paws. Her friends rallied around her, their whiskered faces concerned.

"I'll be fine," Cassie said, glancing at the much too thin Abyssinian model on the cover of the magazine. "I just thought he was the one."

Abigail let out a shuddering sigh. "I thought Wainwright was the one, but we still haven't had a single litter. We don't talk about it, but I know he's fathered kittens before we settled down." Abigail sank down beside Cassie. "I think it's me."

"You'll just have to keep trying," Cam suggested. "Practice, practice, practice. That's my motto."

"We know." Abigail shook her whiskers at the sable-pointed vixen who would raise her tail for practically any tom . . . anytime.

"You just never know when it'll happen," Maureen said, then averted her eyes.

They all looked at Maureen.

"Do you have something to tell us?" Cameron asked, staring at the orange tabby, whose tail went still.

"Well . . ." Maureen kept a low profile. "I'm pretty sure . . . that I'm with kittens."

Abigail's eyes sparkled. "I *thought* your urine smelled different."

"Who are the fathers?" Cameron asked.

Maureen shot her a fang-filled frown. "I'm not that kind of kitty either."

"Suit yourself," Cam said, "I wouldn't be content if all of my kittens came out looking identical. As they say, variety is the catnip of life."

"No one says that." Abigail pulled her head back.

Cameron ignored her. "I've had at least four different fathers with every litter and I'm pretty pleased about it."

"That kind of mating is too rough," Maureen said.

"Too rough?" Cam was astounded and pawed at the scars on her neck left from passionate tomcat bites. "Pardon me, honey, but is there any other kind?"

"Of course there is," Abigail shot her a disgusted look.

"But who's the tom, Maureen?" Cam asked, "Do tell."

"Graeme," Maureen said, still looking away.

"The bar cat?" Abigail's stubby nose wrinkled. "You can do much better than him. He comes from a litter of alley cats."

"Don't judge, miss prissy puss," Cameron said, "those working toms have a rugged charm that these penthouse cats can only dream of."

"I guess you'd know." Abigail pressed her lips together.

After an uncomfortable silence Cassie realized she needed to get her tail out of there. She wanted to be alone, and the tension among her friends was not helping. "Well, congratulations, Maureen." Cassie nuzzled her friend as she turned to leave. "I know you'll have beautiful kittens."

"Thanks, Cass." Maureen nuzzled back.

"Well, I better get going." Cassie headed for the door.

Abigail's human opened the door for Cassie. Before she slipped into the hallway, the woman petted her very softly, as if she knew Cassie was sad and needed some cheering up. Cassie rubbed against her ankles before dragging herself home.

Over a week later, Cassie roused herself from an incredibly long nap. She had been sleeping almost nonstop, preferring to spend her time dreaming of better days, rather than dwelling on the fact that Mr. Big-Paws had cut her loose like last month's collar.

Cassie glanced at the clock and realized it was time for her weekly lunch date with the queens. She laid her head back down, not wanting to face her friends today. Oh, well, they would understand. She wanted to mope a little longer and think about the cat that got away.

The clock seemed to be glaring at her. Both hands pointed upward and told her to get off her lazy haunches and do something. She did need to get out and stretch her legs. Lying in the garden on the roof sounded pleasant. Moments later she was sitting under a wooden bench beside the little pond that should really have had some koi in it when an unfamiliar voice sounded.

"Hello, beautiful."

A cat with light green eyes and slate gray fur sashayed toward her. His ancestry was obviously Russian Blue, and he was definitely new to the building.

Cassie demurred, keeping her body neutral and her tail still. His fine breeding was obvious from his perfect features and shiny thick coat. He moved with a casual fluid grace that imlied a great lineage. She smelled his maleness and fought the instant attraction.

"I am Stefan. I am most pleased to meet you."

"I'm Cassie, nice to meet you too." She took in his foreign accent. His captivating scent was so exotic and musky. It tickled her nose and made her warm in all the right places. He was much smaller than Mr. Big-Paws, but he had an old-world charm so different from the common cats in the city who had only one thing on their minds. "Where are you from, Stefan?"

"The East, over the sea, though I have been traveling a lot in past seasons." Stefan came closer, his the tip of his tail dancing in the air. "Please forgive me for disturbing you. I have been in your city not very long and am eager to learn more of this place."

Cassie had always wanted to travel like Stefan, but she was too comfortable in her home. She'd heard that traveling was often tiring. "You're here on vacation?"

"Perhaps vacation, yes. Though I am considering staying for long time. Many things beautiful are in this country and my human will stay as long as I wish."

Cassie knew where this was heading and decided she was not ready. She rose to all four paws and prepared to leave.

"May I call on you sometime?" Stefan asked, lowering his tail politely and almost hiding his disappointment.

She wanted to say yes, but it was too soon for her to start dating again. Wasn't it? Her feline-biological clock started to tick loudly in her ears. She summoned her willpower to say no.

"Don't say anything, please." Stefan winked at her, his lustrous eyes full of mischief. "We are neighbors now. How do you say it in this country, see you later?"

Cassie admired his persistence, but she couldn't let herself be drawn into one of those rebound-dating things that never worked out. She should just prance off and not reply, but that would be rude. Especially to a foreigner who had just arrived in the city. "Yes. See you later."

Stefan's eyes followed her as she left the garden. She could feel them. As she went down the stairs, Cassie started to miss Big-Paws even more. *Maybe it could work out between us? Maybe he just got scared? Maybe if I go to him now, he'll want me back?*

The door to his penthouse suite was open. Cassie gingerly approached the door and peeked inside. Harsh carpet cleaning chemicals replaced the usual smell of leather ottomans and those strangely intriguing cigars Big-Paws' human liked to smoke. The place was empty save for a housekeeper's cart and the nice woman who always shut off her vacuum when cats passed her in the hallway. It was true that Cassie had planted the original idea to shut off the ear-splitting machine, but even after that, the woman continued to be thoughtful.

Cassie realized she was doing a good job of avoiding the truth as she surveyed the penthouse. Mr. Big-Paws was gone. He wasn't going to ask for her back. It really was over. Cassie felt as though she were sinking into the carpet and had to get out of there. Now. She had to go back home and take a nap that would last for days. Maybe weeks. Perhaps it would be better if she gave up on the idea of kittens all together and just got spayed like a lot of the other cats.

She sulked toward the staircase, her tail feeling dead and lifeless. Stefan appeared, his eyes filled with concern. "What is wrong? May I be helpful to you?"

"No. Thank you." She didn't want to tell him. After all, they had just met.

"Later, perhaps, we will have dinner. I will be in my new place of living all night." Stefan motioned toward a door to a posh penthouse suite facing the park.

Cassie made it back to her place and hid under the bed. She fell asleep after wondering where Big-Paws had gone. She missed him, especially the times when he would wrap his tail around her legs and they would fall asleep together. She awoke in the darkness and crawled out from under the bed. Her stomach was empty, and her food bowl was too.

Damn. Her human must not have come home—again. The silver laptop with the fruit symbol on it was on the desk, so she couldn't be out on business. She must have spent the night with one of those fashion photographers that she was so fond of mating with.

Stefan did say to drop by for dinner. Cassie found the custom-made penthouse cat door open and soft music playing inside. It sounded like one of Tchaikovsky's sweeping piano concertos. She poked her head into the spacious room. It had modern décor with two cognac-colored Ekornes chairs in front of a huge flat-screen TV, brushed metal tables, plush couches with a very relaxing pattern, and thick sand-colored carpet that had only a hint of the just-off-the-roll smell.

"Welcome to my new home." Stefan's eyes beamed as he greeted her. "Come in. Come in."

"Thank you." Cassie entered the lavish apartment, noticing how low and perfect for hopping onto the furniture was. As they passed the soft couch, she smelled gunpowder and money beneath the cushions. Perhaps Stefan's human had heard how rough the city sometimes was and decided to keep a gun close by.

"Are you hungry?" Stefan asked.

With impeccably embarrassing timing, her stomach growled. "Maybe a little."

"Follow me."

In the marble-floored kitchen, Stefan showed her a silver bowl with small black fish eggs. "Mmmm, caviar."

"Beluga, of course," Stefan said, "I find it more palatable than Malossol. Don't you agree?"

"It smells delicious." Cassie took a bite and was hooked. "Would you like some, Stefan?"

"I've already dined, thank you."

She finished the bowl rather quickly as he explained that

his human was at some nightclub and would probably be there all night with business partners.

"Care for something to drink?" Stefan indicated a saucer of water.

When her tongue touched it, Cassie noticed something different. It was extremely pure and had a clean taste so lively and different from the plastic-flavored bottled water she was used to. "This is excellent."

"It's from a pristine spring in my Motherland, shipped in glass bottles to preserve the taste. Common brands are so bland."

Stefan came over for a taste beside her, and their tongues almost met by the edge of the bowl. Cassie pulled away, licking her upper lip.

"The view from my balcony is quite nice," Stefan said. "Would you like to see it?"

Cassie followed him and was stunned by the twinkling lights of the high-rises and the perfect view of the lush park.

"I'm pleased very much that you are here." Stefan, glanced at Cassie, his eyes luminous in the night.

"Thank you for inviting me."

Stefan lay down on a soft rug, while gazing through the railing. He invited her to join him with a flick of his tail.

With her full tummy and the pleasing music, Cassie could not help herself. She lay down beside Stefan and breathed in air that smelled of the rich earth and sweet leaves in the park. She could definitely get used to this.

The next day, around noon, Cassie excused herself, and Stefan showed her out.

"It was most pleasing to see you, Cassie. I hope to see you again soon."

"I'd like that too." Cassie blinked at him, then sauntered away, giving him a good look at her hind end. After all, it was her best feature.

When she returned home, an anchovy that had been recently packed in extra virgin olive oil lay on the welcome mat. Her tail stiffened. It had to be from Big-Paws. He was the only one who knew of her strange weakness for oil-packed anchovies rather than the mundane salt-packed variety.

She sniffed around for the musky scent of Mr. Big-Paws, but a fresh layer of the reeking flowery perfume from the lawyer lady down the hall masked the area well enough that she couldn't pick him out.

Cassie picked up the fish, tasting the bold and rich flavor enhanced by the toasted hazelnuts and caviar that it had been packed with. She made her way out the hall window, along the ledge, and onto her balcony. She wished she had her own custom cat door as she avoided the pigeon droppings on the stone parapet. She went into her apartment with its view of the street, and hid the fish under the bed, wondering if it really had come from Big-Paws.

The next three days were a flurry of activity in between long luxurious naps at Stefan's apartment. The Russian was excellent company, always putting her first and making her laugh. She loved showing him around the building and spending time with him. Late one night they strolled through the rooftop garden. He stopped her by the pond.

"See anything different?" Stefan's whiskers twitched.

Cassie glanced into the water. Orange and white shapes swam back and forth. "Fish? You had koi put in here?"

"It was my pleasure," Stefan said, "especially since you so are happy now."

"They're beautiful." Cassie was enthralled, and couldn't take her eyes away.

"Not as beautiful as you." Stefan brushed against her cheek. Their whiskers met, sending jolts of sensation through all the way down Cassie's tail. Stefan said, "I have traveled very far in this world, but I have never met a feline as wonderful as you."

Their noses met, and his scent overwhelmed her. She was suddenly smelling his rump as he pressed his nose toward her own tail.

Is this the moment? Will we make love beside the koi pond?

Suddenly Cassie backed away, her tail rigid in the air. "I'm sorry, Stefan. It's too soon."

He lay down, his patient eyes fixed on her. "I understand."

She knew that he did. He was so genuine. And yet so mysterious.

Stefan stared into her face. "There will be a right time, and we have so much time to spend together. Especially if you come away with me."

"Where?" Cassie lowered her head in surprise.

"The Orient. Together we can see many koi ponds in beautiful gardens. We'll dine on the freshest sashimi, sleep in the most luxurious places. It will be wonderful."

"When will we go? How long will we be gone?" Cassie worried about leaving her home, but she was excited about the invitation.

"We leave in three days, and we'll be away for at least a month. Perhaps more."

"It sounds wonderful." Cassie glanced at the pond, noticed the ripples in the water. It was all so perfect.

The next day she had lunch with the queens. Abigail, Maureen, and Cam barely touched their food as they peppered her with questions.

"Who is this tom Stefan?" Abigail demanded.

"He's very kind and has the most striking eyes. He's Russian Blue, from Archangel, Siberia. A very good breed. His lineage stretches back before the court of the last czar."

"Is he a good lover?" Cameron raised her ears.

"We haven't done that. Not yet." Cassie twitched her whiskers.

"When are you going to see him again?" Maureen asked.

"Maybe tonight," Cassie said, "I'm going to tell him my answer."

"Answer to what?" Abigail asked, looking a bit worried.

"He asked me to go on a trip with him. To the Orient."

"You just met him!" Maureen exclaimed, skepticism causing her teeth to show.

"I know!" Cassie shook with excitement. "Isn't it great?"

Maureen hissed. "No, it's not, and don't you want to be here when I have my kittens?"

"Of course I do." Cassie glanced at Maureen's tummy, which wasn't showing a bit.

"She's right, honey, especially since you haven't done the deed. You don't want to get stuck on the Orient Express if it's going to be a bumpy ride." Cam paused as a wicked look came over her face. "Come to think of it, maybe you do."

"Cam!" Abigail nudged Cameron out of the way. "Listen, Cassie. You don't know this tom well enough to leave the country with him. Won't you miss the city . . . and us?"

"Of course I will." Cassie sat down. "But I've always wanted to travel, and this is my chance."

"I better check him out," Maureen said. "I'll get in touch with my friend downtown."

"Don't go snooping around." Cassie's ears lay back as she tensed. "I don't need you queens getting in his business and causing trouble. One of the reasons Mr. Big-Paws left is because of how you all meddled in our affairs."

"We barely did anything!" Maureen lowered her tail.

Cassie snorted, remembering how Big-Paws thought her snorts were cute.

"What are you going to tell him?" Abigail asked.

"I don't know yet." Cassie looked at her paws. "I just want to get away from here for a while."

Abigail bumped Maureen with her head.

"What?" Cassie glanced at her friends.

Maureen looked guilty. "Mr. Big-Paws came by two nights ago looking for you. You must have been with Stefan. I'm sorry for not telling you before."

"What did he say?" Cassie asked with raised ears.

"Just that he wanted to see you," Maureen said, "and say goodbye properly."

"Oh, is that it?" Cassie let the faint hope die—as she should have done before. "Where is he now?"

"Gone," Cam said, "like you'll be pretty soon. He's moved on, and so should you. But you better come back and visit."

"You can't leave us for too long," Maureen said, and all her friend's eyes got really big. Cassie knew how much they all cared about her. How could she ever leave and not come back? They were her family. She might even miss her human a little too, and not just because of all the shoes.

That night Cassie stayed home and slept instead of seeing Stefan as she'd planned. She thought about what to do and ignored Stefan's pawing at her door. She wanted one night alone to think. The anchovy under the bed still had most of its scent, but dust bunnies had gotten all over it, dampening some of its appeal.

The next night she made her way to the rooftop garden, knowing that Stefan would probably be waiting for her. He sat beside the koi pond, his tail lazily moving back and forth.

"Cassie." Stefan leaped up. "It's so good to see you."

"You too." Cassie approached and they touched noses.

"Have you made decision?" Stefan pulled back, his eyes catching the moonlight.

"I have." Cassie said, as the lights of the city beckoned

her. She pranced away and jumped onto the wall that surrounded the rooftop to stare at the beautiful buildings with their twinkling lights. Stefan followed, and they both stared over the edge, looking at the precipitous drop over fifty stories down.

This was her home, but it was a big world out there. "I'll go, Stefan. Take me away with you."

"I'll show you so much more than you've ever imagined."

"Not so fast." Mr. Big-Paws jumped onto the wall, his large frame towering over the Russian.

"Y-you're back." Cassie couldn't believe it.

"Go away from here, this does not concern you," Stefan said, showing his teeth in irritation.

"Oh, it does." Big-Paws' ears were flat against his head and he bared his own teeth.

"What's going on?" Cassie asked.

"Maureen got in touch with me." Big-Paws inched closer to Stefan. "Her friend downtown looked up this cat's human. He's Russian mob, on the run from the authorities. And who do you think is the brains behind the operation? Certainly not that human." Big-Paws kept his ears flat. Cassie thought that made his face look strangely savage.

"Is it true?" Cassie asked Stefan, remembering the smell of money and gunpowder under the couch cushion.

"True, yes." Stefan didn't back down. "And knowing this is true should make your friend here worry for his life. I am not a cat to be trifled with."

"Did he tell you he was on the run, Cassie?" Big-Paws asked. "His human will never be able to get back into this country once he leaves. They're after him right now. That's why he's got to leave, and fast."

Stefan's eyes told her that it was the truth.

Big-Paws stalked forward, allowing his claws to click on

the stone. "Is that the kind of life you want, Cassie, being on the run all the time?"

"Humans are easy to replace," Stefan said. "Don't listen to this mixed-breed oaf. He is just jealous that I have you now and he does not. Don't worry, I will find another human to serve us as we travel the world. I always do."

"I've heard enough," Cassie said. She glared at Stefan. "You should have told me the truth." Then she fixed her stare on Big-Paws. "And you came back only after Maureen told you I was seeing another tom. Both of you make me sick."

"You will not come with me?" Stefan asked.

"No." Cassie wrinkled her pink little nose in disgust. "I'm done with tomcats. You're all trouble." She hopped off the wall and sped for the stairs.

A vicious catfight ensued as she reached the steps. They yowled, hissed, clawed at the air, then slammed together. Stefan used his lightning speed to wrap his front legs around Big-Paws' neck, then scratched at the larger cat's vulnerable belly with his rear claws. Big-Paws bit Stefan's ear and grappled ferociously with the gangster cat, trying for a mortal strike.

Cassie couldn't watch anymore. The sounds of the battle faded as she entered the building. A sudden stab went through her heart. *I've given up on love. What am I doing? I just let two toms get away, and one of them I actually loved.* Cassie switched directions, running back toward the roof.

Tufts of fur floated in the air and blood stained the stone. Big-Paws and Stefan were locked in a ball of fury atop the precipice.

"Stop!" Cassie sprinted forward.

Big-Paws didn't react to her appeal. His head shot forward as the Russian hesitated, and he locked his jaws around Stefan's throat. Howling, the gangster threw his weight to one side. Both toppled over the edge in front of Cassie's horror-filled eyes.

The sudden quiet was a shock. Cassie stood there, quivering in every muscle. When she could move again, she slowly approached the ledge. Jumping up, she peered down into the darkness.

They were both gone. She was alone. Their deaths were on her paws. A wail ripped from her throat.

"Don't jump, whatever you do."

Cassie stopped yowling. She looked closer. Bloody and tattered, Mr. Big-Paws stood on the balcony one floor below the roof. There was no sign of Stefan. She knew that from this height, landing on one's feet wouldn't help much.

Cassie met Big-Paws by the stairs a few moments later. They limped into the garden together in silence.

"I came back for you, Kitty." He nuzzled her. Cassie inhaled his musky scent and felt herself getting warm all over.

"I'm so glad you did. I missed you a lot." Cassie buried her nose in his bloody, matted chest fur.

"You're the only queen for me." He licked her face, and she knew he loved her. They would have kittens together, and life in the city would be purrfect.

She was sure. He was the one. Their eyes met and Cassie said, "I think it's time."

"Time for what?" he asked.

Cassie purred, felt the primal heat building into a fire. She licked her lips provocatively and smiled. "It's time to find out if it's true what they say about cats with big paws."

FOR THE BIRDS

Jana Paniccia

Around noontime on Election Day, it was as if a dozen still-living mice began to squirm in my stomach. To try to settle the feeling, I left my aides behind at the E-Day headquarters and pattered down to the bluffs behind City Hall. After raining all morning, the sun was peeking through the clouds, casting a rainbow over the forested river bank opposite. Awe tingled through me, spreading down my back all the way to my toes as I watched the rays of color illuminate the sky.

A sign of destiny?

By the time darkness leached the light from the sky, all the votes would be counted. One way or another, my path would be marked.

"Mr. Churchill. Mr. Churchill!" I twitched my nose, catching the scent of Diefenbaker, my campaign manager, as he barreled around the bend leading from the front entrance of the municipal complex, his white and brown coat all ashambles.

Something official, then. If he'd been coming from the victory—*I hoped*—party set-up, he'd have come up the path toward me and not approached from behind.

"What's happened?" I demanded. I kept my tail steady,

not willing to show any sign of uncertainty. The first thing I had learned early in my career was that good carriage was important even when your nerves felt as if they'd rake your fur into prickly points. I dug my claws into the stonework of the wall protecting unwary visitors from the sheer drop to the river below.

Someone's seen through my façade. They're going to cede the election to Whittington. My life is ruined.

There was no way to keep such fears from tumbling through my thoughts. After all, everyone trusted Whittington. His namesake had had a cat after all—one with posture and poise—a true noble. It didn't matter that Whittington was only a name chosen to give my competitor credibility. Thanks to that blasted story, his moniker was legend.

Certainly, my namesake was revered also. Yet, try as I might, Whittington had the upper paw with voters. Maybe if we were in a time of war, it would be different.

The truth was, the real Whittington's cat had been of noble background, and my competition was as well. He could trace his lineage back to the old country; his ancestors had come over among the first settlers. No wonder the masses were drawn to him. The populace always voted for those with a pedigree.

If they've learned the truth, I won't even have a chance . . .

"Protestors, sir!" Diefenbaker panted. "Down where the vote's being counted!"

"Thank goodness for rats." I said, casting aside my doubts in favor of dealing with Diefenbaker's dilemma.

"No sir. Birds."

Birds?

Crinkling paper caught my attention as an old tabby curled up in a nest of rags and newspaper perked his ears. With his patchy fur set against the muddled shade of the municipal buildings, I hadn't noticed him before. *Wish we could get more of these alley cats off the streets and into good homes. If I get elected . . .*

I couldn't think about that yet. I had to get the office first, which meant dealing with the birds right now, whatever they were up to.

"They've surrounded the Chief Elections Officer and are holding up the vote," Diefenbaker continued, his gold eyes wide.

I sighed. It wasn't easy to plan an E-Day. Picking a time when few humans would notice the absence of their "pets," or the rise in the numbers of felines crossing the city as they hitched rides to their polling locations, was a struggle at the best of times. If protesters were up in paws, or claws, we'd never be able to keep our activity from the other communities at large. Someone would notice. Someone would start asking hard questions.

"What's Whittington doing?" I asked, knowing my fellow candidate would be taking advantage of the situation in any way possible.

"He's already speaking to them, telling the leader that when he gets reelected, he'll be sure to bring their concerns to the City Council. That if they let the voters through to the polls, he'll make certain they get a chance to plead their case."

"And do the protesters believe him?"

"No, sir," Diefenbaker grinned. "As one put it, 'You're a great talker. Too bad you're not so great at keeping promises.' "

Good. At least they won't be using him as leverage.

This protest could not have come at a worse time. If the votes didn't get through and counted, the election would be discounted and postponed until next year. It would take that long to set up another ballot and get the word around.

Maybe I shouldn't have put all my catnip in the same place. I'll never keep my secret another year . . .

I swept my tongue over my chest, thinking. A hollow ache tugged at my stomach, reminding me of lunch. I hadn't eaten all day, what with making last minute cat-calls to influential voters.

Birds. Most cats considered them fair game, especially the ferals, who had no steady food source. I'd even chased them a time or two, all in good fun. But I'd never hurt one intentionally.

Now Whittington . . . I could easily imagine him pulling a bird out of the sky. I glanced up at the rainbow, still a shimmering arc against the blue. Soon flowers would bring a similar spread of colors to the forest, and the pedigreed and wealthy upper class would make for their country vacation homes. Whittington's ilk liked to hunt. When the summer came, they'd all be out chasing birds with vigor.

That's it! Banning the annual bird hunts—now that was something I could promise that Whittington never would.

It's a sport of the wealthy anyway. Most cats disliked the hunts almost as much as I did. There was a huge difference between chasing for fun and killing for sport, after all.

If I promised to ban them, there were sure to be rumors. Jennings and every one of his newshounds would be out for blood. My blood.

No wonder the news has gone to the dogs. No cat in his right mind would lose his sense of objectivity like that.

But it wasn't the first day of the election contest. It was E-Day, the final day. Surely, I could hold the hounds off long enough for the vote to be counted.

Banning the hunts could be enough to slip me past Whittington . . .

Turning toward Diefenbaker, I neatened my fur again. "I'll have to put in an appearance. We have to get the protesters to move. If the humans notice, there'll be more publicity than any of us want."

"What are you going to do?" my aide asked, his nose coming up as if to scent my response.

"I'll go down there myself. Go give my regrets at our lunch engagement, then meet me there. I want to get the lay of the land before I make my final decision. I think we can offer something worth making voters back us . . ."

"You shouldn't go alone, sir. What if they notice you?"

I flexed my front claws against the stone wall, this time with purpose. "Do you think they will if I want it otherwise?"

Getting to the site of the protest meant winding around the few humans collecting in front of City Hall. At least whatever they were doing with their loud music made an excellent distraction. I pressed on.

Maybe they won't notice the birds, I hoped.

The central voting booths were along the canal just in front of the university. It was always a quiet place in the early spring, making it perfect for our needs. Humans biked or jogged along the waterway; they didn't linger as they did in the height of summer. It was a safe place for voting. Or it would have been if birds weren't trying to attract attention. Hiding the voters bringing mouse ballots was bad enough; hiding flying protestors, especially vocal ones, would be impossible.

At least everyone's eyes would be on the protesters. *The hounds won't be after me right away.*

And while my silvery coat might look distinguished in the municipal chambers, down here I'd pass as a mottled gray street cat, at least as long as no one got close enough to read my collar.

There were more birds than even I could have imagined.

As I came out of the line of trees cutting between the heart of the city and the river, my eyes caught on the hundreds—no, thousands—of pigeons swarming our voting station, a rough-cut stone building. The canal hadn't been used commercially in over a decade, so the wheelhouse was perfect for our purpose. Central, yet unnoticed.

No hope of that, now.

On the other side of the thin iron walkway crossing the canal, a crowd of newshounds barked questions at birds sitting on the fence behind the wheelhouse even as McClung, a Persian and the Chief Elections Officer, also tried to bring calm to the chaos. On my side of the canal, a hundred cats lined the water, several playing with their ballots while they waited. One fat calico appeared calm and contented as she watched the flight of birds overhead, a thin tail dangling out the side of her mouth.

Knew there'd be a problem with edible ballots. Tried to tell them.

As I padded down the incline toward the voters, a young vote counter on the other side of the canal snapped at a passing pigeon, capturing a mouthful of white and gray feathers. A loud squawk filled the air as the indignant bird broke away.

"You're an official. Act like one!" McClung scolded the youngster, her ire apparent. If anyone could settle this crowd, it was the Chief Elections Officer. She hated inequitable treatment, even of birds.

"Please, this is no time for arguments. You know that the votes must be counted today or there will be no hope for an election for at least another year." That was Whittington's silky voice. "Do not judge the future until the mice have been counted. This public display is unconscionable." I found him tucked right in the middle of the newshounds.

Of course. Fat cat can't help seeking the limelight.

"They'll learn. Learn when they see this ruckus. You cats will be stopped. Stopped. One way or another." The bird that spoke was fog-colored and speckled, with one wing a dull brown. An ugly thing, no wonder he looked confident as he settled down on the fence right next to Whittington. No pedigreed cat in his right mind would be interested in taking him out, not unless he wanted a bad case of indigestion, and scorn from his companions at nabbing the ugliest member of the flock.

"Why doesn't everybody just leave the birds alone?" a nearby voter said. "It's not as if most of us need to fend for ourselves. Not even alley cats go for fresh pigeon, unless they're starving."

"That's because those pigeons have helped the strays more than the politicos ever have," an elder cat big enough to be part Maine Coon responded. "Always on the lookout for fresh fish. I've heard they worked out a deal."

"Good for them. It's not like the fat cats will ever do anything."

"Maybe Churchill'll bring change—I have a feeling about him." My ears pricked. This time it was a cat further down the line.

"A bit quiet—doesn't seem the type to rock the boat," another said.

"I . . ." My voice trailed off before I could gain their attention. They didn't understand. I wanted to change things. I wanted to get the alley cats off the streets. I wanted to ensure all cats could get medical attention. I wanted to make a difference.

I needed to.

I knew until the election was over, I couldn't give the

newshounds something to fight over. I had to act the pedigreed cat, the one who won votes just by existing. Any hint of controversy . . .

But if what they all want change? What if they want someone who will speak up?

Maybe the real voters were interested in something more than posturing.

Maybe they wanted to know what I *thought*, too.

It was a strange notion, and one I immediately cast aside. The moment I voiced my thoughts, I'd give myself away. I couldn't do that. I couldn't. I was close to winning. At the last poll, Whittington and I had been neck and neck.

Did I want to stir up trouble?

I'm better off just seeing where the ball bounces. It's too close. These couple of hundred voters standing right here could be the tipping point.

No. I couldn't do it.

Once I was mayor—then—*then* I could start being honest.

"Please. Do we need another year of campaigning? Nothing will get done if you do not let the votes get through. I promise I will do what I can."

As Whittington continued his appeal, I noticed Diefenbaker coming up behind the newshounds. Birds fluttered backward upon sight of my campaign manager. They would know I was close. *Bet they're looking forward to it, too.*

Two candidates facing off at a polling station would be the day's top story.

Before the results are in, anyway.

"And where do you sit?" Jennings questioned Diefenbaker. The newshound would sniff the truth out in no time given the chance. He had an excellent nose. *Can't give him the time.*

"The other candidate doesn't even see this as a priority,

or he'd be here himself. Unlike if I win. If I win, I promise I will do what I can," Whittington said, pushing between the beagle and Diefenbaker.

That was my cue.

"Do what you can?" I said, slipping between the cats I had overheard and padding my way to the walk overlooking the canal. I ignored the yowls of surprise as I passed. "Does that include discontinuing your own practice of hunting when you're off at your summer house near Central Park?"

Whittington wasn't going to stop hunting the birds; it was a truth I knew from three years serving together on council. Maybe I could make this about him and not have to choose sides at all.

"If you got in, you'd drag your paws all winter long waffling over the issue, maybe set up a commission to study the matter further, and then be right back hunting in summer," I accused.

"I keep my word," my competition said, tilting his head so he could meet the eyes of some of the voters. His long black coat sparkled with an elegance I didn't have.

"So why are we even here? If you'd kept your promises, the birds wouldn't have any issues, would they?"

It was as if we were back in the council chambers, with the canal serving the purpose of the Speaker.

"Well, Churchill, all you do is run for office by complaining about my policies. The voters don't even know what you stand for."

Anger burned in my stomach as every voter's eyes focused on me. I could feel the accusations there. They were agreeing with Whittington.

Have I been too quiet? Too complacent?

By hiding my lack of pedigree, have I hidden all my dreams also?

The uncertainty made me pause, whiskers trying to feel

out the position of those watching and coming up short. If I wasn't honest, I still had hope. I could force the argument back toward Whittington. I'd lose a few votes, but I'd still be in the game.

If I told the truth, I could be slaughtered.

The moment stretched as I peered at Diefenbaker, visible beyond Whittington's small frame. What would he want me to do? His stance gave away nothing, no hint of worry.

He trusts me.

Maybe he was the only one who did. No one else gave off that innate feeling of trust. If anything, most of the voters appeared resigned, as if they were waiting for me to dodge the argument.

I had a passion to make a difference in the world—and the voters didn't expect me to do a darned thing.

It shattered my calm.

"I can promise I've never been on a bird hunt." As I spoke the words, the mice skittering around in my stomach finally calmed.

I jumped on to the iron walkway crossing the canal, finally feeling free to speak my mind.

"I can promise that when I'm elected, I'll ban such hunts." It was a promise no pedigreed cat would make. "If we work together, we can see change happen. Work with our neighbors instead of against them. There's enough food and shelter for all, if we'd just join together to find it. We can make this world a better place—one where strays have a place to call home, pigeons can be safe in the park, and the dogs battle boredom by pulling on tuggers and chasing balls. A world where fresh blood isn't chased down and ripped apart."

At that, Jennings let out a bark of laughter.

"You think I'm joking?" I asked.

"If you're voted in, you'll be lucky to change the color of

your collar," Whittington said, leaping on to the walkway, so he didn't have to look up at me. He stuck his wet nose in my face. "What have you said the last month that has meant anything? You think making meaningless promises now will make a difference? No one knows what you really want."

"I thought people knew," I whispered, more to myself than to anyone.

Whittington wasn't a bad politician. The election would be easier for me to win if he was. But he was of the old school and wasn't about to change his beliefs. Other cats seemed to instinctively know that about him and thought I was the same. I had to prove I was different.

"Spokespigeon, can you come down here?" I called, finding the distinctive bird in the flock.

After a moment, the bird descended, finding a spot on the rail just out of both Whittington's paw reach and my own.

"I don't go to the hunting parties," I claimed. "I never have, and I never will." The words were an admission, though the bird wouldn't know why.

Jennings came up the steps of the canal without any of a cat's grace and with all the confidence of a dog chasing after a bone. He let out a bark as he made the walkway and joined the mix.

"Never? Why is that?" he demanded.

I knew the dog could smell the truth, and I gave it to him, knowing there was no hope of keeping my secret now. It was as though someone had let me out of a bag. I was free.

I met Whittington's level green eyes for a moment, then turned to Jennings. "I'd never condone such a thing."

The beagle let out a soulful sigh, full of dawning under-standing. I thought I knew what he was going to say next. For a long moment I waited, my heart going to stone.

This is it. The end of my career.

But for once, the dog was silent.

Whittington wasn't. "You're nothing but a mutt, aren't you—*Whisker McTailzo*?" he spat, using one of the worst forms of address another cat could offer: my human name.

There was more than one hiss in response from the bystanders. Even the newshounds and the birds looked shocked.

"At least I'm an honest one." I arched my back, letting my tail fur spike. If I was going to be buried, at least I was the one causing the avalanche. I relaxed my posture and looked up at the protestors' leader. "Do you have a name, spokespigeon?"

"Bergh," the bird chirped.

"Well, Bergh, if you leave now, even if I'm not elected Mayor, I'll fight for your rights. I guarantee I'll be a constant claw in Whittington's side."

There were gasps as I admitted I might not win. Everyone knew it wasn't good practice.

The bird squawked. "For that deal, we will leave in peace."

Their trust was something, at least.

"No!" Whittington leaped forward, taking Bergh down to the ground with a crisp swipe of a paw.

I lunged, striking Whittington's paw away with one of my own, forcing him to release the protester.

"You think you can ban sport?" Whittington yelled as all the birds took to the air, wings snapping in the breeze. "Might as well try to ban eating mice, or are you against that as well? How about all those mice caught and killed to give you votes? Do you agree with that practice?"

I refused his lure. "Change starts one cat at a time," I said. "All I can promise is that I'll work for it, no matter what happens in this election."

"Which must continue," McClung broke in, taking control. She turned to the cats in line. "If you don't have ballots, please remove yourselves from the premises."

"I'll see you in the council chambers . . . Councillor," Whittington said, not even offering a paw. His eyes were cold.

I turned away. Toward the city. Toward the reality that I'd likely ceded the day to Whittington.

The realization didn't hurt as much as I had expected it to.

As I made my way back toward City Hall, Diefenbaker took up a position at my side. Jennings followed at our heels. At the end of the first block, I realized other cats were following us.

Seeing me embarrassed wasn't enough. They want to see me defeated.

I looked to Jennings, wondering what he would say tomorrow if others killed me tonight. I'd played them false, after all. They had thought I was pedigreed, that I had breeding. What was I really? *A mutt, just as Whittington said.*

"Sir? Look at them . . ." Diefenbaker hissed in my ear.

Without thinking, I did. He was my campaign manager, after all.

I looked, and froze.

While most of the cats following us were grave, a few were smiling. Some even nodded when they saw they had my attention. Not one looked ready to strike.

"What?" The word was less than a stumbling purr in my throat.

"Being part beagle myself," Jennings offered, "I could've told you. Sometimes honesty is enough."

I couldn't blink.

Maybe there'll be a party after all.

"So, what are you going to do next?" Jennings barked as we started padding again.

I knew he meant when the night was over—win or lose—but there was only one thing at the top of my mind.

"I think we might have to consider a new ballot system."

EYE WITNESS

Donald J. Bingle

"You saw this yourself?" Shamus McGee stroked his whiskers absentmindedly as he peered at Willie, sizing him up. Willie was usually reliable, but he hadn't seen head or tail of the snitch for some months now, and things can happen—things that can cause once trustworthy sources to become untrustworthy, even dangerous. The reasons were many: hard times, narcotics, mental illness, religious fervor, old age. He'd seen them all in his decades as a private investigator, and he had to be sure of his information. This was a wild, wild tale—the kind that folks talk about in gatherings on Saturday night or when they meet up during a Sunday walk in the park. His reputation was on the line if he reported to the client that this was actually the solution to the mystery. He wanted to be sure he got it right.

"Absolutely, Shamus. Without a doubt. I mean, I couldn't believe my eyes at first, but when you think about it, it explains everything ... well, almost everything." Willie twitched with excitement, or perhaps worry, about the information he had just imparted. Shamus couldn't be sure which yet and he needed to know.

Willie's tale was a blockbuster, if true. The religious establishment was bound to be apoplectic. Willie would be investigated and denounced at the very least. His name, his history, everything about him would be sniffed out, batted about to see what shook loose, then released to the news-mongering horde in a manner calculated to make sure their frenzied attacks and howls of protest lasted as long as possible.

Shamus would be unlikely to fare much better, but at least he had a long professional reputation and some friends, or at least long-established contacts, in the news dissemination business. They would hold off on him for awhile. Long enough to see how the basic story sold and whether his bizarre explanation of the ultimate mystery was going to win the day. Then, if it looked as though Willie's information was bogus, they would pounce and tear him apart, too.

It was past strange that he had ever even gotten this assignment. He'd been in the detective business a numbingly long time, but he didn't go for the sensational jobs. This, well, this was truly sensational and the oddest case he'd ever worked . . . by far. Most of the jobs were straightforward enough, if not downright routine. Not always simple work or pleasant either, but what you expected in the business. Staking out houses and tailing suspects, mostly catching those who cheated on their supposed loved ones. He'd seen more mates leave home in the evening to go visit some piece of tail than he cared to think about.

The clients wanted to know, but they didn't necessarily want to see what was going on right under their noses— most of his clients really didn't get out that much and couldn't handle themselves on the streets like he could. Sure, there was some excitement in the job—an occasional car chase, that kind of thing. But most of the cases were just sad and pathetic.

He hated the missing children cases the worst. Yeah, he had a few successes in his time locating the young ones—

some even alive—but there were just too many cases of kids plucked away from their homes or getting lost or just turning up missing to make any sense of the world. The religious just said there was an unknowable reason for everything. The lunatic fringe—fanatics who howled at the moon—they all had theories of abduction and such. Heck, their weirdo theories made as much sense as this case—which reminded him, he'd better get down to business. His client was paying him to track down the secret of the mysterious "manna," not daydream about his crummy job.

"Let's go over the entire story, Willie."

"Geez, Shamus, I've already told I saw the whole thing!"

"But I've got to make sure what you saw makes sense. I can't just take your word for it. You know, there's no bonus for you and no future work from me, not next week, not in a blue moon, if you screw up something this important. Heck, you'll be lucky to eat out of a garbage can if word gets about that you lied . . ."

"Lied! You know me, Shamus, I ain't no liar!" Willie's nervous twitch became more pronounced.

". . . or were mistaken about what you saw. You say it all happened in Seattle? That's some distance away. What were you doing there?"

"What does it matter?" Willie's gaze went to the side, then down, looking anywhere but in Shamus' eyes.

"A good detective corroborates every part of the informant's story he can."

"It's embarrassing . . ."

Shamus opened his mouth in anger, but he withheld some of the fury of his words: "So is telling a tale like this and not being able to prove it! What were you doing in Seattle? I need to know and I need to know now. It doesn't help either of us if the first time I hear about it is on the evening news."

"I followed a girl there."

Shamus considered this for a moment. Willie wasn't exactly a catch, but some of the city dames are pretty randy. Of course, the consequences of casual promiscuity were anything but casual. That's one of the reasons there were so many unwanted offspring in the world. He focused back on the questioning. "Does she know you were there, or were you stalking her from a distance?"

"I wouldn't call it stalking . . . anyway, whatever you call it, she knew I was there. She caught me . . . I mean, saw me."

"What's her name?"

"Muffy."

"Geez, Willie, you know those rich suburban types will never go for a cat like you!" Shamus thought for a few seconds, unconsciously humming a monotonous tune. "Let's go back to the mystery, itself, and make sure we have all the appropriate elements."

"Whatever. You're the detective, Shamus."

"Alright. Now in most of the world, everyone fends for themselves. They work for their food each and every day. But then, well, then there's the rich—they live in fancy houses, people tend to their every need, and their meals are served to them on silver platters. My task is to find the source of their bounty. There's no ready evidence of where it all comes from. No one sees it, no one smells it. It sure doesn't walk into the place by itself."

"Wouldn't that be the cat's meow?"

"Yet every day, the servants of the rich take this cylindrical object, subject it to some mechanical purring apparatus, then, there it is . . . food on a silver platter. The priests call it 'manna from heaven'."

"That's the story."

"The priests also say that the servants of the pure of soul pray for provisions. If their prayers are answered, the gods purr, and immediately thereafter food mysteriously appears from nowhere, provided to these rich cats because they are the chosen ones. But you say that's not what really happens."

"Never happened to me, boss, one way or the other, but this Muffy . . . I saw it happen to her when I was stalking . . . er . . . watching her. It made me real jealous . . . and hungry, too. So I got pissed and left. Thought I'd head down to the waterfront and see what I could catch to eat. That's when I saw it. Big place, huge place. I could barely believe it, Shamus. Filled with the best food you ever smelled. Big old boats were coming in filled with fish and stuff, and they were chopping it up and putting it into these cylindrical objects, then sealing them real tight—not like a garbage can lid, boss—I mean, real tight so you couldn't even smell the food was in 'em.

"They called it a cannery. Cans is what they called the cylindrical objects. Trucks full of the stuff were leaving for all sorts of places. I followed one, and it went to a big building where there were lots of these cans and some regular food, too. Servants would saunter in and bring the cans home. That's why you can't see or smell the food coming in—it's sealed real tight. I got one of them cans, and no matter what I did, I couldn't get it open."

"So you're asking me to believe that the servants have created an entire workforce dedicated to catching food and shipping it hundreds of miles to other servants, who magically unseal it and feed it to us."

"That's about it."

This was just too much. Willie had told him earlier that the food was inside the strange cylindrical objects, but he hadn't told him this whole fantastic story about hordes of servants conspiring to make it appear. He could no longer control his disbelief of the entire story. Shamus spat out his words: "But it makes no sense, Willie. Food doesn't keep long enough to travel hundreds of miles. And besides, why would they do that? What's the purring sound? I just can't stake my professional reputation on an explanation so outlandish! I'll be labeled a heretic, for cat's sake."

"But it's true!"

"Sure, sure, Willie. I suppose next you're going to explain the mysterious red lights that have been reported lately, moving erratically at incredible speeds with no sound or source of power."

"Well, a cat in Seattle named MicroSoftie was telling me about something called 'laser pointers' . . ."

That did it. Shamus arched his back and hissed. Willie leaped from the top of the park bench and skittered away through a hole in the fence. "Laser pointer, my tail!" he fumed. "Next thing you know, he'll be trying to convince me that the servants are the chosen ones . . ."

MENTOR OF THE POTALA

Bruce A. Heard

The elegant Birman Tai Pan licks one of his pristine white forepaws, a sign that his work is over.

"Well, Mugs," he sighs, "you've truly outdone yourself this time. It took a bit of doing to get them to give you up, especially since this is the second time you've irritated them. Please try not to do that again. If you do, next time they won't listen to me at all."

He sits on the low branch of a tree with broad, thick leaves, looking down on the Astral emanation of the grizzled, muzzle-scarred gray alley cat regarding him from among the roots. Behind Mugs, a forest of giant rhododendrons slowly bristles into bloom under the soft light of a celestial crescent. A wall of majestic snowy mountains curtains the horizon, their snow-capped peaks contrasting bright against the nocturnal sky.

With shrewd turquoise eyes, Tai Pan examines for a moment the faint aura around his paw, looking at its throbbing, pulsing hues. He then glances at the translucent silver cord extending from Mugs' upper abdomen to the Astral horizon. His own cord disappears in the opposite direction.

"You do understand, of course, that my intervention on

your behalf during this little disagreement will cost you a major favor, Mugs Grayshadow?"

The alley cat winces, then nods. Sighing, Mugs levitates until he is opposite Tai Pan's branch. In midair, he rolls over on his back and offers his belly to seal their bargain.

"Aye, I understand. Though I wonder what you have on them, mate, that they'd let me go just on your say-so."

Pleased with its appearance, Tai Pan sets his paw against the other three on the branch. He shrugs his long sable and cream fur to make certain every hair is in perfect alignment. "Oh, just a small debt of honor in the right place," he answers with satisfaction.

Mugs rights himself, stepping to the branch near Tai Pan and sitting down. His thick ghostly tail coils around his paws. "Oy, that kind of thing's easy for you, the mighty Tai Pan. You've always got the goods. We're settled then: I'm in your debt, mate." He closes his golden eyes and sniffs the crisp, nocturnal air for an moment before rising.

"Gotta be off," Mugs says, and vanishes.

"Farewell, old friend," Tai Pan mutters. "Be safe, at least for now. Let me know when you're in trouble again." He allows himself a satisfied smile. "Business has been very good this month, very good indeed!"

"It's excellent news to hear you are doing so well, Sir Titus de Pannikin!" purrs a soft voice behind him.

Tai Pan leaps to his paws and whirls, ready to pounce. "Who's there?" he calls, seeing no one.

On the Astral Plane, seeing no one can be dangerous.

The silvery outline of an old white cat levitates from behind the broad leaf of a rhododendron. "I am Tara Moondreamer, from the Order of Lamasery Cats," she answers, gracefully landing on Tai Pan's branch. "Surely you remember me from long ago."

Tai Pan admires the composure and control of his visitor.

This is someone who has traveled the Astral Plane for a long time.

He searches his prodigious memory and comes up with a remembrance of a tall emerald-eyed white cat fuzzed by just-focusing kitten eyes. Tara Moondreamer had been old even then, a teacher and companion to one of the lamasery's leaders. A wriggle of unease prods his nerves, but he hides it.

What can she want from me? And what will it cost?

As if hearing his thoughts, an amused expression curls her mouth and makes her whiskers twitch. "Ah, Titus Pannikin, have you already forgotten who you are?"

"I am a businesscat," he returns a bit stiffly, the tip of his tail twitching. "And a good one, too. From where do I know you?"

"You were still learning to extend and retract your kitten claws the last time I saw you," laughs Tara. "Little Titus de Pannikin, lordly even as a kit, you always preferred to lap water from that rare silver cup. Do you still?"

Annoyed at being caught off guard by such a personal detail, Tai Pan settles his paws beneath him, trying to look more at ease. If only he could stop the last third of his Astral tail from flipping back and forth.

"Yes, I still do. But you seem to know much more about me than I do about you, Honored Tara. I am at a disadvantage here."

"Pardon my intrusion, Titus. And I didn't mean to make you feel uncomfortable," she purrs. "I am sent to give you a message. There is something urgent that you need to do."

"That *I* need to do?" His unease grows, as if something from his past has returned to haunt him. "What business does the Order have with me? Someone needs a favor, perhaps?"

"Come now, Titus. You were always meant to be a mentor, not a mere broker of services and favors," Tara chides. "Your Birman lineage ties you and your kind to the Order. Your ancestral duty is one that cannot be traded away. You realize this, don't you?"

"Ah. Tied to the Order," Tai Pan snaps back, now truly annoyed. "I haven't heard of them since I was a kitten." He recalled the group as an obscure brood, mostly concerned with the development of supernatural talents among catfolk and a few carefully chosen humans. "So, what do the ancient lamas and their wise cats want with me now, after forgetting me for all these years?" he asks.

"You were never forgotten," Tara states, staring at the moon-fed shimmers of the snow fields. "We have watched your growth. We've allowed you to ply your chosen trade for many years. And we have bided our time until the right moment. That moment is now." She takes in a deep breath, but says nothing further.

Tai Pan again tries to control his tail, with little success. It now flips in a full half arc. "All right, Honored Tara," he grumbles. "What do you want me to do?" Too late he realizes that she might take his question for acceptance rather than a request for information.

She does. "It is now time you took up your true calling, Sir Titus de Pannikin. The Order needs you to help a human acolyte master the ability to travel the Astral Plane. A simple task for you, really, considering your extensive experience there."

"What?" Tai Pan shudders. "Me, teach a human boy? Let the lamas handle that duty. Surely they have somebody better for this than me."

"No, they don't, Titus." Tara's green gaze becomes icy, reaching into Tai Pan's very soul. "When you were just a kitten, the Order placed you in the household of this human acolyte. Yes, Titus, that was no mistake—it is him you are to guide. You are best suited because you have been with young Norbu since his early childhood. He trusts you. What better mentor can there be?"

Tai Pan grumbles, "You and the Order planned this all along. You allowed me to go into business and forget!"

"True, we did the planning, Titus," Tara answers with some amusement. Her eyes become gentle. "But it was your own greed that made you forget your mission."

"Don't call me Titus," he growls, barely keeping his shoulders from hunching with irritation. "My friends know me as Tai Pan."

"What a pity. Your birth name was so fitting."

He snorts. "That's past history. Please, it's Tai Pan now. Thank you."

"Ah. My time here is at an end." Tara glances at her silver cord, which is taut and trembling. "I must go now, Titus-Tai Pan. But I need to warn you. Be very aware that there are some who seek to harm Norbu, some who are as familiar with the Astral Plane as you are."

Tara hesitates, sighing a little. "It is Norbu's destiny to become an important figure among human lamas, perhaps eventually to lead the Order. If you fail, there will be disastrous consequences not only for the lamas, but also for the rest of the world. Norbu is a key element to a binding that prevents many horrors from freely roaming the Astral Plane. His foes will try to prevent his growth and also his accession into the Order when he's ready."

"So why don't the lamas take on this duty themselves?" asks Tai Pan. "It sounds like something they'd relish."

"They can't act directly. If they did, it would surely reveal the place where he's hidden. That place you know so well. So be on your guard, Titus-Tai Pan. Be discreet. You'll need every claw and every wit you have to succeed."

"Wait, what do you mean?" Tai Pan hops to his feet as Tara vanishes. "How am I . . . ?"

He is left alone in the ice-scented breeze, among the giant rhododendrons growing at the foot of the mountains under the crescent moon.

"This is not good for business," Tai Pan mutters. "Not good at all. But what choice do I have?"

Sighing, he vanishes as well.

A split-second later, Tai Pan's Astral form materializes in a small room. His white feet rest on a worn wooden chest at the foot of a bed that is little more than a thin mattress and blanket on raised slats. Tai Pan sits down, observing for a moment the common-looking Asian boy and the bedroom of the small house they'd called home for most of their lives.

No more than ten years old in human years, Norbu sleeps restfully on his back. He is dressed in soft striped cotton pajama pants that appear to have permanent wrinkles. The blanket lies twisted over one foot and ankle. Two large bookcases, crammed with dusty old prayer books and rolled-up scrolls, stand against the wall on both sides of the head of the bed. Wads of well-thumbed comic books stick out between some of the voluminous tomes.

Tai Pan scouts the room with his heightened senses, making sure no one else is hiding there, either physically or in Astral form. *Although it is difficult to conceal anything in this room, I'd better be sure,* he tells himself. *I love this child. I've been his accomplice in many adventures, both on the streets in this city and within the pages of books. We are good friends. How could I lose him now, or leave him, furthering my business my only excuse?*

Still thinking, he leaps silently upon the small desk sitting against the wall opposite the bed, where bluish starlight filters through a gap in the curtains covering the single narrow window. The scarred wood holds a jumble of school-books, papers, pens, smudged trading cards, and toy dragons undisturbed by his weightless paws. The starlight shines through Tai Pan's immaterial form and puddles upon torn jeans and a yellow T-shirt thrown on the chair next to the desk. Worn-out sneakers and dingy socks lie underneath.

"It looks as it always does in here," says Tai Pan aloud to himself, relieved at finding nothing more obtrusive than dust and starshine.

Norbu mutters something unintelligible. Tai Pan stares back at the boy, whiskers aquiver.

"So, you hear someone speaking in the Astral Plane even in your sleep. That's good. We won't have to start from the very beginning. Now, to pry you out of this physical shell . . . Yes, perhaps that will do it."

Tai Pan jumps onto the bed and tiptoes along Norbu's sleeping body, right up to the boy's face. The faint golden glow of Tai Pan's Astral form reveals the boy's crooked nose and the faint shadows thrown by his thick eyelashes even in the dimness of his bedroom.

"Come on, boy," mutters Tai Pan, his nose almost touching Norbu's. "Time to come out and learn something new now."

The child squirms in his sleep, opens his mouth, and lets out a small snore.

"Uh huh . . . there lies the future of a great order of lamas," quips Tai Pan, amused. "Well, let's try this."

He pads downward a few steps along Norbu's body. With his front paws, Tai Pan reaches through the boy's physical ribcage and nudges his somnolent Astral essence. Norbu mutters more incomprehensible words and straightens his legs. Tai Pan purrs softly in encouragement and quirks his paws, pulling upward. His brow furrows and his ears stand erect as he concentrates.

A moment later, a ghostly duplicate of Norbu materializes just inches above his physical body. A silver cord links the Astral form to the boy's solar plexus. The strong golden aura about Norbu's immaterial shape, added to the pale glow from his silver cord and the starlight from the window, fills the room with a warm, pleasant light totally unlike the harsh brightness of human-made lamps.

"Hello, Houston, we've got liftoff!" Tai Pan feels smugly proud of himself and his pupil. "All right, Norbu, let's keep going. Lesson two."

The boy's Astral form begins to waver and sway. Tai Pan scampers toward Norbu's long feet. From there, he reaches up and grabs a hem of Norbu's Astral pajamas with his teeth.

Tai Pan mumbles, pulling. "Thif' way, 'orbu. Thif' way!"

At last, Norbu's essence slowly glides to the foot of the bed and stands upright, floating an inch or two above the wooden floor.

"Ataboy," says Tai Pan proudly from the corner of the rumpled bed. "Lesson three."

Norbu opens his Astral eyes.

"Good," Tai Pan encourages.

But the boy sees nothing. He hovers, motionless, still in a dream state.

"Now, for the tough part: keeping you wide awake and making you conscious of the Astral Plane itself. Let's try this . . ." Tai Pan pads forward and takes a quick nip at the boy's immaterial backside.

That brings Norbu to consciousness. Confused, he looks around. He screams when he sees his physical body lying on the bed.

Tai Pan exudes every ounce of a cat's extraordinary ability to calm. "No, easy there. Everything's fine." His purring fills the room.

It works. Curious now, Astral-Norbu examines his glowing hands and body. Seeing the silver cord attaching him to his corporeal self, he realizes his situation. He remembers reading about this in one of those old books. With a smile, Norbu observes his room.

He's really looking at things, noticing every detail, thinks Tai Pan, proudly staring up at the boy. *I remember the first time I saw through my Astral eyes—everything appears much more clearly.*

Norbu's eyes come to rest on Tai Pan. "Why can I see through you?" he asks.

Caught off guard, Tai Pan answers, "Um . . . Meow?"

"Weird," says Norbu. Levitating upward, he adds with glee, "Hey, this is cool!"

Without warning, he vanishes through the ceiling.

"Whoa. Oh, wharf rats! Hang on there, boy!" shouts Tai Pan, launching himself after Norbu's silver cord. "Stop!"

He sees Norbu's Astral form in the distance, gliding above the city and turning cartwheels. Tai Pan does his best to catch up, thinking himself to where the child is. As soon as Tai Pan appears next to Norbu and opens his mouth to chastise him, the youngster spies a lamasery, and darts through an open window.

Not a good idea! Tai Pan instantly materializes inside the meditation hall, apprehension filling his mind. He looks for the boy's silver cord. *This is not a good idea at all!*

Norbu's unexpected visit is unwise—an enemy might be watching, even in a lamasery. And considering his minimal experience with the Astral Plane, Norbu is in grave danger.

Above large vats of smoking stick incense, the youngster aimlessly darts in and out of the shadows around the head of a large golden Buddha. *He's returned to his dream state: there is no thought behind his motions*, Tai Pan realizes.

One of the clairvoyant lamas interrupts his prayers when

Norbu's Astral form drifts overhead. He then turns and glares angrily at Tai Pan.

"Sorry about that," says Tai Pan, bowing respect. "He is very young in knowledge."

Norbu vanishes once more. *Oh, hairballs and curdled milk! I should have known he'd go out and about.* Worried and frustrated, he launches himself after his pupil.

This time it takes Tai Pan much longer to track down the boy's whereabouts. Norbu's silver cord stretches in a different direction every time Tai Pan reaches a new location: the school, the playground, the local mall. Tai Pan arrives at a crowded ice cream stand outside the mall just in time to see Norbu zip straight up into the nocturnal sky.

"By the Great Cat's extra toes, will you stop this!" Before darting off in pursuit, Tai Pan takes a moment to quickly assess the people waiting for ice cream. One of them, a bearded and hirsute human male covered with tattoos, looks straight at him.

"You shouldn't be seeing any of this!" spits Tai Pan.

The man gives Tai Pan an evil grin and quickly walks away.

Tai Pan hisses and mutters, "The enemies know Norbu's loose! That's bad! Bad, bad, bad . . ." He takes off into the sky in a hurry, expecting the worst.

Moments later, Tai Pan finally catches up with Norbu at the rhododendron forest near the towering mountains. He levitates just above his student's head, next to the trunk of a large tree.

Terrified and cornered, the boy cowers against the bark. Only ten feet away, a nightmarish creature lurches toward Norbu. Filthy black and purple hair covers its entire body. On its face, jagged lips reveal a wide mouth with slime-dripping fangs above which purulent gray eyes bulge from slits. Standing on three thick spider legs, the monster raises two arms like a praying mantis, and clicks deadly serrated claws.

Landing between his pupil and the beast, Tai Pan shouts, "Hold it! I know you for what you are, Garakk Fearmonger. Leave this boy alone!"

Garakk takes a step back and hisses, "What makes you so sure of yourself, Titus-Detritus?"

"I know your kind. You feed on people's terror. I'm not scared of you, you miserable scum. Your business is done here. Get lost! Go back to that slime pit you call home!"

Garakk reveals its fangs in a taunting grin. It hisses back at Tai Pan, "The boy's soul is mine to feed upon. And I will have yours, too."

The creature lunges. Tai Pan's attention was momentarily divided between Garakk and Norbu, a great mistake. He realized that as the monster's claws ensnared and lifted him.

Tai Pan fights like a beserker, biting and slashing at Garakk's arms. Oblivious to the pain of multiple puncture wounds, the beast lifts him closer to its horrid fangs.

"And now, I will kill you!"

Furiously clawing at Garakks's mouth and eyes, Tai Pan shouts, "I'm not afraid of you! You are powerless against me!"

The monster huffs a sardonic laugh as it tips its head and seizes Tai Pan's silver cord between its slimy teeth. Despite his best efforts, Tai Pan cannot free himself from Garakk's thorny grip, cannot reach far enough to protect his Astral connection.

He shouts, "Norbu! Do something! Help me!"

The boy, terrified, screams and crouches at the base of the tree, his fingers in front of his face.

Hissing and gurgling with success, Garakk rips through the silver cord.

Horror-stricken, Tai Pan feels the essence of his life withering. A cold, numbing darkness submerges him.

Garakk shrieks in triumph, dropping the body and turning toward the child. Raising its claws, it opens its hideous mouth.

"I will take you one small bite at a time," the beast exults, stepping forward.

"Stop!"

The imperious command comes from behind it. Lying on the forest's cold ground, Tai Pan's Astral body regains some of its brightness. His silver cord reforms, but too slowly for his need. With what little strength he's managed to reclaim in the last few moments, he staggers to his feet, trying to look undaunted.

"It takes more than one death to kill my kind, Garakk," Tai Pan announces.

"You can't save him!" gurgles Garakk. "You are too weak!" It takes another step forward. Norbu screams.

It's right, I am too weak. Tai Pan closes his eyes. It is time to call for help. To call in a favor.

His facile mind probes the night. A friendly soul answers, "Already cashing in, are you?"

Two other cats show up in their Astral forms, just as Garakk lifts an arm to strike at Norbu.

"Didn't expect to hear from you so soon, mate!" says Mugs Greyshadow. "And I brought a friend, just in case."

The other cat, a large brown-striped Maine Coon, takes in the situation with a cool glance, leaps over Mugs, and lands on Garakk's back.

"Let's get him!" the Maine coon snarls in a gravely voice, betraying a mind as thick as his fur. With savage fury, he claws away with all fours at Garakk, sending clumps of matted hair flying. The creature flings its spiky appendages backward, trying to reach its assailant.

Mugs turns to Tai Pan. "That's Shindig Haywhisker. He's the bouncer at the Fish Eye Cat Club. He's good." The gray studies his friend. "Oy! You don't look right, mate."

"Thank you, Mugs," replied Tai Pan, ignoring the reference to his diminished appearance and denying any more talk about it by changing the subject. "Your friend is just right for this situation."

"So that's how it is," Mugs says. Stepping forward, he hunches and begins to circle Garakk, studying the beast.

"Some nasty bugger you've got here for us, mate! Seen this before, I have—that's an Astral killer, that is."

Dodging Garakk's claws with an uncanny agility learned from years of street fighting, Mugs hollers, "Better watch its arms, Shin. Wicked, those are. If they catch you, you won't get loose!"

Mugs feints at Garakk several times, looking for weaknesses. Shindig does his best to avoid the beast's claws, while delving deeper into its noisome substance. Blackish blood begins to drip from the beast.

Mugs steps back, looking at Tai Pan with an air of glee as huge switch-claws spring from his front paws. "Just got these, mate! If they don't do the job, nothing will."

He lunges again, slipping under Garakk's belly. With a wail of savage joy, Mugs plunges two oversized sets of switch-claws deep into the repugnant flesh.

With a screech born of hurt, rage, and frustration, Garakk brutally kicks Mugs away and finally snags Shindig. The bouncer rebounds off a tree trunk and flops on the cold ground.

Mugs staggers to his feet. "Oy, something's wrong here! That should have done him in."

Tai Pan's mind races. "He's still feeding on Norbu's fear!"

Mugs yells, shaking his head, "If it's that, I don't think

we can stop him, mate." He looks at his Maine coon friend, just staggering to his feet. "This is the first time Shindig's ever been down."

Gathering his strength, Tai Pan frantically cudgels his memory for bits of information that might help.

"I understand now," he calls to Mugs. "Someone evil summoned Garakk and bound it to kill the boy. Only he can defeat it. Mugs, just keep it at bay a bit longer, will you?"

"Yeah, well, we'll try."

Shin and Mugs launch themselves against Garakk in a frenzy of screaming, hissing, and clawing. Tai Pan staggers toward Norbu and places his paws against the sobbing boy's chest. Bringing his face close to Norbu's, he purrs and says calmly, "Norbu? Look into my eyes. Look at me, Norbu!"

The terrified boy finally pulls his hands away from his face. His black eyes find Tai Pan's. He discovers unexpected solace and courage in the steady blue gaze.

Tai Pan concentrates all his will and strength to force Norbu's mind to stay focused on his words. "Listen, Norbu. Only you can defeat Garakk. That beast's only weakness is its hunger for your fear. There is nothing for you to fear but fear itself. Snap out of it, boy! Trust me, and trust yourself. It's time you did."

Norbu's eyes widen, betraying a new glimmer of consciousness, a new level of understanding.

"That's the spirit, Norbu!" encourages Tai Pan. "Stand up. Be strong. Go now, and cast that thing away!"

Slowly, Norbu stands up. He walks toward Garakk, putting one foot in front of the other. His lips are tight and a frown of concentration marks his smooth forehead.

Garakk glares at the boy after pinning Mugs under one thorny foot. It holds Shindig firmly locked in both claws, turning its head to treat him as it had Tai Pan a moment ago.

Norbu walks toward Garakk almost as if the beastly thing

were nothing more than a pesky fly. Reaching up, he grabs Garakk's arms and shakes them until the monster's body rocks back and forth. Shindig flies from the claws to land hard on the ground.

The youngster stares the monster in its repellent eyes and, full of juvenile anger, hammers each of his words.

"ENOUGH! I-AM-NOT-AFRAID-OF-YOU-ANYMORE! GO-AWAY, AND-NEVER-COME-BACK!"

Garakk snarls at Norbu. It staggers back, dropping Mugs, and tries in vain to free its arms from the boy's grip. It can't move. Feeling its strength waning, Garakk voices a deafening shriek. Norbu stands his ground unafraid, seeing now what a pathetic creature Garakk really is. The beast shakes its head and gives Norbu a spiteful grimace before vanishing in a puff of noxious green-yellow smoke.

"Thanks for the help, mate!" Mugs says as he flicks his switch-claws back in. He then scratches his neck with a back foot and steps toward Shindig to help the bouncer up. "Oy, Tai Pan, we done here?"

"This was a favor well returned," answers Tai Pan. "Your debt is paid, and your account with me settled, old friend. Thank you."

"Good thing, that is. What of the boy, mate?" Mugs looks closely at Norbu. "What's between you and him?" Shin also eyes Norbu with curiosity.

Drawing himself up to his full height, Tai Pan says, "As you put it so well, my friend, that is between him and me."

"Fair enough, mate. Nice doing business with you," concludes Mugs. "Come on, Shin." The two cats disappear into the Astral night.

Tai Pan turns back to Norbu. The boy is watching him.

"What happened?" he asks. "I mean, really?"

Tai Pan chooses his words with care, fluffing his fur as he thinks.

"It so happened you fell into someone's trap. You can't go bouncing around in your dreams anymore. It's just too dangerous. From now on you must learn to stay conscious when leaving your physical body. Careless journeys are a thing of the past. I'll see to teaching you that."

Norbu nods at Tai Pan's caution. "I'm so glad you're here, Titus." As he looks at the snowy mountains, thinking of all that had happened, the veil of dreams once again clouds his gaze. He's exhausted.

"I think you've had more than enough excitement for this night," says Tai Pan. He levitates up to Norbu's waist and presses his paw against the boy's solar plexus to get him started home.

Satisfied with the sight of his student diving back toward his physical body, Tai Pan begins to think. He doesn't expect Tara Moondreamer as she materializes next to him. He steps back a pace, startled.

"Not bad for a first effort," says the old cat, smiling as she gives Tai Pan a moment to regain his equilibrium. "Of course, the lamas were very worried about Norbu running amok in the city for every clairvoyant to see. They trust you'll do better next time."

"This turned out to be a very costly first try—one life and one major favor paid," laments Tai Pan. "I'll be out of business before long at this rate."

"Ah, yes. You lost one life," remarks Tara, "but did you not gain another, with a deeper meaning and a greater worth? Did you not just trade a favor from an acquaintance for another of much higher value?"

"Touché," agrees Tai Pan a bit sheepishly. After a moment of silence, he adds, "I'm just realizing there is no greater wealth than that of true friendship, especially the boyhood friendship of a lama destined for greatness. Thank you for pointing out the obvious, Tara. With that in mind, I think I've just become the richest cat in the world." He stands up, preparing to leave the Astral Plane.

"What will you do next, Sir Tai Pan Titus de Pannikin?" asks the white cat.

His voice lingers on the Astral Plane after he disappears. "If you please, I need to take a long nap. Then I'll plan Norbu's next lesson."

THE GUARDIAN OF GRIMOIRE HALL

Christopher Welch

With his head low to the ground, whiskers straight, eyes glimmering and ears attentive, Delavayne entered the Antique District with uneven, silent steps. Following a trajectory of shadows in the moonlit cityscape, he had unsuccessfully searched most of the metropolis in the last week. Within minutes of treading the concrete of the Antique District, his toes began to tingle.

Grimoire Hall and The Book of Apedemak *must be in this part of the city*, he exulted.

He stalked the alleys and avenues, prowling between ancient structures and around parked vehicles and late-night pedestrians as quickly as his four awkward limbs allowed. His nose twitched, bringing him strong unfamiliar scents.

The smoky sheen of Delavayne's gray fur blended with the city's neon and concrete shadows. He'd also taken arcane precautions to veil himself from the city's feline population. He left little scent to track.

Despite my precautions, a big orange cat almost spotted me earlier this evening. Delavayne had faded into the darkness of the urban corridors.

Funny, how cats perceived even the slightest hints of the supernatural. *What other secrets do you hide from me?*

Delavayne wondered. *What other arcane gifts has the god Apedemak bestowed upon you?*

Delavayne saw a tall tabby farther down the street, strolling toward him. A distinctive metaphysical aura emanated from the cat's body.

This one has answers!

Delavayne ensconced himself in shadows. Smiling, he flexed his claws and prepared to pounce.

Inside the underground Grimoire Hall, Tenja nestled on a pillow reading a book she had borrowed from the shelves upstairs without Clara's knowledge by means of the ka spell. It had been years since she'd read the Poe collection, and it was like visiting an old friend.

Tenja had nearly finished *Murders in the Rue Morgue,* and she was anticipating *The Purloined Letter,* her personal favorite. *I'll recommend this book to Fergus the next time he stops by, assuming his stiff feline pride can be convinced to read a human author,* Tenja thought, the corners of her mouth turning upward. *It is good to know something of the people who claim to keep us. And as poet laureate of the city, he'll appreciate the refrains in* Ulalume.

Tenja's whiskers tingled. Sleek muscles under her white-and-calico coat tensed suddenly.

Something is amiss, her Guardian instincts told her.

No one touched the ancient books surrounding her without her approval. No one. Since early Renaissance times, members of her long-lived family had guarded the precious tomes.

Tenja rose, abandoning Poe as she assessed the situation. Her copper-colored eyes darted across the amber-lighted hall. *The Book of Apedemak* lay on its central pedestal, the scrolls remained safe in their cases, and countless bound volumes by austere feline scholars and philosophers stood in orderly fashion.

Running up the front staircase, Tenja checked the main entrance. It seemed secure. She bounded over to the rear staircase that led to the door into back alley. It was also secure.

Everything was just as it should be, but her whiskers still tingled.

Is something wrong in the Antique District?

Tenja listened at the back door with ultrasensitive ears. She heard fading footfalls in the alley, then after six heart-beats . . . nothing. The threat had passed. Her nose told her nothing.

If there is a real problem, Fergus or Sampson or even some nosy kitten will tell me about it. Kittens are good at finding out odd things.

Still alert for a predator, she returned to reading the mystery of the murderous beast that stalked Paris.

A monster was loose in the city.

The cats that nightly patrolled the myriad levels of the metropolis had alerted feline city elders several days ago that *something* was on the prowl, something never seen in daylight. But the creature could not be traced; even the city's best hunters were luckless in tracking it. That in itself was alarming.

"I myself spotted an odd intruder just a few hours ago during my usual scouting," orange Sampson stated to a citizen's committee. They'd hastily gathered at his call in a pocket park adjacent to a weathered brick office building.

Well respected by the city's four-footed residents for his prodigious hunting skills, Sampson's word carried weight in the cat community. Esteemed elders Clem, Isis, Mittens,

Tambour, Tatiana, Gwendolyn, Ling, Oswald, Percival, Mooch, Fifi, and Sarah awaited his information.

"What manner of creature did you see?" prompted Sarah.

"It was furry and quadruped," Sampson said. "It blended well with shadows, which it rarely left. I couldn't determine if it was canine or rodent, or something else. I saw teeth and claws reflected in the moonlight as it ran past the old City Hall. Its gait is odd. And I caught a glimpse of its eyes." He shuddered. "I'm sure there was a glimmer of black magic, the darkest sorcery."

The elders stared at one another in shocked silence.

"We should have detected its mystical presence as soon as this stranger set paw in the Antique District," Clem finally said. "We're familiar with all male and female witches in our city. Who among them would summon such a threat?"

No one spoke. None could fathom the interloper's purpose.

"It must be an infiltrator from beyond the city limits," Sarah concluded in her soft voice. "It's the only logical—"

Caterwauls from two blocks away interrupted her.
Catfight!

Curiosity was killing Spriggan.

He was barely beyond kittenhood and still awaited his adult coat, which he hoped would be a shade darker than his current cinnamon hue. He had heard his father Sampson tell Sarah earlier about calling the congregation of city elders to discuss monster sightings.

Monsters mean excitement! His tail flicked with enthusiasm.

Spriggan had tracked his father to the meeting, staying just within sight of the orange hunter. He vaulted between awnings and window sills, remaining, he hoped, unnoticed. Now perching on a high ledge of the old office building, he listened to the elders' discussion. An odd chill crept up Spriggan's spine as Sampson described the creature.

Spriggan's fur leaped upright as the catfight erupted.

He saw the committee rush toward the clash. Keeping to the aerial path of awnings and ledges of the urban real estate, he followed.

"Who's fighting? Why?" Sarah asked as Sampson zoomed past her.

"We'll find out soon enough," he tossed over his shoulder.

The elders arrived within minutes and found the conflict already finished. Sampson had discovered the tall tabby barely conscious.

"Fergus!" Sarah screamed, skidding to a halt beside the hunter.

The reigning poet laureate of the city was injured in a most unfeline manner: No true cat fought with such ugly brutality. His tabby coat was flayed in places, his eyes slashed, and his ears shredded.

"What happened?" Sampson asked, shocked. "Who did this?"

"Fiend," Fergus sputtered through a bloody cough as the elders gathered around him. "It seeks . . . *The Book of Apedemak*."

Fergus gasped, and he never inhaled again.

"I'll inform the Guardian," Sampson said, turning away. "Warn the rest of the city's residents."

After a few moments of mourning, the elders dispersed. Sampson turned toward Clara's bookshop.

Delavayne sat in an alley and slowly sucked the blood from his claws. The taste was satisfying, but that was a small consolation. He did not have the book.

The residual amber-hued aura from recent contact with *The Book of Apedemak* had indicated the tall tabby had knowledge of the ancient tome. *You knew Grimoire Hall's location,* Delavayne thought. *You had been there, possibly just an hour ago. And you fought to the death to prevent me from discovering it.* The tabby had revealed nothing, not even after Delavayne had nearly chewed his ears off, blinded him with claw swipes, and almost gutted him alive.

I'm close now, he grinned. *I'll find other cats with the same aura and force answers from them.*

There were other spell books rumored to be in Grimoire Hall that Delavayne also wanted to possess, like *The Felinomicon* and *The Bast Codex.* But *The Book of Apedemak*— the most complete and powerful of feline spell books, blessed by Apedemak the Lion-God himself—held *all* the answers he desired. Once he owned it, he'd become master of the arcane secrets of cats.

The sun will rise soon and bring the shift, he thought, stretching long, as only a cat can. *I'll continue my search in a different manner come daylight.* The tingle in his toes told him to remain in the Antique District.

I'm close, so very close.

As dawn brightened the sky, the sun triggered the shift. Delavayne strolled out of the alley on two legs.

Tenja was fond of Clara because the short, bubbly human did the cutest things.

She keeps the bookstore free from dirt and cobwebs, but she never cleans the coffee pot, the Guardian mused from her cushion in the display window. Tenja cleaned up mice, rats, silverfish, and anything else that ruined books.

And Clara thinks she *owns this old brick building!* It was nestled on a bustling avenue of antique stores, curio shops, cafes, taverns, and small offices. The Society of Apedemak had long ago persuaded their humans to invest in and preserve the old buildings in the area known as the Antique District. The Society itself owned the bookstore above Grimoire Hall, also the structures surrounding their treasures.

Clara kept human patrons occupied while Tenja meditated in the early sunlight pouring through the wide window that declared "Clara's New and Used Books." Tenja passed the time by reading when she was not actively guarding the premises, or boxing with shadows to keep her muscles and wits exercised. Most cats lacked interest in human authors, but Tenja fancied some: LeGuin, Bradbury, Atwood, and especially Poe were among her favorites.

Tenja could not only read the shop's merchandise but literally envisioned the spirit of a book. By reciting a spell, Tenja could see true souls, what the ancients called a *ka*. The spell metaphysically revealed truth, all truth. It also translated literature into a language all catkind comprehended. Tenja "read" books through their spiritual manifestations.

Grimoire Hall's ancient valuables included *The Book of Apedemak*. Its tooled leather cover was protected by a fabric jacket woven from hairs of the golden mane of the Lion God himself.

No one touched that book without her approval. *No one. Ever.*

Tenja smiled to herself, thinking of the collection downstairs that outnumbered the books on Clara's shelves by many thousands. It was good to be the Guardian of Grimoire Hall in the guise of a bookstore cat.

Some time later, Tenja roused from meditation when she heard a familiar voice. Lifting her head, she saw Sampson's wide orange face in the window.

"We need to talk." He sounded concerned.

Sampson eyed the cat flap Clara had installed in the

bookshop's front door. Tenja shook her head. She pointed with her chin toward the rear of the shop. *I'll meet you there.*

Tenja rose, stretched, dropped onto the floor, and ambled toward the back of the shop. Busy with customers, Clara barely noticed her exit. Tenja walked to the last book aisle on the left. A shelf labeled "Cookbooks" held three hardbacks with yellow dogeared dust jackets on the bottom row. It was too low for most humans to notice. Tenja stepped through a concealed door and down the stairs to the Hall.

She strode across Grimoire Hall to the rear entrance. This door was just as well concealed from the outside as the interior one. Only certain cats discovered it. The back door opened into the alley behind the bookstore.

"Greetings, Guardian," Sampson said, nodding in respect when Tenja opened the door. "I have news concerning you and the sacred writings."

Tenja stepped back. "Enter Grimoire Hall, Sampson."

Spriggan had kept surveillance on Sampson since the previous night's events. Curious as always, he now shadowed his father around the back of the bookstore. Spriggan heard the cat Tenja grant Sampson entrance to someplace he'd never heard of. After waiting a few seconds, he slunk closer, and found the secret door.

Spriggan searched for a camouflaged knob or handle. It soon became obvious that the back door opened only from the inside.

There must be another way in, he thought. *Of course— inside the bookstore!*

Returning to the front, Spriggan put a cautious foot forward and poked his pink nose under the cat door flap. He heard humans talking. When they did not notice him, he stuck his entire head through.

A woman was babbling to a tall man with gray hair. She

smelled friendly, and he detected the scent of Tenja on her. *She must be all right,* Spriggan thought. The man had an odor he couldn't pin down, and he must have entered while Spriggan was around back.

Taking his chance, Spriggan darted through the doorway and between bookshelves.

Sampson followed Tenja down the stairs. He had been inside the bookshop before, but he had never seen the amber brilliance—the blessings of Apedemak—illuminating Grimoire Hall. There were no shadows. He was awestruck by the room's magnificence. Here, among the great sandstone columns and velvet drapes, were many of the most important catkind manuscripts ever written. Pillows were scattered around for comfortable reading. The sacred book itself rested on its central pedestal, its golden cover closed.

Tenja spends her life here, Sampson thought in reverence, *patrolling the grounds below and above, protecting these fragile but powerful books from small threats such as mice and insects to beings demonic and insidious. Like the one we face now. It is a difficult job to be Guardian.*

"I have much to tell, all of it strange," Sampson said aloud. He marshaled the details, because the smallest one might mean something to her. As he spoke, her eyes widened with concern.

"Poor Fergus," Tenja said after he finished. "He consulted many texts here before he composed his verses. He was an excellent friend." They were respectfully silent for a long moment.

Tenja broke their silence. "You have no idea if this creature was rodent or canine?"

"All I know is that it's ungainly, perhaps even clumsy, in its stride. But it has stealth and speed and knows how to use shadows as well as we do."

Tenja said nothing, deep in thought. Sampson respected her contemplation.

"It is uncomfortable on four legs, but it seeks *The Book of Apedemak*?" she finally asked.

"Those were Fergus's dying words."

"I think Sarah's hunch about an intruder from outside the city is correct," Tenja mused, flicking her tail. "I have a theory."

"Yes?"

"We have to build a better mouse trap, one with lots of teeth," Tenja said in a low voice. "Let me explain."

After a few wrong turns between the musty stacks, Spriggan discovered the door by the three cookbooks. The frame had a hint of amber light on it.

Spriggan nudged the door open and listened. Despite his sensitive ears, eavesdropping revealed only bits of the conversation. His father and Tenja were whispering.

Tenja must be the Guardian my father speaks about! Did she say something about a trap? Why would the Guardian want to bring the monster here? Isn't this the very place it's searching for?

His father spoke.

Did he say he'd go on a mission of some sort? Did he say "decoy?" Something about misdirection and lying in wait?

Spriggan thought Tenja said something about a mysterious warlock or shapeshifter, but that too was not clear.

"You're sure about this plan, Guardian?" Sampson asked, speaking louder now.

"Yes, this is the best way to rid the city of the menace."

"I'll notify the elders. They will be in their places before sunset."

Spriggan heard his father leave through the alley exit. He firmly closed the door by the cookbooks, mind racing with questions. *What has my father gotten into? Why does the Guardian want the monster to come here? Where is everyone supposed to be at sunset? I need to know!*

Spriggan padded back toward the cat flap in the shop's front door. He was worrying his unanswered questions as he passed Clara and her customer.

"Hello, little one," the man said.

Spriggan looked up, and halted. The man's eyes froze him in place. Surely that was black magic swirling there! *Why is he staring at me?*

Spriggan noticed a funny light, one with the same luster as the luminescence from the hidden door, coming from somewhere. His eyes darted back and forth, and finally alighted on his big paws.

Me—that light is coming from me!

He realized the light was what drew the human's attention, what was making him smile in such an odd way. The man saw the amber glow. Mundane Clara did not.

The customer lunged for Spriggan as Clara shouted "No, stop! What about your book?"

Spriggan shot like a missile through the cat door and out to the street. The man bolted outside on his heels, grabbing for his tail.

Tenja flipped through *The Book of Apedemak*, absorbing esoteric information she already knew. She found comfort and courage rereading the words she needed.

My plan is risky, but I feel confident in my deductions. Even Poe's famous detective C. Auguste Dupin would admire them.

She said a prayer for the Lion-God's spiritual unction and jumped off the pedestal.

Tenja had not alarmed Sampson as they conversed, but her whiskers had tingled and her muscles had tensed again.

The murderer had passed nearby but had vanished once more.

Time to get to work.

Sampson spent until midafternoon contacting the elders. He spoke with Sarah, Clem, Tatiana, and Fifi. They would spread the word to other citizens. He knew everyone would be in position soon.

A better mousetrap indeed, he thought, grinning. *Now, where's Spriggan? He's the only one missing.*

His grin vanished when he realized he had no idea where the kitten had run off to.

Spriggan had no idea where he had run off to.

When he saw the dark magic in the man's eyes, he knew this was the monster who had murdered the poet. His instincts had screamed a single order:

Run!

Spriggan heard the man's footsteps and felt him grab the last few hairs of his tail. Spriggan flipped it away from the murderer's fingers and sprinted like a cheetah, dodging pedestrians and vehicles, crossing a dozen streets, bouncing between the urban obstacle course of streetlamps, trash cans, fire hydrants, and mailboxes. Panting and tired, he slowed, turning around to discover he was no longer pursued.

Where am I?

Spriggan had never been to this part of the city before. It had wide boulevards between glittery steel and glass skyscrapers, unlike the narrow streets and old buildings of the Antique District.

I am one lost kitten, Spriggan sighed. *But I've got to tell my father or another elder that the monster is human. Where are they?*

He looked to the sun for a sense of direction. To his left, the crimson beams of near-evening hovered above the street. So that was west. He remembered that the afternoon sun touched the bookshop's display window. So that was east, to his right.

He headed eastward.

Sniffing, listening, and looking for familiar things with every step, Spriggan slowly retraced his path. He passed many mundane humans, most of whom either spoke on phones or had music plugged into their ears. But Spriggan did not see a single cat. Anywhere.

Where is everyone? he wondered. *Where have they gone? Something is very wrong if I can't find another cat in this city.*

He strode the strange streets for a long time as the sun lowered in the sky. His concern evolved into fear.

Am I alone? Did the monster kill everyone? Am I the last cat alive?

His nose worked furiously, and he kept close to buildings and their lengthening shadows to steer clear of threats. Finally, he came upon an avenue of closely built brick buildings he recognized. He was only a few blocks away from the bookshop.

Spriggan felt safer returning to the Antique District. But there were still no cats he could see. His heart beat a little faster.

"I've been waiting for you."

Spriggan whipped around. Peering into a narrow alley, he saw a man whose eyes flickered oddly. And he had a confusing scent.

Spriggan was dumbfounded. *I couldn't smell him! I walked right up to him!*

"We need to have a little talk," Delavayne demanded. "Now."

"Who are you?" Spriggan squeaked, uncertain if the monster could understand him. "Why are you after me?"

"I want information," Delavayne said, stepping onto the sidewalk. The last violet rays of the sun illuminated his face. "*The Book of Apedemak*. Where is it?"

Spriggan stared at the human. His ears flattened. Both fear and defiance kept him silent.

"Tell me."

Spriggan did not move. Night dropped its cloak on the city.

"Very well, little one. Let's see if you're as brave as that tabby cat was," Delavayne said as the shift began.

Spriggan's cinnamon fur stood straight up as he watched those horrid eyes suddenly slide ground-ward. The human melted into another shape.

Glimmering irises and fangs in the dark were enough.
Run!

Spriggan's mind raced as fast as his feet. *Where do I go? Where? The Guardian! She wanted to lure the monster back to the place where that book is. That's where I'll go!*

He knew without doubt that the shape-shifter would follow as he wheeled and flattened into a run.

I hope the Guardian's trap works!

Sampson padded the silent streets alone. Everyone was in place. Now he played decoy to flush out Fergus' slayer. Sampson had been walking for hours.

Why isn't the lure working?

He had planned on the amber aura that still radiated from his body to attract the interloper. No luck.

Wait!

At the intersection a few blocks ahead of him, Sampson saw Spriggan running full-out. Seconds later, he saw a swift but ungainly cat in pursuit. They streaked past.

"No!" Sampson leaped after them as fear and anger collided in his heart.

Spriggan's muscles began to ache, and he felt himself slowing. The sounds of panting from behind kept him racing toward his destination.

Run!

Spriggan rounded a corner and saw the bookstore. Turning at the last moment, he dived through the cat flap. He sprinted down the far left aisle, and heard the small door slap again as the shapeshifter followed.

Spriggan found the cookbooks shelf and slid on the hardwood floor, scrambling to make the sharp turn down the stairs. The doorway was wide open.

Open?

He didn't have time to think about it. Spriggan whisked down the steps, feeling his pursuer too close behind as he rushed into Grimoire Hall.

The Guardian stood in the amber-lighted room. Spriggan was not surprised to see a shocked look on her face.

"The monster's followed me!"

"Hide and don't move," Tenja responded.

Panting, Spriggan jumped behind a pillow in the nearest corner. He peeked beyond its fringe as the Guardian confronted the intruder.

Unlike Spriggan, Tenja was not surprised that the monster entering Grimoire Hall looked like a gray cat.

"Halt. Tell me your name," Tenja commanded.

"Delavayne." The gray halted, looking around. His eyes coveted every book and scroll on the shelves and pedestals. "You must be the Guardian. I've been searching for Grimoire Hall for decades."

"This is a place for cats only."

"Am I not?" He lifted a paw as evidence.

"No. You're an intruder, a shapeshifter, a warlock, and a murderer. You have the likeness of a cat, but you don't have natural control of four legs. You don't understand what it means to be a cat."

"But I *want* to understand what being a cat means," Delavayne said. "I want to understand in every way. That is why I want *The Book of Apedemak*."

Tenja glanced at the central pedestal, then back at Delavayne. "Explain yourself."

"I was not born a cat, true. But I desire every feline secret."

"Why? To use such knowledge in the human world?"

"Precisely," Delavayne's eyes sparkled with greed. "I want to know how cats store sunlight in their eyes so they can see at night; how cats see spirits and sprites everywhere; how cats can steal someone's breath while they sleep; how to leap over a corpse and make it rise as a vampire; how a pride of cats can drive old women insane; how cats can change luck from good to bad and from bad to good; and I want to know how to live nine times. Furthermore, I want to know *everything else*."

"You think there's more?"

"Don't be coy. Those secrets I mentioned are what humans have either figured out themselves or what cats have let slip during thousands of years of close relationships. But I desire to know every other arcane secret—all the secrets that cats have not revealed to humans! And all of *those* are written down in *The Book of Apedemak*, I'm sure. Cats, by nature, have always been more supernaturally endowed than humans. I simply seek to change my nature."

"You're a murderer. Your nature won't change with knowledge, magical or otherwise." Tenja held her ground like an embattled queen. "No one touches that book without my approval. No one."

"You cannot stop me."

"I'll try."

Delavayne pounced.

Spriggan watched the battle with wide eyes.

Delavayne's claws swiped at Tenja, but she dodged the attack. Tenja, half his size, struck back, but Delavyne blocked.

They tackled each other in a frenzy of claws and fangs. The tumbling gray and calico kaleidoscope of violence became streaked with red. Growls and caterwauls reverberated through the hall.

Delavayne fought like a drunken brawler, brute force more important than finesse. His foreclaws were deadly but imprecise. Tenja twirled and pirouetted, her counterstrikes a martial ballet.

Sure footed, Tenja broke away. Delavayne whirled, quickly landing a heavy blow to her face. Tenja rolled across the room and did not rise. Blood showed on her mouth.

Laughing, Delavayne raced to the tallest pedestal and the powerful grimoire it supported.

"Finally, it's mine!"

Is the Guardian defeated? Spriggan was horrified, until Tenja caught his eye and winked. She was playing possum.

Delavayne leaped atop the pedestal and greedily caressed the protective gold cover before flipping it open and reading the first page.

"What is this?" he said, puzzled. "Apple pie? A recipe for apple pie?"

Flummoxed, he read the next page. "Apricot dumplings?" He flipped another, and another. "Linguini, meatloaf, pork chops, zucchini." He slammed the book closed, and screamed, "What sorcery is this?"

That distraction was all Tenja needed. She jumped beside Delavayne, turned, and seized him on a cat's only weak spot, the scruff of the neck.

He howled as they dropped to the floor.

Sampson pounded into Grimoire Hall.

With relief, he spotted Spriggan peeking over the cushion. The kitten was safe, albeit bewildered. Then he saw that Tenja's plan was working exactly as she intended, despite the change in decoys.

"Guardian," Sampson's voice rang with doom. "They're ready."

Tenja pulled the screaming Delavayne towards the back stairs, attended by Sampson and followed by Spriggan.

"Let me go!"

Delavayne writhed in every direction, but escape was impossible. Despite his twisting, Tenja dragged him up the steps, through the hidden door, and into the alley behind the bookshop. She tossed him hard onto the asphalt.

Delavayne wavered to his feet, bleeding from many wounds. Snarling, he headed toward Tenja, who stood back-lit by Apedemak's blessings in front of the door.

Delavayne stopped suddenly in midstride, looking around.

"Who are you? What do you want?" he snarled.

Sarah, Clem, Isis, Mittens, Tambour, Tatiana, Gwendolyn, Ling, Oswald, Percival, Mooch, Fifi, and hundreds, maybe thousands, of other city residents surrounded him. They stood silent on trashcans, in windows, on ledges, and on rooftops.

"You can't stop me," Delavayne howled. "I am too close to success. After all these years, I am too close."

The cats remained silent, staring at their enemy.

"What do you want?" Delavayne screamed, his tone revealing fear for the first time.

"We want you," Sarah said softly, padding forward. "We've been waiting for the Guardian to drag you out, murderer."

Tenja recited the *ka* spell under her breath. It manifested the aura of Delavayne's true soul for all the cats to see.

"What are you doing?" Delavayne hollered. "Stop it!"

The cats growled and hissed as they saw his *ka*. Delavayne's soul was a wicked, shriveled thing; it had beady eyes and a narrow snout, somehow both serpentine and rodentlike.

The citizens got a good look at Delavayne's *ka,* sniffed its scent, and committed his supernatural essence to their memories. Thousands of eyes narrowed, thousands of fangs glistened, and thousands of haunches tensed.

Delavayne looked around again, and again. He was trapped. Like a mouse. He had one course of action left: retreat. He backed up a step, then another.

"The grimoire will be mine," he hissed. "I'll return."

"You will never come back to this city," Sarah said. "Because you will never leave it."

Spinning, Delavayne shot out of the alley.

The citizens, grinning, gave him a head start. Then, as a pride, they sprang after him.

"Will he get away?" Spriggan asked, worried.

"No," Sampson answered.

"What was he? Cat, human, or monster?"

"He was a murderer and thief, the rest is irrelevant," Tenja answered as she limped back into Grimoire Hall. "I think most humans wish to be a cat at some point. Delavayne was an extreme case." She began washing a perforated ear.

"You knew the monster was a cat, didn't you?" Spriggan asked.

"I deduced that someone who discovered the existence of *The Book of Apedemak*, and desired it so obsessively, would disguise himself as a cat. It became obvious to me by Sampson's description—stealth, speed, teeth, and claws—such could only be a cat in this city. That is the primary reason why none of us could detect Delavayne when he first arrived. Nobody could fathom such a horror resembling themselves. It runs counter to feline esteem and our sense of pride. I suspect an olfactory veiling spell at work as well."

"What about the book?" Spriggan asked.

"I switched it," Tenja said. "The idea came from a story by Edgar Allen Poe titled *The Purloined Letter*. It's about hiding important documents in the most obvious places. I deduced that Delavayne would overlook that shelf completely once the door to Grimoire Hall was opened."

"*The Book of Apedemak* is upstairs?" Spriggan asked, shocked. "On the cookbook shelf? We ran right by it?"

"Yes." Tenja began to wash a long scratch on her belly.

"Guardian, may I retrieve it and put it back in its place?" Spriggan asked. His tail flicked with enthusiasm.

"No," the Guardian said. Seeing Spriggan's disappointment, Tenja smiled. "You have proven yourself to be both brave and quick witted, Spriggan. The Lion God smiles upon you, I believe. One day when you are older, you may take a glimpse at its pages."

"One day seems very far away," Spriggan sighed. Sampson led his son up the steps and through the door.

Later, after Tenja had replaced the great books on their pedestals and bathed her wounds again, she sat on her favorite pillow.

"Now, where was I? Ah, yes. For you, my friend Fergus." She started reading *Ulalume*.

AFTER TONY'S FALL

Jean Rabe

Luigi had a dense, blue coat with silvery tips that gave it a lustrous sheen. Like all of his kind—Luigi was a Russian Blue—he had large, round eyes the shade of a just-misted philodendron. His head was broad, his rakish ears sharply tapered, and he was fine boned, yet powerfully built.

Luigi had the most regal appearance of any cat in my acquaintance.

Though I knew he could trace his ancestors back to the Royal Cat of the Russian Czars, he claimed to be Italian—and I'd never heard anyone argue the point.

Luigi spoke with a thick accent, sort of gravelly like Marlon Brando in the Godfather movies. He lived in a spacious apartment above an Italian restaurant in an Italian neighborhood that humans had dubbed "Little Italy."

"Don Luigi" the cats in the 'hood called him.

I just called him boss.

He'd named me Vincenzo the day I came to work for him—that was a wintry morning nearly three years past when he'd caught me nibbling on some Fettuccini Alfredo that had been tossed into the garbage behind the restaurant. He offered me a job, and I was quick to accept.

"You're very kind," I told him. Now I can say it in his preferred tongue: *Sei molto gentile!*

The boss never asked my real name. Probably, like T.S. Elliot, he figured it was only right that we cats have three—my original moniker, Vincenzo, and Vinnie the Mouser.

The latter is what I usually go by. Has a nice ring to it, don't you think?

I'm not really Italian either, being a Bombay, or Burmese, but I love the food. Lasagna, ravioli, gnocchi riplieni, cappellacci al vitello e spinaci, and tortellini campagnola are regular dishes on my menu.

Last night it was vitello barolo—oh-so-tender veal with portabello and shitake mushrooms in wine, with just a touch of cream. The night before that was my favorite—calamari riplieni, sweet squid stuffed with cheese and bread crumbs in a delicate tomato sauce.

Per questa sera . . . I've no idea what will be on the menu tonight. *Per domani sera* . . . or tomorrow night for that matter. But I'm certain I will find everything tasty. *Mi piace l'italiano*, after all.

It is a good life, being Don Luigi's number-one cat—his enforcer, confidant, and appropriator. In exchange for my loyalty and service, the boss makes sure that when I say, *Sono affamato*, I'm hungry, I am given something good to eat. Too, he has provided me a fine, dry place to sleep, on a thick velvet cushion in the attic above his apartment. From this lofty perch I can hear the boss's natterings with Guido, Nino, and Uberto, the Siamese triplets that collect the Don's take from the businesses in Little Italy. I can hear the passionate yowls from his late-night trysts with Mariabella, the Himalayan madam from around the corner, and with Tessa Rosalie, the sleek orange tabby who recently moved into the flower shop across the street.

Best of all, I can hear the boss play.

I'd not heard a cat tickle the ivories before coming into the Don's employ. The boss's tail is muscular enough to join his paws and make chords on the keyboard of a 1920 walnut Italian Florentine baby grand. The boss only plays the music of Italian composers; he says playing anything else is a waste of time. He just finished the main theme from Giacomo Puccini's *Manon Lescaut*. Before that he performed a piece from the unfinished *Turandot* and a few dozen bars from *La Boheme*.

It's like Heaven opening up when the boss plays, the rich notes swirling around the apartment and rising into my attic, consuming me and bringing tears to my eyes. No other sounds are so enchanting.

I live to hear the boss play.

He explained to me once that Italy gave the world the best composers and the best instruments, that piano is a short form of the Italian word *pianoforte*, which in turn comes from the original Italian term for the instrument—*clavicembalo col piano e forte.*

I couldn't care less what you call the thing . . . I just love the way it sounds when the boss sets his paws and tail tip to it.

In the back of my mind I can still hear the notes. I've set my pads in time to the imagined music as I head down the street, looking over my shoulder once to see him looking out the window . . . not looking at me, but surveying his domain.

"*Buon compleanno!*" I hear him call to the long-legged Bengal on the sidewalk. Happy birthday.

"*Congratulazioni!*" he shouts to the Persian outside the used book store. I'd heard she'd recently had kittens.

Imparo l'taliano . . . I've been learning Italian ever since ingratiating myself with the boss, and I'm pleased that I've gotten quite fluent. *Mi piacerebbe visitare l'talia un giorno di questi!* Yeah, I would like to stroll down the sidewalks of Italy with the Don someday and sit high in a balcony during a performance of Gaetano Donizetti's *La Fille du Regiment*.

He promised to take me and Guido next year if things work out all right.

I hear a shrill call, and my head snaps around. It's Bianca, the beautiful bicolor Ragdoll I visit when I go to Madam Mariabella's. I know that Bianca shares her affections with whoever meets the madam's price at the cathouse, but she claims to have a special spot in her heart just for me. I'd love to take her to Italy with me and the boss, but I know it's going to be a business trip, and so dalliances won't be allowed.

I flick my tail at her in a friendly greeting and then pick up the pace. I'm not as fast as I used to be, but I can push my muscles when the need arises. You see, I've got quite a way to go on this particular mission, which is why I set out before sunset. It means I'll be eating late when I get back; I've done that numerous times before, and so far it hasn't upset my delicate digestive tract.

I smell things along the way—the trace of Bianca and the other females at the cathouse, some clearly in heat; the daily specials from the flower shop . . . so many scents I can't differentiate one kind of bloom from another; the sharp and bitter pong of soap from the laundry; and rotting fish from the alley off S'hang's Sushi Bar, which has no place being in Little Italy. The farther I get from the Italian restaurant, the worse things smell.

So I concentrate on the sights instead, the garish, clashing colors of window boxes and signs, the graffiti scrawled here and there, the freshest in day-glow green.

And I focus on the sounds . . . car horns blaring from blocks away, babies wailing, a boy hawking newspapers on a corner, the slam of a door. There's music spilling out of an upper floor window, some rapper spitting out hippity-hop words like they are pieces of bad meat—Lay-Z or Forty-Cents, I can't tell them apart. They're certainly not in the class of the boss's *pianoforte* playing, and so I ignore the thumping racket.

I stick to the shadows whenever possible—being dark has its advantages when you're into a bit of skullduggery. And I continue on my way, remembering the boss's gravelly words:

"*Vada dritto! E poi giri a destra!*"

Go straight—all the way down to the fire station—then turn right. It would be a whole lot of straight again after that—blocks and blocks and blocks of it.

The boss hadn't needed to give me directions, as I'd been to the museum once before when I had a fling some years back with an Angora who lived in the area. Wonder what's become of her? I shake my head to chase away the sweet memory.

I was proud that the boss had entrusted this very special assignment to me. It deserves all my attention.

"You get this for me, Vinnie, this one precious thing, and I'll reward you well," he told me this afternoon. "I have the other three. I just need the fourth to complete the set."

I well knew that he had the other three; he'd shown them to me, taking them out of the chest and lovingly running his whiskers across the old paper before replacing them.

"I just need the fourth. The missing piece. You understand? It will complete the year." His large, round eyes didn't blink. This missing piece was terribly important to him.

I told him I understood.

"*Buona fortuna*, Vincenzo," he said.

I don't need luck, I'd mentally returned. I'd just need a big plate of pasta upon my return. Maybe I could order up something special—polpo alla griglia, octopus charcoal-broiled and dabbed with balsamic vinegar and olive oil. Yeah, that would hit the spot after a long mission like this.

The sun was all the way down by the time I'd left Little

Italy behind and reached the museum. It was closing for the day, and I watched from behind a fir tree as the school groups and retired folks spilled out and down the steps. If I timed it right, I could snake my way between the young ones' feet and slip inside the lobby. A good plan, I decided, but then I quickly dismissed it when I noticed there were two guards at the entrance, and one of them had a gun at his waist. Better not to take the chance that one might scoop me up or shoot me.

I hacked up a furball that had been bothering me and shimmied around the side of the monstrous building. Well, truth be told, it wasn't that big a place, but it was the most imposing structure in this part of town, all cement and iron, ugly and drab. A monstrosity of a building would be a better term.

The sounds of the city intruded—more car horns, people shouting. I shuddered: There was a dog barking nearby. I hated dogs almost as much as I hated rap music. I heard a door slam, and then another, a van from the sound of it, and I poked my head around the back corner to see a cleaning crew getting out of a rust-dotted Chevy Econoline. There were four men, all dressed in gray coveralls, and after picking up buckets and boxes, and after the smallest perched a boombox on his shoulder, they headed across the employee parking lot and to the museum's backdoor.

Buona fortuna was mine indeed.

I hurried, as much as I could because the trip here had winded me, and was just able to dart inside before the door closed. Lights still glared from the ceiling and bounced off a tile floor that, as far as I was concerned, didn't need to be polished. No shadows to hide my furry sable self, I ducked into the first open doorway and discovered a janitor's closet. This hiding place would do until they turned off some of the lights and the museum staff filed out. I just had to make sure no one shut the door on me.

As I rested and waited, I dreamed about Bianca and her pretty spots and about what I might have for dinner. An appetizer of vongole gratinate, juicy clams, would stop my belly from growling. I also thought about Italy, the real Italy that the boss would take me to, not the Little Italy we lived in. I heard music, muted, more of that rap crap, and the gentle shushing hum of what I guessed was a floor polisher or vacuum. The steady click of small heels in the hallway beyond this closet and the regular opening and closing of the back door told me the curators and secretaries and such were leaving.

Finally, all I could hear was the rap, and it was so soft now that I had to strain to pick it out. The cleaning crew had moved farther away, so I was relatively alone in the museum.

In a short while I would have the final piece to the boss's magnificent puzzle. He would be a very happy cat, and I would have my pick of anything off the menu.

I left the closet and hugged the wall, following it until a great room opened up before me, bathed in the soft glow of security lights. Suits of armor were spaced here and there between glass cases holding weapons and pieces of jewelry. A glittering crown sat on a pillow that I thought might be comfortable. A scepter lay next to it. The object of my quest was nowhere to be seen . . . but my keen eyes lit on something that would help me find it. I padded toward a placard touting the rotating displays.

Not all cats can read, but I found it a necessary skill to acquire in the boss's employ, and so I had let Guido teach me two summers past. The placard read:

Special Exhibit
The Life, Times, and Works of
Il Prete Rosso, the Red Priest
Second Floor, Main Hall

I passed by the elevator and took the winding staircase, careful not to slip on its newly polished marble steps. Rap music drifted down from above—the cleaning crew had obviously preceded me.

One man was wielding a big floor buffer, moving it from side to side in time with the godawful beat. Two were dusting the wainscoting that ran around the room and down the hallways that led away to the north and the south. The third man was in the bathroom; I heard the toilet flush.

Occupied, they didn't notice me. I drifted from one display case to the next, slinking as much as possible. I looked through the glass of a low shelf, squinting in the dim light to see decorative red and white and green satin ribbons, and to make out the words on a card in front of a battered violin:

IL PRETE ROSSO, THE RED PRIEST: A VENETIAN PRIEST AND BAROQUE MUSIC COMPOSER, ALSO A VIRTUOSO VIOLINIST. THIS VIOLIN WAS THE LAST INSTRUMENT HE PLAYED BEFORE HIS DEATH.

A card in the next case read:

BORN MARCH 4, 1678, IN VENICE, THE DAY AN EARTHQUAKE SHOOK THE CITY. HE DIED JULY 27 OR 28, 1741. HIS FATHER, GIOVANI BATTISTA, WAS A PROFESSIONAL VIOLINIST AND FOUNDER OF A TRADE UNION FOR MUSICIANS, WHO TAUGHT HIM TO PLAY. HE BEGAN STUDYING FOR THE PRIESTHOOD AT AGE FIFTEEN, AND HE WAS ORDAINED TEN YEARS LATER. IT IS BELIEVED THAT HE WAS CALLED *IL PRETE ROSSO* BECAUSE OF HIS RED HAIR.

The next case, where a small painting was displayed:

IN 1704 HE WAS GIVEN A SPECIAL DISPENSATION FROM

CELEBRATING MASS BECAUSE HE WAS ILL. RECORDS SHOW HE SUFFERED FROM SOMETHING SIMILAR TO ASTHMA. TWO YEARS LATER, HE LEFT THE PRIESTHOOD AND CONCENTRATED ON COMPOSING MUSIC.

Music! That's what I was looking for. And not that damnable rap crap. One of the men had turned it up louder. I couldn't understand the words, and it was hurting my delicate ears.

I continued searching the room.

Another card, this in the largest case; I had to stand up on my back paws to read it:

LE QUATTRO STAGIONI, THE FOUR SEASONS, IS HIS BEST KNOWN WORK. THE SET OF FOUR VIOLIN CONCERTI BY IL PRETE ROSSO, ANTONIO VIVALDI, WERE ORIGINALLY PUBLISHED IN 1725, EACH IN THREE MOVEMENTS. ON DISPLAY HERE IS ONE OF THE ORIGINAL WORKS, BELIEVED TO BE PENNED BY VIVALDI HIMSELF, TRANSCRIBED FOR PIANO.

Concerto No. 3 in F major, *L'autunno*, Autumn.

That's it! I practically shouted out loud.

Tony's Fall.

The boss had sent me here to this ugly museum after *Tony's Fall*, and there it was in all of its tattered parchment movements—allegro, adagio molto, and allegro again, on the top shelf of the display . . . where I couldn't reach it.

The card went on to explain that the matching piano music for the other seasons—spring, summer, and winter—had been lost through the ages. But they weren't lost. They were safely kept in a chest in Don Luigi's apartment above the Italian restaurant that must be serving something absolutely delicious at this very moment.

My stomach rumbled, and the floor buffer sounded louder. The machine was sweeping closer.

"A kitty cat!" called the man gripping the handles of the infernal machine.

"A dark cat. A big one." This came from the one just emerging from the bathroom. "Don't let it cross your path. That'd be six years of bad luck."

"Seven," corrected one of the men dusting the wainscoting. "Seven years of bad luck, just like if you broke a mirror."

I summoned my strength and bolted toward the floor polisher, the pads of my feet slipping and sliding and threatening to send me sprawling. One leap and I was riding on the base of the thing, shushing back and forth as the man wielding it cursed in a language I could not fathom.

I reared up and hissed at him, digging my rear claws into a strip of rubber. I hissed and snarled, laid my ears back and appeared menacing. I well knew how to act menacing—after all, I am the boss's chief enforcer.

"It's crazy!" one of them shouted. I couldn't tell which one hollered. I was holding on for my proverbial dear life, as the buffer-wielder rammed the machine first one way and then another trying to dislodge me.

I hissed again, but it was a panicked hiss, not a mean one. Doubtless he could not tell the difference, though, as he jerked the machine forward and back, faster now, and then out of control, nearly causing me to lose what I'd eaten for lunch. One more jerk and the buffer-wielder slipped on a newly waxed patch of tile. The machine shot forward, humming and jostling and then colliding into the largest of the display cases in the hall. An alarm went off as the glass broke, a harsh claxon that drowned out the damnable crap-rap music and was punctuated by the sounds of thick glass shards hitting the buffer and the floor.

I winced when a shard lanced my back, and I yowled shrilly in pain, adding to the cacophony.

The cleaning men were shouting, all in the harsh language I couldn't understand, and the buffer continued to whir, though now it was going nowhere. And faintly, from below, came the staccato barks of what I guessed were museum guards.

Despite the pain in my ears and my back, I was well aware of my *buona fortuna*. I pushed off the whirring contraption and landed inside the now-open display case, climbed up to the second shelf, and then the third, where my prize awaited. Gently using my teeth and front claws, I rolled up *Tony's Fall* and tied it with a piece of ribbon that had been a decorative touch in the case.

All the while the noises continued, the alarm accompanied by a second one that had started somewhere on the floor below. Feet pounded up the stairs, and my mind whirled with thoughts of escape. I hadn't given any thought to that notion as I'd waited in the janitor's closet. I'd been thinking too much about dinner.

Tony's Fall secured, and my teeth securely fastened to the ribbon around the parchment, I jumped from the shelf and onto the back of one of the wainscot dusters. I dug my claws in, finding flesh beneath the shirt, and discovering that the man could shout louder than the rapper who'd begun to sing about jacking fancy cars.

He called to his fellows in the foreign tongue and gestured wildly. In that moment, two guards reached the top of the stairs. Also in that moment, I leaped away and headed toward the bathroom. The door to it had been propped open, and I took full advantage.

I figured there would be a window in here, one that I could use my bulk to barrel through and find freedom. But there was no window, only mirrors and toilets and sinks and a floor that thankfully had not yet been polished. There was also a vent, and this I vaulted to by propelling myself off the register and onto a sink, then up to a pipe. It had been some time since I'd been involved in this much activity, and my sides heaved. But my prize was worth the effort.

Tony's Fall, the last piece to the boss's magnificent puzzle, would soon be his, and a wondrous culinary reward and more promises of a trip to Italy would be mine.

My front paws wrestled with the latch on the vent. They were a sable blur that clawed and tugged and finally met with success.

The rap music stopped just as I shot inside.

The hollering continued.

The alarms still blared.

I heard the sharp click of heels come into the bathroom, knowing this would be one of the security guards; the cleaning men wore tennis shoes.

Branzino alla griglia, Chilean sea bass grilled perfectly with oil and garlic and served warm with beans, might be mine when I deposit this musical manuscript at the boss's feet.

All I need do is shimmy through this duct.

Shimmy.

Shimmy.

Merda.

I was stuck.

I sucked in my breath and pushed, let out my breath and wriggled. *Tony's Fall* still held by the ribbon between my teeth, dangled sideways in front of me.

Stuck.

Stuck.

"I see him! It's a cat!"

"Cat burglar more like." I knew this came from the other guard, though I could see neither of them.

"He's wedged in there pretty good and tight. He's a pudgy one, this cat. Don't know if I can get him out."

Merda. Merda. Merda.

He dug his hands into my side and squeezed, tugging and tugging and finally pulling me out, and then held me in front of him, where my claws couldn't reach, too tight for me to wriggle free. The other guard plucked *Tony's Fall* from my jaws and retreated with it.

Merda. Merda. Merda.

One too many plates of petto di polla alla senape. In my younger years—before I'd found that Italian restaurant—I was lean and would have been able to fit through that duct with no effort.

Merda. Merda. Merda.

"Wonder why a cat would want some stupid old music," my captor mused as he carried me from the bathroom and through the hall, where his fellow was replacing *Tony's* precious *Fall* and attempting to smooth it out and brush away the broken glass. I didn't see the cleaning crew, and thankfully someone had shut off that hurtful alarm.

I fought with the guard all the way to the bottom of the stairs, but it had taken most of my energy just to reach the museum and snare my prize. He tossed me in the janitor's closet and shut the door, told me through the crack that he'd call the Humane Society for me first thing in the morning.

No vent in here. No chance of escape. Even if there was a vent, I doubt I could have fit through it. Too many raviolis. Too many plates of spaghetti and rigatoni. It was blackest-black, the air dead still, and not even my keen eyes could pick through it. I could smell all the astringent cleaning supplies, and my paws brushed against the ropy tendrils of a mop. My nose touched a tool furry with rust.

I wasn't paying attention to the passing of time. My mind whirred with a mix of hopeful and horrid possibilities.

Maybe I could slip by the guards in the morning, when they opened the door to present me to the Humane Society.

Maybe I could dart out between their legs and out the back and return to the safety of Little Italy.

Then I could hear the boss play *Tony's Spring* and *Summer* and *Winter* again, and promise to go after *Tony's Fall* once more. Just a few less tortellini helpings, and I'd be able to fit through that duct.

The godawful crap-rap music started up again, Forty-Cent wailing about a woman who dumped him. I closed my eyes and shook my head and tried my best to imagine the boss's talons and tail tip tickling the ivories.

The music came louder, and I paced, bumping into this and that. Suddenly the door opened, and one of the wainscot dusters flipped on the light switch and stared at me, the dim light of the hall haloing a head of bushy hair. I took only a heartbeat to register his kind face and thin lips, and then I was through his legs.

"I need to find some turpen . . . cat!" He said something else, but I couldn't hear it over the cacophony of rap, which was loudest in the main hall, where the other three were now working.

The cleaning men didn't notice me this time, so intent on bobbing their heads in time with the crap-rap and polishing the cases and the floor.

I shot up the stairs.

A great part of me thought I should instead look for an exit . . . right this very moment. Forget *Tony's Fall*, as I'd already taken a fall for trying to nab it. Get out and tell Luigi it couldn't be had, not this time and not at this museum. There was too much security. I wouldn't tell him about the too-narrow ducts, which were no doubt in violation of some building code. I should turn around and hover at the back door, wait for the cleaning men to finish and open it and head toward their van.

I'd pad back to Little Italy.

But I was, above all else, loyal to the boss. No one tells the Don they'll do something and then doesn't do it. And I'd told him I'd go after *Tony's Fall*.

And so that's just what I was doing.

I don't know where my energy came from, maybe birthed from mind-numbing panic. I didn't want to be caught again; in my heart I knew a trip to the Humane Society wouldn't be humane, not for an aging overweight cat like me. It'd be the needle.

Thoughts of the needle spurred my paws faster.

A moment more and I was at the top of the stairs and slipping to the side of the closest Red Priest display case. The security man who'd nabbed me earlier was there, along with another short fellow in a similar uniform. They were picking up the shards of glass. The short one stopped and talked into a little radio he pulled from his pocket. I didn't pay attention to the conversation; my heart was hammering so loudly I could barely hear Forty-Cent shouting the lyrics from the boombox below.

The glass shards they collected glimmered in the pale lighting of the hall.

So much glass.

A pity I was responsible for the mess. I glanced around. Only the two guards; it wasn't a terribly large museum, and so probably this pair constituted the entire night force. There would be many more people working here come morning. Through a trio of narrow windows on the east wall I saw that it was late, the sky black and moonless and filled with a scattering of stars.

I waited.

And after several minutes I slunk around behind the display case. The guards were moving; one of them picking up a bucket filled with the broken glass. They'd made no attempt to secure *Tony's Fall*, but I was certain that would be taken care of before the doors opened in the morning.

"Damn music." This came from the one who'd caught me. "Wish they would play something else. Boz Scaggs, Elton John."

"Country," the short one said. "I like Gretchen Wilson, and that blond from Sugarland, and a little Faith Hill thrown in for good measure. Now *that's* music."

Did none of them have any taste? What the boss played was music. Real music. He produced notes so sweet and Italian that they didn't need someone singing along to dilute them.

"Got someone from Consolidated Glass coming in a few hours." Again, my once-captor spoke. "We've gotta get this case fixed and hooked to the alarm system before breakfast. Gotta get the cleaners up here one more time for another pass with the sweeper."

"Martina McBride has got pipes, I tell you. Heard her once at the county fair grounds. Dolly, she's okay, too."

"Nah, Bruce Springsteen."

The security guards continued their discussion of modern music as they finished their tidy of the room. Each took a different hall away from the gallery, and I took the shortest path back to the broken display case. With no alarm to worry about, I leaped onto the top counter, my leg muscles still fueled by fear of the Humane Society's needle. I had to roll the sheet music up again, and this time I secured it with two ribbons. Then I was down the stairs again, and quick to hide behind a suit of plate mail.

I tried to catch my breath—a difficult thing to do considering my chest felt tight and on fire, my mind remembering the security's guard hands squeezing my well-padded ribs. Someone was running a vacuum cleaner. I couldn't see it, but I saw a long, red cord plugged into the wall that mean-

dered like an old snake down a corridor. There was wainscoting along that hall, and a man was polishing it. That left
two unaccounted for. But they had to be nearby, that jarring
hip-hop refrain was echoing off a wall, a woman's voice this
time. Her rhythmic wail felt like pins against my sensitive
ears.

Once more I thought of that lethal needle.

I flexed my claws nervously, unsure of what course I should
take. Then indecision was ripped from me; the security guards
were coming down the stairs.

I summoned all the strength remaining in my fatigued
muscles and sprinted across the floor, slipping and sliding
over the fresh wax and nearly caroming into a suit of samu-
rai dragon armor. One of the guards must have spotted me,
my original captor, I'll wager. I barely heard his shout above
the woman rapper.

"That cat!"

My chest and legs burned, my heart hammered even faster,
and my paws somehow found just enough purchase so I
could speed down the hall and past the hated janitor's
closet . . . and then through the back door that one of the
cleaning men was opening. I thought he smiled at me as I
galumphed past.

I didn't wait to see if anyone else spotted me, though I
knew I should have. I took a risk heading straight back to
Little Italy with my hard-won prize. What if one of the security guards had followed me? What if I had led someone
straight to the Italian restaurant and to the wooden stairs at
the back that led up to Luigi's spacious apartment? What if
they'd discovered the rest of Tony's Seasons hidden there
and confiscated all of them?

But that didn't happen. I was "free and clear," as they say.

Sitting outside the door, I closed my eyes and thanked
God and Bast that this fat cat burglar had escaped unscathed.

I must have dozed or dropped off from sheer exhaustion, as when I opened my eyes the sky was lightening and full of birds. I heard a car horn, and then another.

I scratched at the door, still holding the ribbons in my teeth. After a moment, the boss let me in. I deposited the sheet music at his feet in much the same manner as one might drop a treasure at the toes of a human.

He grinned.

"Come, Vinnie," he said. "Let me order you something fine to eat. I will play this for you while you decide what you want."

He reverently carried the music to the piano and unrolled it, settled himself on the bench, and looked at me.

"An Italian tomato salad," I said, having already made up my mind. "With a few diced peppers, lots of celery, and a little basil. A small salad, Boss, and have them hold the anchovies."

Don Luigi was into his fourth playing of *Tony's Fall* before my scant meal arrived. The sweet notes were worth everything I'd been through.

I climbed the stairs to the attic and gacked up a hairball, curled on my cushion, and listened.

The boss was just starting in on *Tony's Spring*.

I told you earlier that it's like Heaven opening up when the boss plays, the melody swirling around his apartment and rising into my attic, consuming me and bringing tears to my eyes. No other sounds are so enchanting.

I live to hear the boss play.

INK AND NEWSPRINT

Marc Tassin

Sophocles paced in front of the rack of newspapers, his fluffy gray tail swishing back and forth with the precision of a drum major's baton. Ears back, he padded across the shop's asphalt tile floor, turned at the comic book circular, and headed back the other way. Passing the counter, he glared at the big round clock on the newsstand's wall, its plexiglas casing coated with dust.

Ten after nine.

Ten after nine and still no sign of Coffee Man. For three years, Coffee Man had arrived at 8:50 AM every day. Coffee Man always carried a fresh cup of coffee from the diner next door, always of the exact same variety, some sort of cheap Colombian blend Sophocles deduced from the aroma, and always black. He purchased a *New York Times*, and he always paid for it in coins. But for the past two months, no sign of him, and Sophocles found this pointedly disturbing.

It wasn't the man's absence alone that bothered the old gray British Shorthair. Customers came and went at the little newsstand. It was all part of life. In his fifteen years, he'd learned that much at least. Rather, it was Coffee Man's absence combined with the absence of Too-Much-Perfume Woman, Guy-Who-Doesn't-Bathe, Muddy-Boot-Man, and countless others. (Although to be honest, Sophocles didn't miss Muddy-Boot-Man, who made a terrible mess every time he came in to the store.)

The disappearances were all part of a growing trend, one that slowly materialized over the past five years. Where once the shop was a bustle of activity in the morning, now the little bell over the door had fallen almost silent, ringing just a few times each hour.

Sophocles twitched his nose and narrowed his eyes. With the exception of Herbert, the old man who worked the store's counter, Sophocles didn't trust humans. They were notorious for their inability to maintain a regular schedule. Things always "came up," as they liked to put it, and interrupted proper and respectable routines.

He stopped his pacing to survey the newspaper rack. Publications from around the country and the far corners of the world shared space. *The London Times*, the *Detroit Free Press*, the *San Francisco Chronicle*—Ehgleman's Newsstand had it all. At Ehgleman's, customers weren't limited to the one-sided, local point of view. The expatriate wasn't reduced to getting irregular, and certainly inaccurate, information by phone or letter from friends across the sea. Certainly not.

No, at Ehgleman's the customer could find the facts, plain and simple, printed in a sharp 7.5 point Nimrod Cyrillic font, on sensible yellow-white newsprint. That was, after all, what the news was all about. The facts, clearly stated, in a form you can sink your claws into.

And yet, Sophocles thought, the people no longer came.

Checking the clock, he saw that it was quarter-past nine. Sophocles sighed and plodded over to the big plateglass windows at the front of the store. With a bit of effort, he hopped onto the wide sill. The east facing windows made for excellent morning sunning, something Sophocles did daily at 9:15 AM sharp. He stepped onto the little cushion Herbert had placed there for him, turned a few circles to loosen the stuffing, and then settled in.

Sophocles watched the crowds passing by, rushing off to their jobs, towing children to daycare, balancing steaming cups of coffee while negotiating the sea of people moving along the sidewalk. No one even glanced at the wooden bench in front of the shop, the paint on its slats faded and chipping. Herbert had placed it there years ago, back when people actually sat and read their papers right after buying them. On most days, the bench remained empty. People just pushed past, using the bench, at most, as place to set a briefcase while negotiating the removal of a phone from a pocket.

As Sophocles sat gazing out the window, mulling over his troubles, a strange thing happened. Someone *did* sit on the bench, a young man wearing jeans and a t-shirt. No more than thirty, Sophocles estimated, although he was never very good at guessing their ages. Like the others, he had a coffee, a rather large one at that, but he didn't carry a briefcase.

Sitting there on the bench, the man reached into his pants pocket and pulled out a hand-sized device. A phone, Sophocles thought at first. He'd seen these little devices proliferate like fleas on an alley cat over the past few years. He could appreciate the desire to remain in contact with others, but voice communication was seldom as efficient as the printed word. It all seemed rather silly.

But as Sophocles watched, it became clear that this was no ordinary phone. The man tapped a button on the front, and the shiny black face of the thing sprang to life. Colorful icons appeared on the screen, some of them animated, all of them begging to be touched. The man made a few deft motions, tapping here and there on the screen, the image flickering as it switched from one view to the next.

And when the man stopped, what Sophocles saw sent shivers through his body. The world spun, and Sophocles struggled to his feet, stepping over to press his face closer to the window.

There, on the screen of the strange and terrible device, was a newspaper. *The London Times.*

That night, the moment Herbert stepped out the door, Sophocles raced to the phone. He batted the receiver from the cradle so hard that it went flying off the desktop and clattered to the floor. Sophocles had to fish it back up by the cord before he could make his call.

He pawed the numbers, let the phone ring a single time, and then smacked the contact back down to hang up. It was a signal he and a friend of his had developed for calling one another during human waking hours. They'd picked it up from other cats they'd talked to at the vet. He'd heard humans talking about the strange calls they get that ring once and no one is there, but fortunately the humans attributed them to telemarketers or trouble with the lines.

A moment later the phone rang and Sophocles answered. "Hello," he mewed.

"Hey, Sophocles. I had to sneak the cordless phone under the bed to call you back. What's the big emergency?"

"Mr. Snuggles! We have a serious problem over here. I need the advice of someone who knows about those *crazy* phone things the humans are all carrying."

Sophocles had hissed the word "crazy." He despised the trappings of modern society, seeing its many technological marvels as little more than showy glitz designed to sap the time and money of the working cat. Probably true for humans as well, but he hadn't given it that much thought. Of course, after today's incident he realized he might need to reconsider.

"Why don't we get together tomorrow and . . ." Mr. Snuggles began.

"No. Tonight. We need to talk right away," said Sophocles.

"Okay, okay, don't choke on a hairball. Look, the boy is going out with his friends in a few minutes. When he leaves, I'll slip out and come right over. Will that work?"

"Yes, fine. Don't delay. This is of the utmost importance."

"No problem. Just try to calm down, and stay away from the catnip. I'll be over as soon as I can."

Mr. Snuggles lived in an apartment a block from the newsstand. He and Sophocles had met at the vet's a couple of years back. Although their personalities differed dramatically, for some reason they hit it off. Where Sophocles was old, almost fifteen by his own count, and loved all things traditional, Mr. Snuggles was young, a mere kitten in Sophocles' eyes at three years, and he loved everything new and exciting.

Sophocles propped open the bathroom window for Mr. Snuggles, then busied himself counting copies on the magazine rack. If anything was low, he had to make sure to sit near the copy and mew tomorrow, so Herbert would remember to restock. The man was frustratingly unobservant at times.

An hour later, Mr. Snuggles arrived.

"Hey, Sophocles," he said, his coppery eyes glinting in the half-light.

"Oh, thank goodness you're here," Sophocles said.

Mr. Snuggles made his way around the room, sniffing the corners and taking the place in.

"Man, you're lucky. I love this place, Sopho. The ambience is fantastic. It's like stepping back in time. I mean, look at this," he said, hopping onto the counter and sniffing at a clear plastic jar of candies. "You guys even have squirrel nuts. Seriously, Sopho, where do you even order squirrel nuts? I didn't even know they still made them. Places like this are an endangered species."

Sophocles joined Mr. Snuggles on the counter and swished his tail under Mr. Snuggles' nose.

"If you'd stop rambling on, you'd find out that this is exactly why I called you."

"What do you mean?" Mr. Snuggles asked.

Sophocles hopped from the counter to the desk behind it, and dragged a heavy binder out from between two bookends shaped like the front and rear of a Spanish galleon. With a bit of effort, he flipped open the cover, then pawed through the pages until he reached a section near the end.

"Look," he insisted.

Mr. Snuggles hopped over as well and glanced at the page. Columns of numbers filled it from top to bottom, with a startling number of them written in red ink.

"Wow, this is amazing," said Mr. Snuggles.

"Isn't it?" sighed Sophocles. "Shocking, I know."

"Yeah," said Mr. Snuggles. "I don't think anyone has done their books by hand in the past twenty years. I mean, sheesh, Sophocles. Haven't you guys ever heard of Quick-Books?"

Sophocles snapped a paw down on the page.

"Not that, you imbecile, these balances. We're hemorrhaging money. In the past five years alone we've lost almost 60% of our regular customer base. For a while, I thought that perhaps another newsstand had opened nearby, but now I *know* what has happened."

Mr. Snuggles quirked his head, a half-smile on his face.

"Oh, really? And what did you discover?"

Sophocles jumped to the floor and marched over to the

magazines. With a flick of his paw, he knocked a copy of *Smartphone & Pocket PC Magazine* from the rack.

"This," he said, pointing to the cover. "This is the problem."

Mr. Snuggles jumped off the desk and sauntered over. He checked out the magazine cover, which displayed an array of high-end cell phones.

"What?" Mr. Snuggles replied in mock surprise. "Phones?"

"I know! It sounds unbelievable. I hardly believed it myself at first, but did you know," Sophocles lowered his voice in a conspiratorial fashion, "that you can read *newspapers* on these?"

At first, Mr. Snuggles made a shocked expression, but then his eye twitched and he fell over onto the floor laughing. Sophocles stared at him, aghast.

"Wha . . . what's so funny?" he stammered.

"Sophocles," Mr. Snuggles said, "you've been able to do that for years. *And* take pictures, *and* read books, *and* listen to music, *and* send letters . . ."

"Letters?" gasped Sophocles.

This only sent Mr. Snuggles into further fits of laughter.

"Stop that! Stop that at once! This is my life you're laughing at. My store is going to close!"

Mr. Snuggles stifled his next laugh, took a long breath, and wiped the tears from his eyes with the back of one paw. Rolling back onto his feet, he gave Sophocles a look of compassion.

"I'm sorry, Sophocles. It's just that I keep telling you to read the technology sections of those papers you love so much."

"Fah," Sophocles hissed. "That's not news. It's corporate gossip. It has no business in a proper paper."

"You can't hide from it forever, Sophocles. This is the

future. This is why all your customers are drifting away. They don't need newspapers anymore."

"What? Of course people *need* newspapers. Without the news we simply wander in shadow, ignorant of the world around us. Without the news we wallow, confused, with no understanding of our place in the world. Without the news . . ."

"I didn't say people don't need news. I said people don't need *newspapers*."

Sophocles stared, bewildered. Mr. Snuggles sighed.

"Look, Sophocles. Remember when I told you about the internet?"

Sophocles nodded and said, "Isn't that the thing humans use to share mating images?"

"Well, yeah, partly. Okay, mostly, but it's more than that. It's become an interconnected version of our own world. People meet. They talk. They post their own news. Even the newspapers see this. They all offer their news online. With a few clicks, anyone, anywhere, can read news from every-where else in the world."

"But . . . but what about the papers we have here? I mean we offer papers from the far corners of the earth. We already keep people connected to the events of the world!"

"So does the internet, Sophocles, only you don't have to wait until the afternoon print run is complete, or days for those out-of-country editions you carry. You can find out right now, the moment the news happens."

Sophocles walked over to the rack of newspapers and ran a paw over a copy of the *Detroit Free Press*. "And they can get this on their computers, as well as their phones?"

"Yes, Sophocles. Almost everyone can."

Sophocles' head drooped; he sat down, and his tail swished slowly across the floor. When at last he raised his head and gazed at Mr. Snuggles, his eyes were damp.

"That's it then," Sophocles said. "We're no longer necessary."

Mr. Snuggles stepped over and sat next to Sophocles. For a long time they just sat there together, in silence. Finally, Sophocles stood and headed back over to the counter.

"Where are you going?" asked Mr. Snuggles.

Sophocles stopped, head lowered, and gave a long sigh.

"I'm going to run the numbers, see how much time we have."

Mr. Snuggles narrowed his eyes and raised his tail.

"Hold on," he said. "Don't close those books out just yet, Sopho. I have an idea, but we're going to need a computer."

The two cats scurried down the alley behind the shop. It had taken a bit of coaxing to get Sophocles out. From the day Herbert brought him home, Sophocles lived within the confines of the newsstand. His only forays into the outside world consisted of trips to the vet and a couple of accidental lockouts during his more adventurous youth. A close encounter with a taxi, however, convinced him of the folly of such explorations, and he soon settled into a safe and comfortable pattern of life within the shop.

Now, Sophocles found himself in the unpleasant position of making the block-long trek to Mr. Snuggles' apartment. It was all he could do to keep up with the younger, livelier cat, and he had to remind Mr. Snuggles repeatedly to slow down. Each time they passed an opening onto the alley, Sophocles instinctively stopped. Engine noise, distant sirens, pungent unfamiliar odors, and the strange pink-orange light of the street lamps left him cowering in the shadows.

"Relax," Mr. Snuggles encouraged him. "I do this all the time. It's perfectly safe."

In the end, the same thing always pushed him onward. His shop. His talk with Mr. Snuggles had finally driven home the reality. His shop would not survive much longer. Six months, a year at most. He'd managed to hide this truth from himself for a long time, but saying it out loud somehow made it real. This reality burned within Sophocles' mind— no other idea had burned this hot in a very long time.

If there was a way to save his shop, by his tail he would do it. And if it required him to travel a block, hell, two blocks even, then he would make that sacrifice. Taking a long, deep breath and holding it, he dashed across the alley opening.

Soon they stood behind Mr. Snuggles' apartment building. Sophocles marveled at how simple the trip had been. Not nearly the horror he'd imagined. A breeze blew through the space between the buildings, ruffling Sophocles' fur. He lifted his head and put his nose to it, taking in the crisp, outdoor air. His muscles twitched with an urge to run, just run and dance amid the trash in the alley. Maybe even hunt.

"You coming, old man?" Mr. Snuggles called.

Sophocles looked up and found Mr. Snuggles standing on the fire escape above him. An overflowing dumpster offered a simple path to the top. Simple, Sophocles soon discovered, for a younger cat. His vigor from moments before faded quickly as he struggled up the pile. A few jumps in the shop were one thing, but this was something else. His muscles burned, and he breathed heavily as he climbed, sometimes clambering with effort, to the top.

Finally, he arrived and found Mr. Snuggles smiling at him.

"What's so funny?" he insisted.

"You, old man. I'll be honest. I wasn't sure if you had it in you. You're pretty tough for an old cat."

Sophocles raised his nose and tail and then sniffed.

"You will find, my kitten, that age has not diminished my spirit. My muscles may not have the same strength as yours, but I assure you I more than make up for it in determination."

Mr. Snuggles smiled once more, then dashed up the fire escape. Sophocles followed, appreciating the relative ease of climbing the stairs. Moments later, they sat outside a window looking in on a darkened dining room.

"How do we get in?" Sophocles asked.

Mr. Snuggles responded by tapping lightly on the window, claws extended. From around the corner, a shapely young Blue Point Lynx appeared. Her body swayed as she walked, ringed tail teasing the air behind her and blue eyes shining. Sophocles started to feel light-headed and realized that he was holding his breath.

"My word," he gasped. "She's beautiful."

"Isn't she, though? Her name is Evette," Mr. Snuggles replied, beaming.

"You never told me you lived with another cat."

"They only got her about six months ago. I'll admit that things didn't go well at first. They almost sent her away. Heck, they almost sent *me* away after I started marking rooms to keep her out of my space. But one evening, after a really big blow out, all that tension melted into something a bit more, um, enjoyable, and we've gotten along great ever since."

Evette hopped effortlessly onto the dining room table, and from there she virtually floated to the window sill. Standing on her hind legs, smooth white underbelly pressed against the glass, she undid the window latch with her front paws.

"Gracious. She's a vixen, isn't she?" whispered Sophocles.

"Hey. Watch it, old man. That's my girlfriend you're talking about."

"Right, sorry. No offense meant, of course."

"Ah, none taken. And you're right anyhow," Mr. Snuggles said, chuckling.

The latch undone, Mr. Snuggles and Evette worked together to open the window. It resisted a bit at first, but once they broke the seal, the weighted lines in the frame took over and the window slid easily open. They closed it behind them, and the three cats hopped over onto the table. Evette padded over to Mr. Snuggles and rubbed her body down his length.

"Hey, lover," she purred. "You didn't tell me you were bringing company."

She gave Sophocles a sly, appraising look that made him feel nervous and excited all at the same time.

"He's an *old* friend," Mr. Snuggles said, emphasizing the word old and smiling over his shoulder at Sophocles. "But he's got a problem, and I've got an idea on how we can help. We're going to need the computer, though. Is everyone asleep?"

"Dead to the world," Evette replied. "The place is ours."

"Excellent. Okay, Sophocles. Come with me."

"You boys have fun," Evette said, bounding off the table and heading for the far doorway. "I told Boots I'd call her tonight."

Mr. Snuggles hopped down and headed out the other exit, and Sophocles followed. The house was filled with so many new and unusual scents that Sophocles had to work to resist stopping to sniff at them. After so many years in the store, he'd nearly forgotten how rich and exciting the rest of the world could be.

In the living room, Mr. Snuggles hopped onto the coffee table. Sophocles did the same, and he found Mr. Snuggles opening a laptop computer. Sophocles had never seen one this close. With the computer open, Mr. Snuggles tapped the power button and the screen glowed, illuminating the room.

"Okay. We need to get online."

Mr. Snuggles sat in front of the computer and began tapping away at the keys with one paw. At one point he placed his paw on a flat bit of plastic near the edge of the computer, swished his paw back and forth, and then clicked a nearby button with the claw of one toe.

A few moments later, the screen filled with an electronic version of a newspaper. Again, Sophocles felt light-headed. He was having trouble breathing, and he instinctively popped his claws, trying to sink them into the smooth glass surface of the table for stability.

"I want to show you something," Mr. Snuggles said, unaware of Sophocles' condition.

A few more paw motions and the screen changed to show an old diner. Standing in front of it was a mob of people holding signs painted with slogans, like "Save Our History!" and "Keep Our City Alive!"

"I read this article," Sophocles said. "October 23rd, 2007. Activists Save Local Diner."

"Exactly. A bunch of those Save Our City people, the same ones who made the stink last year about the "homogenization of our cities." They went crazy when they found out the place was going to close and a fast food joint would take the spot. The place has crappy food and is about as clean as a sewer grate, but people saved it because it represents a part of our world that is fading away."

Sophocles began to understand, but he shook his head.

"This isn't the same. No one is taking over the newsstand. We're just running out of money. Protesters won't help."

"We don't need protesters. We just need to convince people that they're about to lose something important to the city. How long has Ehgleman's been open?"

"It was established in 1946. Mr. Ehgleman had just returned from the war and . . ."

"Right, right. I remember the story. And in that time, how often have you remodeled?"

"Well, Herbert purchased a new cash register when he took over the shop in '65. Oh, and we replaced that light fixture, the one that fell when the people living upstairs had that party in '95."

"That's what I'm saying, Sophocles. That newsstand is like a freaking museum. It's like someone froze it in time. These folks," Mr. Snuggles said, tapping on the picture of the protesters, "eat this stuff up. And if they find out that you might close, they'll swarm the place."

Sophocles thought about this. Something about the plan nagged at him. In some way it didn't feel quite right, but all the pieces were there. It *could* work.

"It's a decent idea," he conceded. "But how will we let them know? Do you have their phone numbers?"

Mr. Snuggles laughed.

"We don't need to call them. Remember how I said the internet can connect people together?"

Not waiting for an answer Mr. Snuggles tapped the keyboard a few more times. The screen changed, revealing a page with a series of dated entries titled "Mr. Snugg's Place." Sophocles narrowed his eyes and stared at the screen.

"What is it?"

"It's my blog. We're going to take Ehgleman's Newsstand into the blogosphere!"

Sophocles stared at Mr. Snuggles.

"You do realize that I haven't the slightest idea what you are talking about," he said.

Mr. Snuggles sighed. "A blog is sort of like an online

diary. You post entries and can talk about anything that interests you."

"I'm not seeing the point."

"Other people can read the blog and post their own comments, and if they like what you wrote and have a blog of their own, they can connect their blog to your story."

"A web of sorts, I see. But why would anyone want to read the ramblings of a rank amateur? No offense, of course."

"Well, first, they aren't all amateurs. Authors, politicians, all sorts of people have blogs. What's more, and I think you'll be especially interested in this, bloggers have started breaking news stories the major outlets didn't even know about. With a blog, anyone can be a reporter."

Sophocles mulled it over. It was like the small press papers they carried on the big circular rack back at Ehgleman's, the papers published in garages and old warehouses by the members of fringe groups or fans of esoteric topics. Still, Sophocles had his doubts.

"This is all well and good, but how will anyone find what you've written? I mean just because you publish an article doesn't mean anyone will read it."

"Fortunately, I've got that covered," Mr. Snuggles said.

Again, he tapped away furiously, alternating between the keys and the smooth plastic square. A moment later, a list of what Sophocles assumed were blogs, appeared on the screen.

"These are the blogs of other cats, all friends of mine."

"What? You mean there are more cats writing blogs?"

"Oh, yeah, hundreds, thousands maybe. Who knows? On the internet everyone is anonymous. Almost anything you find there could have been created by a cat."

Sophocles looked at the computer, dumbfounded. He felt

as if someone had taken his entire world, turned it inside out, and handed it back to him.

"So all I have to do," said Mr. Snuggles, "is email the other cats and let them know what I'm trying to accomplish. They'll link to the story and we'll start building momentum. We help each other out like this all the time."

He turned to Sophocles.

"Now what I need from you is help writing this story. If anyone who knows how to write news, Sophocles, it's you. We'll save your newsstand yet!"

Sophocles just stared at the screen, taking in the dozens of names in the list.

"I need a computer," he said.

Over the next few weeks, Mr. Snuggles kept Sophocles posted about the progress on their campaign. It wasn't necessary. Within a few days of the blogs hitting the web, strange new people started filtering in to the newsstand.

Some were young people with little handheld computers, like the device the man outside the window had used.

"Oh, my god," they would gasp. "Can you believe this place? This is awesome. It's like something out of a movie!"

Others were older, hair steely colored, wearing sensible shoes and worn sweaters.

"My father and I used to come to a newsstand just like this when I was a boy," they'd say. "He'd buy a *Times*, some pipe tobacco, and, if I was good, a comic book for me."

And more than one of them came in with cats held in their arms or in special travel totes they opened when they were inside the door. As their owners explored the store, the cats came over to talk to Sophocles.

"We think it's really great what you're doing here," they told him. "The humans don't always appreciate their history, so it's up to us to preserve it."

Sophocles simply nodded, unsure what to say and unused to so much company after years of living alone in the newsstand with Herbert.

The most important change, however, was that people bought things again: newspapers, cigarettes, maps of the city, penny candy, comic books, magazines. The little bell of the cash register rang over and over, a wonderful music to the swirling dance of life the newsstand had become.

After visiting Ehgleman's, many people drifted next door to the diner, an old greasy spoon in as much trouble financially as the newsstand had been. The boost in customers helped it as well. At one point, the diner's owner, an older woman with a long nose who always smelled of bacon grease, came in to talk to Herbert. The two of them marveled at their unexpected success, wondering at what had changed.

Beaming at their good fortune, they laughed and chatted, eventually becoming good friends and spending many of their evenings together. All the while, Sophocles sat comfortably on his cushion in the window, filled with warm feelings. He and Mr. Snuggles had not only saved the newsstand and the diner, but in the process they had brought some extra happiness into Herbert's and Long Nose Lady's lives.

At one point, Herbert felt that with some of his profits he ought to remodel. Mr. Snuggles nearly panicked, and he made it very clear to Sophocles that remodeling was out of the question. People didn't want a shiny new newsstand. They wanted classic urban grime. It took a fair amount of effort, but Sophocles managed to erase messages from the contractor, lose paperwork, and otherwise interfere with the process. Finally, Herbert gave up on the idea as more trouble than it was worth.

The high point for Sophocles came when the city's major paper ran a story in the Lifestyles section about Ehgleman's, outlining its history and proclaiming it one of the city's

"pulp gems of a disappearing classic urban landscape."
Sophocles was even featured in one of the photos. The most
satisfying part for Sophocles, however, was that he got to
read it right there in the paper, in strong black ink on yellow-
white newsprint.

Sophocles did get a computer. A few carefully placed
technology articles caught Herbert's attention and put the
idea into his head to buy one. Herbert used it twice and
promptly gave up on it. At night, while Herbert was at home,
Sophocles learned its arcane secrets. After a month of effort,
he proudly opened "Sopho's Stories," a blog about the news
and newspapers where he wrote short essays about the state
of journalism and the news media in the modern world.

And yet, despite the now solid financial position of the
newsstand, something still bothered Sophocles. For a long
time it nagged at him, often in the depths of the night, just
out of reach and tickling the back of his mind. Then one
evening, while Mr. Snuggles was visiting, it came to him.

They were sitting together on the desk behind the
counter, going over Sophocles' latest story on the computer.

"I think I finally figured it out," Sophocles said.

"What's that?"

"That thing. The thing that's bothered me from the beginning."

Mr. Snuggles maneuvered the mouse to click the back
button on the computer. The home page for "Sopho's Stories" came up on the screen.

"I'll bite. What is it?"

"We saved the store, and that's important, but we saved it
by turning it into a novelty."

"And is that so bad? I mean, isn't saving the store
enough? Wasn't that what you wanted?"

"No," Sophocles said, lowering his head. "What I
wanted, what I *truly* wanted, was for things to be the same

as they were. I wanted people to care about those little black words on the page. I wanted them to pick up that newspaper, to feel the newsprint, smell the ink, and know that they held the world in their hands, the combined knowledge of sharp, creative minds, working together to bring the truth to the people.

"But I know the truth, now. We saved the newsstand, but we can't save the magic those little black printed words represent. We can't save newspapers."

Mr. Snuggles sat back on his haunches and gave a little chuckle. Sophocles whipped his head around and glared at him.

"Why do you do that? Why do you always laugh at me when I'm feeling the worst?"

Mr. Snuggles shook his head and said, "Sopho, my friend, you are one of the smartest, wisest creatures I know, and yet sometimes you remain blind to the most obvious things."

"What are you talking about?"

Mr. Snuggles scrolled to the bottom of the "Sopho's Stories" page and clicked on a blue link labeled "web stats." A series of bar graphs appeared on the screen.

"According to this," Mr. Snuggles said, "around 10,000 people, or cats maybe, you can't tell, have read your last article over the past two days. That's 10,000 people whose lives you've touched, people whom you've opened doors for, and with whom you've shared wisdom and understanding they might never have discovered on their own."

Sophocles glared. "I'm well aware of the stats, and while I'm pleased people are interested, I don't see your point."

"Sophocles, it isn't the paper that holds the magic. It's the *words*. It's words that give the paper the magic you love, words that saved your store, and words that will preserve that magic for those who come after us."

Mr. Snuggles rose and padded over to a newspaper setting next to the computer. He swiped at it with his paw, rustling the pages.

"Without the words, this paper is nothing but a piece of flattened tree. It doesn't matter whether the words are printed on paper, appear on a computer screen, or, I don't know, get zapped straight into your head. It is, and always will be, the *words* that hold the magic.

"What you love isn't dying, Sophocles. Just the trees those words get printed on."

Sophocles never forgot their conversation. Through joyous occasions, like the birth of Mr. Snuggles' and Evette's kittens the next year, and sad, as when Herbert passed on two years later, that simple conversation stayed with Sophocles and gave him hope.

It was three years after Herbert passed away that Sophocles died. He was 21 by then, and Herbert's son, who had taken over the shop, found Sophocles curled up on his cushion in the picture window, seeming for all the world like he was sleeping.

Mr. Snuggles realized something was wrong when there was nothing new posted on Sopho's Stories that next evening. Others noticed as well, and soon emails and comments were blooming throughout the internet, as admirers of the journalism blog wondered what had happened.

When a second night came with no new posts, Mr. Snuggles knew. He raced over to the newsstand, hurrying down the alley, fearing the worst. When he arrived, the bathroom window was closed, so he crept around to the front of the store.

A little light sat in the front window. It hadn't been there before, and it shone on Sophocles' cushion. Where the old cat should have been sleeping, there was a framed picture of him in his youth, serious and sitting atop a stack of newspapers. The *London Times*, Mr. Snuggles noticed. Beside the picture lay a handwritten note.

"Goodbye, old friend. Take good care of Dad."

Mr. Snuggles posted the news on "Mr. Snugg's Place" as soon as he returned home. The word traveled quickly, and within hours a memorial to Sophocles the blogger appeared on a popular social networking site. A few humans tried to puzzle out the mystery of who the respected news commentator called Sophocles was, but every lead came up short.

Cats, of course, knew.

It wasn't until three days later that Mr. Snuggles found it. He'd missed the message at first—it had been eaten by his voracious spam filter. It was a single email from sopho@sophostories.com, with the subject "To My Friend." The date and time stamp showed that it had reached his mailbox at 3:00 AM on the day that Sophocles had passed on.

For awhile, Mr. Snuggles just stared at it, unsure if he even wanted to read it. Finally, he worked up the courage to open it, and inside he found two simple, magic words.

"Thank you"

BURNING BRIGHT

Elaine Cunningham

Mhari had seen smallcats before but seldom in the wild—if indeed the city's streets and rooftops and small scattered gardens could be so named. Other than the yellow tom the Woman had thoughtfully provided to relieve Mhari of the heat and madness of her first season, she had seen none close at hand. Yet here were three of them—small, short-legged creatures, with tails too long and heads too large for their barrel-shaped bodies—staring fixedly at her from their perches in the talltree just outside Mhari's home habitat.

The nearest one—a gray-striped tom—thrust his nose close to the strong wire mesh. His whiskers twitched as he tasted her scent. "What are you?" he asked bluntly.

That was rude by Mhari's standards, but she knew little of the ways of smallcats. She rose and padded across her climbing gym's top platform to close the distance between them. "I am a Serval cat," she said politely, turning in profile so they could see the distinctive black bars running the length of her graceful neck, the neat black spots that marked the rest of her long, tawny body. "Daughter of Jahared, a freeborn Serval, out of Ahmriel. I am of Ahmriel's third litter, and I bear Papers, a thing the humans seem to value. My name is Mhari. And you?"

If the tom heard her question, he gave no sign. He glanced toward a gray female. "Told you so. African wild cat. Not much of a runner, but agile. Likes to swim."

The third and largest of Mhari's visitors switched his plumed tail in annoyance. He was rather grand, as his kind went, with long black fur that made him look plump and complacent. The white on his face and throat and belly made him resemble the Man who gave Mhari's Woman sparkling gifts and sometimes took her away for the evening. For that reason alone, Mhari was inclined to dislike him.

"Please forgive Frank's abrupt manner of speaking," the tuxedo-clad tom said in a surprisingly cordial tone. "It is his way; he means no offense. I am called Smithwicks, and this is Minx."

"Frank and I tend to take our names seriously," observed the gray queen archly, lifting her hindquarters in a suggestive manner.

Mhari had seen minks before and could perceive no reason for the smallcat's boast. She turned to the dapper tom. "To what do I owe this visit? It must be a matter of some importance to bring three of you to this part of the city."

"Maybe I live around here," Minx said defensively. "Since you're not a male, maybe you just didn't notice me. And, hey—like the saying goes, all cats are gray in the dark."

The Serval did not point out the obvious fallacy in this saying, nor did she observe that the smallcats in this neighborhood, with its fine old trees and walled gardens, were elegant creatures who wore jeweled collars and were seldom seen in the company of common tomcats.

Smithwicks gave the gray female a quelling stare. "It

is . . . complicated. A matter of some delicacy, one requiring expertise we hope you might possess—"

"We need you to go to the zoo and talk to a tiger," Frank broke in.

A frisson of alarm rippled done Mhari's spine. She knew that word, *zoo*. One of the freeborn Serval on the Arizona ranch, her birthplace, had been kept in a zoo for a time following his capture. He claimed the cats were kept in cages of metal and glass, larger perhaps than the elegant habitat Mhari's Woman provided for her but without the privacy Mhari enjoyed. Humans passed by endlessly, noisy crowds of them, chattering and staring—but never a human a Serval could call her own.

Mhari had no use for humans in general, but she and her Woman shared a bond. There were pleasant evenings at home together, a jeweled leash and harness so that they might take lovely strolls, warm afternoons spent swimming and diving in Mhari's stone-lined pool, car rides, weekend trips to a woodland cottage or a seaside house. The Woman talked to her in English and Italian, and Mhari responded in Domestic and Serval. The Woman was highly intelligent; at times, she almost seemed to grasp Mhari's responses. What Mhari had was not freedom, not exactly, but it was not an unpleasant life.

In the zoo, there was only captivity.

"The greatcats can't talk to you?" she said hesitantly.

"Can't or won't," said Frank. "It's much the same thing."

Smithwick narrowed his eyes at the striped tom. "In brief, here is the problem: we cats have been tracking a human, a killer."

This puzzled Mhari. Humans were predators and could not be faulted for following their nature. Still, there were ways and ways. She often sprawled on the white settee beside the Woman, listening to the talking box. The Woman was fond of something called *Law and Order*. It was a wonder to Mhari that humans survived at all, so endlessly and inventively did they kill one another.

"The humans police their own, do they not?"

"Not if they're just killing cats," Minx said spitefully, "unless, of course, the cat has *Papers*. Or unless we cats *make* them care." She met Mhari's eyes with a challenging stare. "But you wouldn't know about that, would you? I mean, your daddy being 'freeborn' and all . . . ."

"That will do, Minx," Smithwicks snapped. "We followed this human as far as the zoo and saw him throw a gun into the moat by the tiger habitat. Perhaps the tiger will have noticed something about the man that may help us find him. If not, Frank's human is a police detective; he can discover what human handled the gun. Again, your expertise is required—we need you to retrieve it from the moat."

"I see," she mused. Thanks to the talking box, she knew this to be true. "Because you are tame cats—"

"Domesticated, not tame," broke in Frank. "No cat is ever tame."

Mhari twitched her whiskers agreeably. "As domesticated cats, you endeavor to help Frank's policeman?"

The smallcats exchanged glances. Mhari scented a subtle change in their mood—a note that was both primal and familiar.

"You wish to find this human yourselves," she said, surprised and impressed. "I did not know smallcats hunted as a pride. It is not the Serval's usual way, but my sire told me that from time to time the freeborn would band together to bring down larger prey."

"We would be honored if you would join us in that, as well," said Smithwicks. "This human must be stopped, and soon."

The notion of hunting humans made Mhari profoundly

uneasy, but the smallcats were right: A rogue had to be stopped, whether he walked on two legs or four. "I would help you if I could, but how would I get to this zoo?"

Three furred heads turned toward the house. Three smallcats sent out a silent, summoning yowl. The light in the Woman's bedroom flicked on, and in moments she stood on the patio, looking about in puzzlement.

Minx continued to talk to the Woman, but her voice was somehow different—quieter, more compelling. The Woman's night robe swirled around her legs as she hurried to the gate of Mhari's habitat. She unlocked it, added kibble to the already-full dish, and left. For the first time since Mhari had come to live in the city, the Woman neglected to lock the gate.

Moments passed as the Serval sat in stunned silence, not entirely sure she could credit her eyes and ears. Suddenly the gray queen's snide comments made a little sense: apparently the smallcats really could "make" humans do their bidding.

A wave of envy arose from some dark place and emerged as a soft snarl. How was it that a flea-bitten stray would command Mhari's Woman, when she, a Serval cat born to a line that had kept company with Italian nobility, could speak unheard?

She would have demanded answers, but the smallcats had already quit the tree. Mhari climbed down from her perch and skirted her pool. She waited by the gate until the Woman's lights winked out, then nosed it open and edged gingerly into the garden. The Woman's personal garden was small—most of the property had been enclosed for Mhari's use—but beyond it lay the city.

The smallcats were already padding down the cobblestoned drive, obviously expecting Mhari to follow. After a moment's hesitation, she did. In a few loping strides, she pulled up beside Smithwicks and adjusted her pace to his.

"What if we're seen?" she ventured, gazing out into the well-lit street. "I am not inconspicuous."

Minx's snort was loud enough to dislodge a hairball. "No worries. With those long skinny legs and that tiny head, you'll just be taken for a stray greyhound. There's a few of them around—the dog track turns out losers to fend for themselves."

"Shut up, Minx," hissed Smithwicks. "If we need to scatter, Mhari, just climb a tree. We'll find you."

"Not if I find her first."

Mhari whirled toward the speaker. Sitting on the high stone fence was the largest smallcat she had ever seen. His long, tawny coat made his weight difficult to judge, but Mhari would put him at over twenty-five pounds—only five or ten pounds lighter than she. A handsome creature, too, with a long white ruff that was almost leonine and a pleasantly deep rumble to his voice. There was nothing pleasant about his manner, however, from the turned-back ears to the lashing tail fluffed to impossible size.

The three smallcats hissed and backed off, positioning themselves behind Mhari. She stood her ground as the big tom leaped to the ground and stalked toward her. He circled Mhari as if he desired to examine her from every angle. She thought it prudent to turn to face him. The smallcats, also prudent, retreated to the shadows of a flowering hedge.

"I heard rumors, but I didn't believe them," the tom said, addressing the cowering Smithwicks. He flicked a glance at Mhari. "Until now. This foolishness stops here."

He leaped at Mhari and wrapped his front paws around her neck—a take-down maneuver she had seen smallcats use on each other. Mhari braced her front legs and tipped her head forward, accepting the sting of claws as he slid off. Too late she realized her mistake—this was the result the tom had intended. Now beneath her, he raised powerful hind legs to rake and tear.

But the tom did not know the ways of the Serval. Mhari leaped straight up, and the strike that might have opened her belly fell far short.

The tom adjusted with admirable speed. He rolled and got his feet back beneath him while Mhari was still gaining height. As she fell, she twisted in the air and swiped a pawful of claws at the retreating smallcat—a move she'd learned from watching someone called Derek Jeter on the talking box—and tore the tom's ear to bloody ribbons.

The moment her paws touched down, she hopped to one side, neatly evading the tom's running attack. She sped him on his way with a blow from one powerful paw. He stumbled, rolled. Before he could rise again, the three smallcats were upon him, biting and tearing.

"Enough," Mhari snarled.

They paid her no heed. She stalked over and picked up the gray female by the scruff of the neck, like some recalcitrant kitten. She tossed Minx aside and glared at the gray's two male companions, who'd left off their attack on the big tom to eye Mhari uncertainly.

"Next?" she said meaningfully.

Smithwicks edged away. "We came to your aid."

"You fell on a wounded cat like jackals."

"There is no need to take that tone," he said reprovingly. "You do not understand all the factors at work. You do not understand the various factions and schools of thought among the city's cats."

"Explain, then."

Frank muttered something about Bast in heat. His tone suggested that comparison to the Goddess was not necessarily a compliment. "We can stand here waiting for dawn and Animal Control, or we can do what needs doing."

"Well said," agreed Smithwicks. "Shall we?"

Somehow they managed to get to the zoo without further challenge. They scrambled up the vines draping a tall stone wall.

The scent struck Mhari like a blow. Not just the smell of animals—she'd caught that scent long before the walls of the zoo came into sight—but the lingering stench of too many humans, too much scat for so little territory, too many chemicals meant to clean away the odor of scat. But what struck her most forcefully was the scent of despair.

There were coyotes living wild near the Arizona ranch. One time an old, mangy dog ventured near the Serval's habitat, probably drawn by the scent of food it could no longer hunt for itself. He'd been caught in an old, forgotten leg trap in the brush outside the habitat. Days had passed before the humans found and killed him. In that time, Mhari had learned of despair and hopelessness. Tonight, she had learned something almost as troubling.

"You smallcats can talk to the humans and bend them to your will," she ventured, "but the greatcats cannot. That is why they can be kept in zoos."

"That is true," Smithwicks said cautiously.

"I cannot do what you do. If I am captured, I will not be able to escape."

"Minx is very persuasive. She will get you out," the black-and-white tom assured her. He glared at the little gray female as if daring her to contradict him. "We'll make sure she does."

Mhari turned toward the artificial cave in the midst of a steel and glass enclosure. Her nose told her there were lions within. "What of the others? The Great Ones?"

"What of them?" Minx snarled. Her head came up proudly. "For thousands of years, we cats have lived among humans. Our bonds with them have evolved over time. Our civilization is complex and powerful, and far beyond your primitive understanding. *Great Ones*. Ha!"

"What Minx meant to say," said Smithwicks, "was that we honor the Ancestors. They have a place in our hearts and our history. But they are not part of our civilization."

"And there's no place for them in the city," put in Frank. Except for the zoo.

Suddenly Mhari wanted nothing more than to be done with this. She leaped down from the wall and trotted across the road toward the long, sterile pool surrounding the tiger's habitat. A foolish thing, since tigers could swim nearly as well as she, and it had little to do with the things that truly kept the great striped cat imprisoned, but no doubt it made the visiting humans feel more secure.

The Serval leaped the low fence and paced along the edge of the moat, looking for a glint of metal under the water. A low rumble, the feline version of a politely cleared throat, drew her attention to the dappled shadows beneath a tree. The tiger sprawled there, watching her with strangely dull, incurious eyes.

"Greetings, little sister," he said. "How is it that you run free?"

His language fell strangely upon Mhari's ears, but it was close enough to the Serval speech for her to follow. "A gun was thrown into this pool. I have come to retrieve it."

"What do you want with such a thing?"

"The man who threw it away has been killing smallcats. They wish to stop him. The gun will help them find him."

The tiger considered this in silence. "Did the smallcats free you? Is that why you do their bidding?"

Mhari was about to deny this, but found she could not.

How would the tiger understand her bond with the Woman? He would see her captivity as no different from his.

She was not entirely certain he would be wrong.

A surge of water rippled through the pool, an artificial tide of some sort. Mhari closed her eyes and listened. Her large ears made subtle twitches and turns as she searched the air for some hint of her metallic prey.

There it was—a clink of metal against the metal, somewhere beneath the water. The Serval dropped into the pool and dived for the bottom.

The pool was unexpectedly deep, but the water was clear and a street lamp shone overhead like an artificial moon. Mhari could see clearly, but there was no sign of the gun. The pool's sides were blue and green, painted in swirling stripes to resemble ripples on living water. Mhari was not troubled by color; she saw it, but she cared little about it one way or another. Her eyes were drawn first and foremost to motion. Other than the occasional push of air and water from some of the holes in the smooth wall, there was nothing to see.

She rose to the surface for air.

"Do not—" began the tiger.

Down Mhari went again, not wanting to hear what he might say. Nevertheless, she heard every word—including that which no greatcat should ever have to speak:

Please . . .

If water was pushed into the pool, surely there must also be a place for it to leave. The Serval paddled around the depths and watched the holes, waiting to see which pulsed with bubbles and which did not.

Yes, there it was—a round opening on the wall near the bottom, just where she'd heard the click of metal. Mhari swam toward it and reached one long, dexterous paw into the hole. She could just touch the gun, but just barely.

Twice she surfaced, and twice dived again, before she was able to ease the weapon from the drain and paw it into the sack the smallcats had hung around her neck. She rose toward the false moon and scrabbled up over the edge of the pool. The heavy sack thudded against her chest as she shook water from her coat.

"I did not mean for him to kill the smallcats," the tiger said softly.

Mhari stilled in midshake. "You *can* talk with humans!"

"This human," he admitted. "How and why, I could not say. Never before has anyone heard me, much less attempted to do as I bid them."

So the tiger was hunting by proxy. Clever of him. Mhari wondered, briefly, what the tiger's intended prey might be, but she decided that was none of her affair.

"Tell me of this human."

The tiger snorted. "So you can hunt him down? No, that cannot be. I need this human."

That, Mhari could understand. She did not know how she would fare without her Woman. The tiger had finally found a human of his own, and of course he would be solicitous of the man's welfare.

A querulous *mrowl* drew her gaze to the top of the stone wall. The smallcats were waiting for her.

And beyond that wall waited a rogue killer.

"Your human is hunting cats," Mhari said. "He is a rogue, and rogues are dangerous no matter what their kind. If you care nothing for the smallcats, consider this: You could be next. I am sorry for your loss, Great One, but this is what I must do."

And then she was running for the wall, the tiger's despairing roar burning in her ears.

*   *   *

Several days passed before the smallcats returned. Mhari was paddling around her pool, diving after the small, bright fish the Woman placed there from time to time. The moon shone full and high overhead. It was difficult not to think of the tiger's brightly lit moat and the cruelty of a pool—and so much more—lying just beyond his reach.

The Serval climbed from her pool, dropping one of the koi on the stone walk to flop and twitch and die. She would eat it later. Perhaps. Her freeborn sire had taught her that no cat could be certain of a hunt—not certain of a kill and not certain of a safe return.

The smallcats paced impatiently outside the fence. "We found him," Frank announced. "In a park between here and the zoo."

"I am ready."

Mhari listened carefully as the gray queen called to the Woman. It took longer this time to catch her ear and bend her will. There was a party in the house, with laughter and music and the clinking of many glasses. Even a voice as powerful as Minx's could not easily penetrate the din.

Finally the Woman stumbled out onto the patio, laughing, her arms draped around a human male. A new male, Mhari noted with approval. It was past time for a change.

This one did not seem to fear her as the portly Man had done. He came down the path to Mhari's gate with the Woman. He even entered the habitat, something no visitor had done before.

The Woman called to her in English and Italian. Mhari came over, dropping to her haunches several paces beyond reach—and just beyond the flagstone she had carefully prepared.

"See, she likes you," the Woman cooed. "I told you she would. The Serval cats are very particular, and Mhari is a fine judge of character."

Mhari sat still as the male cautiously advanced, his hand held out so that she could take his scent. No need—the stench of alcohol rolled off him in waves. She waited until he neared the flagstone, then told Minx what to do.

A piercing feline yowl rent the quiet night. The man, startled, pulled up short and stepped directly onto the stone with the tiny cave dug beneath one side. It teetered, he stumbled. Mhari darted away to hide in her rain shelter.

"At least you got to see her close up," the Woman said, sounding disappointed. "She can be skittish. I doubt she'll come out until morning now."

Show him the habitat, thought Mhari.

"But since we're here, let me show you her garden," the Woman said. She laughed lightly. "Mhari lives better than most people!"

They walked over to the pool and found the koi, still alive. The Woman exclaimed over its suffering and toed it back into the pool.

Odd behavior, but it provided all the diversion Mhari required. She ran for the gate and slipped out into the moon-bright night.

Other cats joined them in the park. Mhari could hear them in the trees, moving more slowly and less certainly than squirrels. They crept through the underbrush, too—a dozen of them, a score. More.

The man they sought sat huddled at the base of a thick-bodied talltree, his knees drawn up against his chest and his arms wrapped around them. He rocked back and forth, groaning and muttering to himself in no language Mhari could comprehend.

"This is too near the path," said Smithwicks in a worried tone. He cast a glance toward a nearby lamp post. "And there is too much light. We must not be seen."

"The human will not move, not even for Minx?"

"I'm good," the gray cat said grimly, "but even I can't reach him."

Mhari tentatively reached out as she had heard Minx do, but she fared no better. On impulse, she reached out to the human in Serval. If he could hear tiger speech, perhaps . . .

She told him what to do. The smallcats did not seem to hear, much less understand.

But the human heard. He leaped to his feet, looking around wildly. He lurched toward the path, then stumbled back, shielding his eyes from the bright lamplight.

"The light?" he muttered. "Go into the light? But I'm not dead yet . . . am I?"

"No, move *away* from the light," Mhari urged him, still speaking Serval. "Into the jungle."

She was not certain where that word came from, but it had an electrifying effect on the man. He spun toward the wooded area, eyes narrowed, and dropped to his belly. He began crawling toward the trees, pausing once to bat away a nonexistent swarm of bugs, and twice more to cringe and throw his arms over his head.

Mhari watched him with puzzlement and something approaching pity. Clearly, this human could hear wild-speech—not perfectly, but in small twisted bits. For some reason, his quiet-ears could hear what the domestic cats could not perceive. And if his slow, tortured progress toward the woodland shadows was any indication, he heard and saw other things, too—things wilder and more fearful than a tame-born Serval cat.

Suddenly Mhari understood why the Woman had returned the koi to the pond, to live until it died. A swift, clean death was a blessing. And sometimes, life was no blessing at all. No creature should have to endure the suffering this wild man knew.

She stepped out onto the path and called to him. "You are sick, brother, and confused, and very tired. What you have done, you did not intend. You deserve ease. If you wish, I will give it."

The human scrambled to him feet and patted himself down with quick furtive movements, his eyes fixed upon Mhari. "Too small, too small," he garbled. "Don't shoot the smallcats, you fool. The big cat. The wild cat. The great cat."

He produced a familiar-looking gun from the folds of his filthy coat and pointed it at Mhari. The weapon spat fire, and Mhari's shoulder blazed and burned.

A wail of pain escaped her. She fell where she stood, dimly aware of the brush of fur against her flanks and the thoughtless jostle of many small bodies as the smallcats rushed past her.

They swarmed the wild man like large, deadly rats, biting and tearing. His screams were terrible, but they did not last long. The smallcats lingered on.

And then, just as quickly, they were gone.

A small, rough tongue rasped over Mhari's face again and again. It was rather pleasant, and so was the soft thump of a furry head against her neck. Except for the pain in her shoulder, Mhari was quite content—

The pain roared back, loud and angry. She gasped, and the sudden intake of breath carried a familiar scent. A moment passed before Mhari's groggy thoughts could focus enough to identify it: the big tom who had tried to stop this thing.

She forced her eyes open. Yes, it was the handsome cat she had fought and vanquished. If he wished to settle scores now, she could do little do stop him.

"Get up, Freckles," the big tom urged her. "We have to move *now*."

Mhari heard it then—the deep, reverberating thumps of a horse's hooves. She had seen horses in the park during some of her walks, always ridden by a policeman.

She struggled to her feet, allowing the big tom to guide her into the bushes. He found a small hollow beneath a fallen tree and gently pushed her into it. A good choice, Mhari thought dully. Shelter. Defensible.

"The smallcats will find me," she murmured.

The tom touched his nose to hers in an oddly comforting gesture. "Don't you understand? The smallcats, as you call them, set you up. If I hadn't found you, the police would have found that crazy man dead of an animal attack, a gun lying beside him and a large wild cat dead nearby. They probably wouldn't have looked any further."

He twitched his whiskers in frustration. "I've been trying to stop this. Maybe this man was a threat, but cats killing humans? Imagine the repercussions! I thought Smithwicks's gang recruited you for muscle. I had no idea . . . ."

The tom's voice trailed off. He glanced over his shoulder toward the place where the wild man's torn remains lay. "No thinking creature deserves such a death. Not even one whose thinking is somehow twisted."

"Perhaps, especially not such a one," Mhari said softly.

"Agreed."

"I did not attack him. I did not tear him apart or eat his flesh." For some reason, it seemed important for the tom to know this. "But I would have killed him had he desired a quick death."

The male blinked, apparently surprised by her candor. "From what little I saw of the man, that would have been a kindness."

"May I know your name?"

"Jason," he said absently as he scanned the woodland shadows. "Listen, I think you'll be safe here for a while. I know where you live. I'll do what I can to get word to your human. But you have to stay here, Freckles—any human with a gun is likely to shoot at a cat your size."

"My name is Mhari," she said. "And I would be pleased if you would visit me from time to time."

That made him smile, albeit a little grimly. "Let's get you home first."

The night passed and most of the next day, and still no one came. No smallcats, no Jason, no Woman. Weak with pain and thirst, Mhari was almost glad a small, yapping dog found her hiding place. She was almost pleased to see the grim-faced humans in their Animal Control jumpsuits and long poles with loops at the end. She was almost relieved to have the relative comfort and safety of a small metal cage. And surely no water had ever tasted so sweet. One of the humans stuck something sharp in her hip, and she slept. When she awoke the next morning, her hurts had been cleaned and wrapped. Even though they planned to kill her.

Like the koi, Mhari would be permitted to live until she died.

Her Woman came later that day, bringing the portly Man with her. He waved important Papers and blustered on and on. Some of the things he said were sensible. All of the blood on Mhari's fur was her own. The man had shot Mhari, but there was no evidence that she had attacked him. The Woman had insisted upon something called an autopsy, which proved that none of the wild man's many wounds came from a Serval's teeth or claws. There was evidence of other animals, and many of the small bites had been taken before the wild man died. And apparently there was no trace of something called "human DNA" in Mhari's scat.

The round, loud Man talked and talked. Mhari still did not like him, but she could see that he impressed the humans at Animal Control. Mhari's Woman signed many papers. Thick wads of money surreptitiously changed hands. Finally the Woman was allowed to open Mhari's cage and strap her into her jeweled harness.

The Woman sat in the back seat of the car with Mhari on the way home, while the Man drove. She stroked Mhari's coat and talked and talked, but for once Mhari did not hear. She did not hear English or Italian. She would not have heard even if the woman suddenly spoke Serval, for her own thoughts were too loud, and too troubling, for her to hear anyone else's.

Mhari understood why the smallcats "set her up," to use Jason's term. They wished to protect themselves and their civilization. Perhaps they suspected that the wild man could hear the tiger. Perhaps they suspected that the wild man was doing the tiger's bidding, acting as the wild cat's agent in the city. And as Smithwicks had said, there was no place for the greatcats in the city.

Perhaps they thought there was no place for her in the city, either.

Perhaps they were right.

The Woman leaned down to give Mhari a careful squeeze. "I'll be much more careful about your gate," she said. "It just isn't safe for a Serval to wander the city. You'll stay in the house with me tonight."

"No, I won't," Mhari said. Her Domestic was strongly accented by Serval, but perhaps the woman would understand. After all, hadn't her ancestors kept company with Serval for hundreds of years?

The Woman sat up, smoothed a hand uncertainly over her hair. "But it's such a lovely day, isn't it? It would be a shame for you to stay indoors on such a night as this will be." She laughed a little. "Perhaps I'll stay in the habitat with you."

"No. You won't."

"But of course I can't." She sighed and turned away to watch the city pass by.

Despite her best intentions, the Woman didn't quite secure Mhari's gate that night. The Serval waited until the waning moon was nearly set, then she slipped through the quiet streets to the zoo.

The tiger was still lying beneath his tree. Mhari wondered if he had bothered to move at all in the days that had passed.

"Your human is dead, Great One," she said respectfully, "but not by my tooth or claw. I did not understand until it was too late. Forgive me."

"And you understand now?" he asked, but in a way that suggested he had little interest in her answer.

"I think," she said hesitantly, "you were trying to get him to free you."

That got his attention. His ears went up, and he gathered his hind legs beneath him as if he might actually consider rising. "In a sense, yes, that is so."

"Life will never be as you once knew it. I have wandered the city, Great One, and have learned that there is no place for us here. For the Serval, much less the greatcats, freedom is death."

"Freedom is death," the tiger repeated softly, "*and death is freedom.*"

Mhari thought this over until she understood it fully. Until she understood what she had taken from the tiger and what she must give him.

"I had kittens once," she told him. "Savannahs, they call them. The sire was a smallcat, so they are not quite Serval. But they are beautiful kittens, lithe and lovely. They are not smallcats, not quite, but it seemed to me that the humans heard them, a little. I will bear another litter, and I will wean them to the knowledge of what must be done. In a generation, or perhaps two, my young can speak to the humans, and you will be free."

The tiger's yellow eyes brightened, then blazed. "Their seasons come early, these smallcats. One generation, perhaps two . . . . It is not so very long."

She dipped her head and then padded away to seek Jason and breed the tiger's death. And echoing in her mind were heartfelt words—words no Great Cat should ever have to say:

Thank you.

TO CAT, A THIEF

Robert E Vardeman

After dark, all cats are gray, Robie thought over and over as he struggled to drag his bag of cat food along the littered alley. He kept to shadows as much as possible, hiding his snowy white chest and the mittens on his front feet. The rest of his matted fur was a mixture of gray, black and orange—the only legacy he had received from his long gone father. His mother had been a long-haired Himalayan, but although his fur was long, it lacked the silkiness he remembered of hers before she was run over by one of the noisy, smelly human machines.

Another few yards, he thought. *That's all. A few more feet until I find where the stray cats are hiding.*

He had found the homeless cats a few days earlier in an alley behind an apartment building. He had given them what help he could, but it had been little enough that it tore at his conscience. The mother cat, a scrawny tabby, tried to nurse six kittens and had barely enough milk for two. Mother and litter alike were slat-thin and starving. Life in the city had been hard lately, even for a clever, quick cat like Robie. These others needed his help, and he was willing to give it to them.

He hunkered down as lights raked the brick wall over his

head. He pulled in his feet and pressed his chin to his chest to hide his reflective white fur until the humans left. The rattle of their machine, the crunch of glass under the stinking rubber wheels, the gaseous filth spewing from the rear, all sickened Robie. His nose twitched, and he opened his mouth as he sampled their scent to memorize it. When he had a chance, he would get even with them for disturbing his peace—and his rescue mission.

Loud music blared from inside and the human guiding the machine smelled of burned hamburger, tobacco, and something else strong and nasty. Robie filed all this away on an already long list deserving retribution. Everything about that human was annoying and mostly illegal even by human laws.

The machine clanked down the alley and onto the street, finally allowing Robie to once more grab the sack in his teeth and begin pulling. The bag of dry cat food tipped the scales at ten pounds, only a little less than he weighed. He had stolen it from a place down the block. Determination kept him sliding the bag along the alley until he came to the cardboard box turned to face the brick wall where the mother and her kittens were hidden from prying human eyes.

He released the bag and reared up on his hind legs, his long ringed tail twitching in indignation. The female already had eaten and lay on her side so her kittens could have their meal. Robie's nose worked hard, and he found himself wanting to share her new edibles.

"Where did you get the canned food?" he asked.

Lazily, the female lifted her head. Her whiskers twitched. For the first time there was a hint of vitality to her movement, and her pale yellow eyes were no longer cloudy. The succulent canned food had revived her better than his dry food ever could have.

"Another cat brought it for me," she said. "I was sleeping and the little ones can't really focus too well yet. A savior, bringing me food when I needed it most."

Robie sniffed some more. This was not only canned food, it was high-end victuals. The sort of food the hoity-toity fat cats up in the penthouse apartments ate.

"I brought you some more," he said.

"Thank you, Robie, but I don't need it right now. Later." The cat purred and lay back down as her kittens finished their meal and crowded close for their postprandial nap. Mother and kittens fell asleep together.

Robie dropped back to all fours and considered scattering the bag of food across the alley. A slash of his claws and the plastic-coated paper would rip open. What good was it for him to be the most agile, daring cat in the neighborhood if he wasn't allowed to use those skills? He had gone through a tiny pipe that pressed his whiskers close to his face, climbed up a chain—a *chain!*—and broken into a store to get this food. There wasn't another cat feline enough to sneak in using such skills. He was the best!

His anger died at the idea of wasting good food. It wasn't the female's fault someone else had brought her nourishment before he could return. Someone else giving it to her did not diminish his skill or daring.

But someone else was muscling in on his philanthropy. Why should a talented cat go out of his way to help others if it wasn't appreciated because such charity came too late?

"A challenge," he purred. "A challenge to supply the best food. Fancy food from cans? I can equal or top that. I know I can."

Robie left, tail high as the idea of how to soothe his wounded pride took form. He walked into the street and looked up at the ten-story building. Getting to the top floors where the richest humans lived with their pampered slaves would not be too hard. Getting back down with the goods posed a huge problem.

I'm clever enough to solve it after I get the loot, he decided. Robie pressed against the warm brick building and glided around the corner bonelessly, waiting for the front door to open. After five minutes, he dropped to his belly and thrust his paws in front of him like an Egyptian god. Then he put his head down on his legs and went to sleep for another ten. His nose alerted him before he heard or saw the approaching human. Robie rose, stretched, and waited with seeming indifference, as if he expected a mouse to pass by. As the human fumbled in her purse for the keycard that electronically opened the door, he readied himself.

A quick gray blur, sinuous and twisting, he entered the apartment lobby without the human ever noticing. Robie thought about rubbing against her legs, but he restrained himself. Instead, he passed his paw over his forehead and the scent glands there, but did nothing to follow and mark the female. She was unscented—free-range human. He shook himself, having more important things to do than claim this woman as his property.

The elevator doors slid open, and she entered. Robie considered his chances, then decided he would be seen. Even if he wasn't spotted, worse things might happen. Trapped in that cage, unable to open the doors or move between floors, meant he was fair game for the Animal Control kidnappers. Of all the friends he had ever had, not a one had returned after the AC gangsters snatched them away. Other cats had told him stories about markers—RFIDs—implanted beneath their fur. Robie wanted to avoid being cornered or caged at all costs.

The elevator hissed upward on its magnetic drive. It caused his fur to stand on end. Robie slunk along the wall to get away from the elevator, staying close to the floor to avoid being seen on the ever-present security cameras. He had no idea who watched them all the time, but whoever did could howl for the AC kidnappers to come—and they would.

He worked his way around the small upstairs lobby, hardly more than a dim shadow moving toward an emergency door. The humans were meticulous about some things, if not their personal grooming. Marking exits with the white letters and red lights afforded him a way to get to the upper floors. Rich people always lived on upper floors. Robie came to the door with its single handle high up.

He had watched, and he had learned. Robie gathered his legs under him and launched himself with all his strength. He easily reached the handle. He quickly placed one paw on top of the other and swung down, his full weight bearing on the latch. For a moment he hung there, fearing that he wasn't heavy enough to open the door. Then he felt a metallic click, and the door swung away. With a quick midair twist, he landed on his feet in the stairwell.

Robie had entered a different world from the lobby, with its disinfectant smells and the constant inward rush of air from the street that ruffled fur and made his whiskers twitch. Here was a shaft of concrete quiet. He felt the distant throbbing of machines working lower in the building and took some solace from them. He barely remembered, but the rhythmic sound was like his mother's heart beating as he lay next to her. Scents were more vivid here, mustier and distinctive, but not unappealing.

Gingerly placing one paw on the metal step leading upward, he waited. The small vibration he'd made would not attract any human's attention. They were so isolated with their feeble hearing and puny senses of smell that he could walk past any but the most astute—or allergic. At that thought, Robie had to thrash his tail about in irritation.

How dare they start sneezing when I come into a room? I'm as clean as I possibly can be, living in the alley and fending for myself. And others.

Robie stopped when he reached the top of the stairs. Getting through this door would be a little easier since the silver panic bar would yield to a good leap. He had to try three times before the lock snapped open and his weight carried the door inward just enough for him to get through. Landing on soft feet, he sniffed and then began walking down the middle of the corridor as if he owned the building. The scents coming to him were heady and confusing, but he quickly found where a cat resided. Stepping back and looking up convinced him there was no easy way inside. The complicated lock on the door was meant to keep everyone out.

He lightly jumped to a table at the end of the hallway and poked his nose at a window. It took several minutes for him to figure out how to get a paw underneath the partly opened window and lift it enough to slip under. Robie glanced out and down. Ten stories. The street below was filled with the smelly, noisy machines humans dashed around in rather than depending on their own legs. Stride sure, he walked along the six-inch wide ledge, went around the corner and admired the stone gargoyle set at the corner. He rubbed against that corner to scratch just the right spot on the middle of his forehead.

Purring, he continued his exploration and immediately found the window to the apartment where he had scented another cat. Opening this window would take a little more skill since there was a motor attached. His quick claw caught at a wire, and he stopped. The motor and a burglar alarm were already disconnected. Someone had made it too easy for him. The window opened easily, and he jumped down on feather-light feet to explore.

He inhaled deeply and caught the female's scent. A pang of worry almost caused him to reverse his course and leap for the window. The entire apartment had been marked as property by the other cat, but it was such a beguiling scent that he had to continue his exploration. He found the female's bed and poked his nose under the soft blanket.

How decadent. She actually sleeps on a blanket!

Robie continued poking around but did not find where the female must be napping, although signs of her presence were everywhere. Toys. Fancy feather toys that looked like birds dangled from rubber bands. Robie had to bat at one, enjoying the feel of his claw taking off a feather.

She doesn't get to hunt real birds, he realized. He felt a little sad for her. Then anger grew at her decadent lifestyle.

He turned a corner. A bowl filled with refrigerated water from a humming electrical unit waited for her. Beside this fountain of pure elixir was her china food bowl. He sniffed and knew he had to find the pantry. The food that had been delicately lapped from this bowl was gourmet quality. The kittens would benefit from it when their mother dined in style.

I'll show that mangy interloper who can provide the best food for a mother and her kittens!

Robie prowled about and stopped to stare when he found the litter box. Tiny yellow plastic fingers waited at the rear of a veritable sea of litter. He stepped into the box and the urge to urinate and excrete overcame him. A few quick scratches buried the evidence, but when he jumped out a growling sound caused him to spin, arch his back, and hiss.

The yellow fingers stroked forward, finding the clumps he had left and whisking them away into a trough that somehow closed. The fingers retreated and once more the litter was clean and the automated box waited for the next visit. Robie had to shake his head at such opulence—and restrain himself from using it again. He lowered his back and let his fur return to normal as he continued to prowl.

A few quick sniffs led him to the pantry. The door stood ajar. A quick paw opened it all the way. He let out a yowl of pure delight when he saw a plastic bag already loaded with food. Opening the cans would be easy enough but getting them down ten stories without being seen presented a problem.

He dragged the loot from the pantry and then looked around the apartment. It took a few minutes to pull down a feather bird on its rubber band. He tucked that into the bag, then batted toys into it from all the rooms. The kittens would be playing with them soon.

A kitten does not live by milk alone, he told himself, grinning. Robie continued to scout the apartment and finally jumped onto a table by the door laden with pictures. The humans did not impress him. They were all the same, but the 3-D picture of the human holding a Siamese stopped him dead in his tracks. Pressing his nose so close his whiskers rubbed the frame, he studied the blue-eyed, purebred Siamese.

His heart raced. Never had he seen a female so appealing. Robie rubbed his chin against the picture and purred. He bumped his head against the frame and sent the picture tumbling to the floor. The glass shattered into a thousand pieces but the picture remained intact. Lightly dropping to the floor, he stepped through the glass and rubbed against the picture again. Now that the frame mechanism had broken, it only gave a 2-D image. Robie carefully put his paw on the human's face and caught the edge of the picture with his teeth. A toss of his head tore the picture so that he carried the lovely female and the human remained on the floor.

Robie added the picture to his treasure trove in the kitchen, then sat and stared at the bag. He would definitely be a legend when he returned to the alley with this. He could pass out food to more than the mother and her litter. Any stray cat wanting food could dine like a prince.

Like the princess that lives here, he added. Robie looked around the apartment once more, wondering where the Siamese was. Kept cats lived longer but only at the whim of capricious humans. Had her human taken the lovely Siamese to the pound? Why, he couldn't say, but what they did was always a mystery.

Deciding the Siamese still lived here—scent and incredible toys and food and refrigerated drinking water proved it—he slid his head through the handle on the bag and began his slow progress to the window. It took all his strength and cunning to rearrange the chairs and tables so he could make the ascent to the window ledge in easy steps when, otherwise unburdened, he could have easily jumped.

Robie peered down into the street, then edged outside. The ledge was hardly wide enough for the bag he dragged. More than once he had to stop and use back paws and even his tail to keep the bag securely on the ledge. If it slipped, he would find himself with a noose around his neck ten stories up. Such a fall would eat up all nine of his lives. He wasn't sure how many were left, anyway, since he hadn't kept count.

Carefully putting his feet down two at a time, Robie walked along the ledge. His confidence grew with every step. This was going so well. Then it happened.

The ledge gave scant warning that it was at the breaking point. Without his weight as well as the loot on it, the ledge might have remained in place for many more years. As he stepped, the concrete made a grinding noise that caused him to rear backward onto his hind legs just as it tore free. The concrete tumbled down to the street below. Robie found himself on his hind legs like a human, fighting to keep his balance.

With a deft twist, he turned and flopped belly-down on his stolen treasure.

Now what do I do?

Robie arched his back and started to step across the bag he was dragging when he felt the distinctive tremors, like the one that had preceded the other part of the ledge collapsing. Scrambling fast, Robie got over the sack with its food as the spot where his hind feet had been crumbled.

He let out a screech that turned into a strangled whine when the bag tumbled down with the ledge. His feet were on solid ledge but the sack's two handles strangled him. The weight around his neck pulled him flat. Robie chanced a quick look ten stories down. Cats had survived such a fall.

I won't make the fall at all. I'm too good for that!

All he had to do was lower his head and let the sack fall. Determination hardened within his mind. That would be a breach of duty. His honor would be gone. How could any proud cat hold his head up after losing such good food?

With a snort of determination, he heaved hard and strained to stand. The bag dangled under him. Robie began retracing the path he had already traversed, his neck muscles knotting from the exertion. When he reached the corner with the gargoyle, an idea came to him. He used its stony skull as a lever to pull up the bag. He turned around, got all four feet against the far side of the gargoyle, and pushed hard. The sack inched upward and then flopped down once more on the ledge.

Am I THE cat! Robie purred with pleasure. He had done more than survive. He had kept his loot from getting away from him. Neck stiff and chafed, he passed the open window. Robie took a final deep whiff of her scent and pushed on.

Uncertain where he was going, Robie circled the building until he saw it. A rope dangled from a pulley on the roof. Exhausted from hauling the bag behind him, he judged distances and wondered if the rope would extend all the way to the ground. Why else would it be here? The crazy humans always did things impulsively, but he had to give them one thing. They built apartments and bridges well.

Robie got his back feet under him, estimated the distance, then leaped powerfully. His front claws raked the end of the rope, scrambling for purchase. When his claws caught hold, he felt himself falling. Fast. Faster. He swung close to the rope and dug in his back claws, making sure he had maximum grip.

And the rope ran faster and faster, taking him toward the ground. He looked down and then back up. He had fallen six stories. Seven.

With a twitch, he let the bag of food fall free. He caught sight of the picture he had stolen. Although it wasn't in 3-D and lacked the proper scent, he felt his heart twitch. Then he reacted with the full speed of his feline reflexes. Jumping from the rope wasn't easy since there wasn't anything to push away against, but he succeeded in landing in a Dumpster atop piles of trash.

He sank to the bottom, claws working hard to halt his descent. Then he fought to surface in the sea of garbage and stood for a moment, triumphant, on the metal edge before hopping down to paw through the fallen bag. Some of the food cans had burst open. He made sure the picture wasn't soiled, then began dragging the loot to a spot where he could jump onto a box and let out his "Come and get it!" yowl.

Within a few minutes a dozen stray cats crowded close.

"Eat up. Enjoy yourselves," he called. Robie watched in satisfaction as the scrawny cats, some with ribs poking against their fur, hungrily ate what he had brought.

He shouldered a couple aside and found unopened cans. Using a quick claw and a push with his other paw, he opened these for his adoring crowd, too. Then he gathered the feathered toys and batted then around, deciding on which he liked best. These he gave to the mother with her kittens.

"You're so good to me, Robie," the female said, pushing aside what he had brought. "But the other cat's already brought all the toys we can use. More food, too."

Robie's fur rose.

"The other cat?"

"You didn't think you were the only savior for us in this alley, did you?"

He howled loudly and turned away, angry. Not only did this interloper give food, he also supplied toys and other things that made life just a little better in the alley. Robie found one stray who remained after the feast to bat an empty food can around. He listened to its clanging as it struck a brick wall and rebounded.

"You get food from the other cat?" Robie asked.

"Sure, we all do. Usually better than you get us, but this time, well, you outdid yourself," the stray said, taking one last sniff at the licked-clean can before strutting off, tail high.

Robie flopped onto his belly and fitfully groomed himself. What was the use of risking his life to get food for the starving when they didn't care? Worse, they gave all the credit to another cat who furnished even better food.

Looking up at the tall apartment building, Robie felt a surge of determination. He hissed and stood, arching his back. The anger wasn't at the recipients of his charity or even at the other cat who always trumped his largesse, but at the humans. Forcing decent cats to starve in alleyways was terrible. If any of Robie's wards—and he had to think of them as such—strayed too far from this alley, Animal Control would swoop down on them. Those few who returned would carry RFIDs to constantly trace them. More than a simple ID implanted beneath their fur, the chips tracked and charted, spied and probably even listened into conversations.

It was the humans' fault. Cats ought to be free to roam as they chose, climb trees, and daintily pick through garbage unhindered. Robie remembered the last time he had climbed a tree, and snarled. The humans' park a few blocks away had become a deathtrap for stray cats: Animal Control prowled through it like packs of dogs. He had ventured over there a few months ago and had almost been caught in one of their traps.

Robie wasn't sure, but he thought that moment when the trap closed prematurely was when he had vowed to never let another cat go hungry if he could help it.

He looked at the picture of the Siamese and batted it about until he got it standing upright against the building wall. It had been so alive when it was in its frame and in 3-D, but it had also shared half with a human. The human had looked at the Siamese as a slave. No matter how fine the prison, that apartment was still a prison.

Refrigerated drinking water!

The thought of such a sweet-smelling Siamese in that pleasure prison caused his tail to ruff. Robie stretched until his back arched high, then he set off again for that apartment with only a quick look back to the picture for inspiration.

He wasn't sure what he was going to do, but at the least he could get more food for the alley strays. There had been all kinds of cans in that pantry, enough for a dozen cats. Robie purred as he thought of actually seeing the Siamese too, even if he had to dodge her human to do it. He threaded his way through the maze getting back into the stairwell. This time he knew better than to waste time in the hall, and went directly to the window leading out onto the ledge that would take him around the building to another open window.

As he stepped out, he inhaled, and froze. The faintest whiff came to him. He was close to the Siamese. Robie turned around and studied the window. *This is an air-conditioned building*. The temperature was set a little low for his taste. *So why is a window open?*

He shrugged it off. A crusading feline like him deserved luck now and then. Robie curled around the corner and went directly to the open window. The scent of the female came stronger now.

She's home!

Robie slipped into the apartment and sampled the air in all directions, looking for humans and listening for another cat. Curiously, he did not hear her. He jumped to the floor and made his way to the pantry. Her scent here was stronger.

"You're in the pantry. Getting food?" Robie flicked out his paw, pulling open the door. It was dark inside, but he saw as easily as he did outside.

"Are you in here?"

The words barely purred past his lips when he heard a quick padding behind him. He started to turn, only to be bowled over. He rolled into the pantry and came to his feet. Too late!

The door clicked shut.

"You should never have come back," came a voice as pleasant as he had imagined. "It's not right that you steal food from my lady."

"What's your name? I saw your picture."

"I know. You broke the frame."

Robie dropped to his belly and thrust his paws out under the pantry door. She touched one paw tentatively from the other side. He purred.

"You tore the picture in half, too."

"I wanted a picture of you. I'm Robie."

"I . . . oh, why am I doing this? I'm Grace."

"Grace," he said, letting the name slip out slowly, lovingly. "A name befitting you. All Siamese are graceful."

"Not all," she said. "I want you to promise never to come in here again. You'll ruin everything."

"Ruin?" Robie yanked his paw back. "Do you need so much food?"

"Of course not. My human spoils me, but you can't steal it. It will cause problems."

"Problems," Robie snarled. "What do you know of problems in your fine nest at the top of an expensive building? You've got water that comes from a *cooler*. You don't have any problems."

"I have a conscience. Don't you?"

"Are you going to starve if I take another bag of your food?"

"Why'd you come back?" Grace sounded peeved now. Her words almost hissed at him. This made Robie all the angrier at her.

"For you." He hesitated, then added, "For more food."

"All right, enough of this. I've got you trapped. If you promise to leave and not come back, I'll let you go free."

"You'll give me my freedom?" he scoffed. "I'm free. You're the one in a prison. It's a posh one, but you're the captive held by fancy food, clever toys, and chilled water."

"Promise."

Robie paced around inside the pantry, knocking over things and creating a ruckus. When some of his anger passed, he went back and flopped by the door.

"What if I don't?"

"My lady will find you and turn you over to Animal Control."

Robie heard just a tremor of fear in Grace's threat.

Is that because she wants me?

"Let me out and we can talk this over."

"You have to promise to leave and never come back. You'll get us both into big trouble."

"I can stay in here for a long time," Robie said. He batted a can of food off a low shelf and used his claw to pop it open. The fragrance intoxicated him. He was sure Grace smelled it, too, and knew what he was doing.

"You're incorrigible!"

"How sweet of you to say that." Robie sampled the canned food and wondered how Grace stayed so thin. If he had food like this available, he would eat until he exploded. Going to sleep with his chin on the food bowl would be the next thing to heaven. It would be heaven if Grace were beside him.

"Someone's coming! Oh, it's too late!"

Robie's ears perked up when he heard a grinding sound and muffled curses. Grace's human seemed particularly clumsy. He puzzled over the noise a moment longer, then heard two humans speaking in rough voices.

"We might get more for the cat than anything else in this dump."

"Shut up and help me open the safe. Who wants to steal a damned cat? The grinder's not taking off the lock like it's supposed to."

"The cat's a purebred, I tell you. My ex raised 'em. Worth a fortune. Maybe more than the cheap ass knickknacks around here."

"Help me get this safe open!"

Robie heard Grace let out a squeal of anger. He slammed himself against the pantry door and backed off. The door was too solid and the lock too secure for him to barrel through. He stepped back, then jumped to a high shelf so he was level with the knob. Opening this was easy for a cat accustomed to breaking and entering. His claws left deep scratches on the knob as he gripped, dropped with his full weight and turned. The snap lock opened and the door swung wide.

"Damn, look at that. Another cat's—"

This was as far as the burglar got before Grace clawed his face. Robie saw blood spray from the triple wound she left on his cheek. Hitting the floor running, Robie shot forward and leaped, claws working furiously at the man's groin. Between this attack and Grace's quick paws, the man had met his match. Grace hit the floor and spun about, shoulder to shoulder with Robie.

"These aren't your humans," Robie said. It wasn't much of a guess.

"Thieves."

"Not my kind," Robie said. "They steal and keep it for themselves." He looked around. The injured burglar swung a short pry bar back and forth to keep them away. The other one fumbled with a cloth bag. Robie judged how difficult it would be to add a few more claw marks to the first human's face and maybe take a bite out of his worthless pink hide.

Grace looked at him curiously, then turned toward the open window.

"Follow me," she said.

"Anywhere," Robie answered. They jumped to a table but did not go out the window. Grace hesitated long enough to claw at a small gray box.

"Now." She sinuously moved, a blur of cream fur, out onto the ledge as the two burglars began arguing. Robie was immediately behind her.

"You set off the alarm, didn't you?"

"I had disabled it and left the window open."

"Why?"

"We need to get down. Those two are going to fight like cornered rats."

"I've fought cornered rats," Robie boasted.

"I'm sure you have," Grace said, looking back at him. He caught the twinkle in her bright blue eyes. They were slightly crossed, but he had never seen more beautiful ones. Ever.

"How do we get off the ledge without going back into the room?" Robie doubted the rope and pulley would provide a way to the ground a second time.

"How brave are you?" Grace stopped at the corner of the building just past a gargoyle. Without another word, she jumped out into space.

Robie howled and hurried to where she had stood only an instant before. Then he saw what she had done. Grace leaped out toward a flag pole, caught the rope and swung around, landing on a ledge two stories below. She looked up at him, waiting.

He never hesitated. For an instant he thought he had jumped too far, then his claws caught the tattered rope and he was afraid it wouldn't hold his weight. Robie swung back and forth once before letting go. He had to scramble to join Grace on the ledge.

"That was fun," he said, not sure if he meant it.

Grace turned and walked way haughtily. A window was open just enough for them to slip under, letting them into the building again.

"From here it's easy getting out." Grace showed him a niche at the corner that led into the stairwell.

They raced to the ground floor, Robie barely beating her.

Out of breath, they flopped on the concrete and enjoyed the coolness on their bellies. Robie hopped to his feet and found Grace's way out of the stairwell—another small niche. He wondered how he had missed these design flaws on his first excursion into the building. Within minutes he was out on the street and racing for the alley.

Sirens sounded in the street and caused him to hunker

down. The human-infested Animal Control machines rolled up with red and blue lights flashing. Grace's alarm had reached the right ears.

He walked down the alley, howling to gather the stray cats. They looked at him with new respect, as if they knew what he had done. The mother cat perked up, and her kittens looked at him, eyes open wide.

"You bring us more food?" the mother asked.

Before Robie could answer, Grace said, "Not this time. Soon."

Robie spun on Grace.

"You were bringing your own food to them," he said, realization dawning on whom he had been competing with to furnish food to the needy.

"Don't be silly. Of course not. My lady would notice right away and put me on a strict diet if a lot of food was missing. That's why I didn't want you stealing my food. I steal from others in the building."

"You were the one who left the windows open so you could get in and out."

"I disarmed the alarm, too, but I had to turn it back on." Grace craned her neck to see the two burglars being led out of the apartment building and put into the noisy machines.

"Are you going to keep bringing food to the stray cats?" Robie asked.

"Am I? No," Grace said.

"Why not?" Robie waited for the answer he hoped to hear. And he did.

"*We* are."

He rubbed up against her and purred loudly. What a pair they'd make!

THE SCENT OF DEATH

Elizabeth A. Vaughan

One took the blow on the back legs and was tossed off to the side of the black expanse. The noxious scent of the human's rolling death faded from the night air even as the rumble faded from the earth. One lay still, in the moment. Perhaps the damp seeping into one's fur from below was just tainted water.

Or so one could hope.

The pain hit between one breath and the next. The blow had been glancing, but it had sufficed. Dazed, numb, all this one could do was pant. The cold bit through too-thin flesh and ragged fur. One should not have tried to cross the black expanse; others had died trying. But the prey was fat and slow on the other side . . .

There had been too few kills in recent days, and the scent of snow was in the air. One did not have the strength to recover from this blow, and it made little difference. Eyes closed, this one waited for the pain to end. The scent of Death was in the air.

Soft paws padded close. Death came quietly to this one's side, sleek and silent.

It was time. One was grateful for surcease to come.

"There is a task that needs to be done."

Not quite what this one expected Death to say. Forcing pain-dulled eyes to focus, one saw a sleek brown tabby sitting close beside.

Golden eyes gleamed in the night. "Do this task, and receive aid."

"Or die?" One hissed, and then regretted it as the ribs grated, causing more pain.

"Or die." The other confirmed with a flick of an ear pierced with gold.

That One was not Death. A twitch of whiskers and a breath through one's open mouth brought the scent of burning sands, bright suns, and the weight of a thousand lives. Her name was not to be spoken lightly. "Lady Guardian, death is not feared."

"Regardless," She purred. "The task needs doing."

One closed one's eyes. This life or the next, it mattered little. "Lady, I will do it."

Voices then. Human voices and hands. Lifting this one, with warm cloths that smelled of calm. Pain flared at the movement, but one endured and did not lash out. One caught a glimpse of the Lady, still seated, poised and calm, her tail wrapped around her paws. "Rest," came her purr.

This one obeyed.

The damp expanse became a warm room with many humans. Things were done to this one that one does not choose to recall. All indignities were suffered patiently. One had a task to fulfill, after all.

Strength returned, but not freedom. One has seen others through windows, who spoke of warm laps and sweet feedings, but one had wondered at the price. One now knew the cost, but it was just as well. There had been many long, empty hunts and cold nights. The cage was metal, but the cloths were clean and warm. Food appeared, waste disappeared. Scratches of the head and neck were frequent, and many kind voices.

Time passed, and the cage opened to allow one to roam within. Thanks were expressed in the traditional ways, with swipes and purrs and nose kisses. One found the price of comfort to be bearable, as one watched the snow fall outside.

Words were used, such as "good kitty" and "gentle soul." Names were called, for it seems that humans are obsessed with names. One sensed that decisions were being made, but one was untroubled. The Lady held one's life now, and She would do Her will in Her own time.

One waited, patient.

The time came when one was lifted, collared, and taken to a new place. A warm place that smelled of waiting. One twitched one's whiskers and peered out of the moving cage, uncertain. There were smells of resignation, sorrow, and illness, and the faintest scent of Death.

A brown-skinned human looked within and greeted this one in a soft voice. Taken into a room, one emerged from the cage to step on papers and scattered sticks. One particularly liked sticks. A quick bat, and it flew from the surface to land on the floor. One sat, tail wrapped around quick paws and was pleased.

"Bastet."

This one turned, ears perked, eyes wide, surprised to hear a version of the Lady's name on the lips of a human. The brown-skinned woman chuckled in a warm voice, even as she bent to retrieve her stick. And so it was that this one was named by the alpha female of the place of waiting.

The humans obeyed their alpha, and called this one by one of Her sacred names in the days that passed. One was uncomfortable at first, and waited to be punished for this audacity. But punishment never came. So this, too, must be part of the Lady's will.

As She wished.

The patterns of the place were learned quickly and accepted. Humans came and went, tending other humans that lay in large expanses of softness, each in its own room. One wandered the halls, careful of those that traveled in small rolling deaths. They did not smell, but one watched one's tail closely and took great care nonetheless.

Many feeble hands stroked and scratched, with words of praise. One twined carefully between legs and purred, proud to be a source of consolation. The rhythms of the days were pleasant and unchanging.

One also enjoyed the quiet times in the place of the alpha. The brown-skinned woman spent a great deal of time staring at her box and scratching at papers with her sticks. One sat with her and purred. One was content.

Until one night, when the Death stalked within and claimed a human that lay in softness.

Noise and confusion filled the place. Tears and disarray resulted. Disorder in this one's ordered world. It was unpleasant. One was not fed on time, and the waste did not disappear. Even the alpha was perturbed.

It took time for the patterns to settle only to have it happen again, and again. Each time, the scent of Death was in the air well before the human was taken. Each time the humans reacted in surprise.

Was it possible that *they did not know*?

One almost fell off one of the high counters at the very idea. To have no warning? To not scent Death on the air? To fear it? Even *prey* knows.

This was a jest, a bad one. Such a thing could not—

"*They do not know.*"

One was not so proud as to believe that She would speak

so, within the depths of one's mind. So this one pulled within oneself and contemplated the humans as they went to and fro. Curled and silent, one watched the rhythms of the place of waiting, the comings and the goings, and the deaths of the ones that lay in softness. Each time, there was the scent within the halls. Each time Death stalked. Each time, the humans were taken by surprise.

They did *not* know.

Poor creatures. Was not life hard enough?

One hid beneath the alpha's place of sticks, on the warm box. One contemplated, eyes half closed and paws curled in. One finally concluded that the humans did not scent Death's approach and therefore could not prepare, could not antici-pate. One wondered at their deficiencies.

"Bastet, you okay?"

One blinked to see the alpha leaning down, staring be-neath into one's place of concealment. One was warmed by her concern and emerged with a long stretch and a loud purr, to offer reassurance.

For the Lady is a Guardian, and She had placed one here to serve. Disruption was not to be tolerated. One now knew one's task and was prepared.

So it was that the next time the scent of Death was on the air, one perched on the corner of the softness, where the human in question lay. One waited, patiently.

In walked one of the humans, with their things, and ex-pressed surprise at this one's presence.

One howled. Loudly. Not the soft greeting, not the cry of anger, no this was the yowl of attention, the lower note that carried a warning.

"Lord in heaven, what's wrong?"

"Sophie, what was the noise?" In walked the alpha, as one had hoped.

"I have no idea. I walked in to get Ms. Martin's temperature, and Bastet howled to wake the dead."

"Then why isn't Ms. Martin awake?"

Their attention focused on the human in the softness. It was but a moment before the alpha spoke. "Call the Doctor, Sophie. I think Ms. Martin is starting to slip away from us."

Satisfied, one jumped down and padded from the room.

In this regard one served for some time, but eventually the mere fact that one was perched on the edge of the softness was enough to let those who also served know that Death stalked. Once in a great while, they fought back. But for the most part, death was welcomed and the warning gratefully received. With time to prepare, all was orderly. There was still sorrow, to be sure. But life is sorrow, even for a human.

So, one served, and served well.

Until one night, Death appeared with no warning, glaring at this one. "What do you think you are doing?"

One half opened an eye to contemplate Him. As the Lady took the guise of a cat, so this one took the guise of a human, dressed in black and pale. One did not even twitch a whisker.

"One serves."

"Well, you can damn well stop."

One rose and stretched slowly, carefully, and then settled in to groom one's nether regions.

"Cats." Death said in disgust, and disappeared.

The laughter of the Lady Guardian sounded deep within in one's head.

One continued to groom, smugly.

So it was, that the pattern of life was restored. The alpha praised this one, and there was a new food, called treats, and that was well.

Others came and made a fuss over this one, but one fled

them and their "cameras" and "microphones." One was not amused. One had a task. The alpha sent them away.

Outside, the leaves emerged, and one watched as the prey danced outside the glass, young and old alike. One felt no need to hunt but would occasionally make the hunting sounds and bat the glass, scattering those without. It served no purpose to allow prey to become complacent.

Nor can one become complacent about Death. He is everywhere and nowhere, and one should have remembered that. It was not just the humans lying in softness that needed warning.

One blames oneself for one's failing, but the scent grew over time, creeping in as prey rots. Until finally the odor was too strong to be ignored.

But this scent lay on the alpha.

One sat straight up at the realization and fixed the alpha with a stare. This was not one who lay in softness, yet the scent was there, unmistakable. Warning must be given, but would she comprehend?

One leaped to her place, ignored the sticks that lay about, and padded over. The alpha was staring at her box. "You hungry, Bastet? I'll feed you in just a minute. I have to get these reports out—"

One yowled.

The Alpha's head jerked around to stare at one, her dark eyes wide. "Bastet, what's wrong? Who—?"

One yowled again, staring at her intently, with a soft prayer to the Lady Guardian that this human would fall within her protection. The sound that rose from this one's throat grew more anxious, for the alpha was respected and admired. Let Death stalk elsewhere.

The alpha's eyes grew thoughtful. She reached for her phone, speaking of lumps ignored and an appointment. She grabbed up her things, turned off her box, and left.

One batted at the sticks, arranged the papers to one's satisfaction, and settled for a nap. One had done what one could do.

Death appeared.

One opened one's eyes and contemplated the man, all in black, glaring at oneself. Had he been a cat, his back would have been arched, ears flat. "You go too far."

"Are you prey?" one demanded.

"What?" Death hissed.

"Are you prey, to leave your scent markings so clear and make the hunt easy?" One flicked an ear. "Lazy, foolish prey, easily tracked and seen. No wonder—"

"SILENCE," the man thundered.

One yawned, displaying all one's teeth, unimpressed and uncaring.

"Cats." Death snarled, and vanished.

One stood, stretched and circled down to nap. The hunt would be more challenging now, the scent harder to find. It was well. None should become complacent.

Even Death.

The Lady Guardian's satisfied purr filled one's ears as one drifted off to sleep.

THE PERSIAN, THE COON, AND BULLETS

Matthew Woodring Stover

She was screaming. She'd been screaming for a while already. I'd been hearing her since Farside of Leaper's Bridge, so naturally by the time I made it to Knifewall, there was already a pretty good mob. It took me longer than usual, because I had to make a wide detour around a human gun fight—the Same Clothes People and the Calico People, at it again, as usual—and around the blast zone of the Calicoes' exploder, where there was too much fire and stink even for a hardened street tom like me.

She had a serious voice, one I'd been able to hear even through the humans' shouts and shooting, and I was a long way from the only one listening; the mob at Knifewall was the biggest I'd ever seen—I knew maybe only half the cats there, maybe less. She was pulling them in from all over the Zone.

"I'm *hungry*! It's *cold* out here! Where *are* you? I'm *hunnnnngry!*"

I spotted the Coon lounging in a weedy shadow near Knifewall's sunside corner, wiping his face with a spit-wet paw. He saw me looking and yawned. I shouldered through the crowd to the base of the wall so I'd have some shade on my way over. Nobody gave me more than a courtesy hiss.

The cats who didn't know me took their cue from the ones who did, and got the hell out of my way.

"Hey, Coon." I settled into the weeds just out of reach. The Coon and I had a pretty good understanding, but there was no sense taking foolish chances.

He kept washing. "Drags. You want something here?"

This was as close to a respectful greeting as anybody ever got from the Coon. He didn't even have a name; everybody called him the Coon because that's what he was, a Maine Coon, more than half bobcat, fully four times the size of your average street tom. He was a legend in the Zone. He and I had gone some rounds back when I was a little younger and a lot stupider, and while he had given better than he got—he's near enough twice my size, and I'm a big damn cat—he still carried a scar or two with my name on them. I liked to think he had some respect for me. But I was probably kidding myself.

When I was younger, I used to dream that maybe the Coon was my sire. Getting my belly good and ripped cured me of any pretensions to noble lineage. He'd made it clear that if I'd been his kit, he'd have snatched me out from under my dam and eaten my head. And he might have been telling the truth. The rumor was he'd done it before. Rumor was, he never let a tom kit live. And, y'know, that was okay with pretty much everybody.

One of him was enough.

I tilted my face sidelong toward the yowling beyond Knifewall. "That what I think it is?"

The Coon looked away and flicked one ear. "We'll see. Skids is on his way up."

I shook my head at the mob of toms lurking around the wall. "Likely be sanguinary come nightfall."

"Sangwinwhatthehell?" This from Hacky, creeping up by my tail. Hacky had been sidling along in my wake as he usually did, pretending to hunt a beetle, but he wasn't any better at pretending than he was at hunting, and he did both of those better than he kept his mouth shut. "Drags? How come you use all them big words nobody knows? I mean, what's that sangwi-somethin' mean, Drags? Hey, Coon—Coon, you don't know either, huh?"

The Coon just kept washing. He had a good vocabulary—better than mine, I bet, that giant head of his leaves plenty of room for brains—but he didn't like showing it off. Especially not in front of dogbait like Hacky. Why show off when you're the king?

"You'll find out what it means," I told him. "And back off from my tail, Hacky. I won't say it again."

He flinched. "Sure—sure, Drags. I don't mean nothin' by it, you know that. You know I'm not gonna start somethin'. Not with you."

"Which is why I haven't eviscerated your face, you follow?"

"Sure—uh, yeah, I mean, I *think* so—"

"Shut up." The Coon stood up and stretched, looking toward the rim of Knifewall. "There goes Skids."

Knifewall is three or four times taller than my best jump, and that's just the stone part; even if I could get up there—which would be damn hard for me in itself, what with my tail how it is—I'm still way too big to slip through the tangled coils of knife-wire that added another good leap's-worth on top. Skids, though, was small as a kit, and a scrawny one at that; some Siamese blood on his dam's side kept him trim and quick. He was agile as a wolf spider and could run faster than most cats can think. He'd clawed his way up the pale shrapnel scars that pocked the outside of the wall and now delicately threaded his way into the knife-wire until he could see over the lip into Inside.

"Ohhhh, *yeahhhh*!" he howled. "Oh, damn my balls! It's her! It really is! Oh, *wowww*!"

That was too much for the mob. They all started singing back to her. *Come out here, kitten! I'll keep you warm! Hey, baby, if you're that hungry, I got somethin' to feed ya! We're right outside, sweetheart—come on out and join the party!*

"Her?" Hacky looked confused. Or maybe just stupid. How do you tell the difference? "Her who?"

"The Persian." The Coon shook himself, and stretched again, and started to saunter off toward the river. "I'm gone."

"The *Persian?* For real? The Persian's *out?*" Hacky had his tongue half out of his mouth, flemming as if she were presenting right in front of him. "Is it true what they say about Persians? You think?"

I got up. "Coon—you're leaving? Are you *non compos*?"

"She ain't even in heat."

"Sure she is, Coon," Hacky said, still flemming so hard he was starting to drool. "Persians is *always* in heat. That's what they say. Ain't that what they say, Drags?"

"No objections here, if you're going, but I admit to feeling, well—" I didn't have a handy mouthful of word, but I didn't need one. The Coon knew what I was talking about.

"Don't like crowds, kit." But if that were the real reason, he'd have stalked off without bothering to answer. Looked to me like he was trying to talk himself out of something. Or into it. "And this ain't my territory."

"Feculation, Coon, it's *nobody's* territory."

"Not cat territory. You know whose it is."

"I do?"

"You if anybody."

"You mean Bullets." Just saying his name gave me a low, slow shock that started from the back like I'd got my crippled tail dipped in icewater. I had to sit down and think a second or two to figure out how I felt about this.

"Bullets?" Hacky had gone all hushed and wide-eyed. "I heard he was dead."

"He ain't."

"Okay," I said. "So it's Bullets."

"You did that pretty good, kit. Almost like you ain't scared."

"It's been a while." I mostly ignored the frozen ache from the base of my tail. "Is he still a bachelor?"

"Nope." The Coon's eyes slitted, as if he were thinking of ripping me one for suggesting he'd so much as ruffle his scruff over a bachelor. "He's gone alpha. Mobbed up."

"His own mob? Oh, that can't be good," Hacky moaned. "Hey, Drags—wasn't you the cat who—"

"Yeah, that was me."

"And he's the dog that got you by the—"

"Shut up." This from the Coon. He gave me a look that from another cat, I might have thought was sympathy. "You're thinking, Drags. I can see you thinking."

"I'm thinking," I agreed. "I'm thinking sunshadow's growing. I'm thinking Bullets and this new mob of his'll be on the hunt by half-light. And I'm thinking that this is not necessarily a bad thing. For us."

"For cats?" Hacky looked as puzzled as a kitten chasing his first spotting laser. "I don't see it."

"Not for cats," the Coon said slowly. "He means us as in *us*. Just us."

I cocked an eye up to where Skids was snarling a string of curses as he tried to back out of the tangles of knife-wire. "I mean," I said, slicking my right paw to smooth behind my ears, "that these gonad-brains have less chance of getting the Persian to come outside Knifewall than I have of dancing on the moon. I mean that when Bullets gets here, any cats stupid enough to still be mooning around this area will be on a balls-first trip down a dog gullet."

"But you know something?" Hacky said hopefully.

"I know Knifewall."

The Coon started to look interested. "You're from in there, ain't you?"

"Yeah."

The Coon favored me with the kind of look a few hundred birds and rats in the Zone had seen with the last light of their eyes. "You know how to get Inside?"

"Sure." I slicked my left, too, and swiped my other ear. "Wanna come?"

"You got it, right?" I confess to being a bit nervous. It was getting dark, and I could still hear the gun fight going on over toward Leaper's Bridge. "Both of you?"

We were at the fringe of the mob gathered at Knifewall's sweep-fence, which was as tall as the wall and had gaps in it just big enough for the humans to poke guns through if they felt like it, too small for a cat to squeeze through. But from here, the mob could *see* her, all stretched up to scratch the door of one of the Inside buildings, and they were going wild.

Hell, I was too. Long and plump and white as the moon, a giant cuddle-pillow of silken hair . . . but the sensuous ruffle and play of all that hair let you see a hint of the real muscle underneath. Sweet steaming *dog* turds, she was a beauty!

So I've always had a bit of a thing for Persians. So what? *Everybody* has a thing for Persians.

But she was on the far side of Knifewall's sweep-fence, and the humans standing Inside didn't look like they were inclined to open that fence for us any time soon.

I've never figured out why humans like sweep-fences (and sweep-doors) better than flip-doors or lift-doors; if I were a Making-Things creature instead of a Killing-Things creature, I'd make drop-doors, where they'd just slide right into the ground, and come back up to close. That's the only safe kind, because by the time they're up far enough that they might catch your tail, they're too high to jump up on anyway. But whatever.

"You just got to understand humans," I said, once I got my breath back. "That's the thing. You got to know how they think."

"Humans *think*?" The Coon sounded scornful, but he was listening.

"Sure they do. More or less. Look at the stuff they build—"

"Scat, Drags, *termites* build. Humans just have more complex instincts, that's all. Everybody knows they don't really *think*."

"Yeah, the Coon's right," Hacky chimed in. "That's just—what's the word, Drags? You know, the one where you think regular animals are almost like cats?"

"Ailuromorphism. But it's not. I didn't say humans are smart as cats—they're no smarter than dogs, if that. If they were *smart*, we'd be working for them instead of the other way around. Look, I know humans. I used to have some of my own."

Hacky's eyes went wide. "You useta be a *house* cat? What happened?"

I tilted an ear toward Knifewall. "I had a house on Knifewall's Inside. Got hit by a flying exploder. Just an accident—houses get hit by flying exploders every day, especially Inside, because of all the Same Clothes People. You know how Calico People and Same Clothes fight all the time? Well, some of the Calicoes' exploders can actually throw stuff through the air. You've seen 'em. They can throw stuff a long way—and sometimes what they throw is another exploder, and they're usually throwing them at the Same

Clothes. That's what hit my house. Killed both my people.
Their whole litter, too."

"Aww," Hacky sniffled.

"It was a long time ago."

"I hate it when animals get hurt. Even though I got none
of my own."

"Well, y'know, everything's a trade-off. A properly trained
human is a great pet, but they're a lot of work. Too many
house cats just let their people go feral—I mean, look at the
Zone, right? You think humans would kill each other all the
time if they'd been properly socialized?"

The Coon was getting bored. "How should I know?"

"Here's the thing about humans. In a lot of ways, they *are*
dogs. They run in packs, right? They associate by breed—
Same Clothes go with Same Clothes, Calicoes with Calicoes, Cleans with Cleans, Musties with Musties, you know
what I mean—they share food with each other, the whole
thing. But, best of all, they're creatures of *habit*."

"Habit?"

"It means they do predictable things at predictable times,
Hacky. You must have noticed. Same as a dog will take his
perimeter tour mostly the same times every day, and usually
in the same direction."

"Seems like a pretty stupid way to live."

"Sure, to us. But you have to remember, they're not cats.
It's a lot of work for a human to think things over and decide
what to do. So they just do over whatever they've done before.
Each human has his own pattern, wake up now, crap here, eat
then, y'know, whatever . . . but once they join a pack, they
take on the *pack's* habits."

"You're talking about wheelers," the Coon said. "That's
how you know the humans are about to open the swing-
fence."

"Every time there's a gun fight between here and Leaper's Bridge," I said. "Any time now."

Hacky looked around. Half-light had taken over the sky, and he was getting twitchy. "How do you know they'll be here before Bullets?"

"Easy. Hear the guns?"

He listened. So did the Coon. "No."

"That's how I know. In fact—" Being too dignified for any display of triumph, I only sighed like I was irretrievably bored. "—I hope you're ready, because here they come."

Getting Inside turned out to be the easiest thing I did all day. The mob of toms scattered when the first wheeler rolled up. It's a natural instinct—wheelers are loud, their face-lights are brighter than street lamps, they stink, and they'll crush you flat without even noticing you—but if you're just gonna follow your natural instincts, you might as well be a dog. Or a human.

I went first, but the Coon and Hacky, to their credit, were right behind me. Just as the swing-fence started to open we streaked through, which took some timing because the wheelers didn't even slow down. And when the humans started to push the swing-fence shut, the few toms brave enough to make a run at following us found the narrowing gap full of Coon.

He was puffed out double his already gigantic size, and his tail stood straight up, and he didn't even have to unleash that bobcat snarl of his because the other toms took one look at him and decided they had more important business on the Outside.

Which was more or less the reason I invited him along.

Knifewall's Inside was mostly how I remembered: a big cement meadow where the wheelers screeched to a halt, high stone-faced houses, that kind of stuff. But there had been some changes, which looked to be mostly the result of catastrophic remodeling courtesy of the Calicoes' flying exploders. The Bleach & Ammonia House—the one where feral humans took their hurt and dying packmates—had some major chunks of its front face missing, leaving ragged dark gaps like the eye sockets of a cat three days dead.

The face-lights of the wheelers cast so much glare that I couldn't see into the shadows, and the wheelers were still growling and the humans were shouting and carrying each other and generally creating so much confusion and commotion that I got separated from the Coon and Hacky, and I couldn't hear the Persian anymore. There was some blood on the ground, here and there, which reminded me how hungry I was, but I stayed away from it. Humans are funny about blood, and if they see you lapping at it sometimes they just snap and come at you with their boots. Sometimes they even shoot their guns at you, which is a lot scarier than you think it's going to be, up until it happens to you the first time.

So I mostly tried to stay out of their way and waited for the wheelers to settle down and shut off their lights, which left me hanging in a shadow at the corner of the sweepfence. I passed the time getting myself cleaned up, which is how I happed to be just sitting there when the first dog hit the fence.

He was big and he came fast and he hit hard enough to rattle the whole fence. "I can see you!" he shouted, jumping up and raking the metal with his forepaws. "*I can see you in there!*"

"Yeah? Can you smell me, too?" To help him out with the smelling part, I stood up and showed him my butt. If my tail had worked better, I would have given him a good close look at my anal glands and maybe a marking squirt in the eye, but I guess he got the point anyway.

"Gonna *kill* you! Gonna kill you and *eat* you!"

"Maybe in your next life, pooch." I sat down again and bit at a flea on my haunch, which made him even crazier, of course, and his shouts devolved into wordless yaps of fury, which brought more dogs at the gallop. I stayed where I was and didn't even bother to look as they threw themselves at the shivering fence; the more dogs hanging around out there, the less I had to worry about any more toms sneaking in to cramp my action.

I was making a pretty good show of nonchalance, right up until the barking stopped as though the whole mob'd had their throats slashed at once.

The silence brought up my scruff, and the voice that broke the silence brought up the rest of my back.

"That you in there, Drags?"

I didn't need to look around. I hear that deep, calm, bone-evil voice every day. In bad dreams.

"Drags, look at me when I'm talking to you."

With as much composure as I could summon, I turned toward him. I wanted to stalk carelessly away, but I knew that taking the first step would break my nerve and I'd be scuttling for the nearest storm drain like a sewer rat caught out in daylight. "Bullets," I said. "Been a while."

"Yes." He had the side of his vast dirty tan face pressed against the fence, his good eye gleaming black like fresh blood by moonlight. Even my nightmares had forgotten the sheer size of him—that great box-head of his alone was bigger than my whole body. He had a long, slow, quiet way of talking, almost like a giant cat. "How's the tail, Drags? That is what they call you now, isn't it? Because of what I did to your tail?"

"The tail's fine," I lied. I summoned enough false insouciance to sit, because if he watched me stand much longer, he'd see that my expressionless tone had more to do with how the severed muscle at the base of my tail had left me half-crippled than with any actual calm. "How's your eye?"

"Still gone," Bullets said. "And the socket hurts every time I think of you."

"Flatterer."

"Not as much as my mouth, though. And my stomach. They ache for you, Drags." His tongue was out now, and he was panting that canine thunderstorm of hunger, just as I remembered. "I'm drooling for you, Drags."

"You drool for everybody."

He chuckled, dark as midnight in an abandoned basement. "I know where you are, now. There's only one way out of there. When this fence opens, I'll be waiting."

"You do that," I told him. "Patience is a virtue, y'know."

"In cats." Bullets grinned at me. "So is flavor."

"I think I'm gonna be a house cat again. You want me, bitch, you might as well just whistle."

"You think," he said. "But I know."

"Know? What do you think you know?"

"I know what you're gonna find out, smart cat."

"Hey—hey *Drags*—" The hiss came from the shadows under a quiescent wheeler; sounded like the Coon. "Where's Hacky?"

"He was with you."

"He was with *you*."

I got up. Taunting Bullets was fun and all, but this was business. "You don't think—?"

"*Listen!*"

The wheelers had gone quiet. All I could hear was a few human voices from inside the Bleach & Ammonia House and the growing *thwop-wop-wop-wop* of descending thwoppers in-bound. And that's *all* I could hear.

The Persian had gone silent.

"That sneaky little scab-lapper!" I snarled. "Where *is* he?"

"That's what I'm askin' *you*."

"Dammit, she's not even in *heat* —!"

"Maybe Hacky was right. Maybe Persians're always in heat."

"I'll *kill* him."

"Something *wronnng*, Drags?" Bullets drawled. "Somebody messin' your game?"

I didn't even bother to reply, just trotted over toward the wheeler where the Coon crouched. The Persian had been in that doorway when the wheelers came in, right by that cul-de-sac where the humans kept their metal garbage boxes; if she ran from the wheelers like a normal cat, she might easily have ended up—

"Okay," I said. "Let's split up, Coon. You go that way— over behind the Bleach & Ammonia House, there's a garden where all the Inside cats go. Good mousing there, not to mention chipmunks and even some squirrels. I'll take this side—nothing much here, but after I check it out I can catch up—"

The Coon's great green eyes seemed to glow as they picked up the belly-lights of the thwoppers slowly dropping from the night sky. "I got an idea. We split up and *you* take the Bleach and Whatever, while *I* take Nothing Much."

I sighed. "Okay. We stick together."

Which was when, with a distant *bang* and a nearby *swoosh,* a streak of flame reached up from outside Knife-wall, hit the incoming thwopper, and the whole world exploded.

I don't remember much of what happened right after that. There were entirely too many explosions and gun shots and screaming people running and shooting and bleeding, and the wheelers were blowing up, and the thwopper was just a pile of burning junk in the asphalt meadow.

When it finally got quiet enough that I could think again, I found myself crouched flat under one of the humans' garbage boxes in the cul-de-sac. The garbage boxes had big wheels on them, which left plenty of room underneath one even for four pretty good-sized cats, of which I was one, the Coon was another, Hacky was one more . . .

And there was the Persian.

She was cowering next to Hacky, shivering, filthy with the rotting muck under the garbage box and stinking like week-old fish . . . and if it were up to me, I would have taken her by the scruff and done her right there in the muck, because she was just that hot. She really was. But it wasn't up to me, and it never will be.

"What's *happening?*" she moaned. "What *is* this?"

"That's what I want to know," the Coon growled, with a look at Hacky that made me really damn glad he wasn't looking at me.

"Nothing, Coon!" Hacky squeaked. "Honest! I was just—I was just showing her where to get something to *eat*, that's all."

"He's very sweet," the Persian said. "Not like the other toms."

"The *other* toms?" The Coon and I exchanged ear-flattened looks. Nobody likes finding himself pushed toward the back of a line.

"I've heard," she said carelessly. "Ooh, my coat! What you must think of me, meeting me like this!"

The Coon grunted. "You think anybody cares what you *look* like?"

"You're *horrible!*" She had already snaked away from Hacky, closer to him. "What a brute you are—you must be *very* strong—"

"You'll find out," he said, and I couldn't watch any more.

I crawled forward to check what was happening in the slice of the burning meadow I could see beyond the mouth of the cul-de-sac. There were still some gunshots, but they came slower now, in ones or one-twos.

And through the flames, I saw something that made me mostly forget about the Persian. "Shut up, all of you," I said. "We have to get out of here."

"Don't think so," the Coon said, thick and slow. He was flemming now himself. "That corner behind the box has room enough."

"Ooh, you're *horrible!*"

"You said that before." He opened those massive jaws of his and reached for her scruff. "Didn't sound like you meant it then, either."

I reached over and whapped him, right on the end of the nose. I kept my claws in—because I didn't want to die—but the gesture alone made his eyes pop round and flare like the flames from the wreckage in the meadow. "You back away right now, Drags, and I might just forget you did that."

"Will you haul your brains back out of your ball-sack and *look around?*"

"I got everything I need to see right here."

"Please don't fight, toms. Not over *me*," the Perisan purred, wrapping her tail down flat to hide a hint of wicked smile. "The *last* thing I want is for—"

"*Rake* yourself, sister. This is serious. We can't stay here. Coon, Hacky, just come over here and *look*. Look at the light on the walls to either side—no shadows up above, only shadows down here."

Hacky just shrugged. "So?"

"So aren't you starting to feel a little *warm*?"

The Coon spat an obscenity. "The garbage is on fire. In this box, right over our backs."

"It gets worse. Coon, *look*."

He snarled something wordless, but crawled on over and peered out from under the garbage box. "So? Don't see nothin'. Just some burning wheelers."

"That's right," I said. "Do you understand that what you're not seeing is *Knifewall?*"

He seemed to shrink into himself, then.

"The Calicoes must have exploded it. Or at least made a pretty good hole. Does anybody need me to explain what this means?"

What This Means came into view in the form of a long back-lit silhouette stalking across the mouth of the cul-de-sac. This silhouette was as tall at the withers as most cats can jump, and it had a barrel chest bigger around than most humans' shoulders. Each of its paws was the size of my head, and the clack of its toenails sounded like distant gun shots. It stopped in front of the alley mouth and lifted its head, huffing to taste the air . . .

Then it turned toward us.

"Why, *hello* there, Draaaaags . . . fancy meeting *you* here . . ."

The Persian sniffed. "It's just a dog."

"Sure it is," I said. "Strut on out there and rake his nose. Maybe he'll run away."

"Don't do it," the Coon said. "That's not just a dog. That beast has killed more cats than a bucket of rat poison."

"Hey, hey, hey, Drags." Bullets sauntered on into the cul-de-sac and sat down, his vast mottled tongue lolling sideways, trailing a stretching loop of drool. "Is that you under the burning garbage? Getting a little *warm*, are we, Drags?"

"Why don't you come on over and find out, Bullets? You've still got one good eye. Bring it within reach."

"Oh, I don't think so," he drawled. "Think I'll just sit here and enjoy the smell of cooking cat."

"Bullets?" the Persian said. "That's the dog's name?"

"It's because he's been shot so many times," I said. "I mean, *look* at him."

In the clearer light from the garbage above us, all the white scar patches showed clearly against his buff coat; he even had a pair on either side of his blackish dewlap. Bullets was bigger than any human I've ever seen, and probably tougher, too. "They say bullets can't kill him. Maybe it's true."

"What's a *bullets?*"

I stared at her. "Damn, sister, how sheltered *are* you?"

"Don't snarl at me," she sniffed. "I just—I don't seem to quite understand how things work on the Outside . . ."

"Sniffed it out yet, Drags?" Bullets was laughing now. "Sniffed out what I already know?"

"You'd be surprised what I know." I turned to the others. "All right. Get ready to move. I'll go first and draw him off; I'm the one he wants, anyway. When he starts for me, run like hell for the hole in Knifewall."

"We'll all go at once. Every cat for himself," Hacky said. "Maybe he only gets one of us, and maybe we all get away."

"My tail how it is, I can't leap very well any more. No balance. And I'd be clumsy enough scrambling over the rubble that he'll probably take me anyway." I sucked in a deep breath. "And he's not the only one out there. You gotta look out for her, Hacky. You too, Coon. There's other toms out there. You can all pitch in. It's the only way."

The Coon gave me a sidelong look. "Only way to what?"

"To *survive*, Coon. No more every cat for himself. We have to be more like humans." More like *dogs*, I was thinking, but knew better than to say so. You have to walk before you can spring. "Make what I'm about to do count for something."

"You'd—you're doing this for *me*?" The Persian goggled

at me. She sounded awed. "You're so *brave*—! If only *I* could be brave!"

"There's brave cats, and there's live cats. Stick with the live ones," I said, and went.

Bullets was so surprised to see me burst out from under the garbage box that I was past him before he even got his tail-stub off the ground. But he was fast, incredibly fast for a big dog, and I could feel the asphalt shake in time with the clatter of his toenails as he galloped after me. I zigged and sprang sideways, spinning in the air for a quick reverse, but he was right on top of me, so close I could smell the rotten meat on his breath, and I broke left, rolled, and jigged right, searching desperately for a tree I could go up or a wheeler I could duck under, but that was just instinct—

And if you can only follow your instincts, you might as well be a dog.

Because ahead, only a couple dozen strides away, was a Calico, big as life, and he had one of the long slim guns of theirs already in his hands and all I needed in this life or any of my next was to reach the Calico's legs—but jaws closed on my tail and I let out a screech and I was yanked off the ground and flying through the air and I tried to spin my crippled tail but of course it only made it worse and I crashed into a corner of the Bleach & Ammonia House flank first so hard that I hit the ground on my back and could only lay there, gasping, while Bullets pounced on me, both his huge paws coming down on my ribs, which made a crackling sound like the fake skins humans put food in, and I tasted blood.

And I looked up at him and smiled.

Bullets' jaws opened wider than the whole rest of my life. "What's so funny, dead cat?"

Which was when the Calico's gun made that *brdddow!*

noise, and an invisible boot slammed Bullets in the chest and knocked him past me and down.

"Told you . . ." I gasped. ". . . you'd be surprised."

"How did you . . ." Bullets tried to rise, but blood burst from his mouth and he sagged back down on his side, panting. "How . . . ?"

"Calicoes *hate* dogs," I said. "Don't you know anything?"

I managed to get to my feet. It hurt. "Their long-time-ago breed sire *belonged* to cats. The humans still tell the story of how he cut off part of his cloth-skin so he could go pray without waking up his master, who was asleep on his sleeve."

"So smart . . ." Bullets' panting was going ragged now. "So smart . . . but you don't know . . . don't know about your fluffy bitch . . ."

"Of course I know, you stupid pooch."

"You *knew* . . . ?"

"That's she's a neuter? Hell, so am I. I was a *house* cat, idiot. You think full toms would *cooperate*? But they will now. They'll stick together, waiting for her to go into heat. I wouldn't give a marking squirt for the chances of your pack ever taking another one of *those* cats. Not that it's your problem any more."

"You wait," Bullets panted. "I'll live through this. I'll be back."

"Don't think so."

The Calico walked over, angling his gun down toward Bullets' head.

"Don't—don't do it—" Bullets panted up at him. "Don't—can't you see I *love* you—?"

The Calico answered him with a burst of gun shots.

Bullets, as it turned out, wasn't as gun-proof as his reputation suggested.

The Calico reached down with an empty hand, and I let him pet me. I even purred and rubbed along his legs a little. Sure, the Calicoes had killed my people, but I'm no bigot. They're only humans, after all. It's not like they can help themselves.

When the Calico wandered off, I went and sampled some of Bullets' blood.

It tasted like victory.

FATHER MAIMS BEST

Ed Greenwood

The ghost was a pale blue, which meant that it was angry about something. Or someone. Quite possibly whoever had cut its head off, leaving the wraith floating along after its severed part, forever reaching vainly for that grisly, spectral-gore-dripping ball with both hands. It drifted past us almost blindly, heading for a blank wall that it would no doubt vanish through.

Interesting, but I hadn't time to find out more, just now; it wasn't *our* ghost. That is, one we were being paid to get rid of.

Myself, I'm not sure why living humans so fervently want dead humans—restless humans, or ghosts, in particular—to be somewhere else. After all, they gobble down dead things on their plates all the time, silently gibbering little phantoms and all, and think nothing of it. Unless the beef is tough or the turkey overdone.

But I digress. Not surprising, that; it's what I do. "Sam & Abernathy/Paranormal Investigations and Digressions," say the sign and all the business cards Steve is forever handing out. People always handle them gingerly, for some reason, or even with open, nostril-flaring distaste.

Almost as often as they examine me with pained expressions and start to explain some sort of "no pets" policy. Steve doesn't bother interrupting anymore. He just lets them finish and then explains that we're partners, a team. He's the "Abernathy" part, and I'm "Sam." Samiris-Sekhmet, in full, though that was a *long* time ago. Royal blood, of course, though that meant nothing back then. I picked up "Samratharella" several owners ago, and I prefer it.

Yes, I'm a girl, and yes, I'm a cat. The big black one with the white "skunk" stripe down my flank, courtesy of a swordcane that wasn't quite swift enough to rob me of more than one of my nine lives. Of which I've used up seven, thanks for asking.

Oh, and I'm the brains of this outfit, too. Most humans have figured out by now that cats and dogs can see ghosts, but what they don't know is that all cats can see all ghosts, most of the time; most dogs and most humans can't see them at all or, like Steve, can see them only too late, when they're showing themselves off to lure him into danger—or materializing enough to do him real harm. Dogs and humans can *smell* ghosts, but if you don't know what you're smelling, it doesn't do you much good.

That's one of the reasons that a big city like this one has so many "accidental" deaths. Humans run afoul of ghosts, and big cities have lots of both. When they meet, it's seldom pretty.

Not all ghosts set out to murder, and those who do generally have one particular victim—or sort of victim, like rapists or cooks or men on bicycles—in mind. But in heavy traffic or in places where a fall can be fatal, being startled by a ghost can kill just as effectively as a murderous ghost's dark deeds, and dogs and humans can easily be startled by ghosts. They tend to be able to smell a spook only when it shows itself, whereas cats know a ghost is around long before it becomes visible. So we can track ghosts and deal with them.

Cats born these days are pretty little creatures, most of them, and kin—but that's all they are. We royalty (that is, cats old enough to have known pharaohs and who have managed to keep at least a few of their lives since then) can shapechange and speak in the minds of anyone we touch, not just long-time friendly humans, dogs, and other cats.

Yet if I ever let the wrong human see me shapechanging, I'll probably be throwing away the last few of my lives, right there. Which is why I need Steve. He requires clothes and watches and cash to live in the world of humans: that's why we do this work instead of just letting the passing parade of ghosts be just that, a passing parade. Oh, and he sees to my wants, too. A bit of fish, often, and chocolates every once in a long while.

Steve always sees to my wants. Which is why I'm no longer the lapcat of a certain lady known to much of the city (the seamier side) as "Cinammon Nipples," for reasons that are probably obvious but are another digression and so best left undiscussed for now.

Back to the case at hand. The headless human was the only ghost we'd seen so far in this building, but that wasn't surprising. Old buildings tend to host a lot of murders, violent deaths, and strong emotions—and therefore a lot of hauntings—and new buildings, unless they stand on the site of a thoroughly haunted older building, tend to have fewer.

We were here to investigate a "cat haunting." Or rather, to get rid of a "ghost cat" that had taken to appearing and clawing anyone who so much as sat on a couch or chair, or lounged or lay down on a bed, anywhere in the place. "Here" was an incredibly valuable downtown house (on a trendy corner; "location, location, location") that had just been remodelled into three luxury condominiums. The lady owner was living in the uppermost and was facing ruin if she couldn't soon sell the lower two—and the ghost cat had already scared off a dwindling stream of possible buyers.

Those who looked at the place were either a far more discreet lot than usual, or these prospective buyers were all looking to install grow ops or operate escort services out of the place, because not one whiskery whisper of a ghostly cat had reached the papers.

Jethana Throneshuld had, however, sounded rich, haughty, and darned desperate on Steve's answering machine. That desperation was real, because she hadn't hesitated a second upon hearing his rates, and she wanted him on the job as soon as he could get from his end of the phone to hers.

Which is why we were now climbing the palatial stairs and ornate hallways of The Coachlight, heading for our client's door. There was an elevator, but we both hated elevators, and it was only two flights of stairs. Stairs, moreover, that weren't the usual filthy, chewing-gum and cigarette-littered, urine-reeking and otherwise spartan stairwell, but a soft-carpeted, gilt-trimmed pleasure to ascend.

I could shape human lips and throat to talk to Steve, but I made it a rule to do that only behind closed doors, on our premises. So I trotted along beside him looking like a feline domestic as he did the trenchcoat thing.

Hand in pocket as if resting on a gun, fedora pulled low. Right up to Ms. Jethana Throneshuld's door, whose bell awakened distant grandfather clock chiming noises and then opened by itself, gliding inward with the ponderous velvet silence of something no mere mortal could ever afford.

No wonder she was facing financial ruin. The floor was deep white fur wherever it wasn't glossy marble or set-into-the-floor bathing pools (kidney-shaped, of course, and she had *three* of them) and stretched away from us for what seemed the better part of a mile before being interrupted by a wall. A wall of glossy polished wood that wasn't just panelled; it was *carved*, in a huge and complicated relief scene of stags chasing each other over rail fences in a deep wood. Thankfully the usual human hunters on horses—and their torrent of hounds—were absent.

Steve came to a stop, peeled off his rubber overshoes (and don't ask what troubles he goes through to get such things, these days) and dropped them carefully into the zip-up pocket of his overcoat, to reveal spotless black dress shoes. Our client beamed at that, as she came gliding into view through an archway, festooned in some sort of designer negligée and what looked like a small waterfall of matching white diamonds.

"Ah, Mr. Abernathy!" Her face fell, as she added with considerably less enthusiasm, "Oh, and I see you've brought your pet."

"My partner," Steve said, firmly but pleasantly. "A live cat to sniff out a ghost cat. Should we set to work in here, or does your little problem appear only on the lower floors?"

"Ah, you *do* get to work immediately," Ms. Throneshuld said approvingly, patting his arm in a my-but-I'll-be-enjoying-*this*-soon rich Rosedale cougar sort of way as she passed him, to see to the door. Evidently it didn't close by itself.

After the door clicked closed, she did things to a complicated alarm panel set behind a sliding miniature—an oval painting on porcelain, that is—beside it and came back to him.

I didn't much like the look of her or want to approach her, and the feeling seemed to be mutual, but professional necessities are professional necessities, so I contrived to wander close to those shapely and overly spa-treated legs as she pranced past.

And contrived not to recoil, too. I'd been expecting her to smell of expensive perfumes, with an underlying reek of exfoliants and exotic tree oils, ylang ylang and all the other drek they put in shampoos and lotions these days. Instead, she smelt of death. Not murder or kitchen butchery, but old, dry, dusty death.

When death won't go away, that means trouble. But then, the look in her eyes—not just the "I'll see to you" look she gave me, but the very different sort of look she was giving Steve, was stronger trouble, and more immediate, too. It was the look a hungry cat gives to a witless canary that perches obligingly right in front of it.

"It's probably best," she purred, stopping against his chest and posing so that one bare leg could peek through the thigh-high slits in her designer come-hither-and-tear-this-little-frippery-off-me silks and press against him, "if we start in the bedroom. It's been worst in there."

I'll just bet it has, dearie.

Yes, that was a catty thought, but then, I think everything catt—oh, never mind.

"Sam," Steve said a little dreamily, "will you go in and ah, check things out, first?"

I turned my head and gave him an incredulous look. Had I just heard the lost-in-lust tone I *thought* I'd heard?

He smiled at me. Set take the man! He *was* falling for her! A reeking walking corpse, and—

"Well, isn't *that* something!" Oh, so sweetly. "It's as if she understands your every word! Just like a real person!"

And you'd know all about "real persons" HOW, sweetie?

She and Steve actually put their arms around each other's hips, like a comfortable couple, to stand and watch the cute trained cat obey her master's order.

So I obliged, of course. We're partners, after all.

And we're on the job, too. So . . .

The bedroom was every whit as horrible as I'd expected—zebra-skin throws over folding screens fashioned of beveled tall-as-a-person-in-killer-heels mirrors, only these mirrors had frames plated with gold, not brass, and the zebra skins weren't just a textile design but were real pelts. Those screens flanked an oval pink fourposter bed topped with gilded posts holding up a pink oval overhead ring-frame, and a huge oval mirror was affixed to the ceiling above that. Four upright oval archways pierced the soft orange sherbet walls, all of them curtained off in a clashing shade of pink: bathroom, shoe closet, dressing room, clothes closet.

I batted aside the bed's pink pleated skirting—of *course* it had pink pleated skirting, of a different shade than either the archway curtains or the rest of the bed—to peer under the bed and was gratified to see nothing but an unbroken field of white fur, free of the smallest speck of dust or cobweb. No ghost cat here.

Never leave unexplored territory between you and the known way out. I turned toward the closest archway to the bedroom door: the shoe closet, reeking with expensive leather and the very best dyes. Taking a deep breath while I was still far enough from those smells to keep myself from a fit of sneezing or choking, I prepared myself to come nose to nose with spooks.

Jethana Walkingcorpse probably kept her shoes in neat pairs on shelves—the ones she never used, that is. The others would be in untidy heaps on the floor, strewn all over the—

They were. I padded forward cautiously, springing over a few pairs into a little bare area of fur rug before the real heap began.

Where I stopped, nose prickling. Someone was happening behind me. *Just* behind me.

I spun, silently. The Ghost Cat was fading into view and solidity right in front of me, between me and the archway out of this dead end. It—no, he—was smiling. A smile I knew all too well.

Hello, Little Meat.

I had to touch Steve, or any human, to mindspeak. We all have to, unless we use a spell.

Or we're talking to immediate kin.

Only one of which had ever called me "Little Meat."

The Ghost Cat opened his jaws wide, very wide—long yellow fangs, sharp and deadly as ever—and then smiled at me. Oh, yes, I knew him.

Suddenly I was struggling to breathe, fear like ice around my heart.

It's been a long time, he observed pleasantly, looming up suddenly in the narrow closet as he gained full solidity and his true size.

Montuhotep. He Who Makes War and Is Pleased. Maral-wshbekhtah, to use his later name.

He had another, more mundane title, too: my father.

I hadn't seen him for centuries, but he hadn't forgotten me or what he'd been trying to do to me at our last meeting, and that smile told me he was picking up right where he left off.

Trying to kill me.

Swiftly, messily, and gloatingly. That could have been his motto, had Father ever bothered with such things. He probably would have put it in other words, however. "Maim, Torment or Rape, then Slay," perhaps.

Last daughter, he purred in my mind, *come to me.*

He had killed all my brothers and sisters, and probably my mother before that, by maiming them into immobility and then casting a spell on them that stole all of their nine lives and transferred them into him.

He had tried to kill me, too, but I had leaped in desperation, landed someplace I shouldn't have, and paid the price in a nasty backlash as the spell waiting in that place had shattered Father's life-stealing magic.

I had fled, and he had sought me, chasing me tirelessly for decades. Until there came a time when I saw him no more, padding smilingly along on my trail.

Centuries passed. I'd concluded something fatal had finally happened to him.

No such luck, evidently. He was still very much alive.

My nose told me I was facing no ghost, but a living cat. My eyes told me my father was using magic to become incorporeal and pass through things and then solidify again until turning back into a wraith seemed more useful. Until the spell wore out, or he tried to pass through cold iron and got stunned by the shattering of his spell for his pains, he could probably turn back and forth at will, as often as he wanted.

All royalty had heard of that spell, but it had been far beyond Father's mastery when I'd fled from him. He had been busy then with his nine-lives-stealing; his own invention, that had left him bursting with pride, bereft of almost all his kin, and with more lives than any cat had any right to.

He'd probably used most of them by now, though—which was why he was here smiling at me. The stealing spell only worked on royalty who shared his bloodline, a breed of which I was now presumably the last.

Oh, I was terrified. And he knew it.

Tombs and bones, anyone who got a glimpse of me would know it! All over me, my hair was standing on end, thrusting out at the world in all directions like so many rigid little lances.

Father hadn't been the only one learning magic. I knew a few spells, none of them very impressive and only one of them useful in my present situation.

On the other hand, I hadn't known any useful magic—oh, I could conjure a feeble glow, or bring down darkness around myself, but all kittens could do as much, if they were royalty—while he'd been chasing me or earlier. If he still thought me helpless and gloated just a moment longer . . .

Surrender, he told me. *Abase yourself, and receive me.*

Once a tomcat, always a tomcat, first and foremost. His gloating and prancing had given me the time I needed.

"Take me. If you can," I whispered—and vanished.

He launched himself forward, claws flung wide, raking the space where I'd been. He suspected I'd merely mastered invisibility and now, unseen but still in the closet, was seeking to dodge around him.

My spell was something a little more powerful. A translocation, "jumping" my body from the closet to a spot on that broad expanse of furs that I'd examined carefully earlier. Right beside Steve's leg, as it happened, as he tried to ask Walkingcorpse questions as he kept moving, to keep her from rubbing herself quite *all* over him.

He stared at me—my sudden appearance, and my hair on end in terror—in astonishment, jaw dropping open, and her surprise was hardly less.

I didn't wait for further reactions but raced past him like a storm wind, sprang to the sliding miniature and clawed it aside, landed thumpingly hard beneath it, and sprang right back up again to push a particular trio of the buttons I'd seen her push.

In response, the door clicked open—just as Father burst out of the closet and streaked across the room toward me.

"There! The Ghost Cat!" Throneshuld cried, almost triumphantly, pointing. "That's *it*!"

Then I was out through the tiny gap between door and frame and running for my life, with Father bounding after me, eyes ablaze with anger and excitement.

"Sam?" Steve shouted, real alarm in his voice. "*Sam!*"

I heard his shoes pounding across the floor after me, in the instant before the door shut itself again, muffling a shout from him that was loud and angry. And no wonder; he'd never seen me frightened before, in all our time together, and I'd just left him helpless. *I* was the ghostsniffer and expert, and without me he was just a man in a hat and coat who knew how to bluster.

He was probably as frightened now as I was. Perhaps more, because humans get *so* frightened of the unknown. Whereas I knew *exactly* what I was afraid of.

Thinking of which . . . I risked a glance back. Father was gaining on me.

Bast take him! I'd thought in a flat-out race I—being younger, sleeker, and a lot lighter—would be faster. I always had been faster!

Wherever he'd been, he'd evidently been doing a lot of running, or getting stronger, or learning some sort of magic that lent him greater speed.

Oh, *jackal dung*, as some of the priests had been wont to say.

I sprang, batted the elevator button in passing, and kept right on going. I hadn't the time to wait for its ponderous door to roll open, even if it was waiting on this floor—and it was far more likely sitting at street level, two floors down.

Nor did I really have time to use the stairs—not when Father could "fade" through flights of them, to appear below and wait for me. Or could he? Surely its frame would be iron, underneath the carpeting and the sound-deadening sandwiches of foam and wood I'd smelled beneath it. I—window!

That window had *not* been open when we'd come up, but it was open now. I sprang, trusting in my claws on the wooden sill to slow me enough to keep from hurtling helplessly out and down. The sharp stink of fresh cigarette ash told me why the window had been opened. The caretaker with the vacuum who'd been fussing in the lobby when

Steve and I arrived had been smoking, and had dumped—or more likely flicked—the evidence out this window. I followed, quickly.

The ledge I'd seen from the street was more ornamental than useful; certainly no human could have walked along it, even one who knew the wall-clinging spell I had. Yet wires ran along it—what happens when television satellite dishes are added to older buildings as cheaply as possible—which should keep Father from "fading" through any walls to get me. He'd have to follow me, and he was a lot larger than I was.

Traffic honked, below, covering most of his snarls of anger as he thrust his head through the window and saw where I'd gone. By then I was well along the ledge, passing Steve and our creepy dead or undead client again.

"Oh, you *must* stay, Mister Abernathy," she was telling him, arms around him so ardently that he'd have real trouble trying to do anything else. "You can stay in one of the unused floors below us, or better yet my guest room, to try to solve my little problem. You can find your Sam *and* rid me of my ghost cat."

Steve was frowning and shaking his head—but it was a frown of bafflement, not anger at her. "I—I—Yes, I must *absolutely* deal with your problem. Yet lacking my partner, I'm temporarily at a loss regarding the best way to proceed. She was crucial to, ah, 'flushing out' your ghost, you see, and—"

"Then stay, and we can talk this over. Coffee? Or something stronger, perhaps? Surely together we can think of . . ."

Father was out on the ledge, flattening himself against the wall almost bonelessly, and I couldn't tarry any longer.

I'd run out of ledge anyway, because I'd run out of building. If I followed the ledge on, around two corners, I'd probably be able to jump off it, out into the tree I'd seen rising behind The Coachlight as we'd approached it.

Well, Steve certainly seemed smitten. Perhaps Waking-corpse, too, had magic—to ensnare men, in her case. Why else would he be interested in so old and crude a flirt? She was energetic in her seduction attempts but about as subtle as a dog in heat.

I'd done it *much* better. Steve had been head-over-heels for me as a human and eager for each new session of sweet hot lovemaking before he'd ever known I was a cat who could shapechange. As I said, we're partners.

Now, however, he'd just have to fend for himself. I had bigger problems. Such as staying alive long enough to warn him about the true nature of Haughty Ms. Walkingcorpse— or anything at all, ever again.

Night was falling, of course.

Providing the right lighting for a lady cat to be chased by her murderous father, far across the city.

At least, I hoped I'd last that long.

The tree was old and gnarled; its branches sagged but held. Squirrel-like I scampered down them, then headed for the ground, well aware that Father would be right behind me.

Flattening himself out ribbon-thin must mean working a magic that made him temporarily boneless, because it certainly slowed him down. When I raced away along the top rail of a fence, he was two backyards behind me.

I had to stay ahead. He needed me trapped in a confined space, or immobilized, to have time to cast his life-stealing. If he could bite the back of my neck, or get a good swipe at me with both sets of front claws, he could manage the maiming he was so infamous for, and I would be paralyzed—and doomed.

Life had suddenly become so simple—and so precious and hard to keep hold of.

So, just how well did he know this city? How well did I?

The difference between those two answers was probably all that was going to keep me alive for long.

He was gaining on me, fast.

I turned a corner, ran out of fence, sprang onto one of those crazy "spiderweb on a pole" backyard laundry racks, and from there plunged deep into the soft soil of a flowerbed, not wanting to bruise anything this early in the chase.

"Early" I hoped, that is. I scrabbled my way onto firmer ground and ran, streaking through a cat door and right up and along the back of a dog that had been waiting outside it to bully some other cat.

The dog barked and twisted furiously, its roaring din nigh deafening, but I doubted it would last more than a swift bark or two against Father. If he bothered to fight it at all.

I raced across several yards, not bothering to try to hide or misdirect by zigging here or zagging there. Right now, just moving quickly was all that was keeping me alive.

Stay near iron barriers, stay near iron . . .

The dog shrieked in sudden pain, and fell silent. Father.

He was keeping close. Which meant I had to get out of this neighborhood, away from the darkness and the trees that every cat instinctively welcomes and turns to, and into the bright concrete noise of the downtown. Where there would be more cars and people walking; more obstacles.

I darted across a road right in front of a surging taxi. Its front wheel came so close to clipping me that it numbed the end of my tail. There was a littered sidewalk beyond, and one of those two-rows-of-offset-vertical-board fences. I went left, toward the busier street.

It was a long way to the corner, and it occurred to me that if Father had caught sight of me and dared to risk himself that much longer in the traffic, he could "cut the corner" diagonally and catch up with me.

So I found an old dented drainpipe with many straps to hook my claws into, and got aloft, fast.

I hadn't even made it to the lowest window-ledge of the apartments above this shop when I heard a furious scrabbling below. Father's weight was too much for his claws to hold him in his haste; he was slipping, old paint flaking away in a little cloud. Slipping, but not falling.

I wasted no time in watching or taunting but just got myself along those ledges, leaping from one to the next, and around the corner. Where a handy tree-limb let me ascend to the next row of ledges, which would put me higher than the aging shingle roof of the next building along.

Father was faster than ever. There came the crash of a window being thrown up behind me, and a man's voice shouting, "It *was* a cat! And here's another!"

Father hissed in the man's face as he raced past—and was startled to find that one human, at least, was just as fast as he was.

The man had been reading a book, and he thrust it hard into Father's ribs, or tried to. He got Father's rear instead and slammed it off the ledge into space, the rest of Father following it.

To land heavily atop the store awning below. It was as rotten as most of them, and it tore, but Father wisely kept his claws sheathed, and climbed up out of the small hole, to wade along the dirty canvas.

I made the next shingle roof and paused to snatch my breath and plan my route ahead.

"Daughter!" Father hissed, reaching the end of the awning and seeing he was facing an impossible leap to reach me; he'd have to jump down instead, and find another way up.

"Last life, Father?"

"I only need one," he snarled, with a testiness that made

me think he just might be on his last one, "to take all of yours!"

I turned away without another word, and ran. This was going to be a long night. I hoped.

And so it was. Time and again Father *almost* caught me, and I *just* eluded him, until we were on streets I knew well and could stay more than a whisker ahead of him.

Not that Father seemed to be tiring. I was, but he seemed as quick as ever. Which is how he caught me.

I'd been running along a lighted marquee, one of the huge sidewalk-overhanging pulsating signs that so few movie theaters still had these days, but every second store seemed to have gained. I hadn't seen Father fade through the wall of a building to ride a wire to the building that had the marquee—so I got a nasty shock when he faded right out of the wall ahead, to crash down on the marquee facing me, his fanged smile as big as ever.

Luckily for me, that's exactly what he did—*crash* down.

Through the glass panel, into the humming heart of dozens of flourescent tubes, some of which shattered and made his hair stand on end. He clawed his way along them anyway, dislodging some from their mounts so they went dark. So they were no longer alive and threatening to cook him, but they were now on a slant. And as smooth as ever. His claws shrieked as they scrabbled, but he couldn't climb toward me.

I turned and headed elsewhere, fast.

Trapped and knowing it, Father let himself fall through a tangle of tinkling tubes—their shards must have been razor-sharp, but pain had never bothered Father—to reach a metal frame beneath them, in the bright white heart of the marquee. He raced along it until he was under the end of the marquee where I was gathering myself for a difficult jump, and he punched his head upward, hard.

Much glass shattered, the end of the marquee fell in and my behind with it, and Father ended up pinned under my weight and the ends of about two dozen tubes. He snarled and shifted furiously, seeking to get his jaws or a claw on me, but he was covered in a shifting layer of sharp glass shards, and all that happened was that his bloodied shoulder touched my bloodied left hind leg for a moment.

And our minds met.

I had always known Father was insane, but plunging through the dark, swirling storm of his mind was still . . . an experience. He *loved* to kill, as well as loving all the other things tomcats do, and truly thought he had been touched and favored by his namesake, Montu, the god of war. He was addicted to the taste of human blood. Not a vampire; he was more like an alcoholic who had to taste strong drink as often as he could. So he clawed or bit every human who came within reach.

He'd been working with AnkhesenAkana for years.

Her, I mean. The Lady, Jethana Throneshuld, though that was just the body she was currently using.

Full working partners. She was some sort of ancient Egyptian undead spirit that he knew no name for, who went on living—I know that's not the right word, but let it pass—by possessing one living human body after another. Her current body, the unfortunate Jethana, was starting to wear out. The condo scheme had been meant to bring new host bodies within easy reach, but it wasn't going to work in time. So AnkhesenAkana had decided the body of someone else— my Steve!—would have to do.

I *had* to get away from Father, to get back to The Coach-light, and I had to do it fast!

Now there was irony, if you wanted it: the failing, hungry-for-life undead, and the cat who has taken so many lives already and has blood afire with life. Yet surely AnkhesenAkana would long ago have wrung his neck and taken the energy within him if it could use that energy. So the lives of cats evidently helped sustain undeath not at all . . .

It had been AnkhesenAkana who got Father his magic. She had no skill for it herself, but from her, er, first life knew where ancient texts were hidden and remembered some details seen when watching others cast spells.

He was a slow learner, it seemed; he kept undoing the incorporeal thing by indulging in his bloodlust. Contact with blood—any sort of blood—turned him corporeal even if he didn't want to become solid.

Which gave me an idea. I had to get to a place I'd visited only once, a place any cat would hate fervently for its noise and perils and overwhelming smells. The city's recycling sorting plant.

I used my best spell again, to get myself out of the damned marquee and away from Father. Steve couldn't wait much longer.

I'd never much appreciated the pale gray beginnings of dawn, and they didn't look very entrancing now. With me exhausted, Father close behind, and the rotten stink of the recycling plant—humans just throw things out; they don't see any need to wash much—hammering my nose like . . . like . . .

No, *nothing* can describe this smell. It was like being blinded.

For a moment I feared Father would turn back, but no prey had ever eluded him before, and having found me after so long, he wasn't going to let me manage to be the first.

Good. I knew exactly where I wanted to be and got there.

The place was full of rats, who sneered at me as they waited for me to fall afoul of one of the many murderous pieces of machinery that were crushing, spinning, stamping, and spewing endless streams of cardboard, plastic, and glass. When I was broken or dead, they'd feast.

I raced past my umpteenth rat—and then whirled around and bit its neck, clamping my own jaws down hard. It died.

Rat in mouth, I turned to face Father.

He'd been following me rather gingerly, and no wonder: I'd reached that rat by running along a pipe high above the cardboard shredder. Which consisted of endless belts carrying waste cardboard to the open top of a large metal chute that dropped into a metal box. Rows of robotic metal knives, each the size of a surfboard, pierced that box repeatedly, amid endless, high-pitched screaming.

So we couldn't hear each other, couldn't smell each other, and were poised above one of the deadliest butchering contraptions I'd ever seen. Luckily, Father's reluctance told me he'd never been here before, which meant my desperate plan just might work.

There was a weight-sorting mechanism at the head end of this, to keep contaminants out. If it worked, I'd live. If not . . .

"Sorry, Steve," I mumbled, around the rat. It didn't taste any too good, but I didn't plan to have it in my mouth for much longer. Putting my head down, I ran right at Father.

He reared to swipe at me with his claws, but I stopped just out of reach—and he obligingly doomed himself, lunging forward to really get his claws into me.

I slammed into him and drove us both off the pipe, scrabbling at it just long enough so that we fell separately into the waiting chute.

The secret was staying still.

I landed on a good big piece of cardboard and sat there like a stone. Which made the cardboard too heavy, tripped a sensor, and the metal "lifts" rose between the knives to thrust up my cardboard from underneath and shunt it sideways, out of the chute, for hand sorting.

At the last moment, I spat out the rat, and watched it tumble down in front of Father. Who had seen his peril and struggled furiously, churning the cardboard until he could turn incorporeal.

As I got put onto the sorting belt, he was grinning furiously at me, a translucent ghost caged in metal but unharmed by the knives slamming through him.

Until the rat struck the knives right beside him, its blood spattered in all directions, drenching him—and the knives got him.

By then I was tearing down the iron stair meant for workers to unjam the knives when necessary, trying not to cry. He was, after all, my Father.

"So passes Montuhotep," I murmured aloud, stopping under the metal that was now dripping blue blood. I stayed still again until his gore had soaked the fur down my back, then did the one last thing I needed to do: I found a small, sharp-ended shard of old metal I could carry in my mouth. Thus laden, I got out of there and gave in to my grief.

I had hated and feared him, but he was my Father. And a cat who had in his day made many tremble. A royal tomcat, the likes of which the world would not see again.

Feeling glum, I hurried back back across the awakening city as fast as I could drag my weary body and got back to The Coachlight's windows in time to see that I was . . . just in time.

Darling Steve. He had worn himself out searching the building top to bottom for me and had finally fallen asleep, all smudges and cobwebs. AnkhesenAkana needed mouth to mouth—and preferably more—body contact to take over his body and had awakened him to try to get him undressed and into bed.

It seemed even ancient Egyptian undead could seethe with frustration. She was trying to make love to a man too sleepy to stay awake and do anything, who was much larger and heavier than she was.

I decided to put her out of her misery by ringing her bell with Father's special code.

And pouncing on her head when she snarlingly opened the door, bounding on from that lofty perch into her lair before she could even pummel me off.

She followed. I did a lot of clawing in the frantic moments that followed and managed to make Jethana Walking-corpse brain herself against one of the gilded posts of her own bed, hard enough to awaken Steve.

Who stared in bleary astonishment as I rolled across the dazed woman's throat, smearing her with Father's blood—and then, rather awkwardly, pricked her with the shard, in the midst of the gore.

Whereupon Montuhotep's "blood of many lives" started to mix with that human body's own blood . . . poisoning the resident AnkhesenAkana.

Inside the now-writhing woman, it started to burn. She wailed helplessly.

"What—?" Steve contributed in astonishment. "What'd you do to her?"

By then, we were both looking at a blood-smeared but quite alive mindless living human woman. Who had seen better days and had a body no longer really suited to the negligée she was—mostly—wearing.

"Let's go," I snarled at my partner. "Get your clothes and *everything*, and let's get out of here!"

Steve blinked at me, and I sighed, took on human form to start dressing him, and snapped, "Or can *you* think of some way to make the police believe all of this?"

CAT CALL 911

Janny Wurts

The rumor that proved to be no rumor at all began with a no-account rat. Scamper encountered the creature, lean as a snake, twitching its whiskers over the rim of the dumpster. No one else was abroad in the midnight alley, just behind the respectable shop front housing Cat-A-Combs hair parlor. Madame Persian's haberdashery was locked. The darlings who sparkled in diamond collars never stirred from their penthouse comforts past sundown.

The gleam in the rat's shifty eyes sparked like sulfur as it bared yellow teeth.

"Hey, Copper!" it taunted. "A dark-doing'sss at large in the city again. Made a moussse eat her newbornsss from dessspair. Ssso also, it missled a dog that ssstrayed and drowned in the river."

"Feckless folk, dogs." Scamper jerked his tail in contempt. Rat's gossip! He dabbed a lick on his orange shoulder and prowled on, supremely dismissive. "Don't have to be puppies to howl and run riot. And mice eat their young in the lean times without any dark-doing's help."

No tip-off had reached the copper-cat dispatcher, back at the police barracks stables. On the hour that Scamper left on patrol, the Chief had been napping, curled on a straw bale, the reports off the streets uneventful enough that no vigilant copper would wake him.

"You'll wissssh you'd lissstened," insisted the rat. "Thessse mice lived in sssugarplum plenty behind the wallsss of the passstry ssshop." With a gnashing of incisors, the creature scuttled. Its last word emerged through the rustle of trash, as it resumed its noisome scavenging. "A nexusss knot'sss forming. My warning'sss the firssst."

"Get flea dipped, pal." Scamper twitched his damp hair, not impressed. Rats lied. The whole scumbag lot were a furtive breed, naked of tail, and too garrulous for scruples or dignity. Scamper flicked his whiskers forward, alert. Though loath to rely on what might be a hoax, he was a street copper down to the bone, born to patrol the back alleys. No use wishing such work was the good life, snacking on tuna fish out of a can.

Still, this was not the dockside, and he, dapper fellow, was no rip-eared tom, assigned to a thug's beat in the slums. The sort of people who started dark-doings seldom strayed from the seedier neighborhoods. No hint of dire trouble blew on the wind. The deserted buildings wore nothing but their usual night-time shadow.

"I'll be declawed," Scamper grumbled, "before I ask the Chief to send a back-up squad on a rat-race!"

Scamper loped past the maw of a parking garage and slipped through the short cut under a culvert. Now across the street, he emerged at the pastry shop, but he found no hysterical mice. Only the drunk he had rousted up, earlier, reeling on his inebriated way. The bum shuffled along, a sad, lonely creature in a tattered coat, mumbling admonishments to his reflection in the street side windows. The fellow seemed harmless. Scamper widened his pupils, just to make certain. He engaged the sixth sense, peculiar to cats, and scanned for any latent anomaly.

Nothing emerged. The residue streamed by the homeless man's thoughts spun off maudlin regrets, not one of them vicious or threatening. Unlike some humans, he blamed no one else for the wretchedness of his condition. His sorry nostalgia stayed self-contained, a wistful murk too diffuse to take fire, or fuse into entangling spite.

Copper-cats hunted the streets for such things. Where acres of concrete replaced living trees, the whisk of the wind raised no rustle of twigs and leaves; here, no falling water or meandering brooks erased the filmy detritus of human afterthought. The work fell to cats, to break the ephemeral ribbons before they burned black and became entangled. That insidious wrack was obvious to felines. Yet people themselves seldom noticed the tempests, unreeled in their wake like thrown litter.

Scamper prowled on. Nothing dangerous lurked here! Surely the feckless rat led him astray. No human seeking a fight walked abroad, and nothing spawned by a late-going hustler held the passion to weave a dark-doing. Nary a trace of wicked intent required a cat scan to chase down and disperse.

"May a plague of fleas chew that rat to perdition!" Scamper huffed, turned left to sweep the back alley that harbored the strip. He stalked past a blinking storefront selling electronic gadgetry and another crammed with tourist novelties.

The recessed doorway beyond sheltered two lovers, breathless with laughter and tender kisses. Contentment lit sparks of delight in their presence. The air danced with showering flurries of gold, wrought by their giggles and happiness. Scamper knew his job. Most agile of his copper colleagues, he pounced on those delectable fragments. Before their shine faded, he batted that merriment into a tingling wad. The finishing touch required cat-magic. Scamper swatted the captured billow of joy under his extended claws.

The shreds scattered. Whirling like falling stars, they sank with a glittering flourish into the pavement.

A cat's eye could discern the faint sheen that remained. Taut whiskers could sense the vibration. Whether a starved feral, or a pampered pet on a stroll, every feline would be tempted to roll with abandon, paws in the air. In back-scratching pleasure, they would soak up the run of sweet luck that now welled from the sidewalk. Serendipity, also, would touch the lives of unsuspecting pedestrians. A school child might find an escaped coin and buy candy. Or a weary mother might sigh with relief as her cranky infant changed mood to delight. Here, an artist might stumble on fresh inspiration, or a worried man might soften his heart and take pause to lend help to a beggar.

The wide world was alive with such wonders. Wherever people shed formative thoughts, the curious nature of cats would make sport with the exuberant residue. They knew to play tag with the colorful aspects, and weave them into the manifest world.

When the couple departed, Scamper shoved off, no little bit smug that the rat's doom-and-glooming had given him a false lead.

A woman rushed past, heels clicking as she bustled into the subway. Her fizz of anxiety sent bubbles of energy bouncing off the lit street lamps. Scamper sensed no threatening darkness swirling behind her brisk footsteps. If she resented her job, she did not hate her boss. Though her day had been riddled with disappointments, she did not nurse any poisonous urge to dump her malaise on her coworkers. Her loose discontent would not form a vortex. No quivering, plucked string of entanglement waited to snag into other folks' unresolved angst.

Scamper detected no stirring of havoc that required destruction with claws and teeth. No suspect thrill raised a hump in his back, or bristled him to spitting temper. Nose working, tail high, he rounded the corner, jinked down the side street, and skirted the packing crates discarded behind the herb shop.

The narrow alley ahead enticed with the rich scent of cat-mint. Most of the neighborhood's swaggering toms had dropped in for a heady nip. The randy chorus at the Cat-A-Tonic Bar surrounded a svelte Siamese. Amorous loungers watched rivals, slit-eyed, while the husky Maine Coon named Bouncer licked his claw sheaths, prepared to break up snarling fights. Tempers ran short, in the late summer heat. The scrappier males were on seasonal edge, hot to test their machismo before the fur-ripping brawling of autumn.

Scamper licked his sharp teeth. As eager himself for a rambunctious change, he marched past, primed to impress the slinky pussies who danced at the Cat-Ass-Trophy Club. Yet tonight, the stair with the balustrade loomed empty. No black beauties or coy little calicoes beckoned him on.

Instead, Scamper found himself knocked on his haunches by cats pelting helter-skelter. Fur on end, the whole kit'n ca-boodle ran in fear for their lives, darting under the sewer grates or streaking for shelter beneath the parked cars on the side street.

Scamper tensed, primed for uncanny threats. He sighted what appeared as a shadow swooping down on his planted stance. Its wet-blanket force struck him, face on, and bowled him head over tail. Scamper twisted. Agile reflexes brought him back to his feet. Scuffed and furious, he had to acknowl-edge the filthy rat's warning held substance. A monster-sized dark-doing devoured the strip, with no apparent clue in the vicinity to reveal how the nexus had started.

"Not on my turf!" Scamper snarled, and crouched. He launched into his best fighting leap. Yet his dagger-clawed swipe missed the coiling disturbance. Again, he was caught by surprise as a tendril snaked out of *nowhere* and clobbered him sideways.

Scamper picked himself up, spitting curses. The dark-doing lurked in the apartments *above*! No thanks to the rat, for withholding that detail. Such ill-news should have been dispatched in the first place, by way of a reliable messenger. Situations always turned hairball, whenever a rat told the truth!

Already, the invasive clot had grown monstrous. Its creeping shadow obscured half the alley, with Scamper unable to count the number and strength of the entrenched entanglements. He backed, green eyes slitted, dodging as another eruption shot off more strangling threads. The skyline above was choked under the pall. No good news: the least gleam of stars should have made the uncanny stuff shrink. Even the street lamps failed to pierce through the density of this anomaly. At large and expanding at a ferocious pace, the thing crowded the stance of the small, copper tabby who was pledged to serve and protect.

Scamper hissed, stiff-legged and holding his ground. He was no coward! But what could he do? The entanglement siphoned off color and life. Deep taproots had sunk into the sewers. Other murky tendrils seeped through open windows, invading the tenements above. Hapless sleepers inside were being snared by the web. The blast of their nightmares was spawning fresh wrack, feeding the uncanny problem.

Scamper's nape prickled. "Doesn't that stink like unburied scat!" He had never seen human beings wreak such an insatiable pall. Though natural fear urged him to turn tail, he flexed his foreclaws and dug in to charge.

"You're not planning to challenge that!" a deep voice admonished, a half-step behind him. "Better to stay safe! A loose grate in the window well opens into the herb shop's basement. My patrons have taken refuge in there. High time that both of us followed them."

Scamper hissed, out of sorts with surprise. "Bouncer! Frag your tail, don't sneak up while I'm on the job!"

The gray Maine Coon cat wrinkled his white nose and strolled abreast, his usual air of muscular unconcern rattled by trepidation. "Do you know what you're doing, alone in the breach? Whatever that is, no question it's screwed the prosperity of my establishment."

"It could do worse than that." Scamper bared his teeth. "Best scarper, pal. This is copper-cat business and no place for a civilian to be risking his scruff."

Bouncer stretched, flexing twenty-five pounds of pure feline brawn, sleeked beneath a luxurious coat. "You're a runt, by yourself," he pointed out, reasonable.

"Size has nothing to do with superior agility," Scamper declared, fiercely miffed. The Chief might assign larger toms to the slums. But in a tight scrap, sure as fire singed fur, the little cats often scored first. "Scram, friend. Now! Take the refugees and your kitty bar elsewhere until I've unraveled this mess."

Bouncer curled his tail tip, amused. "I've no wish to relocate," he said, more than tactfully tart, "or lose the ambience of the Cat-Ass-Trophy Club, if this festering trouble ruins the neighborhood. Howl as you like, that cluster hump's swallowing more real estate for every second we waste in a hissy-fit."

Scamper conceded that unpleasant point. He dared not risk any further delay, or call on the Chief for a backup squad. Late could become never if this dark-doing bloated past reach of containment. Besides, Bouncer's moxie was lion-sized. Every thug dog unleashed in the district slunk out of its way to avoid his punitive claws.

"Survive this," said Scamper, "I'll owe you a leisurely meal at the Catfish Grill."

"My treat, for cold shrimp at the Cater Wall." Bouncer sniffed, still indignant. No copper tabby who defended his digs would be tackling an explosive eruption, alone.

Side by side, the mismatched pair of cats bounded forward, to Scamper's last minute instructions. "Whatever happens, keep your head down! Duck the large tentacles. If you become hooked, fight back and kick as though the murder itself had sunk fangs in your bollocks! Once I pounce, join the tussle and dig into the entanglement. Snap the binding thread, and bolt for clear air. Don't be trapped as the mess comes unraveled."

The pair sprang in step. Then the web closed upon them. A thrill like electricity tingled their hair. The hungry cold of the dark-doing lashed out, insatiable, to overwhelm them. Scamper flattened, while the larger Maine Coon leaped over the obstructive shadow. Wind flicked at their tails, to the rasp of feline claws scrabbling against concrete. Bouncer yowled, then wheeled his bulk across Scamper's path in avoidance.

"Pussyfoot civilian!" the smaller cat snarled. "Quit trying to protect me."

"So neuter yourself!" Bouncer swore, his fur singed where a razor-edged ribbon had grazed him. "Dead is no use to anyone, pal. I know what my hide's worth! Chief would rag me to mince if he should discover I'd hung your cat-sass out to dry."

Scamper was left too breathless to argue. Fool heroics more likely would see them both killed, with the Chief at the barracks left none the wiser.

Bouncer kept pace, undeterred by good sense, as Scamper streaked onward, scanning the turmoil and gloom for an opening to attack. His trained experience and swift reflexes—even Bouncer's staunch strength—appeared sorrowfully over faced. The stygian tangle around them now blinded their keen feline eyesight. Its strangling opacity sucked the very sweetness of life from the world. The cats darted ahead by hearing and smell, forced to avoid obstacles by nothing more than the warning flick of a whisker tip.

How deep did this draining disturbance extend? Fear could not grapple the concept. Scamper sprinted, lungs burning. Dodging past coil upon inky coil, he found no safe chance for engagement. Bouncer wheezed, labored, his heavy coat never bred for exertion in summer heat.

We could die here, Scamper realized, cringing with shame. Should he fail to grapple the blight, it would drag a friend down along with him. The moment was lost, to turn back in escape. The dark-doing's tumultuous chaos had swallowed them, blinding all sense of direction.

Hesitation would become no less fatal. Scamper bunched his hindquarters and pounced, snagging the nearest tendril. Teeth closed and claws ripped, to no avail. His grip met no resistance, no taut wrack of spiteful entanglement. He yowled, off-balanced and bashed topsy-turvy as the ruinous maelstrom closed over him. A growl, nearby, bespoke Bouncer's attack. But greater bulk lent no advantage. The dark-doing writhed, its explosive ferocity unfazed by their combined assault.

Scamper snapped and bit. He lashed with his claws, seeking for the pattern inside the morass: the hard tie of malice that locked two human beings into mutual hatred. Yet his raking search exposed nothing. No knot existed, to break in release. This mangle of animate thought-stream did not harbor so much as a vicious kink.

Something *else* was horribly wrong. Claws and teeth sliced only an inchoate emptiness that seared feline instincts with dread. This dark-doing was like no other before. No trained skill, and no trick Scamper knew could unravel the horrible force of it

Now desperate, the cats grappled elusive, black lightning. Neither could see how the other one fared. Exhausted and tumbling, Scamper thrashed as a tendril noosed over his chest. It tightened, driving the breath from his body and throttling him dizzy.

Last sensation, he felt Bouncer's teeth on his nape, then a tug, before sliding headlong into darkness.

Scamper woke to the scrape of another cat's tongue rasping across his shut eyelids. He blinked, stirred in protest, shook his aching head. As his bleary vision recovered, he focused on a familiar face.

That worried, green eye, mangled ear, and marmalade nose marked with scars bespoke alley origins and roughneck experience.

"Chief?" Scamper coughed and tried to arise.

The older cat's paw knocked him prostrate. "You bit off more than one copper could chew!" Chief's reprimand granted no grace for excuses. "Good thing that Bouncer dragged you to safety!"

Scamper sucked a deep breath. His ribs hurt. His throat stung. He reeked of singed fur and, more faintly, of the sardines the Chief had been munching before being called to the scene. Collapsed in the gutter between two parked cars, Scamper turned his concern back toward the infested alley. "Has the crisis been tamed?"

"No." The chief perked his good ear, his single eye burning cold emerald. "No copper of mine ventures into a darkdoing alone, far less undertakes the flea-brained idea of involving a noncombatant!"

Still on the sidelines, Bouncer lashed his tail, angered by the dismissal. The tip reeked of garbage, scraped up from the street, which further rumpled his dignity. "No runt-sized shorthair tells me not to fight! Certainly not while that gristly horror invades the strip and threatens my turf!"

Which was the boulder informing the pebble: the Chief winced, mollified, as Scamper bit back that his courageous friend was owed thanks for the rescue. Too upset to dwell on his embarrassing mistake, he added, "What was that thing? I bit the thought-shadow down to the core. Nothing was inside! No strand of hatred between human folks had tangled a knot to be severed."

"There won't be one." The Chief sighed, all at once sounding tired. "The dark-doing that's blighting that alley has nothing to do with two humans linked by active animosity. What idiot idea took you in without back-up?"

"A rat's taunt!" Scamper snapped, which was no less than the irreverent truth.

The shifty critter had lied through its teeth, most likely to lure a copper cat into jeopardy. Now maddened beyond the sting of his scrape, Scamper glared in dead earnest. "What created that shadow? How can it exist? What form of *nothing* on the green earth could fuel such voracious unpleasantness?"

"You encountered the horror of human despair," the Chief explained, looking fraught. "People who lose all hope can give up their belief that life matters. All by themselves, they can think empty thoughts and punch such a hole in the world."

"Hole in the *world*?" Scamper blinked, appalled. "Grief like that puts my tail in a pinch, something worse than a roomful of rockers!"

The Chief lowered his bony shoulders into a sorrowful crouch. "People aren't like animals, Scamp. Not as cats, knowing since birth to enjoy every day we are given."

"Dumber than dormice, some human folks," Bouncer

observed in agreement. "They'll stare at a squawk box for hours on end. Or yap into phones, before visiting. I've listened. They'll squabble over conflicting ideas! Puts a snarking kink in your whiskers, overhearing their petty gripes."

Scamper furrowed his brow, stunned to disbelief. The tiniest kitten understood how to live! The seasons cued the innate urge to grow, then to hunt, to mature, and to breed. When the time came to play or just bask in the sun, cats knew to indulge in delight.

"Human children don't have our instincts," the Chief lamented, quietly patient. "They think, sure enough! It's their meddling nature. But their prodigious gift of reason gets muddled if they forget to pursue their own joy. When trouble arises, they neglect to give credence to how they feel, from moment to moment. Immersed in the logic of looking for *why*, quite often they lose their own way." The Chief shook his head. "Worse for them, if they do as they *think* they ought and stop hearing the dreams inside themselves. The pity is, most of them have no clue, no concept at all, of how powerful those dreams truly are."

"They abandon their fun? How do we fight that?" Never had Scamper felt more hampered by the misfortune of his runt size. With no active tangle of discord to cut, surely a giant was needed. What good could a cat do if a human's own reason squelched pleasure and left them to wallow in misery?

The chief licked a paw, scrubbed at his ripped ear, nerves salved by the comfort of washing. "To lift this blight will take extreme courage, not to mention a copper of uncommon wit and agility."

Dawn was breaking, gray, above the sodium gleam of the lamps that soon would be extinguished. In that mixed light, Chiefs flame coat shone dull brown. His eye showed a bleak glint as he added, "We haven't much time. Are you up to the fight?"

"I got my behind kicked. That's nothing near dead," Scamper shot back, insulted. He sprang to his feet, quivering with readiness.

Bouncer also rammed erect, bristling. "You're going back?"

The battle-scarred Chief stood up and brushed past. Lean but dauntless, he skittered across the cracked sidewalk. "We must do just that. And fast! If this case of human despair ends by suicide, a blight will be left in the world. Unless we act first, even cat-magic can't mend the extent of the damage."

"Then I'm coming along," Bouncer declared.

The Chiefs screeching argument fell on deaf ears. No better than Scamper, he could not repress the Maine Coon's obstinate loyalty.

"At your peril, then," the Chief warned, and stalked past the flickering street lamp. His brusque tone continued, plunged into the gloom. "My detectives are fishing for clues as they can. Let's hope they've found what direction the battle must take."

The nexus that had beaten Scamper before now appeared to have swallowed the entire alley. Its hectic growth had not abated, although Chief had dispatched his best reinforcements. Copper cats now attacked the morass in numbers, tearing off scraps with their teeth. For each bite they took, the whirlwind swelled faster. Now fed by its own spinning impetus, thoughts shadows boiled into existence faster than any trained corps could reduce them.

A fat yellow Persian named Sarge oversaw, perched on a trashcan lid to one side. When the Chief sauntered up, he summarized his frustration with a deep growl of annoyance.

Chief's emerald eye glinted. "Report!"

"The whole stinking list?" Fat Sarge yawned, his stiff silver whiskers raked back. "Petty as flea rash! First off, the human perp's female. Nagged the living hair off the head of her mate. The poor, mangled creature finally regained his sanity and got a divorce. Since then, the exwife harps on about his allegedly faithless betrayal. We've logged her whining complaints by the thousands: that he was a drunk who lounged on the sofa, too lazy to hang up the paper roll next to the toilet! Ten thoughts a minute, she insists how she's wronged: that the world's going to ruin; that the rent won't be paid; or that the fancy new shoes for her kid cost more than her child support." Sarge heaved a sigh. "You'd think, overhearing, that no patch of soil grows any flowers. Or that toddlers don't laugh in the park! Who cares a hoot for a label, by gosh? Can a brand-name sneaker matter so much if the kid's going to splash in the mud puddles?"

"Some folks would refuse to hear the birds sing, even if one perched smack on their noggin!" Chief scratched his jaw, worried. "No clue, yet, what abandoned fragment of happiness lies buried beneath the moil?"

"Not so far." Sarge paused, on the case as three coppers strolled up. Each one carried a shred of the darkness, torn off and pinned in clenched teeth.

"Good work!" The Chief accepted their offerings, nailed them under a claw, then smacked them with cat-magic to disgorge the misery of their content. Ears back, the cats listened: through strings of obscenities that maligned the weather, then more annoyed words on the dirt dropped by pigeons, and bills that some wretched bean counter had attached with a surcharge for overdue payment.

The Chief hissed, disgusted. "This depression's entrenched! Defensively held. We'll face a fight, guaranteed, to lay bare the seed of the problem."

"Then you'll storm the core?" Sarge ventured, his yellow eyes bright with concern.

"Yes, but not here." The Chief cast a keen glance at the pall that lapped toward the bins where they held hurried consultation. "The battle must be taken out of this world, and into the realm of true dreams."

Fat Sarge slashed his tail. "Whom can you send?" He and the other old timers still mourned the tragedy caused by the last sorry incident. Then, four copper cats dispatched into the breach had died in the line of duty. Their team leader had not been agile enough to salvage the wrecked dream before the harebrained case of human depression blew his brains out with a shotgun. "Who has the cleverness to slip through a wrack this aggressive?"

The Chief looked to Scamper. "You're the quickest paw we have in the corps. Have you the courage to venture the dream realm? From there, we must try to unravel the thread that's devouring this woman's hope. If we find the source, and if we can rip a hole in the cause, a cat who's quick has to slip through the gap and revive her abandoned enthusiasm."

As Scamper stepped up, Bouncer also shoved in, "If he goes, I stay with him!"

"What's the use?" snapped the Chief. "If I can't tear a large enough breach in the problem, the whole situation will go fur-balls up!"

"Just stop me!" Nose to nose and fur bristling, Bouncer glared until the Chief blinked and backed down.

"I'll hold the rear guard from here," Fat Sarge soothed, in no mood himself to knock Bouncer's bulk back in line. He watched the three felines take up the fray, with the wily Chief in the lead.

* . * . *

The dark-doing had become no less voracious, despite the copper cats' diligence. Scamper was forced to twist this way and that, streaking after the Chiefs orange tail and with Bouncer a bounding gray blur beside him. The hideous blot would have defeated their rush, had their strategy aimed for avoidance. But this stand would not be made here and now, on the solid ground of the world. Chief did not pounce to wrestle but, instead, charged headlong at the morass with the brave intent to pass *through*.

Scamper and Bouncer jumped just behind. Their leap plunged them into the heart of the darkness and hurled them into *forever*. For the dream realm by its nature was boundless, wrought of the fantastical stuff that gave rise to *perhaps, what if,* and *maybe*—every rainbow color, and more, that the wakeful eye could not see. Here was brilliant light that could dazzle or burn. All shapes of foolhardy fancy and delight, and shadows too, veiled in the beauty of enchanted mystery, or ghastly with ugliness.

Dream-stuff, spun by humans who were alive, seethed with spontaneous intensity. But not here, where year upon year of suppression had hampered the impulse of playful exuberance. The woman's despair had eaten away both the bright and the dark. What remained was the clutter and waste of neglect, shrouded in dust and cobwebs. Scamper and his companions picked their way between piles of broken toys. Here they passed a bicycle going to rust and there a rowboat with a hole in it. They rattled through sheets of crumpled paper, discarded ideas piled like fallen leaves. They passed storybooks, abandoned in puddles of tears, soggy pages dissolved into pulp.

Scamper sniffed at the misted air. Its scentless cold numbed his nerve ends. Unlike on the streets, where thought-patterns were vibrant, he had no clue where to begin.

"Listen up!" the Chief urged, set on edge himself. "Somewhere under here there will be a force, an old memory that steals away happiness. We must seek out what's choking the life from this pattern before we can shoulder the fight."

Scamper pricked up his ears, widened his pupils, and sharpened his feline senses. He peered into the future and saw only tangle: a dreary array of boring activity, obligation, and burdensome days. The detritus of passionless memories closed in, sharp and relentless as traps. Scamper was slight enough to slip through, but Chief and Bouncer needed to squeeze to force themselves past the tight spots. The way grew more dangerous. Fog, and then drizzle, drenched the cats to the skin. More than once they shied back from the crash, as loose objects tumbled and threatened to crush them.

Though the cats were only a whisker apart, leaden silence wrapped them in isolation. They became wrung by pervasive loneliness until feline spirits pined for sunshine and wind, even a storm to shatter the dreadful oppression.

"We have to go deeper," insisted the Chief. "No matter how hard, there's no choice. Give in, and we'll never escape this."

Icy rain became a torrential downpour. Scamper shook the wet from his ears, more weary than he could remember. Through the barrage, he heard a voice, far off and terribly faint.

Bouncer heard, too, and the Chief turned that way, shoving into a murk, thick as slush, that hampered his mincing steps forward.

"Look at this!" Scamper scraped at the stuff with his claws, freeing a forgotten tatter of praise and encouragement. Even as the drowned figment emerged, a strident old woman's scolding arose, overpowering the wisp his cat's paw reawakened.

"Scrub your face! Don't touch, you'll break something! That's disgusting behavior. Don't do that, stupid, your hands are filthy! Stop tracking mud on the floor! Didn't your mother teach you any manners? That's a horrible way to treat your younger brother. Never mind if he hit you, be nice! No, you can't have a pet! They carry disease! Never play on the far side of the street, you could be killed by a car!"

"Come on!" The Chief hissed, his fur bristled. "That's the snarling knot we have to tear through. If we can't, the sad woman will let go of life, pushed past the edge by her early conditioning."

Scamper twitched his puffed tail, more than itching to pounce. "Make any kitten toss its kibbles and milk! Couldn't that witch take a breath without nattering?"

"Likely not." The Chief sighed, slinking along on his belly. "Who wouldn't fade, smothered in safety and peace, with the sparkle torn out of adventure?"

The cats crept up on the entrenched bit of thought-pattern. The vortex had formed as a spider's web, spun from repetitive scolding. The center was gripped by an elderly person whose lips never smiled and who wore a starched dress, drab as the rags in a broom closet.

Bouncer growled, fur erect. "Puts the curl in my back! Shall we jump her?"

"She'll have allies," Chief warned. "Other voices, like hers, will arise to defend her over-protective tyranny. They'll reshape the snarl even as we attempt to rip it asunder. The force in that thought-stream won't give way for good. Not till the browbeaten human in charge finds on her own the wild urge to rebel and abandons each one of those moribund rules."

Scamper bared his teeth. "Then how many times must we rip the stuffing out of this fragment of memory?"

"For as long as it takes to breach through," Chief replied. "You'll know when we've triumphed, no question."

The cats pounced. They tore, teeth and savage claws, rending the howling memory limb from limb. When the carping effigy rose from the shreds, they scrimmaged and mangled its head, broke its neck, and raked it to quivering ribbons. Each time, the monster twitched and reassembled. They attacked, over and over again, until they were breathless and battered.

Bouncer was puffing. Chief seemed done in. The harder the cats fought, the more the rain fell. Their mouths burned with the salt-taste of childish tears, and their eyes stung, gritted with the ashes sown by wounding regrets.

Scamper grappled until he was numb. All but drowned by the endless rain, he kicked and raked at the gibbering fragments. No warning prepared him. Suddenly the thought-stuff he wrestled caved in. The firm ground melted under his feet. Then the dream realm around him dissolved and ran molten, hurling him toward oblivion.

"Let go!" yelled the Chief. "That's the hole for your entry!"

Soaked, beyond miserable, Scamper scrabbled at air. He could not control his plummeting fall. Twisting, he tumbled out of the dream realm, unable to salve his wrecked dignity.

The Chiefs cry of encouragement dimmed, lost in the maelstrom now rapidly disappearing behind. "Copper! You have to land on your feet! Keep your wits, Scamp! We'll keep holding the line in the dream realm. But the game that's afoot in the world is now left entirely up to you!"

*   *   *

Scamper landed on gravel with a spraddle-legged thump. Pelted by a downpour and shaken half out of his feline senses, he yowled with rage and soaked misery.

His caterwaul caused a woman to turn away from her teetering stance at the verge of the tenement roof. She was not old! Young and worn, with a tired slouch to her shoulders, she was as wretchedly soaked as the cat, her eyes red from incessant weeping.

"Meow!" Scamper wailed. No way could he make such a drenched creature laugh! The woman's dejection blackened the very clouds. No brilliant idea, amid this aching chill, could lift her dark nimbus of misery. Dense thoughts still poured from her presence like ink. Scamper was too distressed to do battle, far less conjure up the feline inspiration to wheedle her down off the roof.

Scamper squalled again, ears flat in frustration. This woman had learned as a child to hate cats! If he set her ranting, or gave her a scare, she might trip off the brink without jumping.

Worst of all, Chief and Bouncer stayed trapped in her dreamscape, fighting her relentless habit of melancholy, unless the drab cycle was broken.

Scamper shrank down. Huddled, dejected, he glanced left and right. But the flat rooftop provided no cranny for even a small cat to hide. He could do nothing but bawl as the human approached step by step and loomed over him.

"A cat? Oh! Poor thing!" Chilled hands reached down. They stroked his wet copper fur, which was repulsively grimy with dirt and machine oil. "You're shivering! Starving, too. I can feel every rib! Let's take you inside. Maybe towel you dry and see what I have to feed you . . ."

Three weeks later, Scamper crouched in Bouncer's company, companionably crunching on the promised fillets at the back of the Catfish Grill. Chief lounged nearby, licking his chops, when the Maine Coon posed the curious question. "How in feline daylights did you get that woman to revive her forgotten dream?"

Scamper flicked his tail, purring and pleased. "Wasn't so hard," he allowed with a wink. "I chased a rat burglar into the back closet where she'd stashed her art paper and paints. When I leaped on the shelf, I kicked over the tin. Went easy, from there. I just chased the dizzy rodent in circles till I'd scattered her brushes and pigments. Oh, she yelled, sure enough, when she found the mess. But cleaning the spilled colors out of her carpet, she had to remember the fun she once had making pictures. Then and there, she got up and called an old friend from school. Now they go out painting together. Could be the start of a romance."

Scamper spat out a fish fin and chuckled. "Nailed the rat, too."

"Tasty business," drawled Chief, who enjoyed a fresh kill.

Scamper laughed outright. "The tail end is the best! The dead rat brought the woman so much delight, she's now feeding me tuna fish out of the can."

ABOUT THE AUTHORS

Donald J. Bingle has had a wide variety of short fiction published, primarily in DAW themed anthologies but also in tie-in anthologies for the *Dragonlance* and *Transformers* universes and in popular role-playing gaming materials. Recently, he has had stories published in **The Dimensions Next Door, Fellowship Fantastic, Front Lines, Imaginary Friends**, and **Pandora's Closet**. His first novel, **Forced Conversion**, is set in the near future, when anyone can have heaven, any heaven they want, but some people don't want to go. His most recent novel, **Greensword**, is a darkly comedic thriller about a group of environmentalists who decide to end global warming . . . immediately. Now they're about to save the world; they just don't want to get caught doing it. Don can be reached at orphyte@aol.com, and his novels can be purchased through www.orphyte.com/donaldjbingle

Richard Lee Byers is the author of over thirty fantasy and horror novels, including **Unclean, Undead, The Enemy Within**, and **Dissolution**. His current projects include **Unholy** (the concluding volume in the "Haunted Land" trilogy) and the screenplay for *The Plague Knight*, a major movie release. A resident of the Tampa Bay area, the setting for much of his horror fiction, he spends much of his leisure time fencing, playing poker, and shooting pool, and is a frequent guest at Florida science-fiction conventions.

Having lived catless for decades, Edward Carmien is now co-owned by two tabbies, one friendly, one skittish, brothers rescued by and adopted from the local pound. After averaging roughly a story a year for almost a dozen years, he is soundly beating that average, and his work can be found most recently in *Black Gate 12* and other places one can discover by Googling his last name. Ed rides motorcycles (ABC #7573), teaches, canoes, avoids yardwork, shoots photos, tries to keep up with his kids, and does sundry other things in Princeton, New Jersey, where the elm tree didn't quite die out.

Elaine Cunningham spends most of her waking hours reacting to subliminal messages from her two Siamese. She moonlights as a *New York Times* bestselling author of twenty-one books and about three dozen short stories. *Kirkus Review* named **Shadows in the Starlight**, the second book in her Changeling Detective urban fantasy series, to their list of Top Ten SciFi Books of 2006. (Elaine suspects that the list's compilers have cats and further suspects that those cats communicate with her Siamese—probably through MySpace.) She is still busily writing fantasy novels and short stories but is also branching out into historical fiction. And her first editorial project, **Lilith Undead**—an anthology of tales based on the Lilith mythology—was recently published. A former music and history teacher, Elaine now focuses most of her musical energies on the Celtic harp, which is, oddly enough, the only instrument the cats actively enjoy.

Esther M. Friesner is the author of thirty-three novels and over one hundred fifty short stories and other works. She won the Nebula Award twice as well as the Skylark and the Romantic Times Award. Best known for creating and editing the wildly popular *Chicks In Chainmail* anthology series (Baen Books), her latest publications are the Young Adult novels *Temping Fate*, *Nobody's Princess*, and *Nobody's Prize*. She lives in Connecticut with her husband, is the mother of two grown children, and harbors cats.

Paul Genesse told his mother he was going to be a writer when he was four years old, and he has been creating fantasy stories ever since. He loved his English classes in college but pursued his other passion by earning a bachelor's degree in nursing science in 1996. He is a registered nurse on a cardiac unit in Salt Lake City, Utah, where he works the night shift keeping the forces of darkness away from his patients. Paul lives with his incredibly supportive wife Tammy and their collection of frogs. He spends endless hours in his basement writing fantasy novels, short stories, and crafting maps of fantastical realms. His novel *The Golden Cord: Book 1 of the Iron Dragon Trilogy*, was released in 2008, but his current project is *Medusa's Daughter*, a fantasy set in ancient Greece. He encourages you to contact him online at www.PAULGENESSE.com.

Ed Greenwood has published over one hundred and eighty fantasy novels and *Dungeons & Dragons*® game products and is the award-winning creator of the famous Forgotten Realms® fantasy world. His novels include the bestselling *Spellfire* and *Elminster: The Making of a Mage* and their many sequels, the *Band of Four* saga, and the *Knights of Myth Drannor* trilogy, which begins with *Swords of Eveningstar*.

Bruce A. Heard has written many role-playing books and articles, including the *Alternity* Player's Handbook and

Gamemaster Guide, and many articles for *Dragon* magazine. Currently he lives and writes in Lake Villa, Illinois.

Lee Martindale's work has appeared in such anthologies as *Turn The Other Chick*, *Lowport*, *A Time To . . . Outside The Box*, three volumes of the *Sword & Sorceress* series, three of the *Bubbas Of The Apocalypse* series, and three chapbook collections from Yard Dog Press. She also edited the ground-breaking *Such A Pretty Face*. When not slinging fiction, Lee is a Named Bard, Lifetime Active Member of SFWA, a fencing member of the SFWA Musketeers, and a member of the SCA. She and her husband, George, share a Plano, Texas, home with two feline goddesses—Mistletoe and Eggnog—and fond memories of Pixel and Chiya, to whom "Old Age And Sorcery" is dedicated.

Jana Paniccia lives in Toronto, although she tries to get out of the city as much as possible, preferably to visit more places she's never been before. Her short stories have appeared in a number of anthologies, most recently, *Children of Magic*, *Fantasy Gone Wrong*, and *Ages of Wonder*. She also coedited the Prix Aurora Award winning DAW anthology *Under Cover of Darkness*, with Julie E. Czerneda, released in 2007.

Jean Rabe is the author of two dozen books and four dozen short stories. She edits anthologies from time to time, and she loves to tug fiercely on old socks with her dogs. She lives in southeastern Wisconsin, in a pleasant subdivision brimming with dogs and kids. Her hobbies include playing board games, war games, and role-playing games, twirling her toes in her goldfish pond, finding places to hide her growing collection of books, and visiting all manner of museums.

Matthew Stover is the *New York Times* bestselling author of **Star Wars: The New Jedi Order: Traitor** and **Star Wars: Revenge of the Sith**, as well as **The Blade of Tyshalle**, **Heroes Die**, **Iron Dawn**, and **Jericho Moon**. He is a student of the Degerberg Blend, a jeet kune do concept that is a mixture of approximately twenty-five different fighting arts from around the world. He lives outside Chicago with artist and writer Robyn Drake.

Marc Tassin was enthralled by books from a very early age. He marveled that a collection of letters on a page could sweep a person away to another world, change the course of a life, or evoke powerful emotional and intellectual responses. The magic of this literary alchemy is what inspired him to try his hand at writing. In the years since, Marc has written short stories, games, and articles that explore the far reaches of fantasy and science fiction. From the bloody decks of pirate ships to the secret lives of gerbils, he's taken his readers to strange and wonderful places. Marc lives in a small town just outside of Ann Arbor, Michigan, with his wife, Tanya, and their two children.

Christopher Welch is a happily married freelance writer, reporter, and book reviewer originally from Akron, Ohio. He currently lives in Fort Atkinson, Wisconsin, where he works for the local newspaper and news radio station. His poetry, fiction, and nonfiction have appeared in various small press and professional publications. He is a staff reviewer for *Dark Wisdom* magazine and a long-time member of the HWA. He earned a B.A. (with a minor in creative writing) and an M.A. in English from the University of Akron. Despite his severe allergies to them, he still thinks cats are really cool.

Robert E. Vardeman has written several dozen short stories and more than seventy science fiction, fantasy, and mystery novels. He currently lives in Albuquerque, New Mexico, with his teenaged son, Chris, and a cat. Two out of three of them enjoy the high-tech hobby of geocaching.

Elizabeth A. Vaughan is the author of *Warprize*, *Warsworn*, and *Warlord*, the three books that make up Chronicle of the Warlands. She believes that the only good movies are the ones with gratuitous magic, swords, or lasers. Not to mention dragons. At the present, she is owned by three incredibly spoiled cats and lives in the Northwest Territory, on the outskirts of the Black Swamp, along Mad Anthony's Trail on the banks of the Maumee River.

Janny Wurts has pursued her love of imaginative invention in both story and visual form. She has authored eighteen books, a collection of short fiction, and over thirty contributions to fantasy and science fiction anthologies, with most books bearing her own jacket and interior art. She has received the Cauldron Award from *Marion Zimmer Bradley's Fantasy Magazine* for her writing. Her paintings have been showcased in exhibitions at the Hayden Planetarium, NASA's 25th Anniversary Exhibit at the Cleveland Museum of Natural History, and as part of the Delaware Art Museum's permanent collection. Her artwork has received two Chesley Awards and three Best of Show Awards at the World Fantasy Convention.